Praise for Minerva Spe

THE WILD WOMEN OF

THE BOXING BARONESS

"Swooningly romantic, sizzling sensual…superbly realized."

–*Booklist* STARRED REVIEW

A *Library Journal* Best Book of 2022

A Publishers Marketplace Buzz Books Romance Selection

"Fans of historical romances with strong female characters in non-traditional roles and the men who aren't afraid to love them won't be disappointed by this series starter."

–*Library Journal* STARRED REVIEW

"Spencer (*Notorious*) launches her Wicked Women of Whitechapel Regency series with an outstanding romance based in part on a real historical figure. . . This is sure to wow!"

-*Publishers Weekly* STARRED REVIEW

THE DUELING DUCHESS

"Another carefully calibrated mix of steamy passion, delectably dry humor, and daringly original characters."

—*Booklist* STARRED REVIEW

VERDICT: Readers who enjoyed *The Boxing Baroness* won't want to miss Spencer's sequel.

–*Library Journal* STARRED REVIEW

THE ACADEMY OF LOVE series:

"[A] pitch perfect Regency …. Readers will be hooked." (THE MUSIC OF LOVE)

★*Publishers Weekly STARRED REVIEW*

"An offbeat story that offers unexpected twists on a familiar setup."

(A FIGURE OF LOVE)

Kirkus

"[A] consistently entertaining read."

(A FIGURE OF LOVE)

Kirkus

Praise for THE MASQUERADERS series:

"Lovers of historical romance will be hooked on this twisty story of revenge, redemption, and reversal of fortunes."

Publishers Weekly, STARRED review of THE FOOTMAN.

"Fans will be delighted."

Publishers Weekly on THE POSTILION

Praise for Minerva Spencer's *REBELS OF THE TON* series:

NOTORIOUS

★A *PopSugar* Best New Romance of November

★A *She Reads* Fall Historical Romance Pick

★A *Bookclubz* Recommended Read

"Brilliantly crafted…an irresistible cocktail of smart characterization, sophisticated sensuality, and sharp wit." ★***Booklist STARRED REVIEW***

"Sparkling…impossible not to love."—Popsugar

"Both characters are strong, complex, and believable, and the cliffhanger offers a nice setup for the sequel. Readers who like thrills mixed in with their romance should check this out."

—Publishers Weekly

"Packed full of fiery exchanges and passionate embraces, this is for those who prefer their Regencies on the scandalous side."***—Library Journal***

INFAMOUS

"Realistically transforming the Regency equivalent of a mean girl into a relatable, all-too-human heroine is no easy feat, but Spencer (Outrageous, 2021) succeeds on every level. Lightly dusted with wintery holiday charm, graced with an absolutely endearing, beetle-obsessed hero and a fully rendered cast of supporting characters and spiked with smoldering sensuality and wry wit, the latest in Spencer's Rebels of the Ton series is sublimely satisfying."

—Booklist STARRED review

"Perfect for fans of Bridgerton, Infamous is also a charming story for Christmas. In fact, I enjoyed Infamous so much that when I was halfway through it, I ordered the author's first novel, Dangerous. I look forward to reading much more of Minerva Spencer's work."

—THE HISTORICAL NOVEL SOCIETY

Praise for S.M. LaViolette's erotic historical romance series *VICTORIAN DECADENCE*:

"LaViolette keeps the tension high, delivering dark eroticism and emotional depth in equal measure. Readers will be hooked."

-PUBLISHERS WEEKLY on HIS HARLOT

"LaViolette's clever, inventive plot makes room for some kinky erotic scenes as her well-shaded characters explore their sexualities. Fans of erotic romance will find much to love."

-PUBLISHERS WEEKLY on HIS VALET

<u>Praise for Minerva Spencer's *Outcasts* series:</u>

"Minerva Spencer's writing is sophisticated and wickedly witty. Dangerous is a delight from start to finish with swashbuckling action, scorching love scenes, and a coolly arrogant hero to die for. Spencer is my new auto-buy!"

-NYT Bestselling Author Elizabeth Hoyt

"[**SCANDALOUS** is] A standout...Spencer's brilliant and original tale of the high seas bursts with wonderfully real protagonists, plenty of action, and passionate romance."

★Publishers Weekly STARRED REVIEW

"Fans of Amanda Quick's early historicals will find much to savor."
★Booklist STARRED REVIEW

"Sexy, witty, and fiercely entertaining." *★Kirkus* ***STARRED REVIEW***

<u>*Praise for S.M. LaViolette's Books:*</u>

"Lovers of historical romance will be hooked on this twisty story of revenge, redemption, and reversal of fortunes."

★Publishers Weekly ***STARRED REVIEW***

"A remarkably resourceful heroine who can more than hold her own against any character invented by best-selling Bertrice Small, a suavely sophisticated hero with sex appeal to spare, and a cascade of lushly detailed love scenes give Spencer's dazzling debut its deliciously fun retro flavor."

★Booklist STARRED REVIEW

"Readers will love this lusty and unusual marriage of convenience story."

NYT Bestselling Author MADELINE HUNTER

"Smart, witty, graceful, sensual, elegant and gritty all at once. It has all of the meticulous attention to detail I love in Georgette Heyer, BUT WITH SEX!"

RITA-Award Winning Author JEFFE KENNEDY

More books by S.M. LaViolette & Minerva Spencer

THE ACADEMY OF LOVE SERIES

The Music of Love
A Figure of Love
A Portrait of Love
The Language of Love
Dancing with Love*
The Story of Love*

THE OUTCASTS SERIES

Dangerous
Barbarous
Scandalous

THE REBELS OF THE *TON*

Notorious
Outrageous
Infamous

THE MASQUERADERS

The Footman
The Postilion
The Bastard

THE SEDUCERS

Melissa and The Vicar
Joss and The Countess
Hugo and The Maiden

VICTORIAN DECADENCE

His Harlot
His Valet
His Countess
Her Master
Her Beast

THE BELLAMY SISTERS

PHOEBE
HYACINTH
SELINA*
AURELIA*
KATHRYN*

THE WILD WOMEN OF WHITECHAPEL

THE BOXING BARONESS
THE DUELING DUCHESS*
THE CUTTHROAT COUNTESS*

THE HALE SAGA SERIES

BALTHAZAR: THE SPARE

IO: THE SHREW*

Novellas:

THE ARRANGEMENT: The Duke's Treasure

THE BACHELORS OF BOND STREET: A Second Chance for Love

AUDACIOUS: A *Rebels of the Ton* novella

*upcoming book

BALTHAZAR

The Spare

The Hale Saga Series
Americans in London
Book 1

S.M. LaViolette

CROOKED SIXPENCE BOOKS are published by

CROOKED SIXPENCE PRESS

2 State Road 230

El Prado, NM 87529

First printing May 2023

10 9 8 7 6 5 4 3 2 1

Photo stock by Period Images

Printed in the United States of America

This is dedicated to Jeffe Kennedy.

Thanks Pal, I couldn't have done this one without you.

Author Note

Although alternative religious communities flourished in the United States in the nineteenth century, Canoga—the utopian community in this book—is a work of fiction.

Chapter 1

London
1871

The headlines of the newspapers spread across Victoria Dryden's desk shouted and jostled for her attention:

Free love!

Group marriage!

Coitus reservatus!

Romanesque orgies!

And more.

Victoria looked up from the various scandal sheets and met the expectant gaze of Norton Bickle, Hastings Park's ancient butler. "What are all these, Mr. Bickle?"

"Reggie returned from London last night and brought these to me."

Reggie was one of their footmen, a man whose *colorful* past would have precluded his employment in any other aristocratic household in Britain. Doubtless most other people in Tori's position would think her mad for hiring an ex-convict, but she believed that everyone deserved a second chance. She'd had one, after all, and had made the best of it.

"I hope Reggie was behaving himself in the City." Meaning Victoria hoped he wasn't back to his former trade, which was burglary. Or fencing stolen goods. Or perhaps both; she could never remember.

"No, no, he says he went to visit his mother," Bickle assured her. "In any case, I thought you'd want to see these." Bickle fixed her with an excited, almost gleeful, look. "They have found Him, Mrs. Dryden."

Tori didn't need to ask which *Him* Bickle meant. The old butler was talking about the mysterious new Duke of Hastings, the man the ducal lawyers had been seeking for almost two years.

Two. Long. Years.

Years during which there had been even less money than usual to operate the ramshackle old estate and pay the ever-growing mountain of bills.

Years when Tori and all the other servants had feared that the new duke would not be found and that the title would go dormant. Or, even worse, they might determine there *was* no heir, and the long, distinguished line would go extinct. If that happened, the property would go to the crown, and they would all be out of jobs.

For a houseful of servants who were either too old or whose backgrounds were too dubious to find new positions elsewhere, the possibility of no new duke was the most terrifying future they could imagine.

But now they had their duke.

Bickle frowned when Tori did not reply. "You do not seem surprised by my news, Mrs. Dryden."

"I'm not." Tori lifted the letter that had arrived only an hour earlier in the morning mail. It was from the law firm of Cromby and White, who'd been searching for the new duke for the last two years. Tori had been re-reading it for the third time when the old butler knocked on her door.

Bickle nodded. "Ah, yes. I noticed that was from those lawyers, but I assumed it was just another letter rejecting our pleas for more money to pay the bills."

"No, this was a letter informing me of what you already know: namely that the new Duke of Hastings has been located and notified of his position." She glanced at the letter yet again, still not convinced of what she was reading. "Mr. Cromby says His Grace's name is Zeus Constantine Jonathan Hale?" She gestured to the pile of newspapers. "Is that what you read in one of these?"

"Yes. It is quite an unusual name, isn't it?"

Tori laughed at the understatement. "Indeed, it is. Well, you will be pleased to hear that Mr. Cromby made His Grace aware of our desperate financial situation and the duke has arranged to have funds made available to help us prepare Hastings Park for his arrival."

Bickle cast his rheumy eyes ceilingward and mouthed a silent prayer of thanks.

Tori smiled. "I offered my own prayer earlier."

"Did the lawyer give any indication when His Grace might arrive?"

"Oh, did I leave that out? Three weeks."

Bickle gasped. "*Three weeks*!"

"Yes, we shall have to draw up a plan of attack. Quickly."

The old butler looked faint.

"It will be fine, Bickle, you will see," she said with more conviction than she was feeling. Three weeks to ready Hastings Park for its new master would require a great deal of work, money, and manpower. Thankfully, His Grace seemed willing to open his purse, so that should help with hiring more servants, and even workmen to effect a few critical repairs.

Tori turned to the varied collection of broadsheets, newspapers, specials, and pamphlets and flipped through them. There were over a dozen, ranging from the *London Times* to something called the *Penny Illustrated Paper*, which featured a sketch of an exceedingly handsome man with a suggestive smile and a positively indecent gleam in his eyes. The caption below the image said: *The Wicked Spare.*

Tori frowned, confused. “Did you read all these, Mr. Bickle? Most of them don’t seem to be about His Grace.”

“I glanced through them all,” he admitted a trifle guiltily, his papery skin tinting a healthy pink. “And no, they are not all about the Duke of Hastings.”

“Well?” she prodded. “What are all these?”

He cleared his throat. “Do you recall the articles recently published in *The Gazette* about the religious settlement in America—the one in New York called *Canoga*?”

Tori frowned. “Yes, of course I do. But what does that have to do with—” Her eyes widened. “Oh no! You must be jesting. Just because the man in that story had the same last name as the duke doesn’t mean anything. *Hale* is quite common. Besides, the Hale in that story wasn’t named *Zeus.*” Tori cast her mind back. “He was called Shadrach or Abednego or some such thing. A name from the Bible, if I recall correctly.”

“The fellow from those articles is *Balthazar* Hale.” He paused for effect. “*Lord* Balthazar is His Grace’s brother and heir.”

Tori’s jaw dropped. “Good Lord.” She picked up the newspaper on top of the pile, which was called *The Illustrated Paper.* “So that is why they’re calling him The Wicked Spare.”

“Yes,” Bickle said, trying to stifle a grin and failing.

“Good Lord,” she muttered yet again. If Balthazar Hale was even half as debauched as he’d been portrayed in those articles, then he would put even the most hardened rake to the blush.

Lord Balthazar had gained notoriety thanks to a multi-installment expose about a religious community in New York state. The salacious articles had captivated the British public, which had a decidedly unhealthy appetite for sensational stories. The author was a woman who’d lived at the colony for twenty years and had recently left. She’d liberally salted her scandalous account with references to her many lovers, one of whom—Balthazar Hale—was twenty-years her junior and evidently infamous in their free-love community for his amorous nature as well as leaving a trail of broken-hearted maidens in his wake.

"Are you telling me that our new duke was raised in this village—what is it called, Canoga?—and is some sort of religious dissenter?" Tori asked, not bothering to hide her astonishment.

"*Yes*, it is called Canoga but *no*, the duke never lived there. And it's not a village, Mrs. Dryden. The people who live there call it a *commune*."

Whatever *that* meant.

"I don't understand. Why were the two brothers raised separately?" she asked.

"According to the story in *The Times*—which I think we can rely on much more than the one in *The Scandal Monger*—"

Tori gave a bark of laughter. "No? Is there really such a paper?"

"It's right there"—he pointed. "Look beneath *The Examiner*."

She located *The Scandal Monger* and grimaced at the gaudy illustration—which depicted a leering, disheveled man surrounded by a bevy of scantily clad women—before looking up. "I'm sorry I interrupted. Please do continue."

"The duke's mother died when he was a baby and His Grace was raised by his maternal aunt and her husband. His Grace's father re-married when the boy was ten and went on to have five more children with his new wife. It is *they* who were raised at the commune. It is rather amusing."

"How so?"

"By all accounts the duke is a paragon of respectability and virtue. While the others… Well, you read about them—or at least you know about Lord Balthazar, I should say."

"Ah." Yes, Tori had read about him. What she'd read was… perhaps not horrifying, but certainly repulsive. Lord Balthazar Hale was the sort of sensualist she despised—a man bent on his own pleasure to the exclusion of all else. Tori had had her fill of such men.

Bickle cleared his throat. "Er, incidentally, His Grace's uncle—the one who raised him—was D.P. Martin."

Tori blinked. "D.P. Martin as in D.P. Martin bank?"

"The very same. As his uncle and aunt had no children, they left everything to His Grace."

"A banker," she repeated, struggling to wrap her mind around that. The old duke must be spinning in his tomb.

"That isn't all," Bickle said.

"I'm almost afraid to ask." Tori was only partly jesting. "What else?"

"His Grace only met his younger siblings for the first time a few weeks ago. For some reason the duke's father never saw fit to introduce his children to each other—or even *tell* them about each other."

Tori shook her head. "How utterly remarkable."

"Indeed," Bickle agreed.

"What sort of man would do that to his own family? And why?"

"The newspaper did not say."

"No, I imagine not," she murmured. "You said there were *five* siblings, in addition to His Grace?"

"Yes, there are six Hales altogether." The old man's lips pursed.

Tori narrowed her eyes. "Why are you smiling like that, Mr. Bickle?"

"Am I smiling?" The normally staid butler's mouth twitched into a smirk. "His Grace's siblings are called—in descending order of age: Lord Balthazar and Lady Io—who are twins. And then there are Lords Apollo and Ares—a *second* set of twins. And, lastly, Lady Evadne."

Tori just stared. "Good Lord."

Bickle laughed. "Yes, my reaction exactly. Evidently their father was a classics scholar specializing in Hellenistic studies." He frowned. "Although the name Balthazar doesn't really fit with the rest, does it?"

"No, it doesn't," Tori said absently. "So, they've only met recently. How interesting."

"Although His Grace and his five younger siblings are newly acquainted—they've known each other barely a month—the newspaper article said the five younger siblings recently left the commune to move in with the duke. Apparently, His Grace spends most of his time in New York City."

"That *is* interesting. Did it say why they moved in with him if they only met him?"

"No, none of the papers had an answer for that," he admitted, visibly disappointed. "It seems… unusual, given that they've lived at the commune all their lives," he added. "I would imagine moving to a place like New York City will be a huge change for the younger siblings."

"Undoubtedly," Tori agreed. "If they've left their commune then what do you suppose the chances are that they will all accompany the duke when he moves here?"

"The paper did not say. Didn't the letter from the lawyers mention whether His Grace would be bringing his family with him?"

"No." Tori sighed. "I suppose we should probably plan for all of them."

"The duke is also betrothed, Mrs. Dryden."

"Ah. Then we will have a duchess, too."

"Apparently they are not marrying until next year as she is in mourning." He paused and then added, "Her name is Edith Barrymore. The only daughter of Lloyd Barrymore."

"The same Barrymore as Barrymore Bank and Trust?"

"Exactly. When they marry, the two empires will join together, or merge, or whatever those business sorts call it, making it the most powerful bank in America."

So, it was to be a dynastic alliance, then. Interesting.

"I don't suppose *The Times* mentioned whether or not we are to prepare a suite for the duke's betrothed?" Tori asked a little tartly.

Bickle chortled. "No, I'm afraid they were not so accommodating." He cocked his head. "It would be rather odd if she stayed here, wouldn't it?"

Tori shrugged. "They are Americans; who knows what is odd to them?"

"Yes, I daresay they do things… differently."

They both pondered those potential differences for a moment.

It was Tori who broke the silence. "I shall write to the lawyers and see if they know who will be accompanying the duke. In the meantime, we should err on the safe side and prepare chambers for seven."

"How in the world will we ever manage such a feat, Mrs. Dryden? There are scarcely two rooms in the family wing that are suitable for occupation."

"According to this letter we may hire the necessary servants and even engage workmen and purchase whatever we need to prepare the house for His Grace."

Bickle sat up straighter. "Indeed? Er, how much might we spend?"

"Mr. Cromby writes, and I quote, *His Grace has said you may spend whatever is necessary.*"

Bickle sagged back in his chair, repeating the words, "*Whatever is necessary*," in a shaky, astonished tone.

"Are you quite alright, Mr. Bickle?"

He nodded, his mouth still gaping. "It is like a dream."

"So it would seem—at least where money is concerned."

Bickle's brow furrowed. "What do you mean?"

How honest should she be with her old friend?

Before Tori could decide, Bickle said, "Are you worried about the ones who lived in the religious cult—er, commune—misbehaving if they move here?"

"I wouldn't say *worried*, but one does wonder how people accustomed to such liberties as *free love* and *group marriage* will fit into our little community." And those were only the terms she understood. Tori would have to look up at least several of the other phrases—especially *coitus reservatus*—when she had the opportunity.

She was especially concerned with Lord Balthazar Hale, whose appalling reputation most certainly preceded him.

But Tori could hardly tell Bickle that she possessed first-hand, unpleasantly intimate experience with men like Lord Balthazar—ones who took what they wanted, no matter what wreckage they left in their wake.

No, she couldn't tell anyone that.

However, as the person in charge of the female staff, Tori would do her *damnedest* to make sure none of the young women who worked for the duke were compromised by his disgusting brother.

"We will have to be vigilant," she said.

Bickle nodded thoughtfully. "Yes, that is always wise when there are young men in a house. But surely His Grace will keep his brother—all his brothers—in check, won't he?"

"I don't know anything about the new duke other than he didn't live at Canoga with the others. What did *The Times* have to say? You said something about him being upright and decent. I certainly hope so, because if he is anything like Lord Balthazar"—she bit her lip before she said something that she would regret about her new employer's family.

"Several of the papers mentioned that His Grace is a war hero and is renowned for his ethical behavior when it comes to financial matters." He smiled. "Indeed, he is evidently referred to as the Puritan of Wall Street for his moral stance regarding investments and such."

"Hmm. Well, that is promising. Perhaps he might be able to check his unruly siblings." Tori wasn't holding out much hope for that. After all, if the two men had only just met each other a few weeks before, how much influence could the duke exert over his rake of a brother?

"It will certainly be… lively," Bickle said.

"Yes, that is true." The last duke, God rest his soul, had lived a very quiet life for decades, spending most of his time in his library while Hastings Park had crumbled around him. The sprawling house had been crumbling long before him, of course, and at least he'd not been a gambler like his father, who'd depleted the estate dreadfully before his son could take over.

And now the title had gone across the Atlantic, evidently to the *Puritan of Wall Street*.

Strict morality wasn't the only characteristic associated with Puritans. It was possible the new duke might possess other, less pleasant, attributes: like narrow, conservative beliefs or rigid, unyielding notions of respectability. If that was the case, then he wouldn't be pleased to discover a mere woman all but running his estate, or at least what remained of it.

Tori had never wanted to assume such duties, but the old duke hadn't engaged a replacement steward after his last one had died, instead relying on Tori to assume several of the more onerous tasks.

Like keeping the ledgers, a chore for which she was singularly unsuited.

She noticed that Bickle's eyelids had begun to drift shut and realized this was usually his time to nap. Although she didn't know his age for certain, she guessed he was in his late eighties and should have retired years ago.

Torie cleared her throat softly and Bickle jolted awake. "Ah," he said, glancing around the room as if he couldn't remember where he was.

"I thought we might speak to the rest of the staff about His Grace's arrival tonight at dinner, Mr. Bickle," she said, gently nudging his memory.

Bickle blinked blearily. "Yes, yes. Very good."

"You and I can discuss our plan of attack and marshal our forces tomorrow after breakfast."

He gave her a relieved smile. "Excellent idea."

Torie watched as he pushed to his feet, his ancient bones creaking audibly.

Once the old man had gone, she went to stare out the window over what remained of the parterre garden. With only old MacLean, the ancient gardener, and his two assistants—both of whom had been grateful for the job as they'd come from a workhouse and required little more than room and board—Tori had needed to make some harsh choices when it came to what parts of the extensive grounds would receive any tending. The fact that Hastings Park's topiary was among the most famous in Britain had helped her make that decision. If MacLean—who was already in his late seventies—didn't teach somebody the fine art of maintaining the exquisite shrubs, his expertise might soon be lost forever. And so the topiary garden was in reasonably good shape while the rest of the formal gardens were in disarray.

Unfortunately, she'd not been as successful when it came to preserving Hastings itself. The rambling old mansion was desperately in need of attention, not just the expensive lead roof that was damaged in a dozen places, but the score of leaded windows, the ancient beetle-infested woodwork, and everything in between.

She sighed and turned away from the rather dreary view, catching sight of herself in the looking glass and freezing. A woman well-past her prime stared back at her. A woman whose pale blond hair was neatly plaited and pinned in a staid fashion and whose best feature—bright blue eyes—now had a webbing of fine lines at the corners.

In her youth she'd been accounted passably pretty. Now, as a woman in her thirties, her lithe, girlish figure had begun to thicken around the middle and her graceful step had become purposeful and plodding.

As the only child of a baronet—albeit an impoverished one—Tori should not have needed to work for her crust these last fourteen years, but one careless decision had put her on this path almost a decade and a half ago and there was no turning back.

As far as jobs went, Tori could not regret her position in the last Duke of Hastings's household. His Grace had been a kind, vague man who'd not cared that his young, widowed housekeeper had arrived with a toddler in tow. He'd been far more concerned that Tori had agreed to assume duties that should have been managed by either the mistress of the house, a personal secretary, or a house steward. Duties like gracefully rejecting unwanted social invitations, keeping his cellar stocked, and—for the last five years—paying bills and maintaining his ledgers.

The gentle pace of life at Hastings Park had allowed Tori to raise Jamie, her son, in a lovely, bucolic area for his first eleven years, until his paternal grandfather had finally acknowledged Jamie's existence and paid for him to go to Harrow, as her son's ancestors had done for hundreds of years.

Regardless of Tori's differences with Jamie's grandparents, she was grateful for their generous offer, even though she missed her son fiercely every single day.

Tori reluctantly pushed away thoughts of Jamie and turned back to the desk, which she had claimed as her own when the old duke had told her she could use his study as he had rarely left the library in the final years of his life. She would need to clear away her things now that there was a new duke coming.

She sorted through the keys on her chatelaine, unlocked the top desk drawer, and took out a letter, this one on much cheaper paper than the one from the lawyers, the contents neither written in copperplate nor proper grammar.

I know you never married. I know that boy o' yours is a bastard and there weren't no army captain.

Find yourself another position.

Or else...

Tori didn't really need to read it because she'd already memorized it, even though she'd only received it yesterday.

Her mind boggled at who could have sent this and why. There was no demand for money, only cruel threats. Who wrote a letter like this? What was the point?

Tori carefully folded up the letter and put it back in the drawer and locked it.

No, not your desk. The new Duke of Hastings' desk.

Although Tori had hidden her concern from Bickle, she was more than a little worried about the arrival of the duke and what that might mean for her.

The allegedly puritanical Duke of Hastings would probably not be amused if he learned that his housekeeper had lied about her name, her age, her dead husband, and her marriage. Not to mention the fact that Tori had used the power the last duke had given her to fill his house with servants who possessed dubious—if not outright criminal—histories.

But all that paled in comparison to the fact that Victoria herself was a wanted felon.

Chapter 2

Three Weeks Later

Balthazar Hale stared out the coach window, but he didn't see the lush green countryside of England.

Instead, he saw the last month and a half—passing in a blur—and all the steps that had wrenched him from his staid, predictable existence and taken him more than three thousand miles to a foreign country and a brand-new life.

Six weeks ago, he'd been the eldest of his five siblings.

Six weeks ago, he'd been an unknown farmer and inventor who was content, if not entirely satisfied, with his position in the perfectionist commune of Canoga, a community that was far from perfect although its members had, for its thirty-five-year history, striven to do what they believed was right and moral.

Six weeks ago, Bal had tossed all that away like so much rubbish, abandoning numerous principles to chase after an inheritance from a grandfather whom he'd never even known existed.

And he had done that at the behest of an older brother he'd only just met.

The sound of feminine laughter pulled him from his marveling. Beside him, his twin sister, Io, held several copies of the disreputable rags that flooded the streets of London, just as they'd flooded the streets of New York City. There might be many differences between the English and their American cousins, but the one characteristic they shared was a love of scandal.

Io raised up the headline so he could read it: *The Wicked Spare Has Arrived*!

Balthazar glared at his twin. "Why are you reading that garbage?"

"Because it is amusing. And creative." She grinned. "And also very naughty."

"Not to mention a passel of lies."

Io playfully bumped his shoulder with her own far more delicate frame. "When did you lose your sense of humor, Bal?"

"I suppose it was right around the time when these bloody exaggerated accounts of my sexual and moral depravity became all the rage." Bal spoke calmly, even though he wanted to rip the paper from her fingers, tear it to shreds, and then throw the bits and pieces out the window of the carriage.

"I hope you don't plan to punch every single newspaper man who approaches you," his sister suddenly chided.

Heat rushed to Bal's face at her unwelcome reminder of how he'd lost control of his temper more than once in the prior weeks.

He turned away from her to stare out the window. "I am not proud of what happened." That was true, but he couldn't deny the satisfaction he'd felt when he'd punched the smirking grins off those newspapermen's faces.

"Papa always said your temper would get you in trouble one day."

Bal snorted at that and exchanged an amused glance with his youngest brother, Apollo, who was sharing the seat across from him with Mr. Corbin Masterson, their brother Zeus's secretary.

"I think it was Bal's fists that got him in trouble," Apollo corrected, and then flashed a rare grin. "Those two punches also demonstrated the cowardice of journalists. They dispersed as quickly as a flock of pigeons confronted by a cat. Somebody should write a series of exposés about *them*."

Bal appreciated his younger brother's support, but the truth was that he really needed to learn to restrain his emotions. While the scurrilous stories had been insulting and frustrating—as had the dozens of newspapermen who'd loitered outside his brother's house in New York City and followed his every step—turning to violence had only generated *more* embarrassing articles.

"I would love it if somebody made up such tall tales about me," Io said.

Mr. Masterson's lips curled faintly at Io's pronouncement.

Naturally, Bal's twin noticed his expression.

"Just what are you smirking at, Mr. Masterson?" Io asked, her tone no longer teasing as it had been with Bal.

"Was I smirking? I'm so sorry, my lady," Masterson said in the same mild voice he always used when speaking to Io.

For reasons unknown to Bal, Io had taken a virulent dislike to their older brother's proper, somewhat starchy secretary. The two had wrangled over any and every subject, beginning in New York City and continuing unabated on the transatlantic journey to England.

Actually, it would be more accurate to say that Io argued, and Mr. Masterson merely *absorbed* her hostility, never looking perturbed, offended, or angry.

Really, the man was unflappable; Balthazar's steam plow showed more emotion than the enigmatic secretary.

And the calmer Masterson became, the more he incited Bal's normally rational sister.

Why the two had ended up in the same carriage together when there had been *three* carriages to choose from was anyone's guess.

Well, that wasn't true.

The one thing that Balthazar, his siblings, and even Masterson—though Bal doubted the other man would admit it—could all agree on was that none of them wanted to ride in the coach that held Zeus's fiancé, Miss Edith Barrymore.

Ares—who was Apollo's twin—and their youngest sister, Evadne, had scrambled to ride with Zeus's valet and Edith's snooty French dresser rather than riding with Edith herself.

That had left Zeus, Edith, and her cousin, the downtrodden Miss Susan Barclay, in the lead carriage. Clearly Masterson had decided that riding with Io was the lesser of two evils.

Or maybe he *enjoyed* arguing.

Bal took the crumpled papers from Io's fist and smoothed them out before turning to the second single-page *extra*—a newspaper term for a one-page special edition. He snorted at the headline emblazoned in huge letters: *Read the Riveting Final Installment of the Story that has Captured the Attention of an Entire Nation! The Wicked Spare and the Jezebel of Canoga! By Tirzah Fowler.*

Balthazar still couldn't believe that Tirzah had sold their friendship by concocting such an outlandish, prurient story.

It was true they'd been intimate—years before—but Tirzah had warped the details of their brief sexual union in such a way that their erstwhile relationship was unrecognizable. Unfortunately, the only *recognizable* part of her story was Balthazar's identity.

The utopian community of Canoga—which eschewed traditional marriage—encouraged their members to embrace their sexuality and experiment freely once they'd turned eighteen. Tirzah Fowler, twenty-two years Bal's senior, had been his sexual mentor, as one's first lover was often called at Canoga.

Bal wasn't so naïve that he didn't realize that such a relationship was shocking to most Americans—even without the spurious details that Tirzah had added. Growing up in Canoga he'd become accustomed to facing condemnation and judgement from the outside world, which often attacked both the principles Canogans lived by, not to mention physically and verbally attacking the members themselves.

Even without Tirzah fanning the flames of public outrage with her lies, outsider interest in the commune had almost always focused on sexual matters rather than more important issues, such as Canoga's gender equality.

But for the first time in his life, Balthazar couldn't blame non-Canogans for the way they were treating him. Tirzah had painted the humble commune as if it were ancient Rome, with their mild-mannered leader—Benjamin Hoyt—depicted as Nero in his final, debauched days.

Tirzah's inventive and lurid tales of sexually initiating virile, eighteen-year-old men—sometimes more than one at the same time—had sold so many copies in New York City that at least three newspapers had ordered additional printings.

If Tirzah had only described Bal's sexual initiation, it would have been bad enough.

But she'd also fabricated tales of mass orgies and other deviant sexual practices, no doubt encouraged by her publisher when they saw what a goldmine they had in the subject.

Balthazar was just grateful the authorities had not come to arrest him for some of the activities Tirzah had described. Thanks to her articles Bal had been spat at, physically attacked twice, and verbally derided times beyond counting on his long journey from Canoga to England—via New York City.

When his brother Zeus had first demanded that Bal and his siblings accompany him to England, he had been furious at the other man's high-handedness. How dare Zeus storm into their well-ordered lives and uproot them?

But after Tirzah's sensational lies began spreading faster than wildfire Bal had been grateful to get away from New York—and even America.

He'd hoped the stories of his degeneracy would lose steam and die somewhere in the mid-Atlantic before it ever reached Britain.

No such luck.

Bal could only pray that things would be different tucked away on his older brother's country estate, which was apparently in the middle of nowhere.

The articles about Balthazar were even worse when contrasted with the paeans the papers ran about his elder Zeus.

While Bal was being excoriated as a vile voluptuary, journalists portrayed Zeus as a man whose ethics and morality were almost Christlike.

On top of all that, Zeus Constantine Jonathan Hale was the new Duke of Hale.

Oh yes, *that* had captured the imagination of the nation. A wealthy American banker who was also a duke? Fully half of New York City's Upper Ten Thousand had flocked back to the City in the sweltering heat of summer to fawn on Zeus's custom-made boots.

The newspapers—both in New York and London—had minimized the fact that Zeus was a fourth-generation scion of one of America's richest banking families, instead focusing on his personal achievements. They'd made much of his sobriquet in the world of high finance: the Puritan of Wall Street, a nickname he'd earned because of his refusal to invest in dubious ventures regardless of how lucrative they might prove.

The journalists had a field day praising Zeus as a shining beacon of selfless heroism while contrasting him to the financier J.P. Morgan, who had paid three hundred dollars to purchase a substitute to fight for him during the War Between the States. Zeus, on the other hand, had volunteered before he could be drafted and had earned the Medal of Honor for saving the lives of two men during the Battle of Gettysburg.

Balthazar had not read a single complaint about Zeus in any of the dozens of newspaper articles he'd seen. The man did not drink to excess, patronize whores, or mistreat his servants and employees. To complete the picture of a living, breathing saint, his brother had rescued a three-legged street cur from certain death and the tattered, ugly hound—whom he'd named Mr. Clemens, to the amusement of the famous satirist himself—

had captured the American readers' hearts almost as much as Balthazar's alleged antics had captured their prurient imaginations.

Not that Balthazar didn't have a place in his brother's story, too. Dubbed *The Wicked Spare*, a mocking reference to the fact that he was Zeus's heir to the dukedom, he'd been repeatedly described as the man who'd left of trail of debauched weeping women—young and old—behind him in Canoga.

Tirzah's articles had also hinted—not so subtly—at Bal's darker, lewder activities. Implying that he had sexual perversions that were too revolting to be printed in newspapers.

The crowds that had gathered at the harbor in New York City to see them off had cheered wildly for the American duke while pelting Balthazar with rotted produce.

Yes, that had really happened. It was difficult to say what had been worse, being struck in the head by a rock-hard turnip or covered in rotten egg.

Bal thanked God that they weren't staying in London but travelling directly to his brother's country estate for the next few months. The British newspapers surely would have better things to talk about than The Wicked Spare by the time the Season commenced.

Wouldn't they?

Bal ground his teeth. Goddamned Tirzah! Every time he thought about the woman his hands clenched to throttle her. And to think she'd had the gall to write him a letter begging him to forgive her for the ridiculous lies she'd told.

I am deeply sorry for all this, Bal. I was told the story would sell better if I just... embroidered a little.

Ha! She'd not just embroidered; she'd stitched an entire damned wardrobe for the grasping editors.

I had no idea the story would capture the imagination and attention of so many people.

She didn't think that tales of raucous debauches and non-stop orgies would fascinate a nation that was obsessed with sex and doubly obsessed with denying that obsession?

I had to do it, Bal. After I left Canoga I realized just how hard life was outside the commune. I'm ashamed to admit it, but I needed the money to secure my future.

As much as Bal had hated to admit it, *that* had resonated with him. Hadn't he sold his own soul—albeit less sensationally and not to a newspaper—for money?

That's true, but you're selling out to protect your brothers and sisters, a helpful voice in his head pointed out.

Bal wanted to believe that was the only reason he was contemplating marriage—a stifling social convention that he had been raised to abhor—but he knew it was a lie.

When Zeus had shown up at Canoga six weeks ago—out of the blue—and introduced himself as his older brother, Bal had been absolutely floored by the news. His father had never given any indication that he'd been married before and had another son.

But that had only been the first of Zeus's many surprises.

Balthazar had also learned his older brother was the new Duke of Hastings, which made Bal and his four other brothers and sisters lords and ladies.

Most shocking of all, however, had been Zeus's disclosure about Bal's grandfather's will.

A grandfather that Balthazar had never met—his mother's father, a wealthy shipping magnate named Horace Sinclair—had left Bal his entire fortune of four million dollars.

Four. Million. Dollars.

Four. Million. Dollars.

No matter how often he repeated those words in his head he simply couldn't believe it.

Even after six weeks he *still* couldn't wrap his mind around such an astronomical sum. He'd never even known that he was related to Horace Sinclair, who'd been a titan of industry on the scale of men like Cornelius Vanderbilt and Leland Stanford.

And all Bal had to do to gain control of all that money was marry a *respectable* woman.

Respectable.

And who decided what was respectable? Why, Zeus, of course, the man in charge of executing his grandfather's will.

Balthazar had known right from the beginning that the matter of what constituted *respectable* would be contentious. Especially since both his dead grandfather and Zeus loathed everything the Canoga commune stood for, which made ever seeing eye-to-eye with his brother all but impossible. He and Zeus simply had no common ground other than a shared last name. They were strangers related by an accident of birth, raised in worlds that could hardly be more different.

But if Bal wanted four million dollars, he had to dance to his brother's tune.

He'd been furious, humiliated, and frustrated all at once.

Furious because a man he'd never even met could have such an impact on his life.

Humiliated because Zeus—who clearly despised the Canoga way of life and looked down on the people who lived there, including Balthazar—was the man who'd be deciding not just Bal's future, but which woman he could spend it with.

And frustrated because he'd known—almost from the moment he'd heard the words *four, million,* and *dollars* that there was no question as to whether he would do as he was told.

Over the last six weeks—as he'd locked horns repeatedly with his brother and his brother's insufferable fiancé—Bal had needed to remind himself that it would all be worth it in the end. With four million dollars he could guarantee that his younger siblings were secure for life. He could ensure that *they* weren't forced into a marriage with somebody who was *respectable*—or made to marry at all, if they didn't wish to do so.

With four million dollars all five of them could finally chase their dreams—whether those dreams led them back to Canoga or to somewhere entirely new.

All that money would allow Balthazar to perfect his new steam plow and perhaps even manufacture it. He could buy a farm of his own—a place he could operate without needing to put every single one of his ideas before a council, first.

Io could use her share of the money to support the many social justice issues that she'd worked so hard to support over the years.

Ares could open his own woodworking shop and make the one-of-a-kind pieces he yearned to make, instead of mass-producing cheap furniture for the manufactory back at Canoga.

Apollo could purchase a property where he could not only breed horses but live away from the demands of neighbors and society, as his introverted nature craved.

Evadne, his baby sister, could publish the lexicon of street cant that she'd been working on for years without having to submit the tome to a publishing house under a male pseudonym.

All Balthazar had to do to give them everything they'd ever dreamed of was get married.

To a woman approved by his older brother.

If his siblings ever learned that Bal was planning to sacrifice his beliefs, and his future, to acquire money for them, they would *never* accept it from him.

And so, for the first time in his life, he was keeping a secret from them—four million secrets—and it was sheer misery. Especially withholding the truth from his twin.

He knew that Io suspected *something* must have happened to convince Bal—who'd been the only one of his brothers and sister to be genuinely content at Canoga—to accept Zeus's offer to come to England and live in their ancestral family home for two years.

She had peppered him with numerous questions—why are you going? Why two years? Why do we have to live in Zeus's house? Why is Zeus giving us allowances? And on and on and on.

It shamed Bal to admit it, but he'd lied to her—he'd had to, if he was to keep his secret—telling her that he was eager to go and encouraging her and the others to accept Zeus's offer, too.

"Bal—look!" Io said, jolting him from his musings.

He looked to where his sister was pointing. "Good Lord," he murmured as he took in the sprawling monstrosity that must be Hastings Park. "It looks more like a walled city than a house."

"There must be at least two hundred rooms," Io said.

"There are three-hundred-and-sixty-one rooms," Masterson corrected in his cool, clipped voice. "It is only four rooms shy of being a calendar house." He hesitated and then said, "They are called calendar houses because—"

"Because that is how many days are in a year," Io interrupted, glowering at the secretary. "Just because we didn't grow up in New York City does not mean we are cretins, Mr. Masterson."

"That is the farthest thought from my mind, my lady," Masterson said mildly.

Bal thought it was fortunate there were over three hundred rooms at Hastings Park; they would need to make sure that at least two hundred of them were kept between Io and Mr. Masterson.

Chapter 3

Victoria stood at the head of the line of servants, beside Mr. Bickle, waiting to greet their new employer and his family.

It was all she could do not to gape like a hayseed at the collection of magnificent coaches that rolled over the rutted driveway toward the house. It had been a long, long time since Hastings Park had seen such luxury, certainly not in all the years that she had lived there.

Bickle made a soft cooing sound that caused a bubble of laughter to well up inside her.

"Yes, it's rather impressive, isn't it? I wouldn't be surprised to see the Queen herself step out of one," Tori said in a voice so low that even Bickle didn't appear to hear her.

Which was just as well; the last thing she needed was to be overheard by a servant saying something so vulgar.

As the carriages slowed Bickle turned toward the fidgeting, gawking line of servants and cut them a stern look. They instantly straightened their spines, turned their eyes forward, and stood still, all except Reginald and Benjamin, the two footmen who approached the carriages as they rolled to a halt.

His Grace's only letter to them—written on his behalf by his secretary, Mr. Masterson, rather than the duke himself—had arrived not long after the letter Tori had received from the solicitors. Although Mr. Masterson had said that Tori should engage any new servants she believed necessary, she had decided to hire only the minimum and leave the selection of more footmen—whom employers often had special requirements for—to their new master.

Mr. Masterson had also indicated that His Grace's siblings would be engaging personal servants shortly after they arrived, so there would be a flurry of prospective candidates taking the train up from a London employment agency later in the week.

It turned out that Reg and Benjy weren't needed after all as each of the coaches had their own liveried servants, all handsome, youthful men who gracefully leapt off the magnificent equipages to open doors and flip down the steps.

The first to emerge from the lead carriage was a very tall, dark-haired man dressed in expensive, but sedate, clothing. He waved away the footman and handed out two ladies himself.

The first woman was his perfect match—sable-haired, willowy, and elegantly clad.

The second was so small that at first Victoria thought she might be a child. But when she turned her face toward them, Tori saw she was an adult, perhaps even as old as Victoria.

One last occupant came flying down the carriage steps, and the man snapped his fingers and the dog pranced over to him, the hound's gait strange given that it only had three legs. The newspapers had loved the story about the new Duke of Hastings's pet—Mr. Clemens—a three-legged street cur that he'd rescued. The hound looked to be a mix of several breeds and was not especially attractive, although his obvious adoration for his master was charming.

Tori was so busy watching the occupants of the first carriage that she didn't realize the other two had disgorged their occupants. Four males and two women—several of them bearing a strong resemblance to the first man, whom she assumed was the duke—converged on the gathered servants.

Bickle bowed as low as his old bones permitted. "I am Bickle, Your Grace, it is truly a pleasure to have you here, sir. I've served as butler for your family for fifty-one years, sir, as did my father and grandfather before me."

"It is a pleasure to meet you, Bickle," the duke said, his accent surprising Tori, who'd momentarily forgotten he was American.

He turned to Victoria and she lowered into a deep curtsey. "Welcome, Your Grace. I am Mrs. Dryden, housekeeper at Hastings Park these past thirteen years."

The man's eyes were the pale frosty blue-gray of a new moon and the expression in them was one of sharp, discerning intelligence. Victoria felt as though she'd seen him before, and then realized there was a portrait in the gallery that bore a striking resemblance to the new duke.

He inclined his head. "A pleasure, Mrs. Dryden. Thank you both for readying Hastings Park for our arrival on such short notice." The duke turned to the tall dark-haired woman who stood beside him. "This is my fiancé, Miss Barrymore." He raised his voice slightly so the other servants could hear him. "Although we will not marry until next year, you will treat her as the mistress of Hastings Park." He gestured to the people standing slightly behind him. "These are my sisters and brothers: Lord Balthazar, Lady Io, Lord Ares, Lord Apollo, and Lady Evadne."

Victoria had eyes for only one of the newcomers.

The newspapers had done an exceptional job with their illustration of Lord Balthazar Hale. But, as handsome as he'd appeared on paper, he was even more attractive in person.

His deep-set eyes were heavy-lidded, almost sleepy, and his sinfully full lips were curved into a faint smile, as if he viewed life with amusement. Both he and the duke were well over the average height for Englishmen, but whereas His Grace was all lean elegance, Lord Balthazar had the chest and shoulders of a bull, his massive size oppressive even though he was standing at a distance from her.

One thing the newspaper illustration had *not* managed to communicate was just how much charm the man oozed, even in repose.

Tori's ex-lover Teddy had been called a rake, but he had nothing on *this* man.

As if he'd heard her thoughts, Lord Balthazar turned to her and met her gaze.

Torie felt a sudden tightening in her chest at his bold, quizzical look.

Just like His Grace, Lord Balthazar's eyes were light. But instead of a frosty blue, his were the brilliant green-gold of an unripe apple. His sensual smile deepened as his eyes flickered over her person.

Tori knew instantly that she was being assessed by a connoisseur of women.

Heat flared in her body, the intense physical reaction one she'd not felt for a long, long time.

Not since Teddy.

Not since she'd been young, naïve, and very, very trusting.

Not since she'd believed that falling in love with a man would lead to something wonderful, rather than pain—physical and emotional—and betrayal.

Tori knew her body's reaction was telling; this man was a rake in the true sense of the word. He was the sort of man who could turn any woman's head, whether she wanted it turned, or not. He was a danger to be avoided at all costs. Tori was too old to be at risk, but she'd recently hired several very pretty maids…

"And last, but not least," the duke said, breaking into Tori's fretting, "this is Miss Barclay, who is Miss Barrymore's cousin." The duke's stern, intimidating gaze softened slightly as he introduced the tiny, rather timid-looking woman who'd ridden in the carriage with His Grace and his fiancé.

She bobbed a quick curtsey and then smiled nervously, her huge blue eyes darting from Tori to Bickle to the duke.

"Where is my reticule, Susan?" Miss Barrymore barked.

Miss Barclay flinched. "Oh, I'm so sorry, Edith. It is in the—"

"I don't need a soliloquy. Go *fetch* it," Miss Barrymore said in a tone that caused Victoria's face to heat in sympathy for Miss Barclay, who quickly scurried back to the coach.

Tori glanced at the others in the duke's party, interested to see their reactions to the little interlude.

The duke was quietly speaking to the ancient gardener, who stood next to Bickle. Lady Io was regarding her soon-to-be sister-in-law with undisguised loathing. The gorgeous twins wore identical, faintly disgusted smirks. The exceedingly beautiful Lady Evadne didn't appear to have noticed the embarrassing exchange, at all. Instead, she was gazing at Hastings with wonder, her obvious appreciation of her new home both charming and heartening among such an intimidating crowd.

And The Wicked Spare was still looking directly at Victoria.

Without her realizing it, he had come closer, until he was barely a foot from her.

His shockingly green eyes were so thickly lashed that the only creature she'd ever seen to match him was her childhood pony, Percy, who'd also had lovely eyes—and Satan's own temper to go with his handsome looks.

As if he could hear her thoughts Lord Balthazar's mouth pulled up on one side, the crooked smile even more devastating than his sensual smirk.

Torie rapidly changed her assessment of him.

He didn't look like her naughty pony. He looked every bit like a fox assessing the inhabitants of the henhouse.

***

Balthazar knew he should stop staring, but his brother's new housekeeper was not the sort of woman one usually found in that position. Or at least not what *he'd* imagined a housekeeper to look like. Indeed, the woman who'd kept house at Zeus's monstrous Fifth Avenue mansion had been gray-haired, barrel-shaped, and hatchet-faced. *That* was a housekeeper.

This woman, on the other hand…

She was garbed all in black bombazine like the chatelaine of some remote castle in one of the gothic novels Eva enjoyed reading.

The severe clothing enhanced, rather than dimmed, her appearance. She wasn't exactly pretty, but she was striking, her eyes an attractive sky blue and her high bridged nose lending her an air of dignity.

While her bodice was long-sleeved and high-necked it could not disguise the lush body beneath the yards of fabric. She was tightly corseted, the difference between her wasp waist and generous bosom sensually appealing. Bal had grown up around women who didn't employ devices to shape their figures, who wore loose garments and kept their hair as short as the men in their community.

Mrs. Dryden, with her idealized female form—complete with long, shiny blond hair that probably reached her bottom when unbound—was almost irresistibly attractive.

Unfortunately, she was looking at him as if she expected him to start ravishing the female servants right in front of her. It was exactly the same sort of censorious loathing that he'd been forced to tolerate in the weeks since Tirzah had painted him as the human embodiment of Bacchus.

Bal snorted. So, the prim looking Mrs. Dryden disapproved of him, did she?

The anger that had simmered in his belly ever since he'd left Canoga and exposed himself to the incessant censure of strangers flared hotter when she pursed her lips and turned firmly away from him, as if Balthazar was a sight too vulgar to be borne.

Bal briefly wished that he was the type of man who would give her something to justify that cool judging look.

Leave her alone; she's your brother's servant.

Oh, he would leave her alone; her and the hundreds like her who regarded him as if he were a monster that had just stepped out of Blake's *Red Dragon*.

"Somebody doesn't like you very much," Apollo whispered.

"You noticed that, did you?"

"Apparently your reputation precedes you. Perhaps I should warn her that it is Ares she should really be concerned about?"

It was true that Apollo's twin changed lovers more frequently than most men changed their stockings. Fortunately—for Ares—he had huge, deceptively guileless eyes and a sweet smile that seemed to protect him from the sorts of accusations and rumors that Bal effortlessly attracted.

"Knowing Ares, he'll tame and bed the judgmental Mrs. Dryden before the month is even out and I will be blamed for it in some newspaper article," Bal whispered.

Pol snorted at that.

They waited while Zeus and Edith went down the line of bowing and curtseying servants, just like the master and mistress in some medieval play. His brother had only been a duke for six weeks, but he'd been a wealthy man with lots of servants all his life, so he was accustomed to having his every whim catered to.

Personally, servants made Bal uncomfortable. After all, he and his younger siblings had grown up doing everything for themselves—from laundry to cooking to mending their clothes. Only when he'd gone away to Princeton for three years had he enjoyed the services of a laundrywoman.

"I've had chambers prepared in the family wing, if you would like to freshen up before tea," Mrs. Dryden said after Zeus had greeted the last of the servants, a little boot black who couldn't have been older than seven or eight.

"That sounds excellent," Zeus said. "Please lead the way."

Hastings Park—his brother's country seat—was an assault to the senses. It was simply too big, too grand, and too much. Bal felt like he needed another three sets of eyes to see even a fraction of the fascinating architectural details and *objets d'art* they passed as the housekeeper led them through the seemingly mazelike house.

Mrs. Dryden gave a fascinating running tour as they went, describing the age of the various additions and the dukes who'd constructed them. Bal knew next to nothing about ancient architecture and was awed by the age of the various wings they passed through.

The housekeeper halted when they reached a long room whose walls were packed closely with paintings.

"This is the original portrait gallery," she said as they all stopped to gape at the pictures that lined the walls all the way to the ceiling. "Of special interest are the portraits by Bosch and Gainsborough, depicting the second Duke of Hastings, Thomas Hale, and the sixth duke, Anthony Hale, respectively."

As ignorant of art as Balthazar was, even he recognized those two names. It was astonishing to think that all these people were *his* ancestors.

"You are very knowledgeable about the house and its contents, Mrs. Dryden," Edith said, her condescending tone grating on Bal just as it always did. He'd often wondered what Hell might be like; after spending eight solid days on an ocean liner with Edith, Bal now had a fair idea.

"It has been my pleasure to learn the history of Hastings and its occupants over the years I've resided here," the housekeeper said. "But there is a great deal that I do not know. You will find the three-volume history of the family in the library of great interest," she added, escorting them toward a set of intricate wooden stairs.

"This one looks a great deal like you, Zeus," Io said, stopping before the rest of them could follow the housekeeper up the stairs.

Zeus paused to look at a portrait of a man garbed in the clothing of perhaps a hundred years earlier. "It does a little."

Bal thought the resemblance was remarkable.

"That is Godric Hale, Your Grace," Mrs. Dryden said. "He was active in politics and served as Home Secretary for Lord Rockingham."

"Oh, look," Eva said, pointing at a portrait that hung much higher and was badly faded. "Twins."

"Twins have always run in the Hale family," Mrs. Dryden said. "Those two were the youngest brothers of a different Godric Hale, one who headed the family during the Civil War. The canvas, along with a great many others, was badly damaged and many were lost when the house was occupied by Cromwell's forces."

"So, the Hales were royalists then," Eva said, looking delighted by that fact.

"Yes, my lady." Mrs. Dryden smiled at Eva, the expression far more open than any she'd turned on the rest of Bal's family. But then people frequently smiled when they looked at his youngest sister. Not just because she was exceptionally lovely, but Eva also emanated a genuine joy that drew people to her.

"This part of the house is one of the older sections and these stairs date back to the early Tudor Era," Mrs. Dryden continued as they followed her up the ornate staircase.

"They are exquisite," Io said. "They look so fragile."

"They are surprisingly sturdy when it comes to human use but we have faced an uphill battle keeping them safe from deathwatch beetles."

"A battle you will no longer need to concern yourself with now that His Grace is here to bear the burden," Edith said.

The housekeeper's back stiffened at the other woman's patronizing tone. "Of course, Miss Barrymore," Mrs. Dryden murmured, her tone suitably chastened.

The remainder of the tour took place in silence.

***

Tori was directing the mountains of luggage to their correct destinations when she heard Bickle sending one of the new maids—a lovely young girl named Eunice—off to Lord Balthazar's chambers with fresh towels and a pitcher of steaming water.

"Do you have a moment, Mr. Bickle?"

"Of course, Mrs. Dryden."

Tori stepped away from the milling servants and ducked into the corridor that led to the unused east wing, opening the door to an unused room and waiting as Bickle made his painfully slow way to join her.

"Yes, Mrs. Dryden?"

"I think we should send only Nora and Patricia to wait on Lord Balthazar, Mr. Bickle."

The old man blinked owlishly at her.

Tori leaned closer to him, "You might recall that Lord Balthazar is the one we read about." When he still didn't look like he took her meaning, she threw subtlety to the wind and said, "I don't think we should trust his lordship's self-restraint with the younger, prettier maids, Mr. Bickle."

Comprehension dawned in his cloudy eyes slowly, like the sun pushing through a persistent fog. "Ah. Er, you really believe we should be concerned?"

"I think we should be prudent, Mr. Bickle."

The butler nodded. "Of course, of course. I shall see to it right now, Mrs. Dryden," he said, and shuffled off to amend his order.

"I wouldn't even send an ugly maid up to wait on me."

Tori yelped and whipped around. "Lord Balthazar! I did not realize you were behind us."

"Obviously." He was leaning against the doorframe, his arms crossed over his broad chest. "As I was saying, I wouldn't send a woman at all; I'd send a man. Several of the more strapping footmen look like they could hold their own against me if I became… amorous." His sensual lips were curved into a mocking smile—which she was beginning to suspect was just his face in repose—but his greenish gold eyes were as cold as the Outer Hebrides in winter.

Tori's face was so hot that she swore there was a red glow in the corridor. "I'm sorry, my lord. I didn't mean to—"

"You didn't mean to be overheard, I'm sure. But you meant what you said. Don't compound matters by lying, Mrs. Dryden."

Tori shut her mouth with a snap.

"You're probably wondering what I'm doing here."

She had been wondering that, but she'd already made enough of an arse of herself, so she said nothing.

"I came looking for one of my pieces of luggage and took a wrong turn and got lost. I wandered through several miles of hallway and somehow ended up here." His eyes glittered with dark amusement. "It's almost as if fate lured me here." He pushed off the doorframe and strolled around the quaint, octagonal chamber. "What an interesting space, almost… cozy. With the addition of a few chaise lounges and some comfortable settees this would be the perfect room for an intimate… bacchanal."

Tori's lips tightened, her face—impossibly—becoming even hotter. "You are mocking me, my lord."

"Now, whatever would make you think that?" he asked, prowling closer, not stopping until she had to crane her neck to hold his uncomfortable gaze. The smile that curved his lips was not a pleasant one. "Perhaps you should be the one to serve me, Mrs. Dryden? Just to be on the safe side."

"I—"

"Yes," he said, the word a low hiss. "I think that is best. Tomorrow you can deliver hot water and towels. To my *bed*chamber." His teeth flashed, looking very white against the tanned skin of his face. "I get up early, Mrs. Dryden. And I like my water to be steaming hot."

Before Tori could contrive an answer, he brushed past her and went into the foyer where he paused to pick up a valise and then disappeared from view, heading back toward his room and taking the right path this time, rather than lurking in unused corridors and eavesdropping on unsuspecting idiots like herself.

Tori groaned, closed her eyes, and sagged back against the wall, wishing it would swallow her whole.

Chapter 4

Bal was tempted to remain in his room the following morning just to see if Mrs. Dryden really did bring his water up.

As amusing as that prospect was, he'd made plans with Zeus to go riding at first light, and he didn't want to offend his brother when Zeus appeared to be extending an olive branch.

And so, Bal had washed his face in cold water left over from the night before, rather than ring for more.

By the time he and Zeus returned from their very pleasurable ride several hours later, Balthazar's somewhat infamous temper had cooled enough that he didn't summon Mrs. Dryden specifically when he wanted hot water. Instead, he sent a passing footman to run the errand.

Mrs. Dryden did not bring him water the next morning, either. Or the morning after that. He was both amused and irked to notice that the maid who delivered the pitcher and towels had white hair and was a good four decades his senior.

So, Mrs. Dryden was not easily cowed, was she?

For almost three days he didn't catch so much as a glimpse of the housekeeper's pale blond head or stiff bombazine skirts.

Part of that had been because Bal was too busy interviewing candidates for valet. But he also suspected the lovely, censorious Mrs. Dryden might be avoiding him after their little fracas. Given the size of Hastings, a person could easily hide and never been seen for years.

Engaging a personal servant had been a unique and not entirely pleasant experience. When Zeus had originally said that Bal and his younger brothers needed valets, he had resisted the notion. But even the relaxed country schedule at Hastings Park required changing his clothing at least three times a day, not to mention the matter of bathing—which was a time-consuming affair as the old house did not have running water.

And then there was the issue of determining *which* clothing should be worn where and when and with what.

Last, but not least, was the almost full-time job of maintaining said garments, most of which cost more than the average servant would make in several years of labor. He'd always dressed humbly and had washed his own clothing at Canoga because their community did not make distinctions between women's or men's work. But the clothing Zeus had dragged Bal, Ares, and Apollo to expensive shops to purchase in New York City was not the sort you could scrub in a tub and hang on a line.

And so, Bal had reluctantly accepted that while he might not want a servant, he definitely needed one.

That said, he didn't want a valet like Zeus's man—a pinch-faced, bloodless, slave to propriety named Beaks.

No, if he was forced to engage a personal servant—a man who would see even more of Balthazar than his past lovers had—then he at least wanted that person to be somebody he liked and not just tolerated.

He especially wanted somebody who didn't look down on him, which was not an easy feat as he was quickly learning that many servants were even more snobbish than their masters.

Balthazar had to sit through seven interviews before he found the applicant who met his specifications. Daniel Napier was only two years older than Bal but had already held a position for an older baronet, who'd given the man a glowing recommendation.

Napier had enough experience to make up for what Bal lacked, but not so much that he would attempt to badger or boss him.

Between settling in and interviewing, the first week at Hastings Park was busy and filled with adjustments both large and small.

By the second week, however, Bal realized that he would quickly go mad from boredom if he didn't find something to occupy his time. At Canoga he'd been in charge of farming and, in his spare time, he'd tinkered with his various inventions. His days had been full and long, and he liked keeping busy.

Bal would be in England for at least two years—which was the amount of time his grandfather's will allowed him to find a wife before the four million dollars went to the Presbyterian church. He needed some sort of employment that didn't involve bending his elbow at the village pub with his younger brothers every evening.

Which is what he was doing right now—for the third time in less than a week.

"Can I get you anything else, my lord?

Bal looked up from his pint to find Joanne Fletcher—the friendly, attractive widow who owned the King's Quarrel—leaning over his table.

It did not escape his notice that her bodice was exceptionally low cut and filled to bursting.

Nor was he unaware that she'd been casting sexual lures his way since the first night he'd entered her establishment. He could see in her welcoming gaze that she believed the stories she'd read about his rampant sexuality and was eager to test the truth of them. It wasn't the first time a woman had looked at him in such a way—as if he were some sort of rare specimen that required close examination—no matter that he did nothing to encourage such attention.

Balthazar lifted his half-empty glass and said, "Yes, please. A round for me and my brothers."

A loud cheer erupted in the corner of the tap room—where there was not one, but four occupied dartboards. A half-dozen men dressed in farming garb were watching Ares and Apollo pit their considerable skills against each other. His brothers were identical twins, at least when it came to looks, and always garnered attention whenever they went anywhere together.

"You seem busier tonight than the last few times I've been here," Bal said when the woman lingered.

"Aye, men in town to help with the harvest. They'll be here for the next several weeks."

"There are not enough workers in the area to bring in the crops?"

"Not these days. Many of our young men have gone off to work in the cities." She cut him a cautious look and then added, "Much of the land hereabout has been neglected and overworked and the harvests for many years haven't been good enough that farmers can keep their boys at home. Many can't afford the workers that come to harvest, either." She shrugged. "People pull together and lads from miles around help with their neighbor's harvesting."

That was the way it had been in the area around Canoga, too. Not that anyone had ever come to help their commune harvest. But the farmers who'd lived around Canoga had volunteered to help their neighbors. They worked together and then celebrated together, putting on a large harvest festival and dance every year. Neither of which any Canogans had ever been invited to. Not even after Bal had helped several farmers assess soil problems on their land did any of the locals ever extend any friendship.

But perhaps things might be different here.

"How does a person know who needs help?" he asked Mrs. Fowler.

She smiled, her eyes wandering over his upper body and her lips curving. "Fancy doing some real man's work, do you?"

Bal laughed, not bothering to tell her that he'd worked as a farmer all his life. "I would give it a go."

Her smirk deepened and she looked toward the crowd at the dart board. "Small Jimmy!" she called over the din.

A man who stood a good head taller than any of his fellows broke off from the group and came striding toward Bal's table.

"Wantin' me, Jo?" He waggled his eyebrows suggestively down at the winsome widow, who leered right back up at him and jabbed him in the side with a sharp elbow.

"Mind yer manners, Jimmy or your ma will hear about it. Where is the work tomorrow?"

The giant—probably a few years younger than Bal—slid him a curious look. "Handy with a falx, my lord?"

Balthazar was amused to hear the ancient word for *scythe*. "I can cut and bind wheat."

Jimmy grinned, the expression even more vulpine than the one he'd just cut Mrs. Fletcher. "We'll be at Pendleton's for the next three days just after first light. And then on to Brower's after that."

"Thank you, I just might join you."

The younger man thought that was amusing, laughing as he went back to join his fellows and no doubt spread the news that The Wicked Spare would try to keep up with strapping English lads.

"Walter Pendleton is one of His Grace's farmers," Mrs. Fletch explained. "His only son died in the Crimea and he's been a widower for a good fifteen years."

Bal knew what she meant: the farmer was probably worn to the bone with nobody at home to cook and clean for him, not to mention help bringing in a harvest.

He threw back the rest of his ale and smiled at her. "I'll stand that loud group in the corner a round," he said, sliding more money across the table. "But I'm afraid I've changed my mind about another for myself, Mrs. Fletcher. If I'm going to keep up with Small Jimmy and his mates in the morning, then I'd better get some rest tonight."

***

Victoria hopped down from the gig and took the basket from beneath the bench seat where she'd tucked it.

The day had been unseasonably warm and this was the last delivery of five that afternoon. She felt every bit as wilted as the hydrangeas that grew alongside the short walk leading up to the Brower's small but tidy farmhouse.

Before she could even knock on the door it opened.

"Good afternoon, Mrs. Dryden." Doris, the Brower's spinster daughter looked flustered, her normally pale cheeks darkly flushed.

"Is aught amiss, Miss Brower, you are in high color," Tori said, unaccustomed to seeing the mild woman look so lively.

If anything, her question seemed to cause Doris's flush to deepen. "Oh no, nothing amiss. Please do come in, Mrs. Dryden."

"How is your mother today?" Tori asked as she handed the basket to the other woman in the cramped but cool entry hall.

"The heat has made her tired and I'm afraid she is napping, even though she tried to stay awake for your visit."

Tori followed Miss Brower into a pretty parlor which she suspected the Brower women only used when they received her.

For once, the heavy drapes that were always closed to protect the furniture were open, showing a view of the small back yard that she rarely ever saw.

It was immediately apparent to Tori why the drapes were open when she witnessed the scene that was playing out at the edge of the large field that lay just beyond the Browers' yard.

Miss Brower gave a nervous titter as she followed Tori's gaze to the dozen or so half-naked men who'd gathered around Mr. Brower's wagon to partake of something in a barrel—ale or possibly cider.

Tori had lived in the country all her life so the sight of shirtless farm workers during the summer was not something that surprised her, especially around harvest time.

But her eyes were immediately drawn to one bare torso in particular and she couldn't pull her gaze away.

"The duke's brothers have come for three days to help Papa," Miss Brower said, her voice breathless as she stood beside Tori and stared out at the gods that appeared to have come down from Olympus to frolic on her family's farm. "Every. Day." She repeated in an awed tone.

"Indeed," was all Tori could manage, swallowing to moisten her unaccountably dry throat.

They enjoyed the view in companiable silence.

Tori had no idea which of the men had captured Miss Brower's attention, but she could not pull either her thoughts or her eyes away from one man.

Even amid a group of muscular, half-naked, sweat-slicked farm laborers Lord Balthazar Hale stood out. Not just because he was taller and broader than almost everyone except for Jimmy Parker, but also for the perfection of his massive, sun-browned torso.

She spared a quick, grudging glance for his two younger brothers and saw they were similarly blessed and yet they did not draw the eye the way Lord Balthazar did.

You mean they don't draw your *eye.*

Tori could not argue with that.

The hot afternoon sun had sheened his golden body with sweat and when he laughed at something one of the men said, the muscles in his shoulders and abdomen rippled enticingly beneath his skin.

When he lifted his cup of ale, his throat flexed as he swallowed, and a few stray drops of liquid slid down his chin and glinted in the sun.

Beside her, Doris grunted softly—as if something had knocked the air from her lungs—and murmured, "Oh."

The other woman's stunned reaction gave Tori a good idea which man she was ogling.

A sour, unpleasant emotion that she recognized as jealousy twisted and turned in her belly. Tori gritted her teeth at the jarring feeling, furious with herself. What right did she have to be jealous of Lord Balthazar Hale?

None.

Besides, who could blame Doris for staring at him? The man might be a repellent, immoral, womanizing rake, but there was no denying that he was magnificent.

"How long have you been standing here?" Tori asked.

"Only about half an hour," Doris said. But then added after a long pause, her tone embarrassed by also slightly rebellious, "I was upstairs for most of the day. The view is better from up there when they go out to the field."

Tori turned to the other woman, who slowly pulled her attention away from the lovely view and met her gaze, her cheeks scarlet.

She didn't know which of them started laughing, but once they'd started, it took a while to stop.

"Even Mother came out to watch for a while yesterday," Miss Brower admitted once she'd wiped the tears of mirth from her eyes and caught her breath. "It quite perked her up. She said she hasn't felt better in years."

Tori was still chuckling when she turned back to the window, her jaw sagging at what she saw. Lord Balthazar had set down his glass and was stretching his arms over his head, the action setting off an awe-inspiring display of masculine perfection as the muscles danced beneath his taut brown skin.

Doris groaned. "Oh, dear God in heaven."

Tori could not have said it better, herself.

Lord Balthazar didn't lower his arms completely after he'd finished stretching. Instead, he reached up and rubbed his broad chest, his big hand massaging the slabbed pectoral, fingers kneading the tightly woven muscle, as if he were sore.

Tori swallowed. And then did it again, her breathing loud in the small room.

One of them—Tori wasn't sure if it was her, or Doris—made a choked squeaking sound when Lord Balthazar's hand slid with painful slowness down his chest and over his chiseled abdomen, his fingertips dipping beneath the low-slung waist of his sinfully thin leather breeches.

Tori held her breath as his hand lingered for a moment. *Go lower,* she urged, thankfully only inside her head.

Her prayers went unanswered.

Instead, he absently rubbed his flat belly with those long, sensitive-looking fingers and then dropped his hand to his side.

Tori wrenched her gaze upward.

And saw that Lord Balthazar Hale was looking right at her.

She froze like some forest creature suddenly confronted by a hunter. *Turn and run*! the part of her brain devoted to self-preservation shouted.

No, stay, the much louder, reckless part ordered.

Tori stood frozen with indecision, unable to pull her gaze from the provocative creature beyond the glass.

As if he could read her indecent, hungry thoughts—and was amused by them—he grinned.

And then he winked at her.

***

Balthazar cocked his head and squinted. At first, he'd thought it a trick of the light—that it was just the farmer's spinster daughter watching from the window.

The woman had gawked non-stop for the past three days, her presence at the upstairs window of the cottage provoking many of the workers to naughty behavior now that they knew they had an audience, and a female one at that.

But it wasn't just the farmer's daughter in that window right now.

It was the prim, proper, and judgmental Mrs. Dryden in there, right beside her, ogling the shirtless workers.

Ogling Balthazar, in point of fact.

Bal knew his physique was not as classically perfect as his younger brothers or as slim and elegant as Zeus's more aristocratic form, but he had a big, almost brutish, body that seemed to appeal to plenty of women.

And based on the way Mrs. Dryden was staring, she was one of those women.

His mouth curled into a smile and—before he could stop himself—he put on a little show for her, rubbing himself in a way that emphasized his best physical attributes.

It was difficult not to burst out laughing when her jaw dropped.

It was also difficult not to harden at the worshipful expression on her face.

By the time he finished his brief performance both women were gaping.

Mrs. Dryden's wide eyes slid up his body and met his.

Bal knew he shouldn't tease her, but he did it anyhow.

Even from this distance he saw her eyes go wide when he winked at her.

And then she spun around and disappeared from the window, no doubt thinking to flee without having to face him.

"Oh, no you don't. Not so fast," he muttered beneath his breath.

Bal grabbed his shirt and yanked it over his head before quickly slipping on his waistcoat and coat, not bothering with his buttons.

His clothes were old—ones he'd brought with him from Canoga—because the work was too hard and dirty to wreck any of his new, expensive garments. His buckskins were ancient and they'd been patched often. They were worn thin in so many places that they would probably not be of use for much longer. The cuffs on the shirt he wore were frayed almost to ribbons and his waistcoat had once been navy blue but had faded to gray. He'd not thought to see anyone other than other farm workers and the spying daughter today. And yet who should arrive to see him in his dishabille but the queen of judgment, Mrs. Dryden herself.

He grabbed his battered work hat and jogged toward the house.

"Wait, Bal! Aren't you coming with us to the Quarrel?" Ares called after him. "We're going to swing by for a quick pint before we go home for dinner. Jimmy is going to take on Pol—the best two out of three."

"Not today," Bal shouted over his shoulder, running full out when he caught a flash of a black skirt on the far side of Brower's cottage.

"One moment, Mrs. Dryden!" he called out when he skidded around the corner of the house in time to see her scramble rather inelegantly up onto the bench of a little gig.

Her shoulders stiffened and she turned slowly until she was facing him.

"Lord Balthazar," she said, eyeing him primly, as if she'd not just been staring at him like a lecher at a brothel peep show.

"Are you going back to Hastings, Mrs. Dryden?"

She hesitated for a long moment before cautiously saying, "Yes."

"Good. You won't mind giving me a lift, then?" He strode around to the other side of the cart before she could answer and climbed up, lowering himself onto the narrow seat beside her, amused when she jerked away from him as if she had just touched a hot coal.

But like a hermit crab trying to pull into a too-small shell, there was nowhere for her to go on the narrow bench.

"It's a tight fit, isn't it?" He bared his teeth at her, amused and annoyed by the way she shied away from him, as if he were going to tear off her clothing and start making love to her in broad daylight.

Not that the thought didn't have its appeal.

Her ivory throat flexed as she swallowed and her coral pink lips pursed into a line, until their fascinating color bled almost to white.

She stared doggedly ahead and clucked her tongue, skillfully turning the gig in a tight circle.

Bal knew he was behaving badly sitting so close to her—and he probably stank, as well. He should probably crawl into the small cart bed to give her more room, but something about her pursed mouth and critical gaze brought out the devil in him.

"What brings you to Brower's farm today, Mrs. Dryden? Just sight-seeing?"

Her mouth pursed even tighter and the little he could see of her cheeks beneath the wide brim of her hat was a healthy pink. "I always visit Mrs. Brower on the last Friday of the month, my lord."

"Oh? And why is that?"

"She is bedbound and the Browers have only their daughter to cook, keep house for them, and act as nurse to her mother."

"How selfless of you."

Her head whipped around at his mocking tone. "It is no more selfless than you and your brothers volunteering to help with the harvest."

"You sound almost affronted that I am helping."

She scowled. "Why on earth would I be *affronted* that you are helping?"

"Because it is much easier—not to mention enjoyable and self-righteous—thinking of me as being completely devoid of any good qualities."

"That's nonsense!" she retorted, and yet her clenched jaw and fiery skin told Bal a different story.

"If it helps, you can attribute my volunteering to self-indulgent boredom rather than any real altruism," Bal assured her, and then smirked. "After all, a man can't spend *every* hour of the day deflowering virgins and engaging in orgies, no matter how much he might like to."

She turned on him, her blazing blue eyes appearing almost violet against her red face. "I suppose you are enjoying mocking me, my lord."

Bal leaned close enough that he could see the myriad shards that made up her irises, hundreds of different shades of blue—some so pale they were almost white—and the narrow, dark lapis halo that bound them all together. "Yes, I *am* enjoying myself, Mrs. Dryden."

Her lips parted and she held his gaze, reminding Bal of a hare enthralled by the bright light of a lantern.

And then she hastily turned away, once again giving him her flawless profile.

"Oh, by the way—you are wrong," Bal said.

She hesitated a long moment before grudgingly asking, "Wrong about what?"

"You were wrong when you said that our volunteering to harvest was as selfless as what *you* were doing."

Her head swiveled toward him. "Why isn't it?" she asked, her brow furrowed fetchingly as she stared at him, the old nag that pulled the cart clearly able to take itself back home without any direction from her.

"Because *you* already have a job, while none of us are working—we have nothing but time." His eyelids drooped. "And you know what the Good Book says about idle hands, don't you Mrs. Dryden?"

Her flush deepened at his teasing. "I owe you an apology and this time I shan't allow you to stop me from giving it, my lord."

She sounded so resentful that Bal had to bite back a smile. "Very well," he said. "I'm listening."

Evidently, she couldn't look at him while she apologized, so Bal stared at her elegant profile while her jaw flexed, as if she had to masticate the words into submission.

"It was precipitate of me to make those assumptions about you based on what I've read."

Bal laughed. "I like that: precipitate. So, what stories are you talking about, specifically?"

She fixed him with a horrified look and then gave a soft snort of unamused laughter. "Oh, I understand. You want me to *describe* the lewd acts for your entertainment, don't you?"

Bal grinned. "Of course, I do."

"You will have your pound of flesh, won't you?"

He could have told her he wanted a great deal more than a pound of her flesh, but she looked so damned angry he thought she might haul off and slap him if he kept on teasing her.

"Apology accepted, Mrs. Dryden." Bal knew he didn't sound entirely sincere, but then her apology hadn't been exactly heartfelt, either.

Mrs. Dryden cocked her head, clearly suspicious about his abrupt about-face. "I'm not sure I believe you, my lord."

Bal shrugged. "Fine, so then I repeat my question: Why don't you tell me what sort of antics you read about that convinced you I was so ungentlemanly that I would molest female servants? If you describe the alleged deeds to me—in sufficient detail—then I can confirm or deny whether they are true." He paused, smiled, and met her livid gaze. "I could also answer any questions—or offer demonstrations—if a particular depraved act is unknown to you."

"I *do* hope you are amusing yourself, my lord," she said frostily.

"Don't worry; I am."

"I don't appreciate being a figure of fun, Lord Balthazar."

"And I don't appreciate being treated like a rapist based on nothing but rumor and inuendo, Mrs. Dryden," he shot back, no longer smiling.

***

Tori clenched her jaw and faced forward. It was obvious that his reputation was a sore spot with him—and justifiably so—but she didn't know how to get past the misunderstanding that stood between them.

Especially since you don't really believe he is as innocent as he claims to be.

That's not true! I don't think he is a rapist, Tori protested.

No, but you still believe he is a conscienceless libertine.

Unfortunately, Tori couldn't deny that assessment.

The gig trundled along while they sat in awkward silence. Tori had never been more physically aware of another human being in her entire life. She'd known the duke's brother was a big man—any fool could see that—but she'd not understood just how *overwhelming* he was until their bodies were mashed together on a narrow seat. And he seemed even bigger now that he was angry.

It irked her to admit it, but he had every reason to be angry. Tori might have apologized to him earlier, but she still had reservations—serious ones—about his character. Unfairly, or not, she simply could not forget or dismiss all those lascivious details she'd read about him in the newspapers.

Tori also had to admit that in the weeks since the Hales had been in residence, she had not heard so much as a whisper of Lord Balthazar behaving badly.

It was entirely possible—in fact, probable—that the numerous accounts had exaggerated his lusty propensities.

But if the newspapermen had inflated Lord Balthazar's reputation for raking, they had severely underestimated his appeal for women of all ages.

At least based on the behavior of the women in the village, and even the female servants at Hastings Park, a good many of whom speculated endlessly about the man. She knew for a fact that more than a few women actively engineered situations where they might encounter him, or even just watch him.

You mean like you did today? the sly voice in her head taunted.

I didn't know he would be working at the Brower's farm! Tori protested.

The voice just laughed.

Balthazar Hale was—in short—a masculine version of a mythological siren, the sort of man who lured women to their doom without even trying.

Tori had already been lured to her doom once before—thank you very much—and she'd paid for that momentary lapse for the past fourteen years.

She had no intention of being seduced a second time, no matter how enticing the lure of Lord Balthazar's song.

Tori knew all too well that sex, and all it promised, was an illusion, a mirage that men like Lord Balthazar employed to trick women into giving them what they wanted.

All she had reaped the last time she'd given in to the bewildering, lustful demands of her body was physical discomfort, social ostracism, and a surprise nine months later.

And so she gritted her teeth and ignored the brush of his hard body against hers as he shifted on the seat, stretching out his long legs, the muscles of his thighs bulging and straining against the thin leather of his breeches.

"Sorry," he said, after he bumped into her while stretching his shoulder. "I'm sorer than I should be. Weeks of sitting and doing nothing has already begun to take a toll on my body." His low voice vibrated through her. "I was actually grateful for an opportunity to work off some of my pent-up energy. I received just as much benefit volunteering as those farmers did from my work—more, probably."

Tori sincerely doubted that, but she appreciated the olive branch he was offering. "You may have benefited, but it was still very kind of you and your brothers to help at the Brower farm."

"We were not the only ones helping; the squire's two sons were there, as were several other villagers. Volunteering is part of belonging to a community. But enough about that. Tell me, Mrs. Dryden, I know you work all the time and do good deeds in your spare moments, but what do you do for *pleasure*."

Inevitably, her face flamed at the emphasis he put on that word. Thankfully, she was not looking directly at him.

"Nothing out of the ordinary, my lord."

"What *is* the ordinary?"

She gave an exasperated huff and turned to him. "Needlework, knitting, reading—you have sisters, I'm sure you know what I mean."

He gave her a slow, sly smile. "One of my sisters is a public speaker who extolls the value of orgasms for women and distributes condoms in her spare time. The other researches scatological terminology."

Tori's lips parted, but she had no response, the words *orgasm* and *condom*, neither of which she'd ever heard spoken aloud, echoing in her head like clanging bells.

"Mr. Brower seems a bit old and frail to be working that farm alone," Lord Balthazar said, sparing her from having to respond.

She blinked, her brain scrambling to change directions. "Er, yes," she said after a long pause. "I daresay His Grace will have many changes to make when it comes to his tenants, and I doubt the Browers will remain in their cottage for much longer."

"Where will they go?"

"It has been many years—even before I came to Hastings Park—since any of the farms have changed hands," she admitted. "But I know that people who were too old to work used to spend their last years in one of the small cottages that were built for that purpose. But so many of those have fallen into ruin that I'm not sure if there is anywhere for them to go."

"The farms have not changed hands because new tenants would not wish to take over such dilapidated buildings and such neglected land?"

Tori nodded. "That is part of it. And then there is the fact that many young people have turned away from a rural way of life and are flocking to towns and cities. Farming, I'm afraid, is no longer viewed as a desirable way to spend one's life."

"It is much the same back home," he said. "The life of a farmer is a hard one and they are vulnerable to not only the vicissitudes of the weather, but political and economic shifts also hit them harder than other segments of the population."

His practical statement was almost surprising as his sexual innuendo had been. Tori opened her mouth to ask him how he knew about such matters, but then realized it was not her place to question the brother of a duke.

"What were you going to say, Mrs. Dryden?"

"How do you know I was going to say anything?"

"You have a very expressive face."

That was not good news. Not at all. Tori would need to work on controlling her emotions with this man in the vicinity.

"Tell me," he said.

"It was nothing earthshaking," she assured him. "I was just going to say that it sounded like a subject you are familiar with."

"I don't suppose the scandal sheets mentioned that I possessed any intelligent thoughts about agriculture and the economy—or anything else, probably. After all, neither subject is very… salacious."

"No, indeed it is not," she retorted tartly. "You *said* earlier that you forgave me, my lord."

Lord Balthazar fixed her with that lazy, sensual smile that scrambled her wits as effectively as a whisk and said, "I forgave you, but I haven't yet forgotten. That might take a while longer, Mrs. Dryden."

Chapter 5

Ah, there you are, Bal!"

Balthazar looked up to find his twin glaring at him in an accusing fashion. "Why do you sound so vexed, Yoyo? Where else should I be?"

"Oh, I don't know," she said irritably, hitching her hip up on the side of the massive desk he was using and cutting him a narrow-eyed look.

"What did I do? Why are you glaring at me like that?" he asked.

"If you tell me this is an unladylike way to sit, I will scream."

He grinned, set aside his pen, and lounged back in his chair. "Aw, you poor darling, has Edith been chewing on you again?"

"That woman is like a dog on a bone; she never stops nagging. That is why I came to you for help."

"Oh no! You're not dragging me into one of your fights. I've gone to great pains to craft my life so that I might avoid the woman." Bal didn't mind his role as the family peacemaker, but he was getting to the point where speaking civilly to Edith took its toll. He wasn't sure how much longer he could be courteous to his brother's fiancé. If his sister wanted to wage war against Edith, she could fight her own battles.

"Well, this is *your* fight, too, Bal," Io said, reading his mind in her unnerving twin fashion.

He sighed. "What is it now?"

"It's about Eva."

"Has Edith said something cruel to her?" he demanded. Eva was as sweet and loveable as a kitten, and Bal would thrash anyone who hurt his little sister in any way. Well, he couldn't thrash his brother's fiancé, of course, but he would find a way to punish her if she'd hurt Eva in some way.

"Do you really believe that Eva can't manage Edith without her big brother's help? No," she said before Bal could answer. "This is about Eva's birthday. It is at the end of the month."

"I remember; it will be the big twenty-one. What of it?"

"I asked her how she wanted to celebrate, and she said a masquerade ball."

Bal couldn't think of anything else to say except, "Huh."

Io scowled at him.

"What?" he asked.

"Just because it doesn't sound like *your* notion of pleasure does not mean Eva shouldn't be allowed to enjoy it."

"I never said she shouldn't have a masked ball. I agree—Eva can enjoy whatever she wants." *No matter how asinine*. Bal wisely kept that thought to himself.

"I think we should give her that dream for her birthday."

"Go forth and do so—you'll get no argument from me."

"*Edith* says masquerade parties are common and vulgar.

"This is not *Edith's* house—at least not yet. Did you ask Zeus if he agreed? You know Eva has him wrapped around her little finger. He will say *yes*, I'm sure of it." It was true, Eva could do no wrong in their brand-new older brother's eyes. It was one of the things about Zeus that made Bal believe he might come to like the other man.

"I can't ask him," Io said, snatching up a stack of documents and commencing to riffle through them in a way that put them all out of order.

Bal gently took the papers from her hands and replaced them where they'd been. He sighed. "What happened, now?"

"Zeus is not happy with me."

"Why?"

She shrugged.

"What did you do, Io?"

"I didn't do anything, Bal." Her expression turned vicious. "It was that rotten snitch Mr. Masterson."

Why didn't Bal guess as much? "What did *he* do?"

"I was looking for a house to lease in London—for when the Season begins—and he found out and told Zeus. Zeus called me to his study—like a recalcitrant child—and told me that he would sever my allowance if I attempted to live alone." She snorted. "Can you believe that? He lures us all away from Canoga and then threatens to cut off my only means of support now that he has me in his clutches."

Bal swallowed his frustration; it never paid to become short-tempered with his twin.

Instead, he forced a bland expression. "Why are you looking for a house of your own, Yoyo?"

"I am *not* going to live with *Edith* for the remainder of our time in Britain, Bal. I'll go mad and kill someone. Probably Edith. What?" she demanded. "Why are you sighing so heavily and looking at me like that?"

"Because I agree with Zeus on this matter." He winced at her infuriated shriek and lifted his hands. "*Listen* to me before you go off like a pyrotechnic display. You know *nothing* about London—or about England—for that matter. And a woman on her own—"

"A *woman* on her own? Since when have you made distinctions between men and women, as if we are helpless and witless? You've not been gone from Canoga two months and already you've begun to think of women as weak, inferior creatures who need a man to survive!"

"I'm not saying anything of the sort, Io, and you know that. I'm saying that a woman who lives on her own *here* will be viewed as"—Bal struggled to find the right word. He finally shrugged and said, "Well, you'd be viewed as scarlet, for lack of a better word." He frowned. "Or possibly *fast* is more accurate."

"*Scarlet*? *Fast*?"

"Please don't shout, we're just talking."

"I cannot believe you agree with that draconian, gothic, barbaric *toad*."

"Come, Io. That's a bit harsh. Zeus has been—"

"Oh, not *him*. I'm talking about Corbin Masterson."

Bal had his own suspicions about his sister's vocal, almost hysterical, dislike of their brother's saturnine secretary, but he knew his opinion would anger her even more.

He raised a staying hand, hoping to stop the barrage before it could begin. "Fine. I will talk to Zeus about a masquerade party. Alright? Bloody hell," he muttered. "Anything to end this bickering."

She gave him a coy smirk, her irritation miraculously gone. "Good."

Bal snorted. "You knew I'd do what you wanted if you started an argument with me, didn't you?"

"Of course."

He grabbed his twin and yanked her close, rubbing his knuckles on her head until they were hot from the friction. "Apologize," he ordered.

"I'm sorry!" Io squirmed and thrashed, trying to get away and failing. "Balthazar, please!" she begged as he made her short hair into a bird's nest.

"Say it," he ordered, unwilling to cease his punishment and release her until she complied in the time-honored Hale siblings fashion.

"We are twenty-five-years-old, not five. You can't be serious—" She shrieked when he commenced tickling.

"Say it!"

"I b-beg for mercy oh supreme, perfect being!"

Bal gave a triumphant laugh and let her go. "There, that wasn't so bad, was it?"

She hurried away from him and over to the mirror that hung over the fireplace. "I hate you. Look what you've done!" She scowled as she tried to fix her hair.

"You won't be able to get those knots out," he warned, opening the top drawer of the desk and taking out the scissors. "Here, let me help you."

"You're no better than Ares or Pol," she muttered, and then scowled harder. "Well? What are you waiting for?"

"I beg your pardon?"

"You said you'd go talk to him."

"I didn't mean right *now*. I'm in the middle of something."

She glared.

Bal groaned. "Fine, I'll go now." Because she would ensure that he got no peace until he did what she wanted.

Sisters.

***

"*That* one is going to cause problems," Auntie Max said as she stared out Tori's tiny sitting room window.

Victoria knew who *that* one was before she even glanced up from her needlework. Sure enough, her dearest friend was pointing at the duke's betrothed, Miss Barrymore, who was inspecting every inch of the garden—just as she was doing in the house—with her downtrodden cousin Miss Barclay trotting behind her, scribbling in the little notebook that had probably fused to her hand as she used it so often to jot down her mistress's frequent commands.

Although the Americans had only been in residence for a month it was becoming increasingly clear to Victoria that she would probably need to find some other place to live once Miss Barrymore married the duke. Perhaps she'd need to leave *before* their wedding if Miss Barrymore had her way. Her *way* was—for reasons unknown to Victoria—a burning desire to see Tori gone.

"Jealousy, that's what it is," Auntie Max said.

Maxine Rowell wasn't really her aunt, but almost everyone who lived in and around the village of Symington referred to her as *Auntie Max*.

"She has no reason to be jealous of me, Auntie. She is beautiful, wealthy, well-born, and betrothed to one of the few available dukes in the realm."

Maxine Rowell made a rude *pfffft* noise that made Victoria smile.

As she turned back to her work her gaze slid across the letter she'd been reading when Auntie Max had shown up—uninvited but not unwelcome.

Tori had hastily shoved the missive into her needlework basket and one corner of the cheap paper was sticking out.

It was the second threatening letter and—to her way of thinking—the grammar, if not the handwriting, seemed strangely improved.

What do you think the new duke will say when he learns who you really are?

Leave Hastings Park now or I will let the truth be known.

What would her neighbors say if they knew the truth about her?

What would Auntie Max—who'd been her staunchest champion since Tori had taken the housekeeping position thirteen years ago—do if she knew what sort of person Tori really was?

"You don't need to stay here, my dear."

Tori looked up from her unhappy thoughts at her friend's voice. "I'm sorry?"

"I said that you don't need to keep working here if she is making your life a misery."

"No," she agreed, "I can always find a new position, although I should hate to leave you behind."

Maxine's rather sharp features softened. "I would hate to lose you, too." She hesitated, and Tori knew what she was going to say before she said it, "I do wish you'd consider Malcolm's offer. I know he is my nephew, and I am his *very* fond aunt, but I don't think I am exaggerating when I point out that he is a fine, upstanding young man who would take excellent care of you and Jamie, which is what you both need and deserve. I should *so* love to have the three people I adore most in the world together, Victoria."

It wasn't the first time the old woman had laid out her heart's desire—or even the fifth—she'd been steadfast in her urging for almost three years.

"I know you care for Malcolm," Auntie Max went on, "and I could die happy knowing you were together. Isn't it possible—"

Tori set aside her work and leaned close, taking the older woman's fragile hand in hers. She sucked in a breath. "My goodness! Your fingers are so *cold* Maxine—are you not feeling well? And what is this talk of *dying*?"

Maxine gave a dismissive flick with her free hand. "Oh, I am fine, my dear. Just old."

But Tori wasn't sure that was the truth. Maxine had always been thin, but she seemed to be slowly disappearing.

"Are you *sure* you can't love him, Victoria?" Maxine asked, her eyes suddenly burning.

Tori gently squeezed the other woman's slim hand. "I'm sorry, Maxine, but I am sure. I care for Malcolm deeply. But only as a friend."

Maxine sighed but nodded. "I know, I know. But an old woman may hope, mayn't she?"

Tori hated to disappoint Maxine, who'd taken her under her wing all those years ago, when Tori had come to the small village of Symington afraid of what her future held and very, very alone in the world.

Back then Maxine's husband—the Reverend Rowel—had still been alive and the older woman had been quite a force in the small community. She'd used her influence as the vicar's wife to dispel some of the unsavory rumors that had circulated about Tori when she'd arrived to take the housekeeping position at Hastings Park.

There was a light knock on the door and Tori called out, "Come in."

It was one of the new housemaids, a very young woman named Penny.

"Sorry to disturb you on your half-day, Mrs. Dryden, but His Grace wants to see you in his study at your earliest convenience."

"Thank you, Penny."

The girl dropped a curtsey and silently shut the door.

"Hmph," Auntie Max said, and shook her head.

Victoria bit back a smile at her friend's disgruntled huff as she put her needlework back in the basket, shoving the threatening letter to the bottom in the process.

"If you do this now, my dear, you'll never have any time to yourself," the old lady warned. "Begin as you wish to go on, my mother always said."

"I doubt I'll be *going on* for very long," Victoria muttered as she tidied herself in the mirror beside the door.

"What's that, Victoria?"

"I said that I can hardly expect the duke not to ask questions when he's barely been here a month, Maxine." She turned back to the older woman, who looked more than a little annoyed on Tori's behalf.

Auntie Max grumbled. "I suppose that is true. Oh, wait a moment, I have something to give you," she said, reaching for her large purse and rooting around for a moment before pulling out a small paper-wrapped box. "This is for James when you go to see him. I made him a batch of toffee."

"How lovely," Tori said. "You are too good."

"You don't eat it all yourself, now. I know what a sweet tooth you have."

Tori laughed. "It's a good thing you've wrapped it so securely—I won't be able to get into it. He will be delighted." She pulled a regretful face. "You barely got here and I'm leaving. I'm terribly sorry to run off just as we've been—"

"Hush, now. You go do your job and do not worry about me." She pushed up from her chair using the cane she'd started using perhaps a year ago.

Victoria experienced a sudden pang of fear; just when had the other woman become so *frail*? Maxine was her closest friend in Symington, more like a dear, dear aunt or older sister. But she *was* getting on in years, as much as Tori didn't want to accept it.

Almost suffocating with affection, Tori gave the other woman a quick, light hug. "I'll come see you when I'm in the village on Wednesday."

"Well, of course you will," Maxine said, her cheeks flushing at Tori's uncharacteristic show of affection. Although they were close, they'd never been given to physical demonstrations of their love.

Once Tori had seen the older woman off, she shut the door to her tiny cottage and made her way down the narrow path that led to Hastings.

Tori was fortunate to occupy the small house, which had once belonged to the gamekeeper, back when there'd still been one. The last duke had not cared when Tori had asked to move into the cottage but she suspected that the new duke would soon hire a gamekeeper, and then she would need to move into the housekeeper's apartment, which had no private kitchen or garden.

You might be moving farther away than the housekeeper apartment if those threatening letters turn into actual deeds…

She grimaced at the unwanted thought but quickly schooled her expression and smiled and nodded at the veritable army of gardeners the duke had hired.

Tori knew that Bickle lived in terror of being replaced. Personally, she thought the old man deserved retirement after so many years, but his wife had died fifteen years before and his two sons lived far away with families of their own. Just like Tori, Bickle's work was his life.

Unlike Tori, however, Bickle was not deceiving their current employer as to his identity.

Even if the duke could find it in himself to forgive Tori's deception—not to mention the fact that she'd filled his house with rehabilitated former criminals in the guise of servants—she had already seen and heard enough from Miss Barrymore to know the strict, exceedingly religious woman would not countenance a lying, immoral thief for a housekeeper. Miss Barrymore had already demonstrated her moral rigidity when she had complained to Tori that she'd seen one of the stable lads chatting with a scullery maid.

"*I will not tolerate that sort of fraternizing among the servants, Mrs. Dryden. I do hope you discourage such behavior*," she'd scolded after summoning Tori to her chambers to upbraid her, keeping her standing before her chair as if Tori were a serf. Not even the former duke had treated her in such a demeaning fashion.

Was this why His Grace was summoning her now? To add his criticism to his betrothed's about servants fraternizing with each other—as if talking now constituted a crime.

Tori considered the options before her. It might be wise to seek a new position now—to leave before whomever was threatening her made known their information.

Whenever she thought about those letters the same questions whirled around in her head: *Why would somebody write such letters? They weren't even blackmailing her, which seemed odd. What was the purpose? Just to drive her away? Who would want her gone from her job so badly?*

Tori sighed. This sort of problem was not what she needed right now, not that she'd want threatening letters at *any* time. As much as she'd missed her son, she was grateful that James hadn't stayed the summer with her. Normally he had spent his holidays with her at Hastings but this year he'd been invited to a school chum's in Scotland. She'd not had the heart to say *no*, even though she knew his absence would be painful.

But a child at Hastings in the middle of all this upheaval would have been even more trying than things already were.

Unfortunately, Tori suspected her time at Hastings was speedily coming to an end, it was just a matter of how long her mysterious persecutor would allow her to stay.

***

"Edith does not think such a party is *appropriate*, Zeus, so that is why Io asked me come to you," Balthazar found it challenging to keep his loathing from his tone when he spoke of his brother's fiancé.

For his part, Zeus looked pained. Either he was annoyed at Bal's insistence on using his given name rather than addressing him as John—which is what his brother had always called himself—or because Bal was dragging him into yet another disagreement between Miss Barrymore and one of his siblings.

It was true there had been a great many disputes since they'd entered Zeus's household. His brother's dogged determination to make them a family had begun to fray at the edges even before they'd found themselves trapped together on a ship in the Mid Atlantic. Bal and his younger siblings disliked Miss Barrymore every bit as much as she disliked them. Whether Zeus would admit it or not—and it seemed unlikely at this point—Edith Barrymore had done everything in her power to ensure that dislike by behaving in a condescending, high-handed, and contemptuous fashion toward all five of them.

The animosity had been especially pronounced between Io and Edith, who had been at daggers drawn since day one. Bal feared for his brother's fiancé's welfare if she didn't stop goading his volatile sister. He'd tried to smooth the waters between them on a few occasions, but Io had threatened Bal with bodily harm if he intervened again.

"The last thing I need is a protector, Balthazar. You just look after your own affairs," Io had snapped the last time he'd tried to de-escalate tensions between her and Edith.

Bal always knew he was in the doghouse with his sister when she used his full name.

"What are Edith's reasons for opposing such a party?" Zeus asked after a long moment, pulling Bal from his musings.

"She pointed out that she is in no position to hostess a ball because she's in mourning. When I told her that she'd not be required to lift a finger—that Io and I will take care of it all—she said that a masquerade was beneath the dignity of the Duke of Hasting."

Zeus's frigid blue eyes narrowed slightly at Bal's inadvertent lapse into Miss Barrymore's prissy, hectoring tone for the last eleven words.

Bal hadn't been *trying* to imitate the woman, it just seemed to happen. Probably because Io and Eva delighted in repeating Miss Barrymore's most obnoxious pronouncements for the enjoyment of his brothers. And, fine, maybe Bal, too, found their imitations amusing. Far more amusing than the woman, herself.

"A masquerade ball," Zeus repeated.

"Yes. Io and I thought it might be a nice treat for Eva's twenty-first birthday. Also, a ball would be a fine way to, er, *practice* for the upcoming Season."

Zeus lifted one imperious eyebrow. "And you and Io would make all the arrangements?"

"Yes."

"Have either of you hosted this sort of entertainment in the past? Planned parties or dances or dinners?" Zeus asked, the faint twist of his lips telling Bal that his brother already knew the answer to that question.

"No, but I suspect Mrs. Dryden and old Bickle have plenty of experience between the two of them."

Zeus held him pinned with his uncomfortable gaze; whatever was going on behind those ice encrusted eyes was impossible to read.

Just when Bal began to wonder if the chill had spread to the rest of Zeus's body and frozen him immobile, his brother sighed, uncoiled his tall body, and strode to the door. He spoke in a low murmur to one of the two servants who stood outside any room his brother happened to occupy, which was apparently *de rigueur* as far as ducal etiquette went. Thank God the same wasn't true for duke's brothers. Bal was already struggling to adjust to having a valet constantly in his pocket—and he actually *liked* Napier—he couldn't imagine being trailed by an entire entourage from dawn to dusk.

"I've sent for Mrs. Dryden," Zeus said as he lowered himself back into his seat.

Bal had to quickly suppress a smile. "Ah, good." His interest in the housekeeper had only grown since that ride home from the Brower farm. But the woman was skittish and avoiding him—he was sure of it.

"While we wait, I'd like to talk about your evening jaunts into the village," Zeus said.

Bal frowned, his temperature spiking at the other man's stern, almost hectoring, tone. "What about my *jaunts*?"

"I understand you and our younger brothers have been spending a great deal of time at the King's Quarrel."

He wanted to ask who'd told him, but he could guess as to his source. "Yes, we have."

"And I understand you've struck up an acquaintance with the woman who owns the establishment."

"You *are* well informed, aren't you? Yes, I know Jo Fletcher."

Zeus's lips compressed at Bal's casual use of the woman's diminutive name—something Bal never did when speaking to the randy publican, whose attentions he consistently, but gently, rebuffed.

"This is not Canoga, Balthazar."

"I'm well aware of where we are, Zeus."

"Concepts like *free love* and so forth are neither appreciated nor acceptable here. If you are insistent on carrying on your… *amours*… here, then there will be trouble."

Bal nodded and assumed a pensive expression. "Hmmm. So, no amours. What about just *fucking*?" Bal couldn't resist asking, amused when his brother flinched. "Is that something that is allowed in England? Or is fucking yet another activity reserved for places like Canoga?"

The air between them seemed to sparkle with frost. "You are a duke's brother now, Balthazar. And it would behoove you to behave like one."

"What does that mean, exactly?"

Zeus just stared.

Bal raised his hands. "What? That was a serious question. What do you want from me? Do you expect abstinence?" He frowned and stared more closely at his brother. "Tell me, are you a virgin, Zeus? Because your prudish, judgmental outlook smacks not only of bourgeoisie morality but also of… ignorance. And if you expect virginal behavior out of me? Well, I'm afraid that horse left the barn some time ago."

He'd not believed it possible for his brother's blue eyes to grow any colder. "Debauching our neighbors is not the sort of behavior that I expect from one of my brothers."

Bal could have told Zeus that it had been Joanne Fletcher—a woman who was well-versed in sensual pleasures prior to ever meeting him—who'd been pursuing him, not the other way around. He also could have told him that he'd not accepted any of Mrs. Fletcher's persistent overtures. Nor anyone else's, for that matter. And there had been offers; plenty of them. More than one woman in the area—unmarried *and* married—had made her interest in Bal obvious. He suspected it was the notoriety that attracted them, rather than his actual person.

But that was not his brother's business. None of this was.

He shoved down the anger bubbling up inside him and forced a mild smile, "I'm not to fuck anyone in the neighborhood," he repeated consideringly. "I take it that you want me to satisfy my sexual appetite on the bodies of whores, then? Society's castaway daughters, as it were?"

"Or you might try to simply curb your *appetite* as mature men do."

"Oh. Is that what mature men do? Is that what you do, Brother?" he asked, but then held up his hands at the arctic look on Zeus's face. "Forget I asked."

"I already have."

"How about a compromise? I give you my word that I won't fuck any virgins. Is that good enough?"

"You might also give me your word that you will not use such crudities in my presence."

"You find the word *fuck* crude?"

"As does most of civilized society."

Bal laughed.

"Rather than spending your time slaking your… thirsts, you should be considering the matter of a wife."

All the humor drained from Bal in an instant and he turned his brother's cold look back on him. "I thought I'd just let you pick one for me, Zeus. That's what you want, isn't it, to select some *respectable* broodmare for me to spend my life with? I can impregnate her annually, spend my time socializing with *respectable* men at a proper gentleman's club, and concentrate on growing my fortune—making the four million I sold my soul for into eight million?"

Zeus's jaw flexed. "Nobody is making you marry anyone."

"Are you denying that I'll forfeit all that money if I don't marry a woman you approve of in less than two years?" Bal snarled.

"No, I don't deny that." Zeus narrowed his eyes. "Tell me, Balthazar, does my approval of a woman naturally mean that she would be somebody you would not want to marry?"

"*Tell me*, Zeus, do you not understand that I don't want to marry *at all*? That I've grown to manhood in a community that rejects marriage and all it represents? You can force your beliefs on me all you want, that doesn't mean I will accept them."

"I'm not the one who wants you to marry, Balthazar—your grandfather was." His eyes glittered coldly. "You don't have to marry at all—if you don't want to inherit."

Before Balthazar could say something he was likely to regret, there was a soft tap on the door and Mrs. Dryden entered the room.

***

Tori had expected the duke, but not his distracting brother, whom she'd done an excellent job of avoiding since the day she'd gawked at his shirtless body, an image that haunted her dreams with alarming frequency and shocking intensity.

Seeing the two of them together made her wonder at the unfairness of God to grant so much male beauty to one family—and that wasn't even considering the younger twins, who were objectively even more classically perfect than their older siblings.

Although the duke was the more dignified and imposing of the two men, Tori was, yet again, shocked by her body's primal and unwanted reaction to the younger man.

They both stood when she entered, the unexpected courtesy causing her face to heat with pleasure.

Tori dropped a curtsey.

"Thank you so much for joining us, Mrs. Dryden," the duke said, gesturing to the three chairs in front of his desk. "Won't you please have a seat?"

Ah, so he wasn't going to keep her standing before his desk like Miss Barrymore had.

Unfortunately, Lord Balthazar was standing in front of the middle chair, so Tori was forced to sit beside him no matter which seat she selected.

Once they'd all sat the duke asked, in his rather direct fashion, "Have you planned social functions in the past?"

"You mean dinners, Your Grace?"

"He means parties and balls," Lord Balthazar answered, forcing Tori to turn toward him. He was close to her, almost as close as he'd been on the seat of the gig. He was such a *big* man and dwarfed the large leather wing chair, his long legs sprawled casually, his heavy-lidded eyes even more hooded than usual as he regarded her with that faint smirk that always made her feel as if he was mentally undressing her, although Tori suspected that she was well below his usual standards, and a servant, to boot.

Tori hastily turned back to the duke; her heart beating faster than she would have liked. "I'm not entirely ignorant when it comes to planning large functions," she carefully admitted. "Years ago, His Grace hosted public days and those were parties of a sort. We often received as many as three or four hundred people."

"That's sounds like plenty of experience for our purpose," Lord Balthazar said before his brother could respond.

Tori remained forward facing, her gaze on the duke, unable to read his expression.

"I have a rather unconventional question, Mrs. Dryden."

And then the duke did something that almost caused Tori to fall off her chair.

He smiled.

True, it was so faint she almost missed it, but it was the first smile—or even smile-*like* expression—she'd seen on his stern features. If she'd believed him handsome before, he was positively lethal with a smile, which exposed a dimple on one side of his mouth.

She swallowed. "Yes, Your Grace?"

"My question is about masquerades."

"Er, masquerades, Your Grace?"

Again, it was Lord Balthazar who answered. "Our younger sister wishes for a masquerade ball to celebrate her birthday. Would such a function be untoward, Mrs. Dryden? Would it be… vulgar?"

Tori could not avoid looking at the man when he addressed her directly, so she forced herself to turn—slowly, as one might move in the presence of a dangerous predator.

It was amazing the difference she experienced when talking to the two men. It didn't matter that the duke was the more handsome, wealthy, and powerful; Lord Balthazar did something to her—something that felt almost like a chemical reaction—and she found herself aware of bodily processes that normally occurred unnoticed. Like breathing, for instance. Suddenly she had to *remind* herself to keep doing it.

The man really had the most ridiculously attractive eyes, green and gold—warm colors—completely different from the duke's pale and pitiless blue.

She cleared her throat. "It has been years since I've heard of anyone having a masquerade in our neighborhood," Tori admitted once she'd gathered her wits. "But I believe they are quite the thing in London." She wrenched her gaze away from the younger man and turned to her employer. "I do not think it would be untoward—or vulgar—to host a masquerade, Your Grace."

"There, you see, Zeus?" Lord Balthazar said, his tone triumphant.

She couldn't help jolting at the sound of the duke's outlandish Christian name, which only his brothers and sisters appeared to call him. His betrothed referred to him as either *John* or *His Grace.*

"I told you Miss Barrymore was incorrect," Lord Balthazar added when his brother didn't respond.

Tori wanted to whimper at this unwelcome piece of information.

"Of course, I am hardly the arbiter of what is proper," she hastened to assure the duke, who was looking at his brother with a notch of irritation between his eyes. "If Miss Barrymore said such entertainments are, er, untoward, I daresay she knows—"

A knock on the door interrupted Tori's flustered back peddling.

"Come in," the duke called out, pulling his quelling gaze from his brother.

Yet again both men stood, this time for Miss Barclay. The tiny woman's cheeks flamed in the face of so much masculine courtesy, her step as timid as a deer's as she entered the room.

"I'm t-terribly sorry to interrupt you, Your Grace," Miss Barclay said, her huge blue eyes apprehensive behind her spectacles.

"You are always welcome, Miss Barclay," the duke said, far more kindly than he'd just been addressing his younger brother. "How may I serve you?"

Miss Barclay's slim, pale hands nervously smoothed her ugly gray skirt. "Miss Barrymore wishes to see you when you have a moment, Your Grace."

The duke glanced at Tori and said, "You have told me what I wanted to know, Mrs. Dryden. I appreciate your opinion on this subject, and you have given me food for thought. If you'll excuse me?"

"Oh, certainly," Tori said, scrambling to her feet as the duke strode toward the door.

"A moment if you will, Mrs. Dryden," Lord Balthazar drawled from behind her before she could make her escape.

Tori watched helplessly as one of the new footmen—Phillip, his name was—pulled the door shut.

She steeled herself and turned. "Yes, my lord?"

"Won't you sit?" he gestured to the chair she'd just vacated.

When she hesitated, he added, "Unless I'm keeping you from something more… important?"

She was tempted to retort, *only my half day*, but thought better of it and sat.

"How may I help you, my lord?"

His mouth curved into a wicked smile, although she was beginning to suspect that lips like his couldn't smile any other way than wickedly. "I don't suppose I can prevail on you to stop *my lording* me and call me Balthazar?"

Torie's jaw sagged.

"No," he said, his expression rueful, "I can see by your reaction that you wouldn't be able to do that."

"You wished to speak to me, sir?"

"I want this party for my sister, and I think you can help me convince my brother it is… *proper*."

"It's really not my place to—"

"I'd say you were better suited than any of us Hales—or Miss Barrymore, for that matter—when it comes to deciding acceptable. After all," he added, a sly glint in his eyes, "she lacks your credentials, doesn't she?"

"Er, credentials?"

"Come now, when were you going to tell us that you are the daughter of a baronet?"

***

"Most people are not aware of that connection, my lord." Mrs. Dryden said, having gone rather pale. "How did you hear that?"

Balthazar shrugged. "Like small towns everywhere everyone knows everything about everybody."

"Does His Grace know?"

What an *odd* question. "I have no idea if Zeus knows. Why? Does that matter to you?" He raised his eyebrows. "Are you trying to hide your background?"

"No, of course not."

Bal thought she was lying.

"It's just… Well, it is not common knowledge, my lord. Who told you?"

"I believe it was Mrs. Fletcher from the King's Quarrel who told me. Is it the truth?"

Her cheeks darkened slightly at that information. Judging by the disapproving look on her face, Mrs. Dryden—just like Zeus—believed that Bal and the bawdy publican were lovers.

"It is true that my father was a baronet," she grudgingly admitted.

"So then, you're really Lady Victoria?"

She gave him a look that was almost amused. "I'm afraid that isn't how it works, my lord."

"I thought all peers had titles?"

"Baronetcies are not part of the peerage, and the female children of baronets don't have titles."

"That hardly seems fair."

She gave a startled laugh. "The world is frequently unfair to women, Lord Balthazar."

Why did he enjoy hearing her call him that? He shouldn't. Normally he found the honorific an embarrassing affectation. But with her…

It made him hard.

Or perhaps that was just her proximity—or maybe her disapproval—both of which he perversely found arousing.

"If that was all, sir?" she asked, interrupting his musing.

"Yes, that was all."

She stood and smoothed her hands down her already smooth skirts.

Bal got to his feet almost as quickly, the action bringing them closer together. It surprised him that she was so small. Garbed in black from neck to boots she gave the impression of being a much more substantial woman, but she barely came to his chin.

Balthazar had an excellent sense of smell, and it did not fail him now. Just like that day in the gig, he inhaled her delicious scent and held it in his lungs: lavender and laundry starch, two aromas he'd not found erotic in the past, yet now he couldn't get enough of.

"I was teasing you about the titles, Mrs. Dryden."

"I surmised as much, my lord." She opened her mouth, hesitated, and then closed it without speaking.

"What were you going to say, Mrs. Dryden?" He smiled. "Please, you looked so intense that I am curious."

"I would just appreciate it if you did not share the information about my background with anyone."

Bal's eyebrows shot up.

She hastily went on before he could comment. "If you think the duke should know, then please tell him by all means. But nobody else." She gave a small, self-conscious bark of laughter, suddenly flustered. "Not that I am a popular subject of conversation. Indeed, I'm not quite sure how Mrs. Fletcher learned of my background since I've never told anyone in Symington."

Well, wasn't *that* interesting.

"Why do you keep it a secret?" he asked.

She looked chagrined at his prying, but said, "It is the sort of class distinction that would make managing a large household more difficult, my lord."

Balthazar didn't believe that was really her reason, but he merely nodded and said, "I won't tell anyone. And I'm serious about wanting your help for my sister's party. You see Eva is an anglophile—always has been, ever since she was a little girl. She adored dressing up in fancy clothing as a child"—he snorted— "not that there was much fancy clothing to be had at Canoga." Indeed, for a girl who liked pretty things, Canoga had been a special sort of Hell.

Of all his siblings, Eva had embraced this new, more genteel, life the most. Coming to England was a dream for her. Becoming part of *ton* society was so far beyond her wildest fantasies that he didn't think his little sister had yet accommodated it in her mind. This ball would be an excellent introduction to what the Season ahead would hold for her.

"My sister deserves to have the sort of birthday party she's always dreamed about, Mrs. Dryden." And Bal would be damned if he allowed Zeus's shrewish fiancé to cheat Eva out of such a simple pleasure.

"My lord, you must know that I cannot go against Miss Barrymore's wishes on this issue." Her expression was, for once, not disapproving but imploring. Her soft, cultured voice plucked at something inside Bal, soothing him. In the weeks since he'd first seen her—standing there glaring at him with blazing eyes like some avenging, judging angel—Bal had come to see true beauty in her almost stark features. She was not conventionally lovely, but he sensed an inner strength beneath her reserve that was wildly appealing to him. The man who gained this woman's trust and affection would have something to be treasured, he was sure of that.

And if anyone in the house—besides Mr. Masterson—could convince Bal's prim and proper brother that a dress-up ball was acceptable, it would be Mrs. Dryden.

"Surely a masquerade ball is not the vulgar, horrifying embarrassment that Edith is making it out to be, Mrs. Dryden?"

She opened her mouth and then paused, chewing slightly on her plush lower lip, which was something Bal wouldn't mind doing himself.

Behave yourself, Balthazar, his conscience ordered. *This woman is a servant in your brother's house.*

Oh, shut up. I can do whatever I like in my own mind.

Mrs. Dryden sighed, the soft exhalation almost sensual. "If His Grace decides that is what he wishes then it will be my pleasure to help you with the arrangements, my lord."

Balthazar decided right then that it would be his new priority to make sure his brother made the right decision.

Chapter 6

Dwelling in a rural area, Balthazar decided, was very much the same no matter what country one lived in. The only real differences between Upstate New York and rural England were the accents and weather.

Well, and also the fact that he was slowly going mad at Hastings Park without anything to occupy him.

"You are so fidgety that you are making *me* anxious, Bal," Io said. They were playing their weekly game of chess—a tradition they'd maintained since they'd learned the game at age eight—and Io was thoroughly thrashing him.

Balthazar sighed and laid down his king in surrender. His sister was right: he was too restless to concentrate.

"What is wrong with you?" she asked as she put away the grand ivory pieces of the set they'd discovered in a dusty box in the library, a marvelous room that was, as yet, untouched by Edith's redecorating.

"I'm at loose ends," he confessed.

"I can see that. Go offer your assistance to Zeus. I heard him at breakfast yesterday talking to *Mr. Masterson* about inspecting all the tenant farms, or some such thing."

"Just what happened to give you such an intense dislike of poor old Masterson?" Bal couldn't help asking. "Are you still angry about him telling Zeus about the house in London?"

Io's mouth tightened and she replaced the wooden lid on the chess piece box with more force than was necessary. "That man is positively gothic."

"Why? What did he say?"

"Did you know he was in seminary for a few years?"

"I thought he was a lawyer?"

"He is *now* but before he went to jolly old Harvard with Zeus, he studied to become a minister."

"Let me guess… Presbyterian?"

Io's scowl told him all he needed to know. There were several Presbyterian ministers who had publicly attacked Canoga in the newspapers over the years. Right now—with Tirzah's articles still making waves—the Presbyterian minister John Sears and Canoga's founder Benjamin Hoyt were going at it hammer and tongs in a series of warring editorials that had run in the *Boston Chronicle* and *New York Times*.

The fact that Masterson was a Presbyterian should have made him a natural enemy of Canogans. However, Bal had detected no animus from the man, personally. He suspected there was something else going on with Io and the staid, aloof secretary.

"Tell me, Yoyo, are you deriding Masterson because he decided to focus on the corporal rather than spiritual and immersed himself in the business of accumulating filthy lucre rather than saving souls?"

She scoffed. "I don't care about that. I just think he's managed to meld the worst of both worlds and wields his judgmental Presbyterianism as if it were a hatchet."

Bal kept his own opinions of Masterson—that he was an organizational wizard who seemed to manage whatever Zeus threw at him with ease and aplomb—to himself.

"You need something to occupy you," Io pronounced when Bal didn't take the bait and argue about Masterson.

"I do," he agreed. "But I doubt that *something* is me working with our stiff elder brother. Zeus and I have been rubbing along without killing each other lately." Although most of that was probably due to the fact that they'd not spoken a great deal in the days since Bal had asked his brother about the masquerade—something Zeus hadn't yet approved or rejected yet.

"Besides," he added as an afterthought, "I can just imagine Zeus's reactions to my *radical* opinions on farming."

"You haven't based your ideas on nothing, Bal. You went to university to learn about all that sort of thing—surely that would mean something to him?"

"Probably not." Bal snorted. "Especially since I didn't go to *Harvard* but its pitiful competitor."

Io threw up her hands. "Fine. You can just sit here and stew in your own restlessness." She stood up.

"Where are you rushing off to?"

"I'm going into the village."

"Why? All the shops will be closed now."

Io snorted. "Really, Bal! You've barely been away from home for two months and you think that all women do is shop."

He smirked; there was nothing like annoying his twin to pull him from the doldrums. "You mean you don't need a new frock or a pretty piece of ribbon?"

Quick as a snake she leaned across the small table and flicked his ear. *Hard.*

Bal yelped and rubbed the side of his head. "Dammit, Yoyo, you almost ripped it off my head."

It was her turn to smirk. "You'll never be too big to be disciplined by your twin. And for your information, I'm going to Amelia Temple's house."

Miss Temple was the local schoolteacher whom Io had sought out upon moving into the neighborhood, yet another action that had annoyed Edith, who'd screeched when she'd learned that Io had volunteered to teach at the small school two afternoons a week. Edith argued that such an activity was below the dignity of a duke's sister.

Io had won the dispute handily when she'd pointed out that Mrs. Dryden had informed her that the last duchess had also taught the occasional class in watercolor painting, piano, and French at the tiny school.

Bal wished that his sister hadn't dragged the housekeeper's name into the argument as the poor woman had already attracted far too much of Edith's attention—and none of it good.

Although his brother's fiancé was a beautiful woman, she most decidedly did *not* like to be surrounded by other attractive women. Edith's eyes followed Mrs. Dryden whenever she entered a room and he'd heard her speak sharply to the housekeeper on more than one occasion.

Io replaced the box of chess pieces on the shelf and brushed some dust from her plain, practical skirt. Although she no longer wore bloomers and short skirts, she'd steadfastly opposed anything she termed *frippery*, which meant all her clothing was severe in the extreme, both in cut and color. She was an ardent supporter of dress reform and had rejected crinolines and bustles, no matter how stridently Edith had tried to persuade her otherwise, warning Io that people would mistake her for a domestic servant if she insisted on dressing in such a fashion.

Balthazar thought his twin was so beautiful that the plain clothing only served to make her more attractive, just like a simple setting emphasized an especially magnificent gemstone.

He smirked; Io would cuff him again if she could hear his thoughts.

"What will you be doing at Miss Temple's?" he asked her. "Fomenting revolution? Plotting the overthrow of the government?"

Io ignored his teasing. "She invited me to join her book club. I told her I'd be late—thanks to a *prior* engagement, which was beating you at chess."

Bal stood. "I'll come along—not to your book club," he hastily added when her eyebrows shot up. "I know Ares went to the King's Quarrel earlier, maybe he's still there."

"I hope you aren't going to get up to any *naughtiness*. You know what Edith said about *slumming* with the locals."

Bal ignored the not-so-subtle invitation to bash their brother's fiancé—an activity that increasingly depressed, rather than amused, him—and said, "Go fetch your hat and cloak."

***

After walking Io to the teacher's house, Bal went to the King's Quarrel where he had, indeed, encountered Ares. His younger brother had been pursuing a flirtation with Mrs. Fletcher for weeks, but the lively widow immediately abandoned Ares when Bal arrived.

After gently, but firmly, rejecting Mrs. Fletcher's increasingly outrageous advances for three-quarters of an hour, Bal had finished his pint, cautioned Ares against doing anything too foolish, and headed back to Hastings, taking a different route than the one he'd used on the journey into the village.

Before the mess that Tirzah's articles had unleashed, Bal would have probably taken Jo Fletcher to bed without a second thought. But now her insistent advances irked him. She didn't want *him*, she wanted The Wicked Spare—or she wanted his tail, rather, which she could then nail up on the wall of her bedchamber with all her other trophies. Oh yes, he had Mrs. Fletcher's measure. People said that men were natural hounds, but he'd met a woman or two who could bay at the moon with the best of men.

The amorous widow was probably bored and only interested in Bal for the mild acclaim it would bring her. If he bedded her, Bal would probably read about his performance in a newspaper at some point.

He could see the headline now: *Read all about The Wicked Spare and the Faces he Makes at the Moment of Climax!*

Bal snorted as he crested the slight rise and Hastings Park came into view. He paused to admire it. The old house might be dilapidated and in need of tens of thousands of pounds of repair work, but there was no denying it was a magnificent sight.

A spark of red a short distance from the house caught Balthazar's attention.

Intrigued, he left the footpath and made for the source of the light, which seemed to be coming from the small cottage that servants called the *gamekeeper's house*, even though he knew his brother didn't have such a beast. At least not yet, but the duke was interviewing for the position and had grand plans for hunting next year.

Bal found Zeus's speedy transition from city banker to country lord amusing—even a bit endearing. The man already loved Hastings Park and seemed excited about bringing the old place back to its former glory. Well, Bal corrected mentally, Zeus seemed about as excited as he ever looked, which, admittedly, wasn't much.

The red spark grew in intensity, the glow illuminated a familiar face. Bal couldn't help smiling; it was Mrs. Dryden, and she was smoking. For some reason the tightly laced housekeeper was the last woman he would have expected to have such a filthy vice.

It made Bal even more curious about her.

Her eyelids closed as she inhaled, expanding her impressive bosom as she held the smoke inside her body, her face a mask of sensual pleasure. If somebody could capture that expression and print it on advertisements, Bal suspected cigarette sales would double overnight.

He stepped on a twig and her eyes flew open, her rigid posture even more noticeable when contrasted with the bliss of only seconds before.

She lowered her cigarette to her side, as if to conceal it, and peered into the darkness. "Who is there?" Her expression tightened even more when she saw him. "Oh. Lord Balthazar," she said, her tone flat and pulsing with something that sounded suspiciously like dread. Or resentment.

Bal didn't let her reaction daunt him. "Good evening, Mrs. Dryden." He kept walking, not stopping until he was close enough to smell the surprisingly appealing scent of her tobacco. "I was just walking back from the village and saw the red glow in the darkness. I must admit I'm surprised that you, of all people, have such a naughty habit."

He could see the struggle taking place inside her: talk to the duke's womanizing brother? Or run to her cottage and lock the door?

She exhaled and her posture relaxed, but only slightly, and then she reached into her pocket and extracted a metal case. "Would you care for one?"

"No, thank you. I don't smoke." He smiled. "Believe it or not, it is one of the few bad habits I *don't* have."

She ignored the baited hook and said, "You are wise to avoid it. It's a dreadful habit—and expensive—but I cannot shed it."

"It's rather more prevalent here than it is back home. It's also something one sees in urban areas rather than rural backwaters like the one where I lived."

"I wish I could stop; it's not a very intelligent habit. Whoever was the first person to come up with the unwise notion of sticking a burning object into one's mouth?"

"Whoever it was, they were probably male."

A startled snort of laughter slipped from between her shapely lips. "You believe your gender is more predisposed to doing foolish things?"

"Absolutely." Bal could have told her that he was fending off at least a dozen foolish ideas right at that moment.

"What do you like about smoking?" he asked, genuinely curious.

She blinked at his question, her brow furrowing slightly, as if she couldn't believe he would be interested in her thoughts, as if he was nothing but a rabid sensualist who looked at women as mere bodies to be pursued, conquered, and mounted.

Not that Balthazar would say *no* to any of that, either…

He studied her while she squinted at the burning paper tube between her fingers. In the weeks since arriving at Hastings he'd rarely seen the housekeeper standing still. She was a blur, a whirling dervish who seemed pleased, rather than annoyed, by all the work that accompanied the arrival of a new family. Especially the arrival of Edith, who appeared to view her as yet another personal servant to be ordered around, much like she treated poor Miss Barclay.

"There is the jolt of energy one gets, of course," she said after a moment, reminding Bal that he'd asked her a question. "Strangely, it is both energizing *and* calming." She looked up from the cigarette and he could see that she was embarrassed by her candor. "But it is a filthy habit." She pinched off the end of the burning tube and then laid the half-smoked cigarette back inside the stylish metal case. She gave him a sheepish look. "It is rather revolting to keep them when they've been half-smoked, but they are terribly expensive."

"I have an acquaintance back in America who is working on a machine to roll cigarettes, which will bring the price down considerably."

"A machine?"

"Yes. He is not the only one—there are men here and in Europe who've been laboring away on the concept for years. The one my friend has designed can make upwards of one hundred cigarettes per minute while a skilled roller can make only four."

"My goodness."

"Within a few years I suspect they will all be made by machine. I daresay that will make them much cheaper and more people will pick up the habit."

"One machine will put many people out of work."

Her observation surprised him. "It will," he agreed. "But then what sort of existence is that for a person—repetitive piecework?"

"Some mindless tasks can be soothing. Perhaps the people who make cigarettes like their jobs."

"Perhaps," he agreed. "Tell me, do you like your job, Mrs. Dryden?"

"I do," she said without hesitation. "But then it is hardly mindless and repetitious."

"No. Those are two things it is not," he agreed. "You enjoy it even now, after a noisy, demanding American family has descended on Hastings Park and brought so much more work with them?"

"His Grace is most willing to spend money where it has long needed it," she said, her answer carefully diplomatic. "It is gratifying to be able to bring the house back to order."

There was a long pause, and Bal thought she was going to take her leave, but then she said, "Are you enjoying England, my lord?"

Her question stunned him. Not the question itself, but the fact that she'd unbent enough to exhibit some curiosity about him. Bal knew she *was* curious—he could sense the way her eyes lingered on him on those rare occasions when they'd been in the same room—but he didn't think she was happy about her interest in him, not when she viewed him as a dissolute over-sexed scoundrel.

"Yes, I am enjoying it here. I like the gentle climate and the architecture is fascinating. I also like your accents."

She gave a huff of laughter. "It is *you* who have the accent."

Bal was pleased by her gentle teasing, and his first impulse was to tease her right back, but she was a skittish creature and he suspected that too much familiarity would drive her away. So, instead, he finished answering her question. "I expected there to be a great many similarities, given our shared history. But it is the differences between our two peoples that have surprised me most."

"What sort of differences?"

"It is true that people here are far more reserved, no matter the class. And not only is England geographically smaller, but even the people seem more compact."

Her eyes briefly darted down his body and then back up. "Your family is tall, even your sisters. But surely not all Americans are built on such a scale?"

He grinned. "No, just those of us who are raised in the country with lots of clean, fresh air and room to grow."

"You've always lived in the country?"

"I lived in a city for a few years," Bal admitted as he glanced at Hastings Park, which loomed nearby, a silent, dark goliath. "I certainly never lived anywhere like this before."

"Hastings Park is exceptional even in England," she said, a touch of pride in her voice.

"You've worked here a long time?"

"Yes, almost fourteen years."

Bal's eyebrows lifted. "You must have been a very young housekeeper," he said, and then felt, rather than saw, her retreat from him, not physically, but emotionally, as if she'd suddenly recalled that she was speaking not only to the brother of her employer, but also an unrepentant hedonist.

"I was young when His Grace hired me," she admitted, her manner stiff. "But I'd already kept house for my father. I was experienced enough to manage an establishment this size."

Bal thought she'd become remarkably defensive at the simple question, but before he could ask any questions about her family, she dropped a slight, but graceful curtsey. "If you will excuse me, my lord, I must go close up the house for the night."

"Of course," he murmured, inclining his head and then watching as she made her way past her cottage and then on toward the house. The night was lovely with a full moon and it turned her pale blond hair silver as she moved off, making her look spectral.

What an intriguing woman.

And also a woman who really did not care to answer questions about herself.

Just what was the fascinating Mrs. Dryden hiding?

***

Tori felt Lord Balthazar's gaze as she scurried toward the house like a frightened little mouse.

His effect on her was unnerving. Not since Teddy had she been so aware of a man. And even with Teddy she did not recall being so entirely… unsettled.

Of course, it had been a lifetime ago and she'd doubtless forgotten what it was like to experience such physical attraction.

And then there was the fact that she'd been an ignorant, innocent virgin back then and unconscious of what was happening to her. Now, she recognized the symptoms of her arousal all too well. And just as it had with Teddy, her deceptive body had chosen the least appropriate person within miles to fixate upon.

Well, that wasn't true, Tori thought with grim amusement; she could have chosen one other man who was more inappropriate: the new duke.

The sound of male and female laughter penetrated the kitchen door just as Tori reached out to open it. At this time of night, it should have been empty. Instead, Lady Evadne sat sipping a glass of milk across from one of the new footmen, Phillip, who also had a glass, his empty.

He shot to his feet. "Oh! Mrs. Dryden. Lady Eva—er, Lady Evadne, wanted a glass of milk and had not yet come to the kitchen. She asked me to lead her here, ma'am."

Lady Evadne stood, holding a book and pencil in one hand. "It is my fault that Phillip is drinking milk with me in the kitchen instead of working, Mrs. Dryden. I asked him to sit with me and clear up a few words." She raised the black leather volume. "I am compiling a dictionary of street cant and heard several terms in the village that I didn't understand. Phillip was helping me with them." She turned back to the footman. "Thank you. I shall take this up to my room." She picked up her glass.

"Good night, my lady," Tori said, waiting until the other woman was gone before turning to Phillip, who was getting redder by the second.

"I'm sorry, ma'am. I know I shouldn't be sitting here with her, but I didn't know how to say *no*."

"It is your job to do as the duke or his family asks—within reason, Phillip."

The rebuke was a gentle one, but the young man understood. "Yes, ma'am. Thank you, ma'am."

"You may go."

He scurried from the room as fast as a six-foot-two man could move.

Tori sighed. How was she to deal with issues like that? Over-familiarity with servants had never been a problem she'd had to address before.

That's not true...an annoying, sing-song voice whispered in head. *You were guilty of over familiarity yourself once... Do you remember Teddy, perchance*?

She could ignore the taunt, but she couldn't deny it.

If Miss Barrymore disliked scullery maids and stable boys *fraternizing* then she'd be incensed to hear a member of the duke's family was sharing a glass of milk with a servant.

Tori would have to have a talk with all the staff—it would need to be a subtle yet pointed discussion.

She set about checking the various doors and windows on the ground floor, a process that took a good half-hour. Her mind wandered back to the conversation outside her cottage, where she'd done some fraternizing of her own.

Thus far the Hale siblings had behaved with almost disappointing decorum—especially Lord Balthazar. Part of her had hoped for wild orgies and other signs of sexual excess. But, for the most part, they had been polite and hard-working.

All four brothers were gorgeous specimens of manhood, although the younger three were far brawnier than most men of the *ton*. The eldest, while tall and well-formed, was not as rugged as his siblings.

Both sisters were kind, thoughtful, and considerate to the servants. They were lovely enough to turn the heads of her older, more cynical male servants so it wasn't surprising that Phillip had fallen under his youthful mistress's spell.

Like their brothers, Ladies Io and Evadne possessed a confidence that Tori wasn't accustomed to seeing in women so young. Indeed, she still wasn't as comfortable in her own skin as they were in their early twenties.

And how was it possible to shoulder outlandish names like Zeus, Balthazar, Io, Ares, Apollo, and Evadne and make them appear so very… fitting?

Tori burned to ask them questions about what their lives had been like at that commune. Had they *all* taken older lovers to initiate them in the erotic arts? Or just the brothers?

Liar. You want to ask him questions…

Tori bit back her annoyance as she checked the latch on the conservatory door. Yes, it was true that her curiosity burned the brightest when it came to Lord Balthazar.

That isn't the only thing you burn for.

"*Do* shut up," she muttered.

"I beg your pardon?" a voice behind her asked.

Tori shrieked, jumped, and spun around.

It was one of the twins, garbed in riding clothing even though it was well past eleven o'clock at night.

"I'm sorry, I didn't mean to startle you," he said. "I thought you were speaking to me."

Tori realized she was still clutching her chest and lowered her hand. "I'm afraid you caught me talking to myself, Lord, er—"

His lips twisted into a barely-there smile as he lazily tapped his crop against his boot. "I'm Apollo."

"Thank you. I'm so sorry I didn't know that."

"Don't be sorry, even our siblings can't always tell the difference."

"You are very alike," she said rather stupidly.

"Identical. On the surface," he added, and then gave an abrupt but graceful bow. "I'm off to bed, ma'am. Good night."

"Good night," she murmured, and watched his long-limbed figure stride away until he disappeared up the stairs.

Tori glanced around to make sure none of the other Hales were lurking nearby. It was unnerving to have people in the house after so many years.

Especially unnerving to have one you can't stop thinking about.

Tori wanted to argue with that assessment, but she prided herself on avoiding self-delusion. Who knew why she found Balthazar Hale so attractive when his brother, Apollo—who was so much more… perfect—left her cold?

She sighed as she made her way to the servant door, which she locked behind her with a key that hung from her heavy chatelaine.

She had sensed Lord Balthazar's interest in her that very first day, and she'd known immediately it wasn't the sort of interest that led to anything respectable. Even if his egalitarian outlook would allow him to consider one of his brother's servants as a wife, the man came from a religious sect that didn't even believe in marriage.

Of course, Tori's disreputable past wouldn't allow marriage even if he *were* so inclined.

Still… She'd heard no rumors about the man—nothing to indicate he was deflowering the local virgin population. Perhaps there really was no truth to any of those stories?

Men like him are all the same, Tori—they use women like you. If you think Lord Balthazar isn't cut from the same cloth, then there is truly no hope for you.

The practical part of her tried to latch onto that warning and hold it at the forefront of her mind, but her fertile imagination refused to listen to the voice of reason. And later that night, for the first time in years, Tori had the sort of vivid erotic dream that woke her up panting, and had her blushing the following day.

It also left her more determined than ever to avoid all future contact with Balthazar Hale.

Chapter 7

"*There* you are!" Eva cried out as she flung open the door to Balthazar's private sitting room without bothering to knock.

Bal looked up from thick bundle of paperwork he'd received by messenger earlier that day. "You needed me for something?" he asked absently.

"It's the harvest festival tonight. You told me you'd take me. Remember?"

"I did?"

"Balthazar!"

He winced. "Quiet screeching or you're likely to bring the wrath of Edith down on our heads. Of course I didn't forget," he lied, straightening up the thick stack of documents and tucking them back into their pouch.

"What is all that?" Eva asked.

"I'm considering buying some land."

"Oh. Then you want to stay here—longer than just the two years Zeus mentioned?" Eva sounded happy about that.

"Possibly."

"Good. Because I'm not going back, and I don't want any of you to go back, either."

He smiled, unsurprised by her declaration; living in England had always been Eva's dream. "So, you are still liking it here?"

Eva gave him a look of disbelief. "It is beautiful, the weather is mild, the house is fascinating—as are the people and language—the clothing is lovely"—she gestured to her primrose gown, or walking costume, or whatever it was called and said, "truly, Bal—what is there not to like?" She suddenly pulled a face. "Well, other than Edith. But even that can't crush all the joy out of me."

Bal laughed as he shrugged into his coat. "You are an inspiration to us all, Eva."

Napier, who must have heard Bal's boisterous sister, came out of the dressing room carrying Bal's hat and gloves.

"Ah, thank you," Bal said.

"Good evening, Napier," Eva said, her friendly greeting causing the poor valet to flush to the roots of his strawberry blond hair. "Are you going to the harvest festival? I know Eunice was hoping to see you."

Napier's color deepened and his embarrassed eyes slid to Bal. "Er—"

"I won't need you for the rest of the night," Bal said. "You might as well go enjoy the festivities."

Napier flashed one of his rare smiles. "Thank you, my lord. Perhaps I will."

"Where is Yoyo," Bal asked Eva once the valet left. "Doesn't she want to come with us?"

"She is already there helping Miss Temple with her booth."

"What sort of booth?"

"They are selling used books." Eva lowered her voice. "And don't tell anyone, but they are also giving out birth control pamphlets and condoms."

Bal groaned. "Good Lord! Right here in Symington—with Edith less than a mile away? Is she insane?"

"No more than usual," Eva said.

"I'm serious. If Edith hears of this—"

"She won't. They don't exactly have a banner announcing what they are doing, Bal. They are just making sure that all the young women in the area are well-informed."

Bal agreed with Io's motivation, but the subject of birth control was a divisive one, to say the least. Back home there were movements afoot to make distribution of both information and the prophylactics themselves illegal. He wasn't sure how the law stood on the matter in Britain, but he'd hate to see his sister get hauled off to jail.

He sighed. There was no telling Io what to do—there never had been—so he put the worrisome matter from his mind and resigned himself to posting her bail when and if the time came.

"What about Ares and Pol? Where are they?" he asked.

Eva snorted. "Those two bits of blood and fashion sneaked off right after dinner."

Bal lifted an eyebrow. "*Bits of blood and fashion*? Really, Eva, you're too cruel to our pretty brothers."

Eva looped her arm through Bal's and yanked hard. "Come along, already," she said when he paused to check his face for smears of ink in the mirror. "You look as fine as a Saxon shilling."

Bal laughed. "I thought the saying was *as fine as a fivepence*?"

"A Saxon shilling—which was worth five pence—was superior to many other coins; hence the saying."

"I should know better than to argue with a linguist."

She narrowed her eyes at him.

"I'm sorry," Bal said. "What I meant to say was *lexicographer.*"

"Much better."

"Why didn't you go with Io and man the booth"—he gasped when her sharp elbow jabbed into his ribs— "*Ow*! I meant why didn't you *wo*-man the booth with her?"

"I had yet another fitting."

She sounded so grim that Bal felt sorry for her. "You must be nearly finished with all that?"

"Mostly. It's that wretched court gown. I'd always thought it would be lovely to wear such a dress, but it weighs upwards of thirty pounds, Bal. And one must bow and scrape while wearing it."

"You'll be the belle of the ball."

Eva gave him a scathing look. "You *are* stupid, aren't you?"

Bal laughed. "Why? What did I say?"

"A lady doesn't wear a court gown to a ball. She doesn't wear it anywhere but to fawn on the Queen." She smiled at one of the footmen who was stationed outside Zeus's bedchamber when they passed by. "Phillip! I thought you were going to the festival?"

The footman turned the color of a healthy beetroot and cut Bal a worried look, as if to say that *he* hadn't been the one to encourage such informality. When Bal merely smiled, the younger man relaxed a little and said, "I shall go for a bit after Reg and David return." He hesitated and then added with a cocky grin. "Don't eat all Mrs. Riley's cream cakes before I can get there, my lady."

Eva laughed. "I'll make no promises."

Bal waited until they were out of the house to turn to his sister.

"Oh, please don't scold," she said before he could speak. "I know I'm not supposed to chatter with the servants—believe me, I've been told and told and told. But Bal, I don't have any friends here. It is so… cold here, and I don't mean the weather."

"I thought you were loving it here?"

"I do, it's just"—she bit her lip.

"People have been standoffish?" he guessed. Bal hadn't joined his brother returning any calls, although Zeus had invited him, but he knew his sisters had been forced to both receive and make social calls.

"Lord yes! I've met half-a-dozen young women my age and they've all looked at me as if I've moved here from the moon. I think their mothers all encourage that distance. Everyone is terrified that I'll defile their daughters' lily-white ears with stories of my sexual exploits."

He squeezed her arm. "I'm sorry, Eva. I know this has always been a dream of yours—to come to England—"

"I still love it here," she said quickly. "I'm still adjusting. Especially when it comes to servants. It just seems so… wrong to have these sorts of distinctions. Just because Phillip opens doors and runs errands doesn't mean he isn't a person that I should be concerned about."

"I know, Eva, but it's—well, it's better to stick to the conventions. As Yoyo pointed out to me—quite rightly, I think—it makes the servants more comfortable, too."

She didn't look convinced.

"I'm not scolding just to scold, Little One," he said, using her childhood nickname even though it didn't really apply any longer. At five-foot-eight Eva was the shortest of the Hale siblings, but she wasn't small by English standards.

"Why *are* you scolding then?"

"Because I know you are looking forward to your time in London, but if you keep on this way—"

"I shall be shunned by the entirety of the *ton* for being an American yokel as well as an easy piece?" she asked.

"*Easy piece*?" Bal repeated, laughing.

"It is a relatively new term," Eva explained.

"Yes, and very descriptive, too."

"Don't worry, Bal, I will behave more properly when we get to London, where such things matter more."

Balthazar was relieved that she'd already come to that conclusion, even if he could see that it saddened her to realize that becoming part of the *ton* didn't just mean wearing pretty dresses and attending lavish functions. Eva would, eventually, need to decide whether setting aside her natural egalitarian instincts was worth fitting in.

"I'll likely be shunned no matter what I do, Bal. So I intend to enjoy myself."

"I'm not so sure about that first part, but I cannot argue with the second. So, enough on that subject. You never did tell me where Ares and Pol went?"

"My guess would be that Ares went to see his new lover. Again. He's gone to Mrs. Fletcher every night this week. I only know because I overheard Edith tattling to Zeus about it."

He didn't want to ask if she *overheard* with her ear at a keyhole. He also didn't want to encourage gossip about their brother and his obnoxious fiancé. While he disliked Edith more with each day that passed, he was increasingly coming to respect Zeus—especially for his dedication to Hastings Park—and felt bad taking digs at the man behind his back. Which didn't mean he'd be any less outspoken *in front* of his brother. His anger about the inheritance—especially the part about marrying a respectable bride—had cooled slightly, but he didn't think he'd ever forgive Zeus for riding herd on him as far as marriage and a wife was concerned.

He pushed the unpleasant thought away.

"And where is Pol?" he asked Eva.

She kicked a stone down the path. "Where else?"

That meant their horse-mad brother must be out riding again, even though it would be dark in an hour or so. Something was bothering Apollo—who was always moody but seemed even worse than usual—but Bal didn't really feel comfortable prying. Ares often came to Bal with his problems, but Apollo had always kept his own council. He would have thought Pol was happier here given all the impressive bloodstock that Zeus had invested in, but maybe he'd left a lover back at Canoga and was missing her.

"Do you know what is bothering Pol?" he asked.

Eva snorted. "As if he'd tell me anything. Ask Ares if you want to know—although I doubt he knows his twin's mind, either."

Bal reluctantly agreed with her.

When Eva lifted her foot to kick the stone again, Bal nudged her out of the way and booted the rock down the path.

"You snudge!" she accused, two small hands shoving him in the back hard enough to send him stumbling.

Bal laughed as she cut around him and kicked the stone hard enough to send it spinning into the tall grass beside the path.

"I win," she declared, raising her fists in a mocking victory cheer. Her expression fell when she noticed that her hair had come loose from its moorings. "Look what you've done, Bal," she accused pointing to a lock of hair. She stopped in the middle of the path. "Fix it, please."

"Turn this way," Bal said, and then took the wiry dark brown hair, so like his own, and carefully tucked into back into place. "There," he said, "Good as new. By the way, what's a *snudge*?" he asked when they resumed walking.

"A thief who hides under a woman's bed."

Bal laughed. "You were using it rather out of context then, weren't you?"

"I suppose it is the only thing that Tirzah did *not* accuse you of in those wretched articles."

Bal groaned. "Please don't remind me."

"You're still furious, aren't you?"

"Not furious, but angry, disappointed, and embarrassed." He thought of Mrs. Dryden, and the look in her eyes even now as she imagined him doing the things Tirzah's articles had claimed. He refused to be ashamed of his sexual history—or his beliefs—but he didn't like being viewed as a debauched degenerate.

"Nobody who knows you would believe you toyed with women's affections or engaged in orgies or all those other things."

Bal just grunted.

"Do you like my hair better this way?" she asked, changing the subject before he could respond to her sisterly statement of support.

He turned to look at her, even though he'd just fixed her hair. "It's very pretty."

She smacked his shoulder. "I don't mean how it looks right *now*; I meant do you like it longer better than shorter?"

"I like it this way, but I like it short, too." He shrugged. "It is *your* choice how to wear it, Eva, you don't have to comply with Edith's demands just because she hounds you."

"I know that, Bal. I'm growing it longer for myself, because I'm curious to see how it looks."

The women at Canoga kept their hair short, so his sisters had never worn theirs much past their ears. He knew they both received odd looks for it, so he supposed it would be a relief to grow it longer.

While he didn't appreciate Edith's abrasive methods, he couldn't help appreciating the results of her efforts on his sisters' behalf. They would indeed have suffered ostracism in England if they'd not had her help with their clothing and grooming.

Bal felt a twinge in his shoulder and rolled it, kneading the sore joint with his other hand.

"Did you hurt yourself showing off these past few weeks?" Eva asked.

"Showing off?"

"All that help with the harvesting you did—you and Ares and Apollo."

"What do you know about that?"

"I overheard Judith—she is the very pretty maid with the lovely, curly blond hair—mention that you and the twins were going to one of Zeus's farms to help. She said there were several other girls going to watch because you and the other men had taken off your shirts on your first day of work."

Bal snorted. "I didn't see any observers." Other than Mrs. Dryden and Miss Brower, of course.

"No, everyone was well-hidden."

"Why does it sound like you have personal knowledge of this adventure?"

"Naturally. I went along with them. After all, you and the twins weren't the only men running about shirtless."

"So you went to ogle bare torsos, then. Or to collect more cant?"

"It was an excellent opportunity to do both." She nudged him with her elbow. "I also learned that half the maids are infatuated with you and the other half are in love with either Ares or Pol or both."

"I hope the twins aren't taking advantage of that?"

She cut him a look of disgust. "You should know better than that."

He should. His brothers might like to sow their wild oats, but they would appreciate the distinction between willing, independent lovers—like Jo Fletcher—and women who were employed by Zeus.

Because you've done such a good job respecting that distinction yourself, a sly voice pointed out.

I've behaved myself when it comes to Mrs. Dryden, Bal protested.

Only because you've not had a good opportunity to pursue her...

Bal couldn't argue with that observation.

"None of the maids are madly in love with Zeus?" he asked.

"No, they're all too terrified of *Edith* to even think his name."

Bal couldn't blame them. Their sister-in-law-to-be was an extremely jealous woman and he'd noticed that she took care to never allow even her mousy little cousin to stay in the same room with Zeus too long.

He wondered how Edith would feel when they were in London and going to three balls a night—which is what he'd been told the Season could be like—and Zeus was compelled to dance and socialize with hundreds of attractive, charming women.

Bal decided that wasn't his problem.

Actually, that wasn't really true; Edith *was* his problem. She was a problem for Bal and all his siblings, including Zeus, although his oldest brother appeared oblivious to just how abrasive his fiancé was.

He'd never seen Zeus be either affectionate or annoyed with Edith—nor had he seen her display any emotion toward his brother. To Bal's way of thinking, it was an extremely odd alliance. He knew from the articles he'd read about his brother—rather than from Zeus's own mouth—that Edith's only sibling, Albert Barrymore, had been Zeus's best friend. The two men had attended Harvard together and had both joined the army afterward. Albert had been badly wounded at Gettysburg and had eventually died of those injuries several years after the war.

Zeus and Edith became engaged a year after Albert's death, but before they could marry, Edith's mother had died, leaving her daughter in possession of the Barrymore fortune and making her one of the richest heiresses in America.

Bal wondered if Edith's fortune was all that motivated Zeus. He also wondered if that is what made Edith *respectable*: her money. Would Zeus expect Balthazar to find an heiress? Was that the only sort of woman his brother would approve of—a wealthy one?

"I heard you and Mrs. Dryden rode home together in the gig," Eva said, pulling him from his thoughts.

"My, my, quite the little gossip, aren't you? How did you hear that?" He'd had the housekeeper drop him off before they reached Hastings specifically to avoid such tittle-tattle.

"Plenty of people saw you leave with her, Bal."

"Ah." He should know there was nothing else to talk about in the country but one's neighbors.

"Edith found out about Mrs. Dryden's visit to the Brower's and told her that *she* would assume such responsibilities in the future."

Bal scowled. "What business is it of hers if Mrs. Dryden brings food to a few farmers?"

"Edith says that is the duchess's duty, not the housekeeper's."

Lord. She was *such* an unpleasant woman.

"I've grown to like Zeus, Bal. I just hate to think of him married to Edith."

So did Balthazar. Unfortunately, their opinions weren't the ones that mattered.

He turned to his little sister. "If there is one thing I know about people—whether you're related to them, or not—you cannot tell anyone, man or woman, something if it they don't want to hear it, or make them see things they don't wish to see. For whatever reason, Zeus appears enamored of her. I suspect that if anyone needs to adjust, it will be the five of us once they are married and we are living in *her* house."

Bal didn't tell his sister that he'd probably be doing his adjusting somewhere else as he couldn't imagine living under his brother's roof once Zeus was married.

***

Tori was just setting out the last jars of Auntie Max's brambleberry jam when she noticed a subtle shift in the people milling between the two rows of tented tables. A quick look around confirmed the source of the low buzz of interest: Lord Balthazar and his younger sister, Lady Evadne, had just arrived.

They were looking at something on Mary Swenson's table, which was covered with embroidered items that the ancient lady worked on all year long. The money from some of the booths would be donated to the church to pay for the repair and replacement of the pews, but some of the people relied on the money they earned at the little festival, and Mary was one of them.

"Auntie said you would be here—slaving away in the heat."

Tori turned at the sound of the familiar voice, a smile already curving her lips. "Malcolm! Maxine didn't say you were visiting this week."

Malcolm Rowel, who really *was* Auntie Max's nephew, gave Tori a boyish smile that caused many women in the village's hearts to beat faster. Not only was Malcolm blond, blue-eyed, and well formed, but he was also a lovely person.

And clever, too. His most recent invention—some sort of farm implement—had earned him a great deal of money and made him one of the wealthier citizens in the area. He'd purchased and refurbished the squire's old house specially for his aunt and split his time between Symington and Birmingham, where his factory was.

Maxine doted on him and treated him like a son, as she'd never had any children of her own.

"I'd ask how you've been, Tori, but I can see that you are blooming," Malcolm said.

Tori knew that wasn't true; she'd seen the dark smudges beneath her eyes only that morning in her looking glass. But she appreciated the effort.

"Thank you. You are also looking… prosperous." Indeed, he looked every inch the wealthy man he was. Tori suspected his mind was too occupied by weighty, scientific matters to care about mundane matters like clothing. But his aunt had been riding him relentlessly for years to hire a valet and it seemed her nagging had finally paid off.

He laughed, his cheeks flushing as he glanced down at his garments—an exquisitely tailored tweed coat and elegant wool trousers—which were obviously expensive, but not flashy.

"Please tell me that my valet—yes, I finally gave in to Aunt's hectoring and engaged one—hasn't kitted me out like a peacock, Tori?"

"No, indeed—you are the perfect country gentleman."

Malcolm narrowed his eyes at her. "Why are you smiling like that? Lord, I *do* look like a tosser, don't I?"

Tori couldn't help laughing. "You don't, I promise. So, tell me the news of the outside world."

"I can only report on Birmingham, which is much the same as usual. I've begun production of my new manure spreader—isn't that the sort of subject to make a woman's heart beat faster?"

She found herself laughing again, something she did often around Malcolm, whom she adored. Unfortunately, her adoration—for a friend—wasn't the sort he wanted. He'd asked her to marry him two years ago and told her he would wait, declaring his love. It pained her that she couldn't return his affection and she knew it had gravely disappointed Maxine, who still held out hope for the match. As much as the older woman loved Victoria, she didn't think Auntie Max would be so thrilled for her nephew to marry Tori if she knew the truth about who she really was and what she'd done.

Tori's past was only part of the reason she hadn't accepted Malcolm's offer. As much as she wanted to please both him and Maxine—not to mention Jamie, who adored Malcolm—he deserved somebody who loved him, not just a wife who needed him.

"Good evening, Mrs. Dryden."

Tori's heart leapt at the sound of a certain American voice and she turned to find Lord Balthazar and his sister in front of her booth.

"We've been told that Mrs. Rowel's jam is the closest thing to heaven on earth," Lady Evadne said, smiling from Tori to Malcolm. When Tori hesitated—not wishing to push an acquaintance on the duke's siblings—Lady Evadne, quite literally, took matters into her own hands. She held out one small, gloved hand. "Hello, I'm Eva Hale and this is my brother Balthazar."

Malcolm paused for only a second at the unorthodox introduction. "A pleasure to meet you, my lady. I'm Malcolm Rowel. And you are right about the jam." He patted his flat midriff. "I've personally sampled every batch my aunt has ever made."

The American woman's smile broadened at his friendliness and Tori felt a sharp pang of sympathy for Lady Evadne; her open nature had likely met with more than a few rebuffs among the local gentry, most of whom feared and avoided the newcomers—all except the duke, of course—largely because of those scandalous articles about life in Canoga. Observing her neighbors' bigoted behavior toward the Hales only made Tori feel guiltier about how she'd condemned Balthazar Hale before even meeting him—not that she believed him blameless.

Oddly enough, she hadn't judged his siblings nearly as harshly, even though they'd lived at the commune, too, and likely held the same beliefs as their brother. And the articles had said that women, as well as young men, took *sexual mentors* at Canoga.

That meant Ladies Io and Evadne were probably just as sophisticated in erotic matters as their brothers. Tori knew it was fear of the Hale women's confidence and sexual experience that kept many of the local gentry from allowing their daughters to socialize with the duke's sisters. Respecting the power and wealth of the Duke of Hastings was one thing; jeopardizing their own daughters' futures by allowing them to associate with such scandalous young women was quite another.

"A pleasure to meet you, Lord Balthazar," Malcolm said, smiling at the other man, who towered over him by a good four inches. "I believe we share a mutual acquaintance—David Norton."

Hale's face lit up, his green-gold eyes widening. "Yes, I met David when he came to New York. He stayed at Canoga."

"I know. He was most impressed by your crossbreeding experiments with wheat—not to mention your steam plow."

The two men were quickly engaged in a conversation that included too much agricultural jargon for Tori to understand.

"Bal will talk about farming for hours," his sister said with a look of affectionate exasperation.

Tori blinked at that rather startling information. "He will?"

"Indeed, yes. He oversaw the farming back home—he fed us all. And he is always making things—mechanical things—to diminish the amount of labor needed to operate a farm. And if that isn't enough, he volunteers a great deal of time testing soil—that is what he went to university for. Well, not testing dirt, but chemistry."

"Oh, he went to university," Tori said, rather stupidly as Lady Evadne had just *said* he had.

"He studied engineering, too. Bal is very clever," his sister said proudly. "He does something with chemicals and can tell a farmer what is lacking and what sort of crops to plant. The twins nicknamed him the Dirt Wizard." She laughed.

Tori laughed with her, but it wasn't amusement she felt, it was amazement. None of the newspaper articles she'd read about Balthazar Hale had mentioned farming, inventions, or university. Indeed, all the stories had made it sound as if he *had* no occupation. Well, other than being a sex-crazed Yankee yokel.

Of course, just because he was clever and worked hard did not mean he *wasn't* also a sex-crazed Yankee yokel who—

"Mrs. Dryden?"

Tori jolted at the sound of her name and said, "I'm sorry, my lady, I didn't catch what you said."

"I was just saying that I'd like two jars of the jam, please. Ares and Apollo have such terrible sweet tooths that I will need to keep these hidden."

Tori smiled; the twins' voracious appetites were already legend among the servants at Hastings.

"I noticed that you stopped by Mary Swenson's booth earlier," Tori said as she wrapped up the jars. "Did you find anything you like?"

"Oh yes, loads. She does the most remarkable work. I purchased enough handkerchiefs to have a gift for my sister for Christmas and several for me to enjoy." She laughed. "I'm dreadful with a needle so I'm too mortified to carry my own handkerchiefs."

Tori, who was familiar with Mary's fine work, said, "Her flowers are so lifelike that I always imagine I can smell roses."

"That is exactly what I said to Bal! Of course he just laughed at me. Aren't brothers horrid?"

Instead of confessing that she had no siblings, Tori smiled and asked, "How are you liking the area, my lady?"

"I adore it. All the history, the architecture, the language—especially the language."

"That's right, you are compiling a dictionary."

Lady Evadne's brow furrowed. "Yes, I am, but how did you—Oh, I remember now. You caught me picking poor Phillip's brain in the kitchen over a glass of milk." She gave another of her infectious laughs. "I'm sorry. I know that I've been a terrible distraction to the servants, but they've been such a wonderful source of information for modern cant."

"I can imagine," Tori said drily, recalling some of the *cant*—modern and otherwise—she'd overheard coming from the stables when the men weren't aware she was listening.

The strains of musicians tuning up suddenly filled the velvety night air.

"Is there to be a dance out here?" Lady Evadne asked, glancing eagerly around the town green, which was so full of people you could scarcely see ten feet ahead.

"It will be at the King's Quarrel—there is a room used for dancing on the second floor."

"Bal—did you hear Mrs. Dryden? There is to be a dance."

Lord Balthazar broke off whatever he'd been saying and turned to his sister. "I suppose we should stay on a bit longer, then." He turned to Tori. "Will you be going?"

"Er, I hadn't planned—"

"Oh, do stay for a little while," Lady Evadne begged. "I would love the company."

"Yes, Tori, stay for at least one dance," Malcolm piled on.

"Make that two," Lord Balthazar added. "I would like one."

Tori knew her face would be bright pink at all the attention. "Well, how can I say *no* to all that?"

"When does it begin?" Lady Evadne asked. "Do we have time to look at the rest of the tables?'

Tori picked up the chain that held her watch and opened the protective cover. "It won't get started for another half hour at least. You've got plenty of time."

"Did you hear that, Bal?" Lady asked, interrupting Lord Balthazar, who lifted his hand in in a *just a moment* gesture and finished whatever he was saying to Malcolm.

Lady Evadne turned to Tori. "I've been meaning to tell you how I adore your chatelaine, Mrs. Dryden."

"Thank you, my lady. Mr. Rowel's aunt—the same one who makes this jam—gave it to me many years ago. It used to belong to her, but I have added to it over the years."

"I believe I want one. It would be excellent for keeping a notebook and pencil."

"Then you should talk to Mr. Hires, our village jeweler. He has a booth with a few of his pieces just down at the end of this row of tables."

"Thank you, I will. That's if I can ever get my escort to come with me." Lady Evadne looped her arm through her brother's and tugged.

"I'm coming, I'm coming," Lord Balthazar promised. To Malcolm, he said, "You'll stop by the house and look at what I've been talking about?"

Malcolm flushed with pleasure. "Thank you, my lord. I would be honored to come to Hastings Park."

Lord Balthazar turned to Tori. "Will there be a waltz tonight?"

She blinked. "Er, I should think so."

"May I have the honor of reserving the first one?"

Tori scrambled for an excuse but couldn't find one—not after she'd said *yes* to Malcolm. And so she smiled and said, "Thank you, I'd be delighted."

Only after Tori spoke the words did she realize that she meant them.

***

Balthazar could see that the inventor—Malcolm Rowel—was mad about Mrs. Dryden. The man was also on a first-name basis with her, so the two must know each other well. But at least Bal had managed to get the slippery woman to commit to a dance with him.

It was closer to an hour by the time Eva had finished buying out the remainder of the booths. They left all her goods with Jo Fletcher—who'd finally stopped eying Bal now that she and Ares appeared to have found common ground—and then joined the hordes as they climbed the narrow stairs up to the second floor, which already sounded as if it was going to collapse on top of the first floor it was so noisy.

The country dance was in full swing when they made their way through the crowd that ringed the small dance floor.

"Lord, it's hot in here," Eva half-shouted into Bal's ear.

He nodded and looked across the room, tall enough that he was easily able to see over most of the heads. He caught Malcolm Rowel's eye and the other man lifted a hand to wave him over.

Bal liked Rowell and looked forward to going to Birmingham and touring his manufactory. What he *hadn't* liked was the ease and intimacy between Mrs. Dryden and Rowel.

Although he didn't recall experiencing the feeling before, he suspected that the emotion roiling in his belly—and making him so irritable—was jealousy. Becoming possessive of another person–or getting *sticky* as people had termed such behavior at Canoga—had been frowned upon. Indeed, the council members had been known to forcibly separate people who became too attached to each other and began to expect exclusivity.

Other than his first, brief infatuation with Tirzah, Balthazar had never become especially attached to any of his lovers.

If this is what jealousy felt like, Bal could finally understand why the Canoga elders had warned against becoming *sticky.* He could already see that being assaulted by such dog-in-the-manger thoughts wasn't just irrational, it was also distracting and debilitating.

"Can you see Mrs. Dryden or Mr. Rowel?" Eva asked.

"Yes, this way." Bal took Eva's arm and guided her through the throng.

He smiled through the obligatory introductions to the people standing around Rowel—several of his university friends who were evidently staying at his aunt's house for the week—trying not to be too obvious about looking for Mrs. Dryden.

"You *just* missed Tori—she left only a few minutes ago. She wanted me to tell you that she is sorry she had to miss the dance, but something came up and she had to go back to Hastings early," Rowell said to Balthazar once he'd finished the introductions.

"That is unfortunate," Bal said, the words severely understating his feelings on the matter. He wondered if it was the impending dance with him that suddenly *came up*.

"She works very hard—too hard." Rowel's cheeks darkened, as if he recalled just who she worked *for*.

"I happen to agree," Balthazar said, earning a smile from the other man.

More people drifted over to the group and when Rowell turned to greet them, Bal leaned close to Eva and said, "I'm going to nip out for a little while. I'll be back—don't try and go home without me."

She nodded, clearly loath to break off her conversation with three admiring young gentlemen just to waste time on a mere brother.

Bal slipped through the crowd far more quickly than he'd entered, not having to escort his sister. Outside the throng had thinned but there were still people milling around the closing booths.

He made it to the path that led to Hastings with minimal distractions, wondering just what the hell he was doing running after a woman he barely knew—and one who clearly tried to avoid him—but it was so hard to get her alone at Hastings that he felt he should make the effort now. Bal just wanted to talk to her. Well, fine, that was a lie. He hoped for more than just talk—eventually—but talking would be a good place to start. Her defenses were far higher when she was in his brother's house and—

"Let me go of me!" The angry voice—belonging to none other than the woman he was haring after—came from somewhere off the path. Bal pushed through the thick branches and followed the sound of raised voices.

"What would people say if they knew the truth about you, *Mrs. Dryden*? You'd not be so high and mighty then. Thinkin' you're better'n everyone else when you're nothin' but a—" the sound of flesh hitting flesh cut off whatever he'd been about to say. "*Oww*! You—you *bitch*!"

Bal broke through the trees just as the man lunged for Mrs. Dryden. He took two long strides and grabbed her assailant, snaking his arm around the shorter man's neck and tightening until the stranger's chin rested snugly in the crook of his elbow.

"That's enough," he said through gritted teeth as the man thrashed, his elbows driving back into Bal's abdomen and ribs.

When he didn't stop, Bal squeezed his biceps and felt the man's body go rigid as his air supply was cut off. He glanced at Mrs. Dryden, who was leaning against a nearby tree, her hand at her throat, clutching at the neck of her bodice, which looked to be torn. Her normally neat and tidy hair was wild and loose around her shoulders.

"Are you hurt?" he asked.

She just breathed heavily through parted lips, as if she couldn't get enough air.

"Mrs. Dryden. Are you injured?" he repeated more firmly.

She shook her head, swallowed, and said, "No."

Bal turned to his captive. "If I loosen my hold, are you going to behave?"

The man nodded frantically and Bal released his grip just enough to allow him to suck in a noisy lungful of air.

He looked at the housekeeper. "Will the constable be at the dance?"

Her reaction was swift and intense. "No! Don't take him to Mr. Vickers. Please."

"You know this man?"

"Yes, his name is Gerald Boyd. A disgruntled former employee. He worked at Hastings and I had to sack him for drinking while—"

"That's a *lie*!" his captive rasped and would have lunged for Mrs. Dryden again if Bal hadn't tightened his hold.

"You *behave*, Gerald, and you might just get to sleep somewhere other than a cell tonight," Bal hissed in the man's ear. "Understand?"

The man nodded, his body limp, as if all the fight had suddenly drained away.

"Just let him go. Please, my lord."

He looked up from Boyd to find that Mrs. Dryden had come closer.

"Are you certain?"

"Yes. He is harmless."

"What he was doing to you didn't look too harmless, Mrs. Dryden."

"He just had too much to drink. He was celebrating the end of the harvest. He'll be gone tomorrow—looking for work elsewhere."

"Is that true? You're leaving tomorrow?"

"Two days hence," Boyd grudgingly admitted.

"Don't come near Mrs. Dryden again or the next time you won't be so fortunate."

"Aye, my lord."

Bal released him. "Go sleep it off."

Boyd didn't need to be told twice to leave and staggered from the small copse without a backward glance.

Bal stared down at the obviously flustered housekeeper. "Are you really unharmed, ma'am?"

"Yes, I am fine," she said, her tone suddenly abrupt, her hands moving efficiently to re-coil, pin, and smooth her long, silvery blond hair.

Bal waited for more—an explanation, perhaps. Even a *thank you*.

When nothing was forthcoming, he fixed the increasingly cool and collected woman with an amused, if slightly exasperated, look and said, "Why is it that you dislike me so much, Mrs. Dryden? I thought we'd got past our initial misunderstanding that day in the dogcart, and yet you still regard me as if I'm some sort of dangerous animal."

She recoiled at his direct attack.

Bal refused to retract his question, even though he knew it was abominably ill-bred of him, especially considering the poor woman had just endured a physical attack.

"It is not my place to dislike you, my lord."

"Perhaps not, but you still do." He cocked his head. "You left the dance to avoid me, didn't you?"

"No, of course I didn't."

He cocked an eyebrow.

"You can raise your eyebrow in that odious manner all you want, my lord; *you* were not the reason I left."

"Then why did you hurry off?"

She opened her mouth, hesitated, and then lamely said, "I just recalled there were some things I forgot to do."

"Things?"

"Yes, work things."

"You're lying."

She gasped, clearly affronted.

Bal didn't give her a chance to speak. "I've not molested any maids or neighborhood women and yet you still expect me to turn into a beast because of those stupid newspaper stories, don't you?"

"No, of course I—"

"Then why do you fear or dislike me? Because of what you know about my background? Where I grew up and what my beliefs are?" He smiled at the way her full lips tightened, her reaction telling him he'd struck paydirt. "You're worried that I'll debauch you with my *free love* approach to life?"

"It is not—"

"Oh, I know it's not your place," he said, taking a step toward her and closing the distance until they were barely a foot apart. Her chest—which had been rising and falling rapidly, whether because of her scuffle or their current dispute, he didn't know—froze and her remarkable blue eyes locked with his.

"Why do you care what I think?" she asked in a breathless voice.

"You feel it, don't you?" he asked quietly, and then reached up and caught a lock of hair that she'd missed in her haste.

Her lips parted and warm puffs of air buffeted his chin. "*It*?" she repeated. "Wha-what do you mean, my lord?"

Bal stroked the silky lock, his gaze lowering to her mouth. "Why are you pretending there is nothing between us?" His eyes narrowed. "Or is it just me? Do you not feel the same… spark?"

She opened and closed her mouth, her expression one of confusion and mortification. "I d-don't know what you mean."

Bal snorted. "Even you don't believe your words. I've wanted to kiss you since that day on the front steps of Hastings—when you gave me a look that could freeze a forge." He released her hair and lowered his hand to her bare throat, to where the neck of her bodice had been torn, caressing her with only the tips of his fingers.

She jolted but didn't pull away.

"He tore your dress," Bal said.

"It is nothing," she said in a voice that was barely above a whisper. "Easily repaired."

"Are you sure he didn't hurt you?"

She swallowed and nodded. "I'm sure."

Balthazar was not holding her in place—she was free to leave—and yet she stayed.

"You needn't be anxious, Mrs. Dryden. I do not *take*." He smiled. "At least not unless a woman freely wants to give. Freely, ma'am. You may turn and go and I will not stop you."

She did not move.

"Do you want to be kissed, Mrs. Dryden?"

Her eyes moved to his mouth, lingered, and then lifted again; her nod was so slight it was almost the ghost of assent.

Balthazar didn't know who was more shocked, him or her.

He raised his thumb to her lower lip, testing the warm, pillowy silk before he leaned low and whispered against her temple. "Use your words, Mrs. Dryden. Yes. Or no."

For one long, tension-filled moment he thought she'd tell him to go to hell—but she turned her head until her lips brushed his throat, and then whispered, "Kiss me."

The tenuous tether of restraint snapped and he cupped her face, tilting her head until he could see her eyes and then claiming her with the pent-up desire of the last weeks.

Her lips were as soft as he'd known they'd be—plush and warm and sweet.

But her kiss was… awkward and tentative. Once he got past his surprise, Balthazar reined in his hunger and approached her more gently, more carefully.

He told himself he shouldn't be startled by her clumsy kisses. After all, she'd been a widow for many years and he did not think she was the sort of woman to take a lover, not when she was likely to punish herself for her sensual needs even more than society would do.

Slowly she opened to him, like a bud responding to the heat of the sun, her lush, soft body pressing against his, one of her hands—small but strong—sliding up his chest and coming to rest on his shoulder.

Bal's hands felt enormous and brutish as he gently cupped her slender neck, as if he cradled the stem of a flower. He tilted her to the right angle, stroking between her silken lips, emboldened by the soft, needy whimper she made, her fingers digging into his shoulders as she pulled him lower, closer.

She tasted like sugar and he knew he wasn't imagining it because a few grains clung to her lips.

"Sweet," he murmured, lightly licking at the corner of her mouth.

Her eyelids fluttered and lifted slowly, as if they carried the weight of the world. Her pupils were blown wide, the velvety black encircled by thin blue halos. Balthazar watched with resignation as reality pushed its way through the fog of pleasure.

"Oh," she said, blinking rapidly. She jerked her hands from his shoulders and Bal waited for the inevitable regret to manifest, watching as her eyes shuttered and her expression firmed.

Bal knew a *gentleman* would apologize, but he refused to be a hypocrite.

"That should not have happened," she said, stepping away.

He had no interest in such a discussion so he changed the subject entirely. "What did that man mean earlier, Mrs. Dryden? What *truth* was he talking about? And why would people look at you differently if they knew it?" Bal was a bastard to ask her such a thing—especially when she was still dazed. But, yet again, he refused to retract it.

She flinched at the unexpected question, her lips parting in surprise.

Her blue eyes sharpened, the pupils shrinking rapidly. "It was nothing but the angry ramblings of a drunk, my lord. I must go." She spun on her heel and darted in the direction of the path.

Bal fell into step beside her, holding back the branches so she could pass unscathed.

She stopped and glared up at him. "What do you think you are doing? That kiss was a mistake—and there will be no more of them."

"I'm walking you back to Hastings."

"I'd prefer to walk alone."

"I'd prefer to escort you."

She scowled and stomped back to the path.

Bal easily kept up with her angry, hurried stride.

"I understand you have a son, Mrs. Dryden."

Her jaw moved from side to side and she obviously debated just ignoring him.

Either fond motherhood or common courtesy won out, he wasn't sure. "Yes, I do."

"How old is he?"

"He just turned thirteen."

"You must have been very young when you had him."

"Is that your way of asking my age. My lord," she added grudgingly. Before he could answer, she said, "I am five-and-thirty." She cut him a quick glance. "A good deal older than you, I should think."

"Ten years," he agreed. "I would have put you closer to thirty."

Her mouth tightened and she marched on, but not as fast as she'd been marching just a moment earlier.

"That is kind," she finally said.

"No, it is truthful." The imp that had emerged as he'd held her body and tasted her lips prodded Bal to say, "If you think a few years is a barrier to my interest in you then you've not read those scandal sheets very closely. I like older, experienced women. They make better lovers."

Again, she stopped, braced her hands on her hips, and fixed him with the sort of glare he imagined her using on a recalcitrant servant, or perhaps her little boy when he misbehaved.

Even in the moonlight he could see the pink fire in her cheeks.

"I work for your family, my lord. I don't know how it is in America, but in England, masters and servants do not mix. And the difference in our ages is not a *few years*, but a decade."

She looked so angry at herself for adding that last part that Bal couldn't help smiling. "You're right that I don't know how it is between masters and servants because we didn't have any servants where I grew to manhood. All that mattered to take a lover was whether you found somebody interesting and attractive. As I've already said, years mean nothing to me, no matter how many there are."

Mrs. Dryden opened her mouth and then closed it. Then she abruptly turned on her heel and strode down the path.

"Your son is away at school?" he asked.

"Yes." She must have realized how abrupt she sounded, so she said, "His grandparents have made it possibly for Jamie to go to a good school."

"Jamie—short for James?"

Her lips curved into a smile that looked to be an involuntary reaction to thinking about her child.

"Yes. James Abbott Dryden."

"Abbott? Is that a family name?"

She'd relaxed while talking about her son, but she stiffened again at this question. "Yes, it was my father's name." There was a finality to her tone that decided Balthazar against prying any further.

Instead, he escorted her the short distance home without saying anything else to incite or annoy her, stealing glances at her as she strode determinedly along, her taut jaw telling him how uncomfortable she was.

"You can leave me here," she said once they approached the edges of the vast lawn that bordered that side of Hastings.

"I'll walk you all the way."

She sighed but did not argue.

He escorted her to the servant's door.

"Thank you, my lord," she said, not lifting her eyes to meet his.

"Good night, Mrs. Dryden."

After she closed the door, Bal turned on his heel and started back toward the dance, where he would likely spend the next hour or so waiting for Eva to exhaust herself.

As Bal strolled down the moonlit path, he mulled over the strange scuffle he'd interrupted earlier, trying to remember exactly what it was that Gerald Boyd had shouted at Mrs. Dryden. Something about what would people think if they knew the truth about her.

What truth had he meant?

Why did Bal think there was more to the altercation than a disgruntled employee?

And why did he feel like Mrs. Dryden had lied to him?

Chapter 8

"I think a ball to celebrate Eva's birthday is a fine idea, Balthazar."

Zeus had called Bal into his study after dinner and it was just the two of them.

"I'm pleased to hear it," Bal said. Part of him wanted to poke and prod and see how Edith had taken Zeus's decision, but his brother appeared tired tonight. There were dark smudges beneath his eyes, which looked almost colorless. The only color on him at all was the reddish hue on his cheeks and high-bridged nose, a testament to a great deal of time riding around the estate for a man who rarely spent so much time outside.

"I'll leave the planning of the event to you, Io, and Mrs. Dryden," Zeus went on. "Just have all the bills sent to me." He paused and then said, with a rather pensive expression, "I have never attended a costume party."

"Neither have I. What costume shall you wear?"

"I suppose it would be terribly predictable if I were to dress as the obvious?"

Bal laughed. "What? You mean as the king of the gods?"

Zeus's lips twitched. "Too unimaginative?"

"Perhaps." Bal grinned. "But still damned amusing."

"Will you tell our sister about the party, or shall I?"

"I think you should tell Eva," Bal said. "Just be prepared to have your eardrums shattered with her joy."

His stern brother almost smiled. "Very well, I shall tell her. I trust you and Io will speak to Mrs. Dryden and Mr. Bickle and see what they can do to help?"

"Yes, we will." Balthazar looked forward to having a reason to speak to the enticing housekeeper, whom he'd not seen since their brief kiss in the woods.

Zeus scowled at his heaped desk. "Perhaps you might tell Eva I wish to see her when you leave. It will be a pleasure to make somebody happy before I need to apply myself to all *this*."

Bal felt a pang at his brother's grim expression. Io's suggestion came back to him; should he offer to help in some way?

"I was wondering if you'd come look at several of the tenant farms with me," Zeus said, suddenly making Bal wonder if the other man could read his mind. Or at least his expression.

"What do you want me to look at?"

"The soil, for one. Also, I think perhaps some of these farms are not planting the best crops." He ran a hand through his thick dark hair, which was almost the same color as Bal's. "I will be honest with you, Balthazar, I know next to nothing about agriculture. I could use an expert opinion."

Warmth bloomed in his belly at the other man's praise—something Zeus did not distribute freely in Bal's experience.

"I'm not sure I qualify as an *expert*, but I would enjoy a closer look." He cleared his throat and then added, "I must tell you that the few farms I've already seen have sorely depleted soil."

"You mean the places where you've helped with the harvesting?"

"You know about that?"

"Yes. I am pleased you and our other brothers took an interest, Balthazar."

"Well, it is what I enjoy doing," he said, a bit embarrassed by the other man's praise. "Indeed, now might be a good time to tell you that I am looking at some land."

Zeus's eyebrows shot up. "In England?"

"Yes. I thought since I could be here another two years, I might as well have somewhere I could continue my, er, experiments."

"Do you mean your agricultural experiments or your mechanical inventions?"

"Both, actually."

Zeus propped his elbows on his desk and leaned forward. "You've developed a steam plow, I understand?"

"Yes, but how did you know that?"

"I asked Io about your work at Canoga and she told me about your efforts to acquire more land and financial backing for your plow—back when she was still speaking to me," he added dryly.

"Ah." Bal wasn't sure what to say about Zeus's argument with his twin. It had always been his job to broker peace between his siblings, but he thought his brother and sister would need to solve their own differences this time.

But he *was* surprised to hear that Zeus was interested in Bal enough to ask about his pursuits.

"I would be interested in investing in such a device."

Bal blinked. "Investing in my plow? You mean, to manufacture them?"

"Yes. And I'd also like to purchase one. None of the tenant farmers could afford to buy one for themselves, but it seems like they might be able to afford to *lease* one."

"That is a very good idea. And yes, the money they would save on the labor would more than allow them to lease." He hesitated, and then said, "But what use would you have for one? Other than to lease it, of course. I'd been given to understand the prior duke sold most of the land that used to run with the estate itself."

Zeus's mouth flexed into a frown. "He wasn't the only one to sell off parcels. The last four dukes have been winnowing away at the estate for decades. I'm currently negotiating to purchase back several tracts." He gave Bal a querying look. "Perhaps you'd like to take a look at those, too, and give me your opinion. It could make a difference in the price if I could offer some expert evaluation?"

Bal couldn't help the smile that took over his face. "Indeed, that would be my idea of a treat."

Zeus snorted. "Well, to each their own. I must go into London for a few days starting tomorrow, but how about next week?"

"I have no fixed engagements, so whenever you are ready." It was ridiculous how optimistic Bal felt just contemplating looking at farmland. He really *was* bored.

Zeus glanced at the mountains of documents on his desk with a sour look. "Monday, then. I'm afraid I can only spare half a day given all this"—he waved at the stacks of paper.

"What is all that?" Bal asked, getting to his feet and approaching the desk.

"*These*"—Zeus placed his hand on one mound— "are all documents relating to water rights. And these"—he touched a larger mound—"are relating to tenant farm leases. And these—" he scowled at the largest tower—"are household ledgers and accounts for the past two decades."

"You need to go over all that?"

"I hate to speak ill of my predecessor," Zeus said, "but he appeared to view keeping accounts as if it were something he needed to do only when the whim struck him." He clucked his tongue in disapproval. "He kept his books like a squirrel hoards nuts, which is to say haphazardly."

Balthazar laughed.

"I am not jesting. In fact, I am probably doing squirrels a disservice to say that." He sighed. "So many drafts on the account are mysterious. There are odd payments to a workhouse outside Bradford. And small, reoccurring amounts that have no description at all. Some have payees but make no sense. Like this one that goes out quarterly to Harrow—a private school for boys."

"What is so mysterious about that? Isn't that the sort of place aristocrats send their children?"

"Yes, but the duke *had* no children."

Bal nodded. "Ah, that's true. So, who is it for, then?"

"Who knows? There are so many entries like this. Some are deposits," he added, his banker's soul visibly outraged by such carelessness. "Corbin will eventually ferret them all out, but right now his time is consumed scheduling the most critical repairs before the winter comes and no work can be done. As of this moment there are parts of the east wing where you can see sky through the roof."

It was the closest he'd seen his brother to despair. For once, Bal felt some sympathy for the other man. Hastings Park was indeed in a dire state and there was *so much* of it that needed fixing. Bal had spent the last several months angry about what *he* had to do to receive his grandfather's bequest. He somehow doubted that Zeus had really wanted a title that only brought debt with it.

Everyone, he suddenly realized, had to do things they didn't want.

Balthazar gestured to the books. "I am no expert when it comes to ledgers, but I always kept the ones for the farm at Canoga, and they were neat and accurate. Perhaps I could help fill in some of the blank spaces?"

Zeus perked up so much that Bal had to bite his lip to keep from laughing. "Would you?"

Bal made a decision right then; he would try and deal honestly with his brother and—with hope—find some common ground between them. For months now he'd been too angry about his grandfather's bloody bequest to see straight. Zeus hadn't written the damned will—Horace Sinclair had. It wasn't fair to keep blaming him.

"I am accustomed to being busy from before sunup to after sunset, Zeus. Now that harvesting is over, I am pulling my hair out from boredom. You would be doing me a favor to give me something to occupy my time."

"You should have told me you were at loose ends, Bal—may I call you Bal?"

"All my other siblings do," Bal pointed out. He hesitated and then forced himself to say, "I know you've spent most of your life being called *John* and then the five of us came along and arrogantly changed that—with no permission from you. If you would rather, I can ask them all to call you *John*."

"To tell you the truth, I've become used to it."

Bal raised his eyebrows in surprise.

Zeus flushed and looked almost… shy? Whatever the emotion was, it passed quickly and once again his brother was an expressionless enigma. "I don't mind the name and it seems less… outlandish"—Bal heard echoes of Edith in that word—"now that I live with the five of you." His lips twitched, almost as if he were about to smile, but it didn't quite happen. "To be honest, there is hardly anyone who calls me by my Christian name anymore. I find it more difficult to adjust to *Your Grace* than to Zeus."

"I know what you mean—I still look over my shoulder every single time I hear *my lord*, so I can't imagine how it is for you." Those words, he realized now, were very true. And for more than two long months, he'd not even bothered to imagine how all these changes were impacting the other man. "But yes, to get back to that other matter—please, put me to work."

Zeus picked up a ledger from the top of the pile. "Here is the one from this year. Essentially, what I need you to do is fill in blanks wherever you find them. I suspect that may involve talking to either Mrs. Dryden or Bickle, both of whom apparently managed the accounts since the duke died."

More reasons to talk to Mrs. Dryden? It was like Christmas morning; Bal had to struggle to keep from grinning. "Of course," he said, and took the heavy leatherbound book. "Should I work on these here or can I take them with me?"

"Please, take it. In fact, if you're going to work on this then I'll set them all aside and you may access them as you wish." He gestured to the stack of trunks off to one side of his desk. "There are letters, bills, and documents in *those*, jumbled together by year if one is fortunate. The one on top is this year. Tell me where you want it and I'll have servants deliver it. It will take two men to carry it," he said, reading Bal's thoughts—that he could carry a single trunk—correctly.

"If you could have them bring it to the library, I've commandeered the big desk in there."

Zeus nodded and stood, holding out his hand.

Surprised, Bal extended his own hand.

"Thank you," Zeus said simply, giving Bal's hand a firm shake before releasing him.

"You are welcome."

For the first time since he'd met his older brother, he left the other man's presence feeling more optimistic—both about their relationship and about his future.

He was especially optimistic about his mandate to speak to Mrs. Dryden.

Trying not to grin like a fool, he made his way to the small sitting room that his sisters had taken to using in the evenings, mainly to avoid Edith, who'd commandeered the grander sitting room several doors down.

"Ah, just the two people I was looking for," he said, smiling at Io and Eva. "You should go see Zeus in his study, Eva. He has a surprise for you."

Eva's eyes went wide and her lips parted, the expression rather comical. "A good surprise or a bad surprise?"

"A *very* good one," he assured her.

She tossed aside her needlework and fled the room at a very unladylike speed that made both Bal and Io snicker.

Once she'd gone, Io gave him an arch look. "Let me guess: we shall have a masquerade ball, after all?"

"How did you know?"

"Miss Barclay might have mentioned it to me."

"You mean the timid Miss Barclay speaks without being spoken to first?"

"*Tsk*, Bal, you shouldn't mock. That poor woman." She shook her head. "I don't know how she bears it. And she is intelligent, too—far smarter than her obnoxious, small-minded employer."

"Is she? I've not managed to get more than two words out of Miss Barclay."

"I doubt you've tried very hard."

It was true that he'd not really made much of an effort to get to know his soon-to-be-cousin-in-law. If there even was such a thing.

"She's so timid that she makes me feel as if I am too big, too loud, too intimidating, just too… *much*," Bal confessed.

"You are all those things, *mon frère*."

"Ha. I'm not nearly as intimidating as you."

His twin looked pleased. "Thank you. But I am serious about her, Bal. If you'd been pecked as often and hard as poor Susan has been then you'd know why she is the way she is. Do you recall Dotty?"

Bal frowned. "Er, you mean Eva's pet chicken?"

"Yes. Remember how she was always hiding? And if she ever *did* need to go somewhere she'd dash as if her tailfeathers were on fire."

Bal laughed. "Lovely imagery, Yoyo. Now whenever I look at Miss Barclay I'll see poor hen-pecked Dotty."

"I don't think she is naturally that reserved and shy. I think it is a result of slaving for Edith that has repressed her so severely. Once you get to know her, you'll find out that she is clever and funny. She is worth knowing," Io insisted.

Coming from his picky sister that was high praise, indeed.

"She should find a different job if it is making her so miserable."

"I've tried to broach finding her another position—one with a less exacting employer—but she is loyal to the point of foolishness."

"You can't live her life for her, Io." Bal changed the subject to one that was of more interest—at least to him. "So, about this ball… Do you want to talk to Mrs. Dryden—er, and Bickle—about the party, or shall I?"

Io's eyes narrowed and then her lips stretched into a slow, evil smile. "Well, well, well. And here I thought it was that delightfully brazen publican, Mrs. Fletcher, whom you were chasing."

Bal couldn't believe his face heated under his sister's probing gaze. "I'm not chasing anyone," he lied.

"You are smitten by our brother's housekeeper."

Balthazar sighed.

"I hope you're not thinking to debauch the servants. Zeus would have you staked naked over an anthill if you venture in that direction."

"Thank you so much for the mental picture, Yoyo. And no, I'm not planning to debauch anyone."

Liar, liar, liar.

Io waved an admonishing finger at him. "What was acceptable at home is considered debauchery here."

"Do tell, *Edith*."

She pulled a face and turned back to the piece of needlework in her hands. "That's hitting below the belt, Balthazar. Even so, I shall let you tell Mrs. Dryden the exciting news. Once the two of you have hammered out the plan, tell me what I must do—I will serve as your foot soldier."

He wanted to hug his twin—but to do so would make her even more suspicious than she was already. "I'll go speak to her right now."

"You should ring for her, Bal. That is the accepted mode of summoning a servant."

"Listen to you! To the manor born."

"It embarrasses and ruffles them when you don't conform to protocol," Io said, unbothered by his teasing.

"A little ruffling never hurt anyone's feathers, my dear sister."

"I'll remind you of that the next time I ruffle *yours*."

Before he could reach the door, it opened and Edith entered, Miss Barclay in her shadow.

"Hello Edith, Miss Barclay," Bal said, realizing as he said it that he'd never called the smaller woman by her Christian name, for some reason.

Edith's elegant nostrils pinched slightly, as if she smelled something foul. "Ah, good, you are both here. I need to speak with you."

He bit back a groan but forced a smile. After all, if Bal was going to encourage Io to be more conciliating to the woman then he should put in the effort. "Of course, Edith, come in. Have a seat and—"

"I don't need to sit for what I want to say."

Bal heard a snort of ill-suppressed laughter behind him and wanted to box his sister's ears when Edith's eyes narrowed and her expression became even frostier.

"You have both played on John's sense of guilt and convinced him to host this appallingly gauche function for your sister."

"Guilt?" Io asked, coming to stand beside Bal. "Guilt about what?"

"That is not my affair, but something you may discuss with your brother."

"Then why did you bring it up?" Io retorted.

Bal sighed as Edith began to swell up like a poisonous toad and Io looked ready to do some swelling herself. "What did you come to say, Edith?" he asked, hoping to get this over with.

"I will have no part in arranging the"—her lips twisted—"frolicking, but I insist on being in charge of the dinner before the ball."

"Why?" Io demanded.

"Fine," Bal said at exactly the same time.

Edith ignored Bal as if he'd not even spoken, turning her spiteful gaze on Io. "*Why*? Because I don't wish to shame your brother or myself, that is why."

Io opened her mouth.

"We would appreciate your help, Edith. Thank you so much for offering," Bal said, striding toward the door and jerking it open, ignoring his sister's scorching glare.

Miss Barclay took the hint quickly enough and darted into the hallway, but Edith lingered to deliver a parting shot. "I do hope you have no intention of inviting your teacher friend, or the village hat maker."

Io's smile was frigid. "As a matter of fact, I'm inviting both. I am also inviting Miss Dolan… the village *dress* maker."

"There will not be places set for them at *my* dinner table, so don't embarrass yourself by inviting them to *that*."

"I'm sure they'll weather the disappointment of not breaking bread with you."

Edith opened her mouth—no doubt to deliver something suitably scathing—when Zeus's voice came from out in the corridor. "Ah, there you are, my dear. Did you finish those two letters you wanted me to send? Corbin is taking everything to the post office first thing in the morning." Zeus stood in the doorway, regarding his fiancé and sister with a suspiciously bland expression.

Edith turned to Miss Barclay, who was obviously trying to stay close at hand without standing *too* close to Zeus, which would aggravate her cousin. "I thought I told you to bring Masterson those letters earlier, Susan?"

"Oh, I didn't—"

"Save me your excuses, please." Edith heaved a sigh of profound exasperation. "We needn't stand here in the hallway discussing it. Come along, I shall do it myself."

The two women moved out of sight, the sound of Edith's chiding fading as they disappeared down the hallway.

Zeus turned to Io, his expression as unreadable as ever, and said, "Could I have a moment of your time in my study?"

"Right now?"

"Whenever is convenient for you."

Bal willed his twin to be gracious. Zeus might appear indefatigable, but the dark circles under his eyes said otherwise.

As if she'd heard him, she nodded and said, "Very well. I'll come with you now."

The door closed behind them and Bal let out a sigh. If his brother hadn't come along Bal and Miss Barclay might have needed to physically separate the two women.

Instead of relations getting better between his siblings and Edith, things were just getting worse. Ares and Apollo had both stopped coming to meals. He couldn't blame them, right from the very first Edith had sensed the spirit of rebellion that thrived in his twin brothers and had viewed them with a suspicious wariness usually reserved for rabid animals.

Something needed to happen to put a stop to the escalation in hostilities, but Bal had no clue what he could do.

He stared at the floor blankly at the floor for a moment and then shook himself, taking a moment to remember why he was in the small parlor and what he'd been doing. Ah, yes…Mrs. Dryden.

Bal pushed away worries about Io and Edith and smiled in anticipation as strode toward the door.

At long last he had a reason to spend time with Mrs. Dryden.

And he was not going to waste a second of it.

Chapter 9

Balthazar had not been to the servant part of Hastings before. He'd had no need to seek out maids or footmen because whichever way he turned, he seemed to trip over one.

His brother had engaged in a veritable orgy of hiring almost from the moment they'd stepped foot on English soil. Most of that, he surmised, was due to Edith and her expectations.

During his brief time in New York City Bal and his siblings had eaten only once at Edith's aunt and uncle's house. He'd thought Zeus's mansion lavish, but his brother was restrained compared to Edith's family. There had been a servant behind every chair at dinner and so many courses with the meal that even Ares—who was infamous for his insatiable appetite—had looked bilious after eating so much rich food.

That glimpse into her life had gone a long way to telling him just what Edith's expectations were.

No doubt Hastings Park—ancient, rambling, and decidedly shabby—was driving her batty. He'd heard her ask his brother about knocking down the east wing rather than repairing it. At the time the ancient butler had been in the room and Bal had worried that poor old Bickle might faint dead away when he heard her say that.

Fortunately, Zeus appeared immune to Edith's more idiotic ideas.

Bal took the servant stairs which he knew led from the second-floor family wing down to the kitchen.

If ever there was a stark distinction between the wealthy and working class it was the transformation that took place when Bal stepped into that stairwell.

Like his brother's house in New York City, the servants lived far away from the family wing. But Zeus had constructed a clean, pleasant, and airy structure for his employees. Hastings was ancient and it seemed the oldest, grimmest part of it was where the bulk of the labor occurred.

The narrow hallway that led to the kitchen was gloomy to the point of darkness, the air heavy with the odor of food, ancient damp, and lots of bodies crammed in tightly.

He heard the loud murmur of voices before he opened the door and strode into the room. And then stopped in his tracks as dozens of eyes turned his way.

Bal blinked and took a step back. "Ah, I apologize. I didn't realize you were eating dinner," he said when every servant who was seated at a long table suddenly shot to their feet. "Please, sit down and finish your meal," he said, mortified at having disrupted so many people in the middle of their feed.

Nobody sat and Mrs. Dryden was already in motion toward him. "May I help you, my lord?"

"I'm sorry to interrupt," he repeated, eager to leave so the others would sit. "If you would come to the library when you are finished, I would like to speak to you. Do not hurry—come at your leisure," he added, feeling stupid even as he said it. She was a servant and his family employed her; she would not feel entitled to do anything at her leisure.

"I shall be up in a quarter of an hour, if that is suitable?"

"Very good, thank you."

Bal didn't even see the corridors as he passed back through them, his mind on the scene he'd just left.

The kitchen had been uncomfortably warm and almost dungeon-like with its low ceiling, but it had been clean and well-lit in comparison to the corridor. Mrs. Dryden had been sitting at the foot of the table, Bickle at the head. Before he'd entered the room it had sounded like the din of voices back home at Canoga. Indeed, seeing everyone seated at that table gave him a faint yearning for the family-style meals at the commune, which had always been one of the best parts of the day.

Now his family sat at a table big enough to seat thirty with Zeus and Edith at the head and foot. The conversation was rigidly controlled by Edith, while Zeus more often than not simply nodded at what she said, his thoughts obviously elsewhere, and Miss Barclay was up and down like a marionette fetching things that her mistress needed *at that moment*. Of late, with only Bal, Io, and Eva joining them at dinner, it had been especially grim and cheerless. He couldn't blame Ares and Apollo and understood why they'd abandoned the meals—so neither of them would lose their patience and say what they really wanted to say to Edith.

If that ever happened—and Bal feared it would—Zeus would have to make a difficult choice.

When Bal entered the library he was pleased to see it was unoccupied and slumped into the chair behind his desk, experiencing a sharp yet wistful pang at the scene he'd left behind him downstairs, which had reminded him of his old life. While at times it had been difficult to live with almost *no* privacy, he'd enjoyed growing up in such a tightly knit community.

Even though his brothers and sisters were in England with him, things just weren't the same between them since they'd left home.

It was Balthazar who'd erected a wall between his siblings and himself the moment he'd made the decision to keep his inheritance and the terms of their grandfather's will a secret from the others.

Part of the reason for his secrecy had been shame. Horace Sinclair had been set in his conservative ways and only his oldest grand*son* had mattered. Bal could not believe the old man hadn't even considered his other grandchildren. To give one grandchild millions, and four others nothing was shocking and callous. Bal felt ashamed to be the recipient of so much bounty when the others didn't receive so much as a penny.

And so he'd kept his intention to marry a secret. And now, for the first time in his life, there was a gulf between Balthazar and his siblings. It was especially difficult not to confide the truth to his twin. He and Io had been like one person for the first ten or so years of their lives. Even after they grew older and had interests of their own, they'd still been close.

She would be incensed if she knew what Bal was planning.

Balthazar knew that because he would be just as furious if Io or one of the others had to marry for money. Not only was marriage something they'd all been raised to view with extreme skepticism—especially his sisters, who would lose so many of their basic human rights to a husband under the law—but the thought of marrying to please a dead man, and one who'd viewed his beliefs and way of life with revulsion, made Bal's blood boil.

He sighed and let his head fall against the back of his chair and closed his eyes.

Although Zeus had never said anything more about Balthazar's phantom bride other than she had to be *respectable* to satisfy the terms of the will, it bloody terrified him to think that his brother had a woman like

Edith in mind for him. Not that Bal had ever met anyone—male or female—quite as obnoxious as Zeus's fiancé.

How could Zeus bear to face a future with such a cold, rigid, and unpleasant woman?

A reluctant chuckle escaped Bal as he recalled the first time they'd all met Edith.

Oh, he could laugh *now*, because the last few months had dulled his sensibilities to her caustic personality, but at the time, every single one of them had been livid at her behavior.

The scene was still remarkably vivid in his mind's eye. Edith had lined them up, as if they were soldiers to be inspected, and she their new commander. Her admittedly lovely face had worn a faintly contemptuous sneer as she'd surveyed their country clothing and Io and Eva's short skirts and bloomers.

"Well then," she'd said once they'd all been introduced and allowed to sit. "I don't wish to rush everyone—"

"*And yet here she goes,*" Io muttered so softly only Bal could hear her.

"—but we have only two weeks until we depart for England and—"

"You are accompanying us?" Ares asked.

Their brother's fiancé frowned, clearly not accustomed to interruptions.

Zeus stepped into the awkward silence. "Edith has been gracious enough to consent to offer her assistance. As the future mistress of Hastings Park, it seems only sensible that she and Miss Barclay"—he inclined his head slightly toward the tiny, colorless creature scurrying back and forth between Edith and the rest of them, delivering cups of tea and cookies— "will travel with us to England."

Edith gave Zeus an approving look—as if he were a dog that had just performed a trick—and then turned and barked at her cousin, "Fetch my list, Susan."

Bal had cringed at her sharp tone—and would do so often over the coming weeks—appalled when Miss Barclay had hurried to obey and hand her the notepad and silver pencil that had been on the end table, easily within reach if Edith had just extended her hand to pick it up.

Edith had received the items without so much as a glance at the other woman, her gaze flickering over Bal and his siblings, as if she couldn't bear to look at any one of them for too long.

"I can't help wondering if that is really… proper, Miss Barrymore," Io had said, making Bal want to groan.

"Is what really proper?" the other woman asked sharply.

"You are an unmarried maiden. Should you be cohabitating with our brother, your husband-to-be? Or will you be living elsewhere?" The uplift in her tone on the last part made it clear what *her* preference would be.

Once again, Zeus stepped in. "Edith's reputation is above reproach. And she will have chaperonage in the form of Miss Barclay. While the circumstances are unusual, we have our reasons—socially acceptable and yes, *proper*—for her joining me." He gave Io a stern look to punctuate his words.

Edith nodded, her expression prim. "Thank you, John." She gestured toward her black gown. "I daresay you've noticed that I am in mourning."

Bal hadn't noticed and doubted his siblings had, either, but—thankfully—they all remained silent.

"My dearest Mama recently left this world so I am officially in mourning for another ten months. Of course I shall *always* mourn her in my heart," she added, her pale cheeks pinkening slightly.

One of the twins snorted softly.

Edith had narrowed her eyes at the pair and Zeus had frowned, both of them obviously scenting trouble.

"The wedding will be in England, then?" Eva asked, breaking the tension.

Edith's frown had lightened slightly at Eva's obvious enthusiasm. "Yes, we shall marry at St. George's."

"Ah, lovely." His sister had worn a dreamy expression as she'd sipped her tea and Bal suspected that she was visualizing a grand wedding like something from a romance novel.

"It *will* be lovely," Edith said firmly, giving Eva a regal nod. Her sharp blue eyes had been expectant as they'd wandered over Bal and his other siblings—as if she were waiting for something from them, perhaps congratulations.

When they remained silent, she treated them to yet another disapproving frown and then said, "There are many things that must be attended to before we depart. Obviously the first thing is to acquire appropriate clothing for your sisters before—"

"Appropriate?" Io interrupted.

If there was one word his elder sister loathed more than *proper* it would be *appropriate.*

"Yes, dear. Your garments—as quaint as they are—will hardly do for New York and London. And your *hair*... Well, I'm not sure if anything can be done about that right now."

"Is that so?" Danger had glinted in Io's light brown eyes.

Bal had cleared his throat to break the cobra-mongoose staring match that had developed between the two women. "We all understand that our more relaxed country clothing will not do for city entertainments," he'd interjected before his sister began to verbally carve up Edith as efficiently as she could physically butcher a deer or rabbit.

"We have always chosen our own clothing," Bal continued, forcing himself to smile politely. "But I'm sure we would appreciate any suggestions you might have to offer."

Edith had turned her condescending smile on Balthazar. "As the eldest of your siblings I daresay you are accustomed to being in charge of your family, er, Balthazar" her lips twisted slightly, as if his name was unpleasantly sour— "but you may shift those burdens onto John's capable shoulders now. He is the head of your family and will manage any important matters for you and your younger siblings."

"Says whom?"

Miss Barrymore turned at the sound of Ares's abrupt question.

"I'm sorry, but I'm afraid I don't know which one you are."

"Ares." He flashed her a smile that exhibited plenty of straight white teeth. "The god of war."

Her lips pursed and she glanced down at her notebook, making a check mark before something on the page before looking up again. "You have just raised another important issue: your names."

"What about our names?" Apollo asked in his deceptively soft voice.

"They are too unusual—too... heathenistic to be appropriate for the brothers and sisters of a duke. As you've probably noticed, John has wisely chosen to use his middle name. Perhaps the five of you"—she broke off suddenly and leaned toward the twins. "Is there something wrong with your eyes?"

"Heterochromia." Apollo enunciated each syllable, turning Edith's condescending tone right back at her.

"It means two different colors of irises in the same person," Ares explained with equal condescension.

"It is quite rare," Apollo said.

"Estimated to occur in less than one percent of the population," Ares finished.

Edith's head moved back and forth, like a woman watching a tennis match.

"We are proud of our names," Eva interjected before Apollo and Ares could continue *twinning* Edith into submission. "Although it is kind of you to be concerned about the impact they may have on our social success in London," she added sweetly.

"My sister is correct," Io said, cutting first Zeus and then Edith a defiant look. "We shall not be adopting new names to suit anyone… Edith." Io pronounced the woman's name in the same tone she might use to talk about cat hairballs or garden slugs.

Edith had looked from Hale to Hale, the furrows on her forehead deep enough to plant corn in. "I'm sure you are *quite* attached to your names, but they are rather—"

"Quaint?" Io guessed.

"Your names are fine." Zeus, yet again, had stepped in to divert matters. And he'd done so again and again in the weeks afterward. But the skirmishes between Io and Edith had only become colder and more frequent as time passed.

Bal would have liked to purchase a house where they could have lived away from the source of the conflict, but Zeus had granted them allowances as part of the agreement to lure them to come to England with him and learn about their heritage, with the understanding they would live at the family estate. Bal suspected their allowances would disappear if the five of them moved out of Hastings Park and away from their older brother's supervision.

No, the only way Bal could take his siblings away from Edith's influence was to marry and he should do so sooner rather than later.

Instead of fantasizing about his brother's housekeeper he should be focusing on finding a *respectable* bride before Zeus and Edith married and all of them had to truly live under her dominion.

Seeing Mrs. Dryden in her milieu in the kitchen had brought their differences home to Balthazar in a way that Zeus's chiding a few weeks earlier—when he'd warned Bal about debauching the neighbors—had done.

Victoria Dryden—for all that she was the daughter of a baronet—was still a servant in Zeus's house and Balthazar was now of the ruling class. No matter how intrigued he was by her, he should leave her alone.

That is what he told himself.

Whether he would listen to his own advice was yet to be determined.

Chapter 10

Once Lord Balthazar had interrupted dinner Tori had to force herself to resume her seat and finish her meal under the curious eyes of her staff, as if there was nothing untoward in one of the family paying a visit to their private underworld.

Dinner in the servant hall was later than in most houses. However, they had—even during the old duke's most penurious years—always eaten well, so there had been very few complaints as to the delayed hour.

Tori thought it only common sense to feed one's servants decently. When a master took care of his employees' bellies, everything else took care of itself. The same went for providing one's workers with somewhere pleasant to eat together. While the kitchens at Hastings were old-fashioned, they were at least spacious and a person didn't feel as if they were eating in a cave. She knew of households where there *was* no servant hall, but only a rickety table tucked away in a corner where workers had to take turns gulping down shoddy, cheap provisions.

Tori wanted to hurry to the library, but she forced herself to wait ten minutes before leaving. And if she stopped along the way and checked her appearance in a cracked old looking glass in one of the guest chambers… Well, there was nobody but her to know about it.

"Come in," Lord Balthazar called out when she knocked on the ancient wooden door to the library.

Torie took a breath and steeled herself to speak to the man who'd been appearing almost nightly in her dreams, always hot and sweaty and without a shirt.

With that vision lodged in her mind's eye Tori's heart was already thumping when she walked into the room. It beat even more erratically when saw him again—even though she'd only spoken to him a quarter of an hour earlier—sweaty palms and an oddly dry mouth joining the list of symptoms.

"You wished to see me, my lord?"

He'd stood up when she entered and gestured to the chairs in front of the fire, which burned all year long to keep the damp from ruining the fortune in books the room held. The only area in which the last duke had never stinted was the library. "Let's sit where it is a bit warmer, Mrs. Dryden."

Tori did as he bade her, wondering what in the world he was up to now.

"Thank you for coming," he said, gracefully lowering his imposing body into the chair across from her, which creaked dangerously beneath his weight. He gave her a look of mock concern. "Do you think it will hold?"

Tori couldn't help smiling and the tension she'd been feeling ever since he'd walked into the kitchen earlier dissipated slightly. "I think I should have some larger chairs brought in for you, my lord."

"We American Hales *are* rather beastly, aren't we?"

"I wouldn't say *beastly*, but you are certainly built on a grander scale than the previous duke."

"And yet he looms so large in that full length portrait that hangs in the gallery."

She smiled again. "A matter of perspective, I assure you. He was not much taller than I am."

"I would indeed appreciate some larger chairs in here and also the sitting room off my bedchamber, if there are enough to spare. I daresay Zeus and my brothers would also like sturdier furniture."

"There is more excess furniture than you can imagine stowed away in various parts of the house, although most of it would be considered rather unfashionable by today's standards."

His sea green eyes glinted with humor. "I'll take comfort over fashion any day of the week, Mrs. Dryden." A long, strangely charged silence inserted itself and it was all she could do to keep from squirming beneath his penetrating gaze. "But it wasn't chairs I wanted to talk to you about. My brother has approved the masquerade ball for my youngest sister."

Tori was glad the duke had agreed to the party, even if it probably meant more uncomfortable exchanges for her with his fiancé. Personally, she found the youngest Hale sibling both charming and unspoiled. Even with her rather odd ways—such as her fascination with street cant—Torie thought she was so fresh and lovely that she would take the *ton* by storm when the family removed to London.

"Yoyo—I mean Io—and I will serve as your foot soldiers in the planning, but I'm afraid you must command us, Mrs. Dryden."

"Er, of course, my lord." Tori lowered her eyes, suddenly finding it difficult to meet his open and direct gaze. Instead, she reached for the small notebook that hung from her chatelaine and unlatched the silver cover.

"What a cunning device that is."

She glanced up as she turned to a blank page and took out her pencil. "The chatelaine?"

"Yes. I've noticed them before—especially in New York City—but I've never seen one up close. May I look at what you have on all those chains? I must admit I've been curious."

"Oh, of course." She lifted the chains and held the items aloft.

He leaned toward her, his dark head bowed almost over her lap. Tori could smell him—hints of starch, soap, and clean, slightly salty skin. He wore no cologne. She knew that because there had been a bit of a discussion below stairs among the three new valets, all of whom seemed to fight an uphill battle with their young masters when it came to anything that smacked of dandyism.

All four brothers dressed in tasteful, expensively tailored clothing but none of them wore anything *too* fashionable or extravagant. Their lack of interest in subjects like fashion or hair styles or jewelry struck Tori as attractively masculine.

Teddy had always fussed with his clothing and hair more than Tori ever had. At the time she'd found it amusing but now it seemed shallow. Although why she should hold men to such a standard when she didn't judge women so harshly, she did not know.

"Scissors, I recognize," he said, his long, tapered fingers tracing slowly over the silver chased holder before moving to the next chain. He held the rectangular case for a moment, studying it and when he glanced up, they were so close that she could see that the reason his eyes looked so light was because of all the golden shards mixed in among the green. "A magnifying glass?"

Torie nodded, entranced by the kaleidoscope of colors in his irises.

He held her gaze, his lips curving into a smile. "What is it? You are looking at me so intensely."

"It is nothing, my lord," she said, her voice a raspy croak. Tori swallowed when he still didn't turn away, unmistakable heat flaring in his eyes.

And Tori *knew* that is what she had seen, even though it was gone in the span of a heartbeat, the raging inferno replaced by polite curiosity.

She cleared her throat to speak, but her mind was empty of any words.

He lowered his gaze to the chatelaine and she felt as if she'd suddenly been released from a fierce, invisible force.

What a fool she was to get so giddy from a mere glance! He was a practiced rake and she was behaving like a virgin schoolgirl facing her first flirtation.

"A thimble," he murmured, and then lifted a shiny metal tube next, glancing up at her with a look so mild and guileless that she began to question her own judgment. "What is this?"

"Some needles and a bit of thread."

He moved on to the tiny pen knife, and then, lastly, unscrewed the cap on the crystal bottle and leaned closer to sniff it.

Tori was so flustered by his nearness that it took her a moment to understand what he was going to do. "No!" she said, fumbling with the chain to pull it away. "You shouldn't—"

"Ugh!" He flinched back, his face scrunching up as he shook his head back and forth, rubbing his nose hard with the heel of his palm.

She bit her lip, amused by his reaction. "I'm sorry, my lord. It's sal volatile."

"Ah," he said, taking out his handkerchief to dab at his watering eyes. "So that is what it smells like. I have always wondered."

"I should have told you sooner."

He chuckled and tucked his handkerchief back in his pocket. "I probably would have sniffed it anyhow, just to see what it was like. Do you need to use that a great deal?"

"You'd be surprised how often servants—especially females—get light-headed from not eating correctly or overexerting themselves." *Or cinching their corsets ridiculously tight to catch some man's attention*, she thought but didn't say. Especially as she'd found herself doing the exact same thing lately…

Victoria cleared her throat when he merely stared at her with his too sharp gaze. "So, then, should we make a list of what is to be done, my lord?"

Tori didn't know whether she was relieved or disappointed when he sat back in his chair, his eyelids drooping low.

But, instead of saying something provocative, as she'd expected—and, yes, hoped for—he nodded and coolly said, "That sounds like an excellent place to begin, Mrs. Dryden."

They spoke about ball-related business for the rest of their meeting, making Tori believe that she must have imagined his heated look, after all.

Chapter 11

Balthazar stared at the crabbed handwriting before him and rubbed his eyes before slumping back in his chair. He'd only been going over the ledgers for a few days and already he felt overwhelmed.

Zeus hadn't been exaggerating the randomness of their forebearer's bookkeeping.

Bal had started with the payments to the boarding school, as those at least were traceable. A quick visit to the ledgers in his brother's office showed the payments going back almost three years. They'd been current until this quarter. Either the most recent payment hadn't yet been entered or the money hadn't been paid.

When he'd looked for correspondence relating to the payments, he'd come away empty handed. Money was obviously going to Harrow, but he had no documentation showing *why*.

It was indeed a mystery. Bal decided the quickest way to resolve the issue would be a journey down to Harrow, which was just north of London and only a few hours by train.

Balthazar had a meeting in London next week with a man Zeus had contacted about financing his steam plow—he was discovering that it was good to have a powerful banker for a brother—so he would kill two birds with one stone and visit the school then.

He put a marker in the ledger and shut it. That was enough for one day.

Before he could take out the land survey for the property he was thinking of buying the door opened and Apollo hesitated on the threshold. "I hope I'm not interrupting?"

"No, I'd just finished. Come in—did you need something?"

A slight flush spread over his brother's blade-sharp cheekbones and he lifted a slim stack of papers. "I was wondering if you had time to help me with these."

"I've got time, whether I'll be of any help is another matter," he said, smiling. "Sit down and tell me what you have."

"I've been looking into some property."

Bal took the papers his brother handed him and glanced at them. "You're going to set up a stud in England?" he asked, trying to keep the surprise from his voice.

But Apollo was the most sensitive of his siblings, and heard his unspoken question, anyhow. "I know you will be disappointed to hear this, but I am not so enamored of returning to Canoga as you are, Bal."

Was he disappointed? He wasn't sure. Bal shrugged. "I understand more than you think, Pol. Things have changed rapidly back home—I fear there will be nothing left by the time we return to Canoga." *If* they returned.

Apollo looked relieved. "Yes, that is my thought, as well. I know you are aware of some of my past difficulties with the council, but I'm not sure you understand just how often they rejected my requests for more money or improvements to the stables. I'll be honest, Bal, the restrictions they put on the breeding program were more than a little onerous."

Apollo was talking about the five-person ruling council at Canoga, who approved or denied projects like farming, manufacturing, and cattle raising. Even though the commune voted on a great many matters, decisions about how their money would be invested or spent were generally in the council's hands.

"I understand," Bal said, struggling to come up with a polite way to tell his brother that the allowance that Zeus gave them probably wouldn't purchase very much. "But, er—"

"How will I afford this purchase?" Apollo asked, an amused glint in his eyes at Bal's stammering.

Bal nodded, relieved. "Yes."

"Zeus has agreed to co-sign a loan from his bank if I present a workable proposal."

Bal felt an almost crushing wave of relief at his younger brother's words. Apollo, at least, would not be negatively affected if Bal failed to find a *respectable* bride in time. He smiled at his brother. "I'm so pleased to hear that, Pol."

Apollo's darkly tanned cheeks flushed. "I'm glad. I worried you'd think I was, er… "

"Going over to the enemy's side by deciding to take Zeus's help?" Bal guessed with a wry chuckle.

Pol nodded.

"My opinion of our brother has changed a great deal in the past weeks." He gave Pol a sheepish smile. "And he is helping me obtain financing for my steam plow, as well."

"That is excellent news, Bal. I'm pleased you'll pursue that—it is a worthy endeavor." Pol chewed the inside of his cheek, and then said, "He is not so prickly once a person gets to know him a little. What seems like arrogance is merely reserve. I think he is genuinely interested in helping us."

"Yes, I agree." In fact, it stunned Bal that Zeus—for all intents and purposes a stranger—seemed to care about their futures so much.

"I feel a little bit guilty that we gave him so much trouble those first few weeks." Pol hesitated and asked, "Do you think we should call him *John*?"

Bal grinned. "Don't worry about that—I already asked and he is fine with us using his given name. Although he didn't admit it, I think he might actually enjoy being the king of the gods."

Pol laughed and Bal turned to the documents that his brother had just given him. On top were letters from property agents and owners. At the bottom of the stack were maps showing the location of each stud farm.

He looked up. "How can I help?"

Apollo lowered his eyes, his face creasing into an uncomfortable expression. Bal had some idea of what his brother wanted but didn't want to offer and guess wrong. While Apollo was smart—probably the smartest of the five of them—he had always suffered agonies when it came to reading and writing, although his memory was awe-inspiring and his logical processes infallible.

"Do you want me to look over the accounts or contracts?" Bal finally asked.

Apollo gave him a look of relief and nodded. "Yes, if you wouldn't mind."

"I don't mind at all."

"It will require going with me when I inspect the properties," he warned.

"That's fine—I find myself with plenty of time on my hands now that harvest season is over."

Apollo nodded. "I never thought it would be so tedious to have so much leisure time."

"Yes," Bal agreed. "Too much of a good thing, and all that."

"Exactly. Oh, by the way, Ares said something about Zeus hosting a masked ball for Eva's birthday. Is that true?"

"Yes, that is the plan."

"Ugh. A costume thing, is it?"

He laughed at his brother's obvious misery. "Yes. Would you like me to find a costume for you? Or will you manage your own. Zeus and Ares have already asked me to get something together for them, so it will be no problem to find one more."

"I suppose I have to go?"

"Only if you want our youngest sister to keep speaking to you."

Apollo sighed. "While Eva can be a pest at times, I like her a great deal, so I'll go. And if you don't mind getting a costume for me, I'd appreciate it." He hesitated and then narrowed his eyes, "But don't make me look like an idiot. And absolutely no animal costumes where I end up as the back part of the beast."

"Is that all, my lord?"

"Nothing with a *twin* theme, either."

Bal laughed. "Duly noted."

***

Bickle was sorting the mail when Tori tracked him down. "I wanted to let you know that I am going to the state apartments if anyone needs me."

He glanced up, a faint moue of distaste on his thin lips. "I thought His Grace was not planning to inspect the interior damage in that part of the house until the end of the month?"

"I'm not consulting with him about repairs; I'm going to look for old clothing—for costumes."

His distaste vanished and he smiled. "Ah, yes. *The Ball*," he said, making the words sound like an historical event. "I need to give you the inventory I wrote up for the plate and linens."

"Is it bad?" she asked, already guessing the answer.

"As of right now we could host a ball for approximately thirty-six people."

Tori grimaced. "I foresee a great deal of shopping in my future. Oh, that reminds me, could you ensure those chairs we discussed are brought to Lord Balthazar's room and the library? I shall look for others when I'm poking around today as his lordship suggested that we change out the ones in His Grace's study and his younger brothers' rooms, as well."

"Of course, I shall see to that as soon as I've distributed the mail." He gave her black gown a pointed look. "You'd better wrap yourself head to toe in a sheet. It has been a year since we've last done any sort of cleaning in those rooms. Are you sure you don't want to send one of the footmen to fetch the trunks?"

"I'll wear one of these." Tori slipped on one of the full-length aprons that hung on a hook for anyone to use. "I need to sort through the trunks first—there are too many. Once I've decided which ones are worth hauling, I'll get some help to move them."

"Oh, these are for you." Bickle handed her two envelopes. One was from Harrow School and her heart lurched as she recognized the seal. She tore it open immediately. Her relief that nothing was wrong with Jamie was short lived. The quarterly payment for his tuition had not yet arrived.

Victoria chewed her lip as she considered the letter. Usually, Jamie's grandfather sent the money well in advance so she could deposit it in the duke's account—because she didn't have a bank account of her own—and then send one of the duke's checks to Harrow. The money should have come several weeks ago, but it hadn't yet arrived.

That meant she would have to contact Jamie's grandfather and also write to the school and beg their forbearance.

Tori sighed and turned to the other letter, her breath freezing in her chest when she saw the return address and the signature across the corner.

She glanced up and saw that Bickle was staring at the envelope in her hands as well, his expression one of open curiosity.

Torie's response was a bit more visceral. She'd not received a letter from the Earl of Westmoreland in thirteen years. The money he'd sent to her had always come via his solicitor, never from the Earl, himself.

She swallowed down her dread and shoved the envelope into the pocket of her apron and forced a smile for the old man. "I shall likely be busy for a few hours if anyone needs me."

Tori all but ran from the room, eager to get away from Bickle's suddenly too-sharp gaze. Her mind listed like a ship in a storm as she strode unseeingly through the maze of corridors that led to one of the older parts of Hastings.

Instead of the threadbare runners and shabby corridors, she saw the Earl of Westmorland and his lady wife.

And then she saw Teddy the very last time she'd been with him, his expression guilty but still laced with that patina of amusement that his handsome face was never entirely without. An expression that said life was a lark and that Tori should be amused because *he* was amused, even though her own existence, as she'd known it, had changed forever that day.

And lastly, she saw her son's face. Her beloved Jamie.

What could this letter mean? Surely nothing good—not for her and Jamie. And for it to come at the same time as a dunning letter from Harrow?

No, it could mean nothing good.

Torie woke from her frantic daze to realize that she'd entered the addition that had been built in the late sixteenth century especially in preparation for the queen's visit. The corridors were narrower and darker, the wood and stone saturated with age and the passage of forgotten lives.

She lit the sconce outside the Queen's Chambers with a hand that shook badly.

Read the letter. Read it!

No, she couldn't do that right now. She needed time to collect herself.

Why? You will only shatter again once you've read it.

She couldn't know that. Perhaps it was nothing.

Bitter laughter echoed through her head.

Torie surveyed the once grand room which was now tattered, moth eaten, and dusty. The ruins around her seemed appropriate to what was in the pocket of her apron. Was it her ruin in the envelope? Her son's ruin?

Open it. Read it now!

Tori ignored the nagging voice and stared at the ghostly four-poster bed. For some reason it had no Holland cover. What had happened to it? All the chairs, settees, and chaise lounges were still protected by heavy canvas. Not that it really mattered; it was far too late to save the ermine trimmed velvet coverlet, which had been stitched with thread made using genuine gold. It was hideous, but the cost would have been astronomical.

What does any of this matter?

She sighed and went to the adjoining sitting room, which was now crowded with furniture, crates, and old trunks.

Looking for costumes when your life is tumbling down around your ears is a waste.

Tori briefly closed her eyes and whispered, "Go. Away." She sank to her knees in front of a trunk and lifted the lid. The contents brought a smile to her lips even in her current mood. The clothing was not the age of the state apartments, but from the middle seventeen hundreds.

She removed piece after piece, the heavy brocades, velvets, and silks remarkably well-preserved. The vibrant jewel-like colors and fabrics spoke of a more sensual, reckless age. There were red-heeled shoes with gloriously gaudy buckles and an outrageous headdress made to look like a ship in full sail.

At the bottom of the trunk was an ensemble comprised of periwinkle blues, violets, and silver trim with hundreds of tiny crystals glittering on the ornate stomacher. It was grand enough that it had probably been worn by a long-dead Duchess of Hastings.

The garment was made for a small woman, but with some creative tailoring it could be adjusted to fit Lady Evadne, whose near-black hair and blue-violet eyes would look ravishing with such a gown.

Pleased with her finding, Tori set the pieces aside and returned the rest to the trunk. When she was done, she reached for the next trunk but was arrested by the crackle of parchment.

The letter in her pocket.

She was behaving like a coward and hiding from reality.

Tori stood and went to the closest settee, lifting off the heavy cloth cover before sitting on the ancient, motheaten gold brocade.

She took a deep breath and pulled the letter from her pocket, quickly cracking the seal.

It was only a single sheet but the name at the bottom shocked her so badly that the parchment fluttered from her fingers.

It wasn't from Jamie's grandfather.

It was from Teddy.

Tori remained frozen for several moments, her mind locked up like a ship frozen in ice. The first thoughts that broke through were not encouraging.

If Teddy was writing it meant something had happened to the old earl.

Read it! Read it!

She swallowed and picked up the letter with trembling fingers.

Dearest Victoria:

I can hardly believe I am finally able to write to you—and hopefully soon speak to you—after so many years apart. It is difficult to believe that it has been almost a decade and a half since we last saw each other. We were but children back then and only now have I learned that you have raised our *child, and without me ever suspecting that one even existed!*

How like my father to be so arrogant as to keep you from me. When I think I might have gone to my grave without learning about my son I turn cold inside. You are probably wondering how it is that I came to know the truth now.

My elder brother, Augustus, died three years ago and I became my father's heir. Even then, the old curmudgeon did not tell me about you and the boy. To the very end my father resented the idea that I would carry on the family name.

Tori snorted. So, the earl had received the comeuppance he so richly deserved: a feckless, vain, and self-indulgent heir.

She turned back to the letter.

Julia—that was my wife if you don't remember her name—died over a decade ago. It is still a source of irony to me that she came back into my life and destroyed our marriage, and then left again after less than two years. We had no children, which I do not mourn.

Only on my father's death did I learn about you and the payments he sent for James's education. You must know that I could not help but visit him.

"Oh, God," Tori breathed, her fingers crushing the paper. Why hadn't Jamie written to tell her? Why hadn't the headmaster at the school? Surely a mother deserved *that* much?

She smoothed out the letter, swallowed her fear, and continued.

Don't worry, my love, I didn't tell either the school or our son who I was. I visited on the pretext of endowing a new building. I was subtle and engineered time viewing Jamie both at work and at play. He is a magnificent boy and reminds me of myself at that age, especially on the rugby pitch, where he is confident and strong.

Tori laughed, the bitter sound loud in the quiet room. How like Teddy to see only himself in their child and not appreciate Jamie for his own person.

Oh, Victoria! What a son we have made!

When I learned that my father had found you a place in service I was, for the first time, grateful that he was no longer in this world. My anger at such a travesty was and is intense. How could he dare to force the mother of my child to take a menial position!

Never fear, my love, now that I know of your dire condition you may cast off the shackles that have imprisoned you these long years.

Unlike my father, I will not bury myself in the country; I will live in Town.

That brings me to the most joyous part of this letter. You will come to London and I will set you up in an establishment befitting the mother of my son.

Even amid her horror at being discovered by Teddy, Tori couldn't help giving vent to a snort of disbelief, amused by what an arrogant, self-centered twit he was.

It was too bad that she'd not seen him as clearly many years ago. For years now she'd understood that he was the sort of man who was delightful when it came to flirtation but as sturdy as the rotting cloth in this bedchamber when it came to actual life.

Even though she'd already accepted what he really was, reading this letter drove home the truth more painfully than Tori could have imagined. Remembering how much she had loved him made her feel ill. And weak. And it also showed her that she could never, ever trust her judgement where handsome, charming men were concerned.

She turned back to the letter with a sense of dread.

I know what you will be thinking, my love.

"Oh, I sincerely doubt that, Teddy. Or should I call you *my lord*?"

You are hoping we can finally marry.

Tori snorted. "You vain, self-deluding cad."

Unfortunately, I am no longer the footloose spare who is free to please himself. I am Westmoreland. As such, I owe a duty to my family and my name. I'm sure that when you consider the matter you will see that I can hardly marry a woman who bore an illegitimate child and has spent the last fourteen years working as a domestic, no matter what my heart truly wants. I must marry to satisfy the demands of my station.

That does not mean I cannot take care of the mother of my child, something I insist upon doing. It is both an honor and a duty. After all, if my contemporaries ever learned that you were a domestic, I would be roundly reviled. And so you will leave Hastings Park and go to London.

It is not a perfect future that I offer you, Tori, but it is safety and security. And I refuse to have my son growing up in the servant quarters.

I know you will need some time to arrange your departure. I sent the money for this quarter just today. I will have your assent to my offer before I send the money for the next term.

Lest you think this is a carte blanche, let me assure you that my intentions are honorable.

We both know that our son would be crushed if the world learned about his mother—not only the shame surrounding his birth, but also the unfortunate truth about your time in gaol, and why, exactly, you were there.

I would hate for any of that to become known.

I would also hate to think of any son of mine growing to manhood in the servant quarters at Hastings Park. If you were to refuse my offer, I'm afraid I would have to exercise my paternal rights. We both know it would be easy for me to convince any court in the land that Jamie would be far better off with me.

Think of that reminder not as pressure to comply with my request, but as a stimulus for much needed change.

I await your answer with a joyous and hopeful heart.

Your servant,

Teddy

Tori stared at the letter for a long moment before furiously tearing it in half, and then in half again and again and again, until there was nothing left but tiny pieces.

She wasn't stupid. Teddy's message was clear: either she danced to his tune or he would wreck the quiet, dignified life she'd painstakingly built for her son.

He would try and take Jamie away from her, and he would likely succeed. Tori had no money, no power, and no way to fight such a man.

As for moving her into a house where she could *live in dignity*?

Ha! Tori could just imagine how long his intentions would remain *honorable*.

And even if he really did just want to remove her from a job that shamed him, Tori knew that moving into one of his houses would be the end of her respectability. Even if nothing happened between them, the perceived impropriety would be enough to cast her beyond the pale forever.

Teddy had, once again, taken away her choices.

How could this be happening to her?

Raw emotion tore at her: the urge to laugh hysterically; an almost overwhelming desire to smash things; and a gut-churning sorrow that forced choked sobs from her very soul.

Suddenly, and without warning, Tori was seventeen years old again, her world crumbling around her.

***

Balthazar had not been to what the servants called the *Queen's Wing* of the house before today. Hastings Park was sprawling—obscenely large for one family—and so much of it was crumbling that they had all been advised to stay away from the outlying parts of the building until Zeus could bring in experts to inspect the structural integrity.

Although the sections were called *wings*, it was more accurate to call them spurs, or shoots like those that grew willy-nilly from a tree branch. It was clear that each Duke of Hastings had wanted to put his stamp on the building more than they'd cared about architectural beauty.

Bal had come looking for Mrs. Dryden on the pretext of asking her about ordering champagne. Zeus had brought up the matter when the two of them had been talking after dinner last night. Meeting in Zeus's study to discuss the events of the day—and Bal's progress on the contents of the many crates of documents—had become something of a daily ritual since the day his brother had asked Bal for help.

Zeus was still reserved and aloof in many ways, but he made numerous, subtle efforts to bring their new family closer together. Of course, for every advance Zeus made, Edith managed to take two steps backward.

In any event, Bal had promised Zeus that he would take charge of stocking the cellar for the ball. Bickle had told him there wasn't much in the way of wine or champagne in the honeycomb of rooms that made up the cellar. He said the prior duke had instructed Mrs. Dryden to manage the purchasing of wine after His Grace's steward had died, but there hadn't been enough money to buy much.

And so now Balthazar had the perfect excuse to seek her out.

"She will be back in an hour or two, my lord. She's just gone to the Queen's Wing to sort through some trunks of old clothing. Shall I summon a servant to guide you there?"

"I can find my way."

And so here he was, candelabra aloft, walking through narrow hallways with creaking wooden floors and the scent of ancient beeswax and dust tickling his nostrils. All it lacked was a ghost clanking about in heavy chains.

Mrs. Dryden had lit the two sconces outside the room where she must be working. Just as Bal opened his mouth to call out the housekeeper's name so as not to startle her an odd noise arrested him.

Frowning, Bal paused, straining his ears to listen while he stared in concentration at the carpet runner beneath his feet, which was so old you could see narrow wooden planks through the motheaten holes.

It took him only a moment to realize what it was that he heard: someone was crying. A female someone.

Balthazar hesitated. Either it was Mrs. Dryden or another female servant weeping. Should he intrude on such a moment? What if whoever was crying was physically, rather than emotionally, hurt?

Motivated by that concern, Bal approached the open doorway. He couldn't see anyone from the threshold, so he entered the room, following the crying.

He found Mrs. Dryden in the adjoining room on a settee, curled up in a fetal position while sobs wracked her body with so much violence that he was stunned a person could survive such gut-wrenching anguish.

Like many men, Balthazar was brought low by the sight of a weeping woman. Especially one he was attracted to. Caught between the Scylla of the desire to comfort her and the Charybdis of masculine inadequacy, he hesitated, shifting his feet and causing a board beneath one of his boots to squeak.

Mrs. Dryden's head whipped up, her sob freezing in her chest.

They locked eyes for a moment, neither speaking.

And then she scrambled up, as if preparing to stand.

Bal took a step toward her. "No, don't get up."

She took no convincing to sag back onto the faded gold brocade settee.

"Can I fetch something—or someone—for you?" he asked.

She swallowed noisily, pulled a handkerchief from her right sleeve, and quickly dabbed away her tears. "No, nobody." She lowered her gaze to the floor.

Bal dropped to his haunches in front of her and she lifted her eyes to his. There was still such anguish in her reddened gaze that he instinctively took her hand, pleased when she didn't pull away. Her skin was warm, the pads of her fingers rough like any woman who worked.

He didn't want to ask, but he had to. "Did something happen to your son?"

She shook her head.

"Can I help you in any way? What is it, Mrs. Dryden?" He hesitated, and then said, "Tell me what is wrong, Victoria."

Her breathing hitched at the sound of her Christian name and her lips parted. Balthazar waited, holding his breath in anticipation of what she would say.

But instead of speaking, she closed the distance between them.

And then she kissed him.

Chapter 12

A wave of desire crashed over Tori the moment her lips touched Lord Balthazar's. All her anger, fear, and worries about Teddy were swept away like detritus with the outgoing tide.

Raging, howling need surged inside her, battering her senses.

Yes, this is what I want. What I need. Hold me. Protect me.

Love me.

Lord Balthazar hesitated only a moment before cupping her face with both hands, taking control of the kiss the way he had the first time, when she'd become frightened and pulled away, afraid of her passionate response to him.

Tori wasn't pulling away today.

She melted into his arms, sliding her hands into his thick, silky hair as he tilted her face and consumed her, until her entire body vibrated with want for him.

Tori whimpered when he drew back, her lips following his.

"Shhh, I'm not going anywhere, love. Up," he said, and stood, bringing her to her feet along with him, one hand cupping the back of her head while the other slid down her body to her hips. He shoved aside her bustle, his hand pushing beneath to cup her buttock over the layers of material.

She gave a startled gasp but still did not pull away.

"My God you feel delicious," he muttered against her mouth, nipping and kissing, while his big hand palmed first one cheek and then the other, pushing the fleshy globes together and then spreading them apart, the sensation leaving her feeling both exposed and wicked.

Tori pressed against him like a wanton, unable to get close enough to the long, hard length of his body.

He paused his erotic massage and tipped her face until she was forced to meet his gaze. "Yet again I have come upon you in distress and then kissed you—"

"It is gentlemanly of you to try to spare my feelings, but *I* kissed *you* today, my lord."

His lips curved slightly into that lazy, wicked smile that sat so easily on his handsome face. "Still, my eager response is selfish, especially considering you are upset about someth—"

Torie lifted a finger to his lips. "I don't want to talk about that."

His eyelids lowered and he nodded, sliding his second hand to her hip, squeezing and pulling and stroking while his knee pressed between her clenched thighs, the hard bone of his thigh nudging at her sex. "If you don't want to talk, then let me make you come, Victoria."

The crude but erotic words knocked the air from her lungs and her jaw sagged.

He suddenly grinned. "I'm sorry, that was vulgar, wasn't it?"

She nodded and he laughed softly and then squeezed both her cheeks and gently spread them apart. Her face flamed as she imagined what she must look like—how he was blatantly exposing that most private part of her, not that anyone could see, of course, but still…

"I want this bustle off you—I want to touch your skin with my hands—and my mouth. How does one remove such a contraption?"

Tori blinked, once again stunned by the wave of lust his words evoked. "You—you've never been with a woman wearing a bustle?"

"No." He glanced down at her skirt, tilting his head and examining her with a furrowed brow. "Women don't wear such things at Canoga." He frowned, poking at the horsehair pad beneath the material. "It is like a puzzle. Where does it attach? Is it beneath here?" He stroked a hand around her body and rested it over her abdomen, his hand large enough that his fingers brushed over her mound.

Torie's breathing suffered yet another setback. "Higher. Around my w-waist."

"Hmm." He released her, the loss of his touch leaving her body cold. Before she could ask what he was doing, he strode toward the door, shut it, and threw the bolt.

Tori watched him dumbly, her mind still stuck on the shocking manner in which he'd been touching her buttocks only a moment before. He was earthy and masterful—pure sensuality—and the erotic promise in his darkened gaze was unmistakable. Balthazar Hale was as different from Teddy—and his selfish, hurried fumblings—as it was possible for two men to be.

She knew—without saying how or why—that if she gave herself to him today, she would not be able to stop giving.

Yes, you will. Because you will be gone in a month, giving yourself to Teddy, instead...

Her gorge rose at the thought of even sitting in the same room with the faithless, selfish man who'd written that letter.

No. Teddy only wants me to stop working—to not be an embarrassment to him.

Oh, Victoria. Will you never learn?

Tori was terrified that the cold voice of reason was right when it came to Teddy's intentions.

Lord Balthazar came back to her and stopped a foot away, his expression no longer wickedly amused but sternly sensual. And hungry.

"Lift up your skirts."

Tori felt as if she'd left her body, watching like an observer as her shaky hands obeyed his quiet command, pulling up her skirt and petticoat together.

"Higher, up to your thighs," he said when she paused.

When Tori complied, he dropped again to his haunches and she felt his hands, big and warm, close around both ankles.

"Keep it raised, Mrs. Dryden," he ordered, the rough pads of his fingers sliding up her calves, his touch firm yet gentle. "Spread your feet for me, sweetheart."

Tori's feet obeyed, her body responding to his command before her brain could offer up any objections.

Up and up his hands glided, over her knees and then up over her chemise to the belt that held on her bustle. Once he'd unfastened it, he reached behind her and tugged away the heavy horsehair garment, tossing it carelessly to the side, his hands immediately resuming their distracting stroking.

He looked up at her, his pale green eyes darker than she'd ever seen them. How a man on his knees could seem so commanding, Tori did not know.

"I'm going to put my mouth on you. If you'd rather I didn't, you should stop me now."

Tori knew such things were done, of course—she had taken Teddy in her mouth several times during their brief "marriage," but never had he done the same.

Lord Balthazar smiled slightly and cocked his head when she was too tongue-tied to respond. "Please?" he asked.

A startled laugh broke out of her and his smile turned into an answering grin. "Be brave, Victoria. Let me pleasure you," he said, seemingly unaware of what a delightful picture he made gazing up at her, his long-lashed eyelids heavy with desire.

Torie wanted what he was offering—she suddenly wanted it desperately—and she forced her head to nod, even as her face flamed at what she'd just agreed to.

His lips curved in triumph as he slowly slid the hem of her chemise up with one hand and tucked it into Tori's right fist which was clenched around her heavy black skirt and plain white petticoat.

Tori trembled under his intense gaze.

"Shhh," he soothed. "Do you want me to stop?"

"No," she answered immediately.

He nodded, his intensity gentling slightly. "I promise you will enjoy it. Now hold your skirts up higher for me. Yes, good girl, just like that."

The words should have sounded silly coming from a man who was years younger her, but he was clearly decades older when it came to erotic experience.

He traced a finger along the split seam of her drawers. "I feel like I'm dreaming," he said, giving her another of his charmingly unguarded smiles.

Torie knew what he meant. An hour ago, she'd been chiding one of the housemaids for using good linen to mop up a spill. Now she had her skirts pulled up to her waist and Lord Balthazar Hale was kneeling at her feet.

Truly, one never knew what the day might hold.

She felt cool air between her legs as he parted the fabric, exposing the dark blond curls that covered her mound.

And then, to her utter stupefaction, he buried his nose in her sex, his deep groan vibrating up her body.

A startled laugh slipped out of her and she felt his answering chuckle before he sat back on his heels and cut her one of his sensual smirks. "It feels like Christmas morning."

This time her laugh wasn't choked, but genuine. The amusing thing was that she could picture him as a boy, eagerly waiting to tear into his gift.

Tori barely had time to collect herself before he parted her lower lips, met her gaze, and then extended his tongue and licked her.

***

Balthazar knew he was likely shocking Mrs. Dryden with his behavior, but he simply could not stop himself. To see her this way—still garbed in her severe black servant attire—with her pretty pussy bared to him was beyond intoxicating.

Married people truly were odd. How was it that the deceased Mr. Dryden had been able to keep his mouth off his wife's cunt? And *why* would he have wanted to?

Balthazar had barely begun to plumb her delectable body and he already knew he'd be insatiable. Above him, Victoria shivered and swayed as he licked, nibbled, and kissed. Her fingers clenched and jerked on the skirts she held in a death grip and her knees bent, the long muscles of her thighs jumping from the strain of standing under such a sensual assault.

He reluctantly paused his feasting to say, "Sit on the settee, Mrs. Dryden—lie back against the arm. Yes, just like that," he praised when she obeyed him, her actions those of a sleepwalker, her wide eyes on him in a way that told him to go slower, to be gentler.

The other part of him—the primitive, hungry part that had been lying in wait like a restless, lurking predator and had never really believed this moment would arrive—elbowed the gentleman aside.

Freed from his restraints, Bal nudged her thighs wide when she'd laid her body out for him like a banquet.

He lowered his mouth again and surrendered to the beast inside him, exposing her secrets to his greedy eyes and mouth, dragging his tongue from her opening to the tight little bud at the apex of her sex.

He closed his lips around her clitoris and sucked gently, lifting his gaze as he did so and earning the rewarding sight of Mrs. Dryden biting her lower lip, her eyes riveted to his face as she watched him pleasure her.

Balthazar adored having her attention on him and his balls tightened, his cock throbbing with frustrated need. But his body was more well-disciplined than his mind and his leaking, aching prick knew it would not go where it wanted today.

No, not today.

Today was about Mrs. Dryden. He couldn't take away whatever had made her weep so heart wrenchingly, but he could make her forget all about it for a brief time.

***

Torie could not pull her eyes away from the sight of Lord Balthazar, his handsome face framed by her brazenly sprawled thighs, his tongue buried in her sex, the fingers of one big hand probing at the swollen entrance to her body, teasing, prodding, and finally penetrating.

Her eyelids fluttered at the exquisite stretch and a guttural, needy growl tore from her throat as her building need finally fractured into a thousand pieces.

Her shocking lover gave his own growl, an approving one, his wicked lips teasing, his tongue flicking, finger invading and pumping.

Her body rippled as he assaulted her with sensation, not letting up, but working her toward yet another peak, her spine loosening until she undulated like a river beneath his touch.

Tori had barely floated back to earth when a second finger nudged in alongside the first.

She stiffened at the fullness, her muscles clenching against the intrusion.

His hand stilled. "Is two too much, Victoria?"

Tori didn't answer immediately; it *was* uncomfortable, but intensely pleasurable at the same time.

"Have I hurt you?" Lord Balthazar asked, his eyes still heavy with lust but now concerned, too.

Tori stunned herself by raising her hips, the action not an offer, but a demand. "More."

His slow smile was pure sin. "As you wish," he said, his hand resuming its pumping, his breath hot against her core as he lowered his mouth again.

And then he gave her *more*.

Tori was only vaguely aware when her fingers threaded into his thick, silky locks and tightened, her hips rolling while his lips and tongue and fingers took her apart, until she lost track of everything except her own desire.

Chapter 13

Balthazar knew the exact moment his lover came back to herself and realized what had just transpired, how she'd ridden his face and taken her pleasure, her earthy, demanding response to his love-making the most arousing sight he'd ever seen.

He sighed, reluctant to release her, but he could feel her body becoming rigid, and not in an erotic way.

Bal withdrew his fingers and then deliberately licked them clean while her drowsy eyes widened, her flushed skin darkening several more shades at his earthy behavior. He smiled—no doubt a smug expression—gave her lower lips one last, lingering kiss, and then sat up and pulled down her chemise, covering her, even though he did not want to.

He offered his hand and helped her to her feet, turning away to fetch her bustle and then giving her privacy to pull herself together.

Bal adjusted his erection while he waited, amused by the wet stain on the front of his trousers and grateful that the current fashion for men was long coats rather than close-fitting cutaways. While he'd not ejaculated, he'd come damned close.

Smirking at the unintentional pun, Bal wandered into the adjacent room and looked at the trunks scattered about the decaying chamber.

One was open and a gown lay beside it. It looked like something from the portraits he'd seen of the mid-Eighteenth century. He assumed that with the appropriate undergarments the dress would flare out a ridiculous amount and look like something Marie Antoinette would have worn.

Eva would love it.

A slight sound made him turn and he smiled when he saw the proper Mrs. Dryden was back. The only signs that she'd just had multiple orgasms on his tongue were the bright spots of color on her otherwise pale cheeks.

"My sister would adore this dress," he said, gesturing to the garment on the floor.

Her anxious expression fled, replaced by a smile that was immediate and genuine. "Yes, that was my thought, also. This periwinkle blue and silver will suit her blue-violet eyes and almost black hair."

"Did you find one for yourself, too?"

She pressed her lips together in that chiding way he was begging to crave. "Servants do not wear costumes, my lord."

If she thought the chiding look that she shot him would put him in his place, she was sorely mistaken. Instead, it made Bal's stiff cock ache even harder, causing a bigger stain on his poor trousers.

"Being scolded by you is more arousing than being flattered by other women, Mrs. Dryden."

Her lips parted in surprise, but no more scolding words issued from them.

Bal smiled. "Tell me, why don't servants wear costumes?"

"All the staff will be working that night, my lord."

"I want you to wear a costume."

"You are old enough to know one does not always get what one wants," she retorted tartly, and then her skin scalded when she realized to whom she was speaking. "I'm sorry, my lord. That—"

"Don't apologize," he said, closing the distance between them and lowering his lips over hers before she could object. She was stiff in his arms for only a second before softening against him, her mouth opening beneath his. A shudder ran through her when she realized she was tasting herself on his lips. "Do you like the taste of yourself, sweetheart?" he whispered when he could make himself release her, and then chuckled at her scandalized expression and pulled her back for another kiss.

Only when she'd become pliable again did he stop and stare down into her swollen pupils. "You get to say whatever you want to your lover, Victoria. And you also get to use his name. Say it—Balthazar."

She blinked rapidly, the pulse in her throat fluttering.

"Say it, *Victoria.*"

"Balthazar."

He smiled smugly. "I love my name in your accent. Say it again."

She narrowed her eyes. "Balthazar." The word was amusingly grudging.

"Very nice," he teased.

Her lips pursed and he could see she was fighting back a smile.

"You know I am not treating you this way because you are a servant. I would have done the same thing if you were one of Squire Powell's daughters." He pulled a face. "Thank God you are not."

She *tsked.* "That was unkind, my—er, Balthazar."

"It was unkind," he agreed. "But I will never be unkind to you, Victoria." He claimed her mouth with a breath-stealing kiss and then forced himself to release her.

But before she could step back, Bal took her wrist and set her hand on his erection. "Mmm," he groaned, clenching his jaws at the exquisite sensation. "Why does that feel so much better than my own hand? Surely it should not make such a difference with layers of cotton and wool between my cock and your fingers?"

To his utter delight, she squeezed him.

"God, yes. More," he said, the word an echo of her own demand from mere moments earlier.

She gave him a firm pump and then stepped back. He knew what she would say before she said it.

"I cannot be your lover."

"Because you don't want me?" he asked.

"No, that is not—"

"So you *do* want me."

She made another of those adorably exasperated huffing sounds. "What I want makes no difference, *my lord.*"

"I disagree, *Victoria.* It makes all the difference. The only difference, I would say."

"You are a duke's brother and I—"

"—and you are the woman I am attracted to." He stepped closer to her, once again closing the gap between them, but not touching her this time. "I may be younger than you, Victoria, but I am not inexperienced"—her snort of laughter made him smile— "I'm not speaking only sexually," he chided. "I was raised to accept my feelings rather than suppress them. I can tell you, in complete honesty, that I've not been so attracted to a woman before. Not just physically, but in every other way. You fascinate me. I need to know you. You need to *let* me know you."

"To what end?" she demanded, her tone one of frustration. "Even if you learn everything about me—none of which, I feel I should confess, is especially fascinating—then you will still be a duke's brother and I will still be a duke's housekeeper. What can there ever be between us?"

"Why can't we have whatever we want?"

She stared, her lovely, kiss-swollen lips parted in a way that gave him erotic ideas. "Because…"

"Yes?" he prodded. "Because?"

"This just cannot *be*, my lord."

"It can be whatever we want it to be."

"There speaks a very young man," she retorted.

Rather than be insulted, as she no doubt intended, Bal just laughed. "You are right; I *am* young. But that does not mean I'm foolish—I know what I like and what I want, Victoria. I'm utterly entranced by you. Is that really so terrible?" he asked, lightly tracing the curve of her jaw with one finger. "Is it?"

***

Victoria couldn't think straight while Lord Balthazar was so close and touching her. She felt as if she'd been knocked in the head and had lost the power of speech.

He smiled when she stared at him like a gaping ninny. "Should I pretend that I'm not entranced by you? Would you prefer that? Do you like to play games? Shall I chase you? Is that what you like? Vigorous pursuit and flirtatious—"

"*No*! I don't want any of those things," she said. "But I *do* want you to accept the truth of our disparate stations, my lord—*yes*, I will call you that if for no other reason than to inject some reality into our discussion."

His jaw firmed and his light, teasing manner changed in a heartbeat. The man who replaced that gentle, tender lover was staggeringly stern. "Here is some reality: I am not bound by antiquated notions of class, Victoria. In my world it matters not if you are the daughter of the king or the daughter of a farmer. All that matters is what we want from each other."

It was on the tip of her tongue to ask him exactly what that was.

But she could not make herself ask because she was afraid of the answer. The man had lived his entire life in a religious community that did not believe in marriage. She knew all too well what he wanted and it was fleeting, no matter how pleasurable.

Tori spun on her heel and strode across the room to stare blankly at the portrait on the far wall. She could not believe they were even having this discussion. She glared into the eyes of some long dead Hale, refusing to look at the beautiful, passionate Hale who was standing right behind her.

"Victoria." She felt a light touch on her shoulder.

"What is it, sir?"

"Won't you look at me?"

"No."

His laughter was low and velvety. "Why not? Am I so hideous?"

She snorted. "You know you are not."

"Then why?"

"Because looking at you makes me weak."

He stopped trying to turn her. "Then let us have this conversation your way. With you strong." His warm lips and hot breath brushed her ear. "Why won't you give me a chance, Victoria?"

Yes, why won't you? the selfish voice in her head demanded. *You will have to leave this place—leave the life you've known and built for fourteen years—and become Teddy's kept woman. And you know that is what will happen, no matter how much you want to deny it. Even if you don't become his whore, the world will believe that is what you are. No decent man will want you after that.*

The voice might have been selfish, but it wasn't wrong. She would go to Teddy. For no other reason than she could never afford her son's schooling on her own. Her wages were not enough even if she earned three times what she made now. Sending Jamie to Harrow would never have been possible without his grandfather's money.

Her choices were simple.

She could ignore Teddy's command, which would mean she would have to take Jamie out of school. He would be fourteen soon, old enough to find work. If she did this, she would also need to hope that Teddy didn't act on the threat in his letter. If he did, she would go back to gaol and there would be nobody to rescue her like the last time.

Or, she could accept her friend Malcolm Rowel's offer and marry a man she liked but didn't love, using him just so she could afford to pay for her son's schooling.

Lastly, she could accept Teddy's offer and hope he kept his word—that he only wanted to support the mother of his child—and Jamie would not only receive the education he needed, he would also get a chance to know his father. She might disdain her former, fickle, and feckless lover, bur her son deserved an opportunity to spend time with him.

You can do that and still enjoy something for yourself, Victoria. All your adult life—ever since Teddy—you believed that sexual intimacy was only for men. That for women it was painful and shameful, that the rewards of taking a lover were not worth the danger.

Today a whole new world has been laid out before you. What else could this man give you? If you do nothing, you will never know.

You have time—plenty of time to have something that is just for you… Why should Teddy ruin this for you?

Tori wanted to ignore the insidious voice, but she couldn't.

Lord Balthazar is the duke's brother. What if somebody were to find out?

You will get sacked and your reputation will be in tatters—which is going to happen in any case when you move into a house owned by Teddy.

"Victoria?"

Tori startled at Lord Balthazar's voice. She'd momentarily forgotten that she wasn't alone.

He gave her shoulder a gentle squeeze. "It's alright, sweetheart. You don't need to do—"

"One month," Tori said before she was aware that she'd even thought the words.

Balthazar turned her around to face him. "A month for what?" he asked, his brows knitted in confusion.

"I'll be your lover for a month. But at the end of that time, I will move on to another position."

Rather than look pleased, as she'd expected, his confusion was replaced by displeasure. "Why would you do that?"

"I will have to leave here after what happened between us today, my lord. Surely you must understand that?"

He scowled. "You believe I will importune you if you stay?"

"No, I don't think—"

"I would never force myself on you, Victoria. And I would never tell another soul what passed between us today. If you want, I will leave this room and never bother you again."

"I don't think you would importune me—"

"Then why would you talk of leaving Hastings Park?" he asked, his smiling face suddenly hard, his warm gaze so cold and severe that lying to *this* man didn't seem wise.

But she could hardly tell him the truth, could she?

"I—I just thought it best," she said, the excuse sounding lame to her own ears.

"I cannot believe you'd think it best to leave Hastings because of me. It has been your home for much longer. I would be extremely unhappy if I drove you away."

"You haven't—you won't," she added hastily, at least able to be truthful on that point.

"What are you saying?"

Tori looked into his intense green gaze and lied. "No, I won't leave."

"Good," he said, his stern expression softening a little. "Now, what was this month you spoke of? Why must we put a limit on furthering our acquaintance?"

"Er—"

"Imposing a time limit seems… cynical. I'd like to begin on an optimistic footing."

Tori swallowed and repeated, "Optimistic."

"Yes."

Once again, his gaze seemed to hold her captive, and she had the uncomfortable feeling that he would see into her thoughts if she didn't throw some sort of screen between them.

There is no artifice in this man. The thought shot from nowhere, the truth of it both startling and compelling. Whatever else Balthazar Hale was—a womanizing libertine?—he was honest.

Suddenly her plan to snatch a little pleasure and then run seemed not only mad, but deceitful and even cruel. "I think perhaps this is not a good—"

"No, do not take it away now that you've got my hopes soaring. I will accept your offer," he said, lifting a hand to gently stroke her jaw. "A month. To start with," he added, his mouth curling into that sensual, irresistible smile.

Tori's resolve crumbled like a biscuit dipped in hot tea; she was weak and he was so very, very tempting…

"Victoria?"

"Very well, but we would have to be extremely—"

"Careful," he finished for her. "Yes, I know." He cocked one dark eyebrow. "Just because I've never needed to exercise subtlety and discretion when it comes to affairs of the heart does not mean I am not capable of it." He stroked her chin, grazing her lower lip, his eyes darkening as he stared at her mouth for a long moment before lifting his hot gaze to hers. "What if we fall in love, Victoria? Will you insist on a month then?"

She opened her mouth, but nothing came out.

He chuckled. "Never mind. We shall address that if it happens." His eyes flickered across her face, the expression in them both caressing and speculative. "Planning this ball gives us an excellent excuse to be together, does it not?"

Tori considered his question. A housekeeper and a son of the house planning a party together? It was… odd, but then the American Hales were shaking up the neighborhood in a dozen or more ways, already, so nobody was likely to notice.

She swallowed and nodded.

"Good. Let us take full advantage of that opportunity. And once Eva's ball is over a month from now… Well, then we shall see, hmm?"

Victoria looked into the loveliest green eyes she had ever seen and found herself nodding. "A month."

Chapter 14

"I believe I'll go with you, Bal."

Balthazar looked up from the book he'd been studying to stare at his twin. They were sitting in the library after dinner and he'd been scheming about tomorrow. Well, scheming and re-living that glorious hour he'd spent in the state apartments with Victoria. He'd scarcely thought of anything else since yesterday afternoon. The memory, as arousing as it was, also happened to be damned inconvenient and had led to him walking around with an erection for most of last night and today.

"Why do you want to go with me?" he asked rudely.

"Why not?" Io retorted.

Based on the sly glint in his twin's eyes he wasn't the only one scheming. Lord only knew what Io was up to now.

"What?" she asked, her eyes wide.

"When you say *what* like that, I always know you are up to something. So, Yoyo, what are you up to?"

A slow smile spread across her face. "I'll only ride to Northampton on the train with you and Mrs. Dryden. I shan't tag along with you and interfere with whatever *you* have planned."

Bal could not believe that his face heated under his sister's amused gaze. "I think you are mistaken, Io."

She laughed. "Don't worry about me meddling in your plans, my darling brother. I have my own fish to fry."

If Io was *frying fish* no good could come of it, but then Bal was hardly one to talk, was he? He was planning his own fish fry.

He met his sister's too-sharp gaze. "Fine. We are taking the first train up and the last one back, just so you know it will be early." Bal wanted an entire day with the elusive Mrs. Dryden, no servants bothering her, none of his family asking her questions, no Edith barking orders. Nothing but the two of them.

"Fine," she echoed, and then turned back to whatever she was reading.

Bal went back to his examination of the *Bradshaw's* he'd purchased in the village that morning.

The ostensible reason for the trip was to acquire several necessities for the party. Because there hadn't been a ball at Hastings in over a decade, the last duke had sold all the plate, cutlery, and linens as he'd been desperate for money.

Balthazar trusted Victoria to have a more comprehensive idea of what they needed. His part of the trip was to take her to lunch and perhaps do a little sightseeing and maybe even a bit of kissing if the opportunity presented itself.

Unfortunately, there didn't appear to be much in the way of sights to be seen in Northampton. There was a river and—

The door to the library opened and Bal looked up.

Edith stood in the doorway, her gaze flickering from Io to Bal. "Ah, there you are."

Bal had a sinking feeling as she sailed into the room like a frigate, with Miss Barclay the smaller dingy in her wake.

He got to his feet. "You were looking for me?"

"Yes. Mrs. Dryden told me you were going to Northampton tomorrow. I believe I will join you." She made a negligent gesture toward Miss Barclay. "And Susan, too, of course."

The words *over my dead body* pounded at his lips. But Bal clenched his jaws, thought of Zeus—and his many kindnesses—and forced himself to smile and say pleasantly, "How delightful. What do you need in town?"

"I am most displeased with the samples the draper—who Mrs. Dryden recommended—brought to show me. Lady Spencer assured me the warehouses in Northampton were adequate. If I cannot find what I want then I shall be forced to go into the City."

Bal found it annoying the way Edith—who'd been in England no longer than the rest of them—felt comfortable calling London the *City*, as if she were native born. And her accent—always more of a mid-Atlantic twang—sounded more English with every day that passed.

Edith gestured to the train schedule in front of Bal. "What time are you leaving?"

"First thing in the morning," Bal said, desperately hoping such a savagely early departure would put her off.

Instead, she gave him an approving smile. "Excellent. We shall have the entire day. Come, Susan." Her cousin hurried to open the door for Edith but risked a quick look and smile in Io's direction before hurrying after her mistress.

"That should make for a pleasant trip," Io said, once the door closed behind them.

Bal turned and glared at his twin.

Io burst out laughing. "It will be difficult to canoodle with Edith hanging around your neck."

"Ca-*what*?" he demanded, unable to keep from smiling, no matter how annoyed he was.

"Canoodle," she repeated. "One of Eva's newest discoveries. Apparently it means to snuggle and make love."

There wouldn't be any of *that* tomorrow. Not with Edith eyeballing him the whole time.

"Not quite the romantic outing you were hoping for, was it, my poor twin?" Io asked.

No, indeed it was not.

But Bal was not a man to flinch from a challenge. He'd find a way to be alone with Victoria, no matter what Edith did.

***

Balthazar looked from his watch to his sister to Mrs. Dryden—he needed to remember to call her that, even though his tongue wanted to say *Victoria*—and frowned. They'd gathered in the foyer, as planned, but Edith and Miss Barclay were nowhere in sight.

"Shall I send a footman to check on Miss Barrymore, my lord?" Mrs. Dryden asked.

Bal looked at her—never a hardship—and smiled. "Perhaps that might be—"

Feet—booted and male—came down the ancient wooden staircase and Corbin Masterson appeared, his hat on his head, cane in one hand, and wearing a light overcoat.

"Miss Barrymore has suffered a mishap and sprained her ankle," Masterson said in his pleasant but emotionless voice. "I have her list of warehouses and shall bring samples back for her." He stopped and pulled on his gloves—black, to match the rest of his dour ensemble—his opaque gray eyes fixed on Bal.

Bal had the strangest feeling the other man could see the internal celebration in his head that his words had set off. Not that Edith was hurt, of course, but it would be far easier to shed Zeus's secretary than it would have been to escape Edith.

"I hope the injury is not severe," Mrs. Dryden said before either Io or Bal could muster the proper concern.

"No, not severe." Masterson glanced from face to face and Bal could have sworn his thin-lipped mouth flexed into the ghost of a smile when his cold eyes flickered across Io.

One glance at Io's face—which was twisted into something between a sneer and a scoff—told Bal that his twin would have preferred Edith's company over Masterson's.

Five minutes later Zeus's normally spacious ducal coach felt oddly cramped, the hostility vibrating between Io and Mr. Masterson palpable.

"So, you add interior décor to your formidable repertoire of skills, Mr. Masterson," his sister said in a goading tone the moment the carriage commenced to roll down the drive.

"Do I have a *formidable repertoire*?" Masterson asked. "I wasn't aware that I did. I am flattered that you have such a high opinion of me, my lady."

Io snorted at his calm rejoinder.

An uncomfortable silence filled the carriage for the next few minutes and it was Io, surprisingly, who broke it. His sister was not much for chitchat, but she appeared more than a little irritated and distracted today.

"Were you born and raised in these parts, Mrs. Dryden?" she asked.

"No, I'm from Plymouth."

"You'll have to excuse my ignorance, but I'm afraid I'm not yet familiar with all the cities. Where is Plymouth?"

"It is in Devonshire. On thc coast," Masterson answered before Mrs. Dryden could speak. "One of the original counties listed in Doomsday Book."

"Yes, that is correct," Mrs. Dryden said, smiling. "You've been studying our country, I see."

"My brother tests Masterson weekly," Io said to the housekeeper, her mocking gaze sliding to the secretary. "For every question he gets wrong Zeus bends him over the desk and gives him a swat with a ruler."

Mrs. Dryden's jaw dropped and even Bal was shocked by his sister's words.

Masterson, if possible, looked even more saturnine. "Only three swats this past week—much better than the four I received the week before."

Io snorted and turned to look out the window.

"May I see the list of what we are shopping for today, Mrs. Dryden?" Bal asked in a choked voice.

Victoria all but dived for her purse. "Of course, my lord." She wasn't wearing her chatelaine today but took her silver notebook out of the rather large, practical-looking handbag that was sitting in her lap.

"Thank you," he said when she handed him the little notebook.

Bal's frown deepened as he examined the lengthy list written in her neat handwriting. Good Lord! If he allowed it, she would have them spend their entire day shopping.

That wouldn't do.

Not at all.

He looked up at Masterson, who was engaged in a silent staring contest with Io. "You mentioned going to a warehouse for fabric samples?"

The secretary turned to him. "Several."

"Would it be possible for you to order"—he turned to Mrs. Dryden— "Do you have a list of the linens you want?"

Her lips twitched; she knew what he was doing. "It is three pages below the one you are looking at. You may remove the page."

Bal handed the list to Masterson, who scanned it quickly and nodded. "I've purchased such items for His Grace's house in New York. It shouldn't be a problem. It won't take all my time—is there anything else I might help with?"

Bal gave the taciturn man a genuine smile before turning back to the list and looking for the most boring errands. "Cutlery and plate?"

Mrs. Dryden bit her lower lip and he knew it was to keep from smiling. She fished around in her capacious bag and came out with a fork and a saucer.

Beside him, Io laughed and even Masterson cracked what might have been a smile.

Mrs. Dryden blushed slightly. "I thought it best to bring samples along. The styles of both were specially created for your family, but it has been years since either has been replenished so I'm not sure if the original craftsmen are even still in business."

"Did the last duke live like a hermit, then?" Io asked.

"He did not entertain very much after his wife died. Certainly nothing on the scale of what Miss Barrymore has intimated His Grace will do after they are wed."

Bal could just imagine what Edith was planning for when she had the power of all Zeus's money behind her, not to mention the title of duchess. It really didn't bear thinking about.

"If you have a list I can—ah, thank you," Masterson said when Mrs. Dryden handed him another piece of paper, assumedly with the addresses of the shops. He tucked both into his satchel. "Anything else?"

Bal decided they had to keep *something* for them to do, so he said, "Thank you, that will give us plenty of time to see to the other items on the list."

And also plenty of time to engage in his own plans…

***

Tori didn't know whether to be happy or relieved that there was no opportunity for private conversation on the train. As curious as she was about Lord Balthazar, she'd felt altogether too conspicuous beneath Mr. Masterson's cool, appraising gaze.

The steward-cum-secretary was something of an enigma to Tori and the rest of the staff. Other than Miss Barclay, who was at least a member of the family, Masterson was the only servant who'd come from America who dined with the family.

From what Tori could determine, Mr. Corbin Masterson had gone to university with His Grace and the two men were more than just master and servant, but also friends.

In any event, Masterson was reserved with the other servants and seemed to hold himself apart from the duke's family, as well. He was, in other words, an aloof, reserved island unto himself.

Except for his relationship with Lady Io, which appeared cold at best and acrimonious at worst.

Yesterday, after Mr. Masterson had overheard Lady Io's maid—Moira—say that her mistress had given her the day off because she was taking a trip to Northampton, Masterson had, for the first time in Tori's presence, demonstrated some emotion. If Tori had had to guess, she would have said the man looked furious, although the expression had come and gone more quickly than a heartbeat.

Masterson had fixed Moira with his unnerving stare. "In the future you will accompany your mistress on all her outings, is that understood?"

Moira had gaped. "Er, but she didn't want—"

"What she wants is immaterial. If she rejects your company, you will come to me—or His Grace, if you prefer."

"No, sir! I won't want to bother the duke—or you, sir. I'll insist on going. Er, should I go tomorrow?"

"No. I will accompany her to Northampton."

Moira had waited until the grim-faced man had left before bursting into tears.

Tori didn't envy the girl having to tell Lady Io that she would be *forced* to do anything. Of all the Hale siblings—even the duke—Lady Io was the most vocal when it came to sharing her opinions. She wasn't unkind or obnoxious like Miss Barrymore, but she was firm and more than a little intimidating.

Tori did not think Lady Io knew that Mr. Masterson would have come along with or without Miss Barrymore, and that he wasn't just on this journey to fetch linen samples, but had come to keep an eye on *her*.

Tori had no intention of sharing that information and doubted poor Moira would mention it, either. Already the maid—barely eighteen and in awe of her beautiful, forthright mistress—was terrified of angering Lady Io and losing her first important position.

During the train ride Io and Mr. Masterson both read the books they'd brought, but their brooding presence was a deterrent to conversation and Tori and Lord Balthazar ended up spending most of trip looking out the train window and exchanging desultory comments about the weather.

When they reached the station at Northampton, Lady Io and Mr. Masterson immediately began to argue when the secretary insisted on accompanying her.

Lord Balthazar watched his sister and Mr. Masterson bicker with an openly amused look on his face.

"Bal, please inform Mr. Masterson that I do not need a nursemaid," she said to her brother when it was clear the secretary was going to follow her, with or without her permission.

"It's true, Masterson; my sister no longer requires a nursemaid."

Lady Io scowled at her brother's jocular tone.

Mr. Masterson nodded. "Understood, my lord. I shall not attempt to feed her or change her nappy."

Balthazar choked on a laugh and Lady Io glowered at both men.

Undeterred, Masterson continued, "I am only offering to accompany her." He paused and then made a tactical error in Tori's opinion—unless he *wanted* to irk Lady Io—and said, "His Grace would be most displeased with me if I were to allow your sister to gallivant around Northampton unaccompanied."

"*Gallivant*?" Lady Io repeated loudly.

Lord Balthazar winced, took Torie's arm, and then said to the other two, "We shall be back here for the last train at six-thirty." He then leaned down and whispered, "Quick, let's make our getaway before they start pulling each other's hair and we need to break them up."

Tori snorted at the mental image and allowed him to hurry her from the station.

Once they were on the street he hailed a hansom cab, helping her into it before saying to the driver, "The Mormont Hotel, please."

"A hotel, my Lord? That is hardly subtle, is it?" Tori asked when he lowered himself beside her on the seat, their bodies almost touching.

He laughed. "I'm not taking you there to make love with you, Mrs. Dryden—no matter how much you beg me to do so." He cocked an eyebrow. "Actually, I would need to hear your begging before I ruled out the notion entirely."

Tori pursed her lips and shook her head, aware that she was blushing, something she seemed to do constantly in his presence.

"They serve a delightful hybrid of breakfast and luncheon. I thought you might be exhausted and in need of sustenance after listening to my sister and Masterson argue all morning."

Torie stared at him for a moment longer.

"Why do you look so fierce?" he asked. "Not that I don't find it attractive," he added, his ridiculous bedroom eyes warm with humor.

"If anyone sees us entering or leaving the hotel, they will assume the worst."

"One thing I've learned in my life is that I cannot be responsible for what others think." He gave her a significant look, one that reminded Tori of what *she'd* once thought about him, and without him having done anything to earn her judgement.

Oh, what does it matter? Everyone will believe you are another man's whore in less than a month.

Tori was stopped dead by the thought.

"What were you thinking just then, Victoria?" he asked, his voice low and urgent.

"Er, about this brunch."

He clucked his tongue. "Oh, you fibber."

She gave an exasperated huff. "Don't you know it is rude to ask people what they are thinking?"

"I *do* know it," he admitted. "But my curiosity about you far exceeds my good manners." The smile slid from his mouth and his eyes darkened. "If people want to believe we are taking a room, then perhaps we should give them what they want?"

Tori turned away, facing frontwards.

"Coward," he whispered, sliding his hand between their bodies and then over her lap until he found her hand. He laced warm, strong fingers with her rigid cold ones and leaned closer. "Nobody can see what we are doing."

"I feel as if I have a scarlet *A* emblazoned on my chest."

Again, he laughed. "I am not married, neither are you." He frowned. "Unless—"

"I am not married," she assured him. "But adultery is not limited to those who are married. Any time people are not married and engage in"—she bit her lip.

He gave her a look of exaggerated curiosity. "Engage in what, my dear Mrs. Dryden? Book clubs? Knitting circles? Badminton?"

Tori laughed.

"Or did you mean *sexual intercourse*?" he whispered loudly, causing her face to heat even more. How was this man of only five-and-twenty able to disconcert her so?

She forced herself to be serious, even though it was not easy. "I may be a widow, but that does not mean I am a woman of loose morals, my lord. I have limited experience with this sort of thing."

"So do I."

Tori's eyebrows shot up.

"Why do you look so skeptical? This is the first time I've done anything… illicit, for lack of a better word."

"But you've had plenty of experience with—"

"Sex?"

Tori *hated* how her face scalded.

He grinned, clearly enjoying her discomfort. "There is no shame in admitting that you want to talk about *sex*. Are you curious about my *sex*ual history, Victoria?"

"Stop *saying* that word," she hissed.

Thankfully the carriage drew to a halt in front of the hotel before she needed to answer his question.

He handed her down, paid the driver, and then escorted her into the rather grand-looking building. Tori was glad to see that nobody appeared to pay them any mind as they crossed the large foyer toward the restaurant.

"I have reserved a table for two," he said to maître d'. "The name is John Brown."

The man consulted his ledger and nodded. "Right this way, Mr. Brown."

"John Brown?" she whispered as they followed the man through a dining room that was only a quarter full. "Could you have chosen a *less* believable name?"

"I considered John Smith, first."

She snorted.

"You wanted me to be stealthy, you didn't say I had to be inventive, too."

Tori couldn't help it; she laughed and it felt good to let her enjoyment out. After all, how could she not be pleased that a handsome, charming, and wealthy young man had gone to so much effort simply to have a meal with her?

They studied the menu and then ordered food. And by the time the waiter left with the menus Victoria had begun to hope that Lord Balthazar had forgotten the question he'd asked in the hansom.

But then he leaned toward her and said, "You never answered my question. Are you curious about my sexual history, Victoria?"

Chapter 15

Balthazar knew he shouldn't tease her. He and his siblings had grown up in one of the most sexually permissive environments in the Western world while Britain was every bit as starchy and tightly laced as her queen.

And Victoria Dryden, despite her cool veneer, positively seethed with repressed sexuality. At least around Balthazar.

Rather than become flustered as he'd expected, her lips curved into a wry smile. "You must know that everyone in Britain is curious about you, my lord—Balthazar," she corrected when he gave her a chiding look.

"I do know that. A great deal of that curiosity is hostile and condemnatory."

"You don't need to fear either of those things from me."

Not anymore, he might have teased, but did not.

Instead, he said, "I am delighted to hear that." He glanced up and nodded when the waiter appeared with a bottle.

"Champagne?" she said once the waiter had filled their glasses and departed. "Are you trying to scramble my wits … Balthazar?"

"I like your wits exactly the way they are." He lifted his glass. "To us."

They clinked glasses and Victoria sipped, her nose twitching adorably at the bubbles.

She set down her glass and met his gaze directly. "I really do want to know the truth about you—and yes, I mean your, er, romantic history."

Bal chuckled at her clever avoidance of the word *sex*. "So, you want to know if I left a trail of broken hearts and torn hymens in my wake?"

She'd just taken another sip and Bal patted her back lightly while she choked.

She glared at him when she caught her breath. "Next time you are going to say something shocking, please warn me first."

"Oh, was that shocking?"

She shook her head at him.

"I've never had sex with a virgin. Did I engage in orgies?" He chuckled. "No, although those articles made them sound quite… interesting. Did I have lovers? Yes. In fact, those fabrications were written by an ex-lover. But Tirzah was pressured to embroider on the truth."

"Who pressured her?"

"The newspaper that was paying for the story. She left the colony to marry her lover and they needed funds to pursue a business opportunity."

"So, she just *lied* about you?"

"Yes."

She chewed on that for a moment and then said, "I thought your people didn't believe in marriage—that you practiced something called *complex marriage*?"

"That is true. However, there have been fractures in the commune in recent years, with some people arguing that complex marriage might not be tenable at this point in human evolution."

"I'm not sure what that means."

"It means that it's difficult to adhere to one's ideals when one must coexist with the outside world, which has a completely—often diametrically opposed—set of ideals."

Her expression was thoughtful as she sipped her champagne.

"What part of your ex-lover's story was not a lie?" she asked, looking both mortified but determined.

Good, he wanted her to feel free to ask questions. It irked him that Tirzah's foolish story had colored her opinion of him before they'd even met. The only way to move past that was with honesty.

"While it is true that Canogans are more sexually liberated, we do not engage in one continuous orgy. Or any orgies, at all, for that matter." He smiled at the color the word *orgy* caused to bloom in her cheeks.

"But you did choose Mrs—er, is it Miss?"

"Tirzah will do fine."

"You *did* choose Tirzah to be your first lover—even though she is quite a bit older?"

"Yes. When a member of the community turns eighteen, they are encouraged to seek a sexual mentor—somebody more experienced who will teach them about giving and receiving pleasure. Older women are considered excellent lovers for younger men for a variety of reasons. They tend to be more… direct and emphasize the importance of men giving pleasure first, before taking their own releases."

Victoria raised her hands to her now-scalded cheeks. "Goodness."

"Shall I stop?"

"No," she answered immediately, lowering her hands with a sheepish smile. "It is amazing how you manage to make me feel like a girl although I am years older than you."

"I hope that is a good thing—making you feel younger?"

"It is a… thing, that is for certain."

Balthazar laughed.

"Do go on," she encouraged.

***

"Where was I?" Bal said. "Ah yes, sexual mentors. Not everyone chooses to take a lover when they reach eighteen."

"But you did," Tori persisted.

"Yes. I'd been attracted to Tirzah for a while before I approached her."

"You knew her already?"

"Our colony is small and everyone knows everyone else, at least a little. I knew Tirzah quite well; she was the mother of my best friend."

"Oh! That is—er, well, I'm not sure what to say about that," Tori added, more than a little dumbfounded. "Did your friend know about you and his mother?"

"Yes, of course. We do not consider sex shameful and something to hide, Victoria. We believe there are two reasons for intercourse—pleasure and procreation. In our view, women should be able to enjoy orgasms without living in a constantly pregnant state."

Tori just stared.

He gave her an amused, but not unkind, look and went on, "In any case, at Canoga it is the women who make the decision when to have a child and then she approaches the man of her choosing and asks him to be the father. Of course, a man can always decline that honor."

The thought that women chose men to have children with—outside of marriage—and nobody judged them was simply… unthinkable."

She met his patient gaze. "Have you—did, er—"

"Do I have children?" he asked.

She nodded.

"No."

"Did anyone ask?"

He paused and then said, "Yes, I've been asked."

"Why didn't you?"

He shrugged. "It just never felt like the right time."

"Did it bother you that a child conceived that way would be illegitimate?"

"Yes," he said, not hesitating. "It did—and does—bother me. But I respect the right of others to make a different decision."

"And—and nobody is married who lives there?" she asked.

"It is not the norm."

"So, the children, they are all illegitimate?"

"Most of them. I think the founders were more optimistic than they should have been on that point. They believed that society's position on matters like legitimacy and marriage would have changed more rapidly over the past forty years—which is how long the colony has been in existence—and that people would be more permissive by now. They were terribly mistaken and there is a great deal of… unhappiness among people my age when they go out into the world for either education or work and realize the stigma they must carry, and that their legal status matters a great deal to the people they meet. Or, in my friend Marcus's case, to a woman he fell in love with."

"What happened?" Tori hastily added, "You needn't tell me if it is private."

"I don't think Marcus would mind." He snorted. "In fact, I'm sure he's far more concerned with the stories his mother told to the newspapers than he is with such a tame, yet sorrowful, tale. Marc loved a woman enough to leave the colony. He was offered an excellent position at a Boston law firm. Believing everything had fallen into place, he asked her to marry him. The family investigated his family history and refused their permission. Not only did they oppose the match, but she abided by their decision. And if that wasn't bad enough, her father went to the law firm and told them about his background. They discharged him."

"Because he was illegitimate?"

"That was part of it. His association with Canoga—even after he left the commune—was another part. It was not the first time that friends of mine have faced such intolerance. My siblings and I would have had similar issues to confront if our parents hadn't been married when my mother had us."

"Why did they marry when nobody else did?"

"My mother and father married and lived in Boston, where my father taught at a university. My father didn't move us to Canoga until after my mother's death—when Eva was born."

"Oh, I'm so sorry."

He smiled at her. "It was a long time ago, Victoria. I hardly remember her anymore."

"How old were you?"

"Io and I had just turned six."

"And the duke was from your father's first marriage?" Tori was more than a little ashamed by her probing questions, but too curious to stop herself. After all, who knew when she would have such an opportunity again?

"Yes. My father had married eleven years before he married my mother," Lord Balthazar said, evidently unperturbed by her questions. "Zeus was their only child. After his mother died my father left him with his aunt and uncle." His full lips compressed into a frown and he looked disgruntled. "We didn't learn about Zeus until after my father's death."

"I read about that." Tori gave him a sheepish look. "I thought that most of the information in *The London Times* was probably accurate."

He chuckled. "Probably better than the *London Illustrated Newspaper*."

Tori grimaced. "Oh dear, you saw that?"

"That and others." He shrugged, obviously not wishing to talk about his notoriety. "My siblings and I were not very happy that my father kept Zeus's existence a secret."

"Why do you think he did that?"

Balthazar shook his head, his expression one of bewilderment. "I don't know, but it was cruel to deprive us of each other." He snorted. "Although I have to admit I might not have said that even a month ago."

"What do you mean?"

He gave her a wry look. "I'm sure you can imagine that Zeus and the rest of us don't exactly see eye-to-eye on a lot of matters given our very different backgrounds."

"Yes, I suppose that is true. But—things are better now?"

"Oh, yes. I am beginning to see that his bark is worse than his bite. Besides," he said, with a sigh, "not all his reservations about Canoga and our lifestyle are without basis."

Tori wanted to ask what he meant, but she didn't have to.

"Our belief system is simply unworkable within the greater world."

She wasn't quite sure what he meant by that, but he looked so disheartened that she didn't want to pursue the subject. "Do you miss your home?"

"Sometimes."

"Are you going back?"

He drew in a deep breath, enough to expand his chest—already impressive—to imposing proportions. "I have not yet decided," he said after a long moment. "What I do depends on what my siblings do. Although we were raised communally, we are still very close."

"What does that mean—*raised communally*?"

"It means we didn't live with our parents, but with all the other children. Everyone is aware of who their biological parents are, naturally, but children are encouraged to consider the entire community their family and not cling to a traditional family structure."

"Oh." Tori said, stunned—and not in a positive way. She would have hated to give up Jamie when he was a baby. It had been painful enough to let him go away to school when he was eleven.

"You think that is horrible?" Balthazar guessed accurately. He smiled. "It is alright, you don't need to answer; I understand. I have reservations about it, myself." An odd expression flickered across his face but was gone too quickly for Tori to read it. "Regardless of how I was raised I am very close to my siblings—maybe because I spent the first six years of my life outside the commune—and I would not like to return to Canoga if they all remain here."

"And that is a possibility?"

He considered her question for a moment and then frowned. "I suddenly realized that I have been answering all your questions and asking none of my own."

Tori hated the stab of fear she felt at his words. For almost a decade and a half she'd experienced a similar apprehension—although not quite so sharp—whenever anyone asked about her past.

This man doesn't care about illegitimacy; you could tell him the truth. He wouldn't judge you.

It's not for me that I lie; it's for Jamie.

And Tori could not throw away Jamie's security because she was smitten by a handsome young man.

"There is not much to know," she lied. "My husband was in the army and stationed in India. He died in a cholera outbreak not long after Jamie was born."

"How did the two of you meet? Were you childhood sweethearts?"

It was a struggle to keep the bitterness from face and voice. "No. I was a governess and my husband was a guest at the house where I worked." Tori had told that same lie for years. This time, for some reason, it made her feel vaguely ill to say the words "After we married, I quit working. Unfortunately, our situation was not such that I could avoid taking another job after his death."

Balthazar's chiseled features softened with empathy. Tori had believed his wicked smile was the most appealing expression she'd seen on his beautiful face, but kindness was even more attractive.

Lord Balthazar Hale might have the sensual smirk of a rake and the muscular body and rough hands of a day laborer, but he was unexpectedly sensitive and gentle. He was a sympathetic listener and that made Tori want to confide in him, which scared her. He was the sort of man who made one feel safe and protected. But, in her case, that was only an illusion.

"Tell me, what did that man mean—the one who attacked you on the night of the harvest festival?" he asked, proving that she was *not* safe with that single question.

Tori had been expecting him to ask about Gerald Boyd every time she spoke to him, so she was at least prepared with a lie—and a convincing lie because it was also partly true.

"He was repeating a very old, stale accusation that I was the duke's mistress and that Jamie was his illegitimate son." That gossip had haunted Tori for years after she'd come to work at Hastings. It had taken Auntie Max's influence in Symington to put an end to the persistent rumor.

"Why would people believe such a thing?" he asked, his question that of a man who obviously didn't spend his time engaging in tittle-tattle.

"Many people thought His Grace would not have hired such a young housekeeper unless there was some ulterior reason. While that was partly true, it was not because I was his lover." She hesitated, and then decided to tell the truth—at least some of it. "The Duke of Hastings was friends with the Earl of Westmoreland, who'd employed me when I'd been a governess. And the Earl was a boyhood friend of my father's, so giving me the position was a favor to both the Earl and my father."

"Why did your family not take you in—if you don't mind me asking?"

She *did* mind, but it wasn't anything she'd not been asked before, and by people she liked a great deal less than Lord Balthazar. "My cousin inherited the baronetcy and he and his wife did not wish me to live with them."

He looked displeased by that and she was foolishly flattered that he was affronted on her behalf.

"It is good that at least your husband's family have taken an interest in you and Jamie."

For a moment Tori didn't know what he meant, but then she recalled the lie she'd told about her dead husband's family paying the school tuition. She nodded and sipped her champagne, reminding herself to drink slowly; the last thing she could afford to do was indulge too much around Lord Balthazar.

The waiter approached their table. "Would you care for more champagne, Mr. Brown?"

"No, thank you. Just the bill, please."

Tori glanced at the watch she'd pinned to her bodice, as she wasn't wearing her chatelaine. "Goodness," she said. "We have been here for over an hour and a half."

He heaved an exaggerated sigh. "I suppose it is time to shop."

Tori smiled at his obvious reluctance. "I'm afraid so."

He leaned closer. "Or perhaps I might engage a room upstairs and persuade you to come with me and spend the afternoon in a mutually pleasurable fashion."

Tori swallowed as she met his eyes, which darkened even as she watched. She swore she could see what he was promising reflected in the velvet blackness of his pupils: Tori sprawled naked across a bed, her spine arched in ecstasy while Lord Balthazar stared up at her from between her spread, trembling thighs.

She was so transfixed by the vision—so utterly and completely tempted—that she couldn't seem to speak.

Taking her silence for something completely different, he smiled gently and said, "What shop are you taking us to first, my dear Mrs. Dryden?"

***

Strangely, Bal found he didn't hate shopping nearly so much as he had in New York City. He suspected that Victoria's presence had something to do with that.

"My lord?"

He looked up from the book of samples he'd been staring at to see Victoria holding up two bolts of some sort of filmy material. "Which one do you like better?"

Bal frowned. "What is this for, again?"

"For draping and decorating the ballroom."

"So, this is different than the fabric list I gave to Masterson."

She laughed. "Yes. That was for tablecloths and napkins. So, which one?"

He squinted at the gauzy material. "Are they different?"

"One is *blush* and one is *peony*."

Balthazar rolled his eyes. "Of course! What a dunce I am not to know that. Er, how about the *blush*?"

"My thoughts exactly."

"It as if we were the same person," he teased, and then added, "Mrs. Dryden" when he noticed that the shop clerk was in danger of tipping over, she was leaning so far across the counter.

Balthazar somehow suspected that news of this shopping expedition would fly fast and far.

Victoria gave the clerk instructions for how much material she wanted, arranged for its delivery to Hastings, and then turned to her list, quickly making several ticks.

Bal looked at his watch; they had an hour and a half remaining before they needed to be at the station.

When she met his gaze, he gave her a pleading look that was only partly feigned. "Aren't we done yet?" he said, allowing a plaintive whine to seep into his tone and earning a chuckle for it.

"Oh, we've much, much more to do. I've not yet arranged for the flowers. And then there is the orchestra, and—"

"But we are done for *today*?"

"Considering that you passed off most of the list Mr. Burton, yes, that is all for today, my lord."

"Excellent, because I have something I want to show you."

Her brow puckered with concern. "Er—"

Bal laughed and then *tsked*. "What a naughty mind you have, Victoria. I'm not going to show you *that*—at least not today. Trust me, when I show you something truly interesting, we will have hours and hours to enjoy ourselves and won't be on a street in the middle of an English market town."

"I didn't mean *that*," she protested laughingly.

"Shhh, don't compound the offence by lying, my dear," he chided as he escorted her from the shop. "We are going for a walk by the river. I am told there is a delightful park."

"A delightful park in Northampton?" she asked, sounding dubious. "Are you sure you wouldn't rather see the new guildhall? It was only opened a few years ago. It is said to be an excellent example of Gothic Revival."

He smirked at her efforts to steer them somewhere more public than the small wilderness he'd read about. "Although I have a mania for Gothic Revival, I need to stretch my legs. We have plenty of time," he assured her when she started to check her watch.

"Are you happy with our progress today?" he asked as they made their way through the late afternoon crowd of shoppers on St. Giles Street.

"Yes, quite. And you?"

"Very happy. About to be even happier."

She laughed.

"Why do you do that?" he asked.

"Do what?"

"Cover your mouth whenever you laugh—do you feel guilty?"

She frowned. "Do I really cover my mouth when I laugh?"

"Almost every time."

"I didn't realize that. I think it might be an English response."

"The *stiff upper lip* also means no laughing?"

"We are not so free with our emotions as your countrymen."

Bal could have told her that he was suppressing a great many emotions—and urges—just then, but he didn't think that confession would help ease her concerns about being seen walking about town together.

"Ah, it's through here," he said when they approached a brick arch with iron gates that were propped open.

"Who told you about this?" she asked him as he guided her toward the river.

"I read about it in *Bradshaw's*. I was very disappointed that Northampton didn't have a more romantic setting to offer, but this is what I must work with." He held out his arm. "Come, take my arm. There is nobody here to see us."

She hesitated a moment, but then hooked her arm in his elbow.

"Look, there is a bench—not too close to the water, which I understand smells quite foul thanks to several nearby tanneries—let's sit for a while." He led her to the rustic stone bench, which was sheltered by a cluster of shade trees.

Once they were seated, he withdrew a slender package from his coat and handed it to her.

"For me?"

He cocked his head.

"That was a foolish question, wasn't it?" She stared at the package. "What is it?"

"Take it and open it," he ordered with mock severity, nudging her with the gold paper wrapped package.

She took the gift and gave him a very unconvincing scowl. "You shouldn't have bought anything for me."

"Maybe I didn't buy it. Maybe I stole it."

She laughed. "Shame on you! Besides, I know you didn't steal it because it is wrapped."

"Why shouldn't I buy you something?"

"It isn't appropriate."

"My thoughts about you are even less appropriate." He lowered his eyelids. "Besides, there in nothing untoward about buying one's lover a gift, Victoria."

She stared down at her hands, visibly flustered.

Balthazar thought she was adorable. He had enjoyed the afternoon, even though he would have much rather taken her back to that fancy hotel, hired a room for the day, and fucked her until neither one of them could see straight.

But Victoria was as easily spooked as some of the colts his brother Apollo was so adept at taming without breaking their spirit.

Bal wanted Victoria to want him—to cast away her caution and fear and *take* what she wanted.

That was going to take a while, but it *would* happen.

Right now, however, shopping together was probably a wiser first date when it came to a proper lady like Victoria. And the day had been unexpectedly delightful for all that he'd barely been able to touch her.

She pursed her lips and gave him a mock scolding look. "When did you even have time to buy this?"

"When you were haggling with that poor wine merchant."

"I was not *haggling*."

"Yes, you were, and it was something to behold. I think you must have been a rug merchant or perhaps a Dutch trader in a prior life. I was sure that unfortunate gentleman was going to weep when he finally knuckled under to your price."

"Oh, stop. You don't mean that."

"No, of course I don't," he said, nodding his head *yes* while he spoke.

She laughed again, this time with less restraint.

"Open it, Victoria." He slid a hand along the bench behind her shoulders while she gently stroked the velvet ribbon on the small package.

"This is almost too pretty to open," she murmured.

"You can re-wrap it when you are done, and then open it again."

She gave him a look that was a blend of embarrassment, exasperation, and—yes—even a bit of fondness. And then she tugged off the ribbon and peeled back the thick gold paper. Inside was a lovely wooden box and inside that…

She took the small chainmail purse from the velvet-lined box. ""My goodness! It is beautiful, Balthazar. Oh, and there is even a chain attached."

"It is for your chatelaine," he said, even though that was probably evident.

"This is so lovely." She sounded mournful instead of pleased. And she was staring down at the little purse, rather than Balthazar.

"Why won't you look at me, Victoria?"

Slowly, she turned to him. She was so close he could see the fine down on her jaw and the startling blue facets that comprised her irises.

Her delicate throat flexed as she swallowed, and he knew that the gift had made her shy, as if she didn't deserve nice things. Balthazar resolved to spoil her, both with affection and gifts, and drive the haunted look from her eyes.

"Where did you find it?" she asked.

"It was in the window of the jewelers next to the stationer's shop. I knew you should have it as soon as I saw it. I cheated and sent one of the clerks to purchase it for me while you were making the wine merchant cry."

"It is very thoughtful. Thank you."

"It is my pleasure, Victoria."

She swallowed again, her gaze dropping to his mouth. "Are you going to kiss me?"

"Yes. Unless you tell me not to."

She glanced around.

"We are protected from view by the trees. Only somebody floating by on the river would see us. There is nothing but dense scrub on the other side," he whispered as he drew her closer, until he could feel the heat of her body.

Their hats knocked together and Bal laughed. "I'm not a very skilled seducer, am I?"

"I'd say you are extremely skilled," she said wryly.

Bal took off his top hat and dropped it to the ground before tilting his head to fit below the brim of her straw hat.

***

Tori ignored the warning voices in her head and gave in to her desire. *Just for a little while*, she told herself, even while she shifted on the bench to give Balthazar better access.

He held her in a gentle but firm grasp, his skilled, clever hands maddeningly staying on her face and neck rather than doing what Tori wanted and wandering her body the way they had that day in the Queen's Suite.

Some part of her cringed at how needy she was for this man's touch. It was as if fourteen years' worth of desire had built up and shattered the dam inside her into a thousand pieces. Common sense washed away along with self-preservation, leaving only gut-wrenching need in its wake.

"Touch me, Victoria," he whispered in between nips and kisses.

Tori set a hand on his jaw, and he gave an approving growl, so she slid her other hand into his silky hair. When he claimed her mouth again, she opened and met him tongue-to-tongue.

He made a pleased, purring sound and shifted his body so they were even closer, his arm curving around her to hold her tight, his hand resting dangerously close to her breast. Wanton that she was, she shifted so that his fingers grazed the flesh, which was sensitive even through the layers and layers of clothing.

"Mmm," he muttered, his big hand cupping her exactly the way she wanted.

"I didn't *need* your help, Mr. Masterson!"

Tori gasped and she and Balthazar sprang apart at the sound of the angry, familiar voice, which seemed to be coming from behind the small grove of trees that shielded the bench.

"What you *need*, my lady, is a firm hand," a coldly angry voice retorted. It was *so* cold and angry that Tori might not have recognized it if Lady Io had not just said his name.

Tori locked eyes with Balthazar, who just shrugged and held a finger up to his lips.

"I suppose *you* think it should be *your* hand, Mr. Masterson?" Lady Io shot back.

"Seeing as there is nobody else around to impose the discipline you require—"

"*Discipline*?" Lady Io shrieked. "Perhaps it is *you* who needs a firm hand, Mr. Masterson. Have you ever considered that? Perhaps I should turn you over *my* knee and spank your bottom!" Before the—likely stunned—man could respond, Lady Io hurried on, "I suppose you are going to run and tattle to my brother when we get home." Her angry voice got fainter, indicating the pair was probably moving toward the road.

"Run and tattle?" Masterson repeated in a low, menacing tone. He said something else, but the words were too quiet for them to hear.

"I would like to see you try that!" Lady Io shouted, her retort probably audible several streets away.

Tori released the breath she was holding when it was clear they were gone. "Don't you want to go after her?" she asked when Lord Balthazar tucked a loose lock of hair behind her ear and dropped a light kiss on the end of her nose.

He lifted one elegant black eyebrow in surprise. "Go after Yoyo?" He laughed. "And say what, pray? No, I do not think so," he said before she could answer. "My sister would not thank me for pushing my nose into her business. If she wants my help, she will ask for it." He tilted his head and smiled at her. "I suppose that is another way in which I'm not an English gentleman, isn't it?"

"What do you mean?"

"I mean I refuse to rush to Io's aid, as if she were a helpless damsel in distress." He reached out and cupped her jaw in that confident way that he had—the way that said he'd never once been rebuffed in his life by a woman and didn't expect to happen now—and caressed her cheek. "I am not opposed to rescuing damsels who are in distress, Victoria. So long as the damsel in question *wants* my help." His eyes narrowed slightly, the intelligent speculation in his gaze more than a little unnerving. "What about you, sweetheart?"

"What about me?" she asked, unable to look away from his pupils, which were swelling even as she watched.

"Are you a damsel in need of rescuing, my dear Mrs. Dryden? Shall I swoop in on my white charger and lift you into my arms, take you off to my fortified castle and shelter you from the world?"

Tori wondered if he knew how tempting that offer was. She didn't need to be rescued—she could take care of herself and her child and always had—but never in her life had she *wanted* to hand all her problems over to somebody as badly as she did at that precise moment.

Fortunately, her madness passed.

"I am no damsel in need of rescuing." She drew away from him even though it hurt to break contact with his warm, hard body. "We had better get back to the station, my lord. We don't want to miss the last train home."

Chapter 16

Yet again, Mrs. Dryden was avoiding him. Balthazar felt as if every single time he had any contact with the woman—no matter how tame—she turned into a ghost afterward.

They'd had such a lovely day in Northampton—so he'd thought—but he'd not seen hide nor hair of her in the days since. It was annoying that he couldn't simply seek her out and speak to her as if they were two normal people. This skulking and lurking did not suit him at all. He needed to do something to rectify the situation, but he'd not yet decided what. The fact that it was *her* livelihood that he would jeopardize if he behaved precipitately kept him from doing anything rash.

Balthazar was determined to come up with an idea on this journey to London. There was nothing like a train ride for stimulating one's thoughts.

He strode from the livery to the train station, all but trotting to catch the train because Eva had handed him a lengthy, complicated shopping list at the last minute and made him dreadfully late.

Today he had a full slate of errands in London, beginning with a trip to the boarding school, Harrow, to investigate the mysterious tuition the Hastings dukedom had been paying for the last three years.

Bal was heading toward the first-class compartment when he glanced up and saw a familiar profile in the window of the third-class car.

Well, well, well.

Instead of continuing to the first-class railcar, he turned around and boarded the one he'd just passed.

Mrs. Dryden's eyes went comically round when she saw Balthazar striding toward her.

"Is this seat taken?" he asked when he got to her bench.

She blinked up at him, her large blue eyes looking wary and catlike. "No, it's not." She scooted as far over as possible and he sat, their bodies still touching because the wooden benches were narrow and bloody hard, to boot. Still, he couldn't complain about having to be mashed up against her. Indeed, he would have paid extra for the experience, although her anxiously knitted eyebrows said she did not feel quite the same.

"Did you follow me?" she asked him in a low voice while an older couple settled into the seat in front of them.

"Would you like it if I had?" he countered.

She sighed.

"No, I didn't follow you. I have business in London. What about you?"

"It is my day off."

"And you didn't want to spend it with me?" he asked in an injured tone that was only partly feigned.

"I am going to visit my son."

"Ah, you are excused, then. If it had been anyone else you were going to visit then I would been crushed."

She snorted.

Balthazar glanced around the car. "There is quite a difference between first and third class."

"I am surprised you are on this car."

"I have my *reason*," he said, giving her a pointed look that should have left no doubt in her mind that she was his *reason*. She didn't respond, but Bal thought she was trying not to smile. "Do you only see your son—Jamie, is it?"—she nodded—"one day a month?"

"Yes, it's difficult to get away more often."

"I'm sure Zeus would give you more time if you asked him, Victoria."

"Even if I wanted to stay for longer or go more often, I wouldn't want to disturb Jamie's schedule. He will come home for the Christmas holiday." Her smile said that was something she was greatly looking forward to.

"He was not here when we arrived; he did not come to stay with you in the summer?"

"Not this year. He was invited to a friend's house. It was the first time he's not come home."

"You must have missed him greatly."

"I did, but the sacrifice was worth it. His letters were full of all the exciting things he got to do and see, so I was pleased for him." She narrowed her eyes at him. "Why are you looking at me that way?"

***

Tori knew the question was unpardonably rude, but she suspected Lord Balthazar would appreciate her directness.

His laughter told her that she'd guessed correctly. "I was just enjoying the view," he said, his flattery having the predictable effect on her cheeks. "You mentioned that you grew up in Plymouth. Do you have family there?"

"None but the cousin who inherited my family home."

"The one who wouldn't take you in when you needed it?"

Tori gave him a wry smile, amused by his tone. "Yes, that one." She had to admit she liked how angry Balthazar was on her behalf. Teddy had never thought that her being thrown out of her own home by relations was anything untoward. If her cousin hadn't tossed her out, then she never would have taken that governess position and she'd not have met Teddy.

If, if, if.

"Have I made you sad thinking about your old home?" Balthazar asked, once again displaying that surprising sensitivity.

"No, not sad," she answered honestly. "I try not to regret things that are in the past and I cannot change." Besides, if she'd never met Teddy then she wouldn't have Jamie. And he was the best thing that had ever happened to her.

"What about you, my lord? Do you miss your home?"

"Not as much as I thought I would. Part of that is because my brothers and sisters are here."

"Do you think you will go back? When I asked you about it before you said you weren't sure."

"It's possible there won't be anything to go back *to* after this recent fiasco in the newspapers. My reputation wasn't the only thing that suffered," he added and then shrugged. "I'm in no hurry to put an end to my adventure just yet." He regarded her warmly. "There are some other reasons—one in particular—that I don't miss home."

Tori ignored the fluttering in her belly at his words. While Lord Balthazar wasn't the dissipated hedonist the newspapers had made him out to be, the man was still a skilled and practiced seducer. She would do well not to let his flirtatious flattery go to her head.

She'd never met a man—or anyone, really—who'd made her feel more interesting than Balthazar Hale did. She couldn't understand what it was he liked so much about her. Tori hoped it wasn't just because she was convenient and available, both of which were reasons why Teddy had once wanted her.

He pointed out the window, making Tori realize that the train had left the station without her even noticing. “That is an interesting spire over there. Do you know what it belongs to?”

“That is St. Anthony’s. The church was struck by lightning perhaps a decade ago and the cupola and spire needed to be rebuilt.”

He tilted his head. “It looks… crooked.”

She couldn’t help smiling. “That’s because it is. The townsfolk wanted to pull it down and rebuild it, but changed their minds when it became something of a landmark—and an attraction.”

Tori found herself relaxing and becoming more talkative when it became evident that he wasn’t going to pry or ask any difficult-to-answer questions about her past.

Lord Balthazar had a curious, clever mind and had intelligent comments about the countryside and towns they passed. In fact, Tori had such an enjoyable time that the journey flew past and she was startled when her stop was announced.

She began to gather her things and frowned when Balthazar did likewise. “You still have a few stops to go before you reach the City of London.”

“This is the station for Harrow, is it not?”

“Yes, it is. But—”

“I need to pay a visit to the school.”

“You need to go to Harrow?” she repeated.

“Yes. Why? Is that where your son goes?”

“Yes, it is.”

An odd expression flickered across his face—once again it was too quickly for her to decide what it meant.

“Well, then,” he said, giving her another of his knee-weakening smiles, “we can share a hansom cab.”

***

“The money is to pay the tuition for James Abbot *Drake*—not Dryden?” Balthazar repeated, just to make sure he’d heard correctly.

The headmaster—Mr. Pringle, a bone-thin man in his fifties who seemed elated to have a visit from the infamous brother of the American Duke—as the newspapers liked to call Zeus—nodded and looked down at the file that was open on the desk in front of him. “The payments came from His Grace of Hastings until recently." He looked up and cleared his throat. "There was a bit of a, er, delay with this recent payment but I'm pleased to say that has been taken care of."

"How is that? I've been looking through my brother's ledgers and there is no outgoing amount since earlier in the year."

"No, this one didn't come from His Grace."

"Who paid it, then?"

Mr. Pringle opened his mouth and hesitated.

Bal knew he had no right to demand an answer for that question, but he fixed a stern, inquiring expression on the other man and hoped that look—plus his illustrious connection to Zeus—would work in his favor.

It did.

Mr. Pringle leaned forward slightly over his desk, as if he were going to impart something delicate. "I shouldn't disclose such information but—as His Grace's predecessor paid for so long—I will make an exception. It was the Earl of Westmoreland who paid the tuition. The new earl, that is."

"And that happen recently?"

"Yes. The earl's father died only a few months ago. The new earl paid us a visit just a few weeks ago." Pringle smiled indulgently. "He was a student here himself. Indeed, the Earls of Westmoreland have attended Harrow School for hundreds of years."

"What is the earl's family name?"

The other man's forehead creased at the question, but he said, "That would be St. John, my lord."

Bal thanked the headmaster and left, his mind racing.

Was Westmorland senior the grandfather Victoria had been talking about? If that was the case, then who was Dryden and why was the boy's last name *Drake*?

Just what the devil was Victoria hiding?

Chapter 17

Tori ran through the deluge, praying that she'd not missed the train. She usually took the second to last train because she did not like to drive the gig from the livery back to Hastings Park when it was dark. But she'd lost track of time tonight, mainly because Jamie had been so full of questions about Teddy, who had *not* been as unobtrusive as he had claimed.

Tori had told Jamie the truth about his birth before he'd gone off to school. Well, she'd told him the truth up to the point of giving him his father's name. But she'd confessed that she'd never been married and that there was no Mr. Dryden. It had only seemed right to let him know about his birth.

Now, thanks to Teddy, Jamie knew his father's identity.

It had taken hours to answer his questions. And still she'd said nothing about the offer—or demand, really—that his father had made to her. Tori needed more time to have that conversation. She wasn't sure how to couch the fact that Teddy was insisting on destroying what little reputation she had left. Jamie was young, but he wasn't stupid. And he had a moral code that was far more developed than his father's would ever be. Tori suspected Jamie would not be pleased by the change, and not just because he would miss everyone at Hastings Park. He'd grown up with Bickle and the other servants. They were his family and he would not like leaving them.

But that was a problem for another day.

"You missed it!"

Tori startled at the familiar voice and slowed her steps, turning to look at Lord Balthazar, who was striding toward her, a huge brolly in his hand.

"Where is your umbrella?" he asked, shielding them both with his.

"I forgot it," she said, staring up at him through the streaming rain.

"I didn't think it was possible for an English person to forget their *brolly*."

"Was that supposed to be an English accent?" she asked.

He laughed. "Not very convincing? I'll need to work on that."

"I must look like a wet dog," Tori said.

Balthazar smiled. "You look beautiful." He, of course, was perfectly dry beneath the largest brolly she'd ever seen.

"You were obviously here early enough. Why didn't you take the train?" she asked, already guessing his answer.

"I wanted to wait for you."

"We are stuck here. Together."

"So it would appear."

Tori couldn't help smiling. "You don't look especially unhappy about that."

He grinned. "That's because I'm not."

***

"Here," Balthazar handed Victoria his handkerchief once they'd settled into the cab—not the usual hansom, but some giant, rickety old family coach that had been forced back into life as a hackney.

"Thank you," she said, taking off her hat and attempting to repair the rain damage.

Bal hadn't lied; she did look beautiful. But it was creeping into late autumn and there was a chill in the air, so she was probably more than a little cold.

"Where are we going?" she asked.

"I thought I'd take us somewhere that was so big and bustling that we would be unnoticed," he said. "On our one night in London my family stayed at Claridge's."

"Oh."

"Is that acceptable?"

She sighed, a wry expression on her face. "There is no way to go to Hastings, is there? We have to stay in the City."

"We could always go to a livery and hire a post chaise, but the moon is a sliver and hidden by clouds, so I'm not sure how far we would get. Will anyone worry when you don't return?"

"Nobody will even notice until tomorrow at breakfast."

"I told my family I might stay overnight, so I am not expected. We can send a telegram early tomorrow morning to let them know you will be home in the afternoon. Will that serve?"

She opened her mouth—as if to demur—but then just nodded.

Balthazar leaned forward and took one of her hands. "I am not planning any seduction. We can eat dinner—in a private parlor if one is available, or in one of our rooms if not—and then say goodnight."

She stared at him for so long that he wondered if she'd even heard him.

And then she said, "What if I don't want to say goodnight?"

***

Tori was not an impulsive person. At least not since her last impulsive action—with Teddy—had cost her her job and reputation and left her pregnant.

But something about Lord Balthazar Hale seemed to turn back the clock as far as her behavior was concerned.

She was as giddy as a young girl—that was the only way to describe it—as she waited in the hackney a street away from the hotel to protect her privacy, while Balthazar strode through the rain to arrange their rooms for the night.

Tori had known that he'd do the honorable thing even before he'd reassured her. Although she'd been dodging him ever since their trip to Northampton it wasn't Balthazar she was afraid of, but her own desires.

She felt the strangest sense of urgency when she was around him—or even when she thought of him—as if an hourglass had been turned over and her time was rapidly draining away.

Tori had sent Teddy a letter accepting his offer but demanding more time—and also listing *her* terms. She'd insisted on a written agreement so Teddy couldn't stop paying Jamie's tuition or toss Tori out at will, leaving her homeless.

She'd also made it clear that she was accepting his offer of housing, not a carte blanche.

Teddy had agreed to the contract; he'd not commented on the *carte blanche* issue; and he'd grudgingly allowed her some additional time before she had to leave Hastings Park. As things stood, she would have to leave shortly after Lady Evadne's ball.

So little time.

And what were the chances that Tori and Balthazar would have another opportunity to be together again, alone, like tonight?

Very slim. And she planned to take advantage of it.

Tori looked at her watch, frowning when she saw that he'd been gone almost three-quarters of an hour. Tori hoped there wasn't a problem. Perhaps the rooms were all taken? Or—

The coach door opened and Balthazar climbed in. "Sorry that took so long. The hackney will drop us closer. As you can hear, the rain has only worsened. There are no private parlors but the suites I've reserved connect and there is a dining room in one. Are you hungry?"

"Not really—that is the reason I was late; I was eating with my son."

"We'll order something light for later."

"Thank you—for all this," she said. "I feel foolish that I missed the train."

"Did something happen to distract you?"

Tori hesitated and then shook her head. "Nothing happened. Jamie just had a lot to share."

The carriage turned down an alley and stopped in front of an unobtrusive looking door.

"I told the clerk we required a more discreet entrance," he explained as he hopped out and opened the umbrella and then handed her down.

The door opened even as they approached it.

"Thank you," Balthazar said to the porter.

"It's not as pretty as the main entrance, sir, but it is private," the porter said as he led them up several flights. "Here we are," he said, opening a door onto a hushed, lavishly appointed hallway.

Tori had never stayed in a hotel before and hadn't known what to expect. The room the porter led them to was enormous and the décor was every bit as sumptuous as the newly furnished suites at Hastings.

The porter showed them the various features—including a shower bath, an invention she'd never seen before—and then led them to the connecting door into an almost identical suite with the exception of an added dining room.

Balthazar walked with the porter to the door and spoke quietly with him for a moment while Tori inspected her room.

"I've arranged for some dry clothing so that yours might go to the laundry."

"Thank you."

"The maid should be up with the garments soon. Why don't you get out of your wet clothes, take one of those delicious shower-baths, and then we can meet back here."

Here was the sitting room in his suite.

He strode to the connecting door and opened it. "Shall we say three-quarters of an hour?"

"That will be ample," she said, wondering what she would do with almost an hour.

But a few minutes later, after Tori had shed her soaked garments and stepped into the shower-bath, she thought it might be difficult to leave the steaming paradise ever again.

Only the sound of somebody ringing the bell pulled her out of her heavenly daze. Once she'd wrapped a towel around her hair and slipped into the robe she'd found in the armoire, she opened the door to find the maid Balthazar had mentioned.

"But… what is all this?" Tori asked as she took in the heaping armload of jewel-toned garments the other woman held, the colors and fabrics so luscious that some of them looked like they might even taste good.

"Good evening, ma'am. My name is Mary, ma'am. These are from the modiste shop the hotel employs. The boutique is well-stocked for those times when a guest's luggage is lost or delayed. I was instructed to help you dress, take away the garments you don't want, and also see to any of your clothing that needs tending."

Tori pulled her greedy gaze away from the gowns and opened her mouth to say she only needed her clothes dried and pressed, but what came out was, "I would love your help dressing, Mary. And I hope you can do something with my hair."

Chapter 18

Balthazar was looking over the information he'd received from his brother's bank earlier that day—the documents regarding a loan to commence manufacturing of his plow—when the connecting door opened.

Did his mouth fall open when he saw the vision of loveliness who hesitated in the doorway?

Yes. And Bal was not ashamed to admit it.

"You look…" He shook his head as he took in the sight of her. "There isn't a word to describe how beautiful you look."

She blushed becomingly and gestured to her gown. "You did not need to do this."

"Yes, I think I did."

Her hand fluttered around the necklace around her throat. "You have exquisite taste. I've never worn anything so beautiful."

"I do have exquisite taste," he said, looking at her and not the necklace or earrings, although they were quite pretty, too. They were filigreed gold, studded with topaz stones that had complemented all three gowns he'd chosen. The set had cost more than anything he'd ever bought for either himself, or anyone else. Looking at her glowing face, Balthazar knew that he would have gladly paid ten times as much.

"This is too much, Balthazar. I cannot accept—"

"Hush. It wasn't a gift for you, Victoria. It is a gift for *me*. I am the one who gets to see you wearing it, after all."

She gave an exasperated laugh. "You truly are silver-tongued."

"I only tell the truth. Will you turn so that I might see you?"

She rotated slowly in a circle, the gown making an enticing *shushing* sound as she moved.

Good God. The clothing modern women wore might not be practical like those worn at Canoga, but there was no denying the silhouette they created was pure sexuality. Her waist looked even tinier than usual, the pale, soft swells of her breasts above the snug bodice as beautiful as he had imagined they would look.

Bal realized that his mouth was hanging open and shut it.

"They were all so beautiful that it was difficult to choose."

"Don't choose, then. Take all three."

"No, Balthazar, you can't do that."

"Yes, I can. You will take all of them," he repeated. He didn't want to hear any more demurrals, so he changed the subject. "I'm surprised how much I like that color—not the pink, the other shade—it seems too pretty to call it just *brown*."

She smoothed a hand over the skirt of the gown. "The color is taupe and the trim is rose," she said.

"*Taupe*," he repeated. "Why does it sound so ugly yet look so delicious on you?" Bal smiled. "And it looks especially good when you blush that color."

"The maid said that you chose the gowns and jewelry personally, rather than just leaving instructions for the dresser the hotel employs."

"Yes, that is what took me so long. They opened their little shop for me to peruse. I think I did well."

"You did *very* well." She lifted her hands. "These gloves are the most luxurious I've ever worn."

The were also one of the most erotic things he'd ever seen on a woman; snug, wickedly soft *taupe* kid leather that hugged her arms to just above the elbow. He'd never noticed how seductive that tender flesh between a woman's shoulder and elbow was before.

"They suit you. You look beautiful, but then you always do, Victoria. Tonight, you look *different* beautiful."

"Thank you."

He gestured to the settee that was closest to the fire. On the table in front of it was a bottle of champagne in ice and a selection of fruits and the tiny sandwiches Bal knew were usually served for tea, but which would suit a casual meal in front of a fire.

"I decided we didn't need the dining room, after all. It is warmer here, too.

"It looks delicious," she said, gracefully turning so that her bustle so that she could sit.

"It must take practice to wear that," he said, pouring out two glasses and handing her one before taking a seat beside her.

"You mean a bustle?" she asked, taking a dainty sip.

"Yes."

"When I was a girl, the gowns were even more unwieldly, the crinolines immense—like upside down teacups." She cocked her head. "Why? What do women wear at your commune?"

"Come now, I know you've read about their bloomers," he teased.

"I wasn't sure that was true—I'm not sure what about those articles is true and what is fabrication."

"The part about bloomers is true. They wear short skirts over them and most of the women don't wear corsets." His gaze lowered to her bodice. "They are an interesting garment."

She gave a slightly breathless chuckle. "I've never discussed undergarments with a man—or even many women."

"I want you to feel as if you can discuss anything with me, Victoria."

"What do you mean by *interesting*," she hastily asked, clearly wishing to avoid his invitation to intimacy.

"I mean that I can appreciate the artistry of a corset while still deploring its impracticality." Again, he allowed himself to gaze openly at her awe-inspiring bodice. "There is no denying that it shapes a woman's body in a way that is appealing to a man. My sister Io says that women are the victims of masculine ideations of femininity."

"I'm not even sure I know what that sentence means."

"It means you are making me hard, Victoria."

Her lips parted and her fingers tightened enough on the glass that it shook in her hand.

Balthazar took it from her unresisting fingers and set it on the table. "It means you've only just put that gown on and already I'm thinking of taking it off you." He cupped her chin and claimed her lips, sliding his other arm around the torso he'd just been describing, the feel of tight silk and warm skin like kerosine on the flames of his desire.

He groaned with pleasure when she threaded her fingers into his hair and pulled him closer, her kisses already far more skilled than they'd been that first time. He decided she wasn't inexperienced after all, just out of practice.

Balthazar opened for her and submitted to her increasingly bold caresses while his hands commenced an expedition of their own.

***

Tori was only vaguely aware when he released her chin and pulled her closer. He'd opened his mouth wider and allowed her to explore him thoroughly at her own pace.

His hands closed around her waist. While he could not span her, he came close enough that Tori felt dainty and small, even though she was neither of those things. Although, compared to him, most women would feel delicate.

Balthazar Hale wasn't just tall, he was *big*. He looked massive, but now that she was running her hands over his body, he felt even more intimidating. His chest was like a wall, both in breadth and solidity, and his shoulders and biceps felt as rounded and hard as river rocks beneath the expensive wool of his coat.

Tori tried to dig her fingers into the bulging muscles but it was like trying to push them into stone.

"That feels good," he rumbled, "Harder."

She seized the invitation—and his shoulders—with both hands. Massaging him was like kneading a block of wood, but the noises he made were by far the most erotic she'd ever elicited from a lover.

He caressed from her waist up her sides. When his thumbs brushed over her nipples Tori gasped in pleasure and wantonly pressed her chest against his warm palms.

"Mmm," he hummed against her cheek, his lips leaving a hot trail of kisses to her ear. "I've been thinking of this for days, darling. Why have you been avoiding me?"

"I wasn't—I'm not—*ugh*." She stopped stammering like an idiot, took a deep breath, and said, "I don't know why I did something so foolish."

He shook with laughter and then pulled back enough to see her face, his eyes glittering with desire and humor. "I'll forgive you this once, Victoria." His jaw hardened, his amusement giving way to frank desire. "Don't avoid me again; you drove me half-mad depriving me of even the sight of you."

"No, I won't," she whispered, pinioned by his gaze.

He nodded and then his eyes lowered to her bodice, his fingers caressing over her aching nipples. "Will you let me fuck you tonight?"

Tori tried to gasp and exhale at the same time, which resulted in a mortifying squeak of surprise slipping from her mouth.

He laughed. "I'm sorry. That word is too vulgar for polite company, isn't it?"

"*Yes*," she said when she could stop coughing.

Balthazar grinned. "You should probably become accustomed to it—it's one of my favorite words," he admitted, unabashed. "It is earthy and potent and smacks of raw animal lust. Somehow copulate, breed, or mate just don't have the same appeal, do they?"

Her jaw sagged lower.

Again, he smiled. "I keep telling you I am no gentleman, Victoria. I might have been thrust into expensive clothing and have the word *lord* before my name but I am just a farmer. My upbringing was probably regrettable in some ways, but there are several lessons I learned growing up in Canoga that I will always be grateful for. First, there is no shame in the human body or any of the wonderful things we can do to one another with it. Second, and equally important, women are every bit as entitled to sexual release as men. In fact, you can have half a dozen orgasms in the same time that I can have only one." He chuckled. "You look so shocked."

"This is an embarrassing subject," she admitted, and then hastily added. "But I think it is one that needs to be talked about. You will just need to forgive me if I am not nearly as articulate or forthcoming as you are."

"There is nothing to forgive," he said, his eyes softening, his expression one of affection rather than the almost feral hunger of only seconds earlier. "I am plainspoken and I would ask that you are, too—at least with me. You may ask me anything you want and I will answer." He caressed her jaw, his gaze so worshipful that it sent confusing bolts of emotion ricocheting through her.

He looked, almost, as if he… cared for her, rather than just wanting to satiate his needs on her.

Suddenly it was quite important that she not have to share him—she would only have him for a few weeks, and the thought of him leaving here after tonight and going to another woman—Jo Fletcher, for instance—suffused her with a sort of frustrated anger she'd never felt before.

"Are—are you and Mrs. Fletcher lovers?"

He looked surprised by the question. "I've had no lover other than you since coming to England, Victoria. I have no plans, or desire, to be with anyone else." Heat flared in his dark gaze. "There is something very different about you—about what I feel for you."

"Wh-what do you mean?"

"I mean that for the first time I can understand why people become possessive about their mates. Not the sort of possessiveness that destroys, but the sort that promotes intimacy and protects it." He stroked his thumb lightly over her lower lip. "I don't like the thought of sharing you with another man." His jaws flexed and his nostrils flared even as his sinful mouth curved into a self-mocking smile. "There is a term for that at Canoga and it is called being *sticky*."

The word surprised a laugh out of her. "Sticky?"

He nodded. "There were more than a few couples who were separated when they became too *sticky* and didn't want to share each other."

"Separated?"

"Mm-hmm. They'd be kept apart—not in any way that hurt them—until they could accept that they had no right of possession over the other person. I always thought that sort of affection would be a burden. Now that I feel it"—he shrugged.

"What?"

"Now I think it is uncomfortable because it's not requited. But I would imagine it could be quite pleasurable if the object of one's affections felt the same way." He leaned forward and kissed her, which was just as well because she didn't have a clue what to say to that.

When he pulled away, he sat back. "I want you badly." He took her wrist and set her hand over his groin. His eyelids fluttered and he hissed in a breath when Tori tightened her fingers and stroked him through the thin wool of his trousers.

"Yes," he encouraged, "just like that."

She bit her lip at his helpless groan of pleasure and the way his big body flexed beneath her hand, as much a slave to her touch as she had been that day in the Queen's Suite.

Teddy had never spent a great deal of time kissing her—either on the mouth or anywhere else—during those two months before their disastrous marriage, when she'd lived in his parents' house, they had sneaked away at every opportunity. As much as Tori had wanted him—had believed that she loved him—she had refused to give him her virginity until after they'd married.

For all the good that had done.

But just because she'd not lain with him, hadn't meant that they'd not done plenty of other… *things.* Teddy had never been shy asking her for what he wanted and training her how to give him the sort of pleasure that she was sure men usually only demanded from mistresses and whores.

For the first time in over a decade Tori was glad she possessed such shameful skills.

Balthazar lifted his hips slightly, thrusting into her fist, his jaw tight and his clenched teeth showing between his thinned lips.

It was arousing to have such power over him—a man who was so confident about his own body, and hers, too—that Tori didn't want to stop. Indeed, she wanted to pull his trousers off and see what she couldn't quite close her fingers around.

But he gave a frustrated growl and set a hand over hers, stilling her movements.

"Did that not feel good?" she asked.

"It felt very good. But I want to talk to you before we lose ourselves in each other."

Tori frowned, the fear that was never far away swimming to the surface. "Talk?"

***

The worried look on Victoria's face told Balthazar that she feared what he might ask.

This was a woman who had secrets. Just how many—and whether he should be concerned—Bal had to know.

"Yes?" she said, sitting back and smoothing her skirt with the hand that had just been stroking him with such delicious intent.

"I went to the headmaster's office at Harrow and he told me that the duke—the last one—has been paying your son's tuition."

She looked almost relieved. "I suppose you discovered the payments in the ledgers."

It wasn't a question, but Bal nodded. "My brother asked me to track down some missing information. These payments to Harrow was just one of them."

"I did nothing untoward," she said hastily. "His Grace—the last duke, that is—relied on me to keep his books, so I am the one who entered many of the bills that were paid. I didn't pay the tuition from the duke's money, there were—?"

"Mysterious deposits," Bal finished for her, not liking how agitated she was getting. "I assume those were money from Lord Westmoreland?"

"Yes." She dropped her gaze to her lap, where her hands were twisted together.

"The last earl sent the money, not the current one."

She looked up at that. "The headmaster told you that?"

He nodded.

Her cheeks once again flushed, but this time not with pleasure. "He shouldn't have."

"No, he shouldn't have. But he did. The earl sent the money directly to the school—rather than through you?"

Again, she nodded.

Bal took her hands and carefully disentangled her tight fingers before holding them pressed between his. "Won't you tell me the truth, Victoria? You can trust me."

She sighed. "I was foolish thinking nobody would ever notice those payments. I thought I had more time. The last duke really did allow me to use his bank account to pay the quarterly tuition. I—I don't have one, myself."

"What are you hiding that you think is so bad, Victoria?"

"There was no Mr. Dryden."

He smiled. "I deduced as much, sweetheart. So, Jamie's father is one of Westmorland's sons?"

"Yes."

"And you were never married?"

"We were, actually." She gave a bitter laugh. "For all the good it did."

He frowned. "What?"

"We were married in a legal ceremony. Unfortunately, not until after our rather hasty ceremony did I learn that Teddy, who was Westmoreland's middle son, was *already* married."

Balthazar was too surprised to know what to say.

She nodded grimly. "Yes, it's difficult to come up with a response for that, isn't it? I was rather speechless myself, at the time." She stared up at the ceiling, as if looking for guidance. "He'd married an opera dancer and thought she'd died—or that is what she said, anyway. It turned out that she hadn't died. She'd been very ill and Teddy"—she stopped and gritted her jaws, as if she didn't want to speak the words— "let's just say that Teddy didn't behave very gallantly toward her."

"How did you meet him?"

"Part of the story I told you is true. I was a governess in his family's house. He came down from university—well, he'd been *sent* down for something, he wouldn't say, but now I suspect it probably had to do with this woman."

Bal waited patiently while she considered her next words.

"I'd always managed to avoid him in the past, but during that permanent, er, *break*, from university he pursed me and… Well, I gave in and we became close."

Bal felt a twinge of shame when he realized he could be accused of doing the same thing that this *Teddy* had done to her all those years ago. He told himself that his intentions were far more honorable, but the truth was that he wanted her and would do whatever it took to have her.

He shrugged away his shame and asked, "What happened?"

Victoria gave him a look of mingled resignation and shame. "We were caught together—his mother's lady's maid—and I was given the sack." She glanced at him. "It wasn't as bad as you are thinking," she hastened to add.

"I'm not thinking anything, darling." Except maybe how nice it would be to get his hands around *Teddy*'s neck. "What did you do?"

"Teddy came after me and took me from the cheap lodgings where I'd been living while trying to find work—not easy without a letter of recommendation. He told me he loved me and that his parents would relent toward me after we'd married. After all, our fathers had long ago been friends. It was his mother who opposed the match, but she would come around." She shrugged. "And so we were married.

"He had enough money to hire a place for us to stay and we'd been there for several weeks when he received a letter from his father, commanding us to present ourselves. I'd hoped—well, I'd been foolish and believed this was the reconciliation Teddy had promised. Instead, we arrived at their house only to be confronted by Elizabeth Marlowe—er, Elizabeth St. John—Teddy's *real* wife. In the eyes of the law, I was just some woman he'd"—she broke off and shook her head. "In any event, the earl did something that made the second marriage go away completely—I think it wasn't entirely legal, but he didn't want proof of his son's bigamous behavior. I'll admit I was grateful for that. And so, once again, I was homeless and jobless."

"Why wouldn't they at least help you, Victoria? You'd not done anything wrong."

Her eyes slid away from him.

"What else happened?" he asked, dread building in his stomach.

"When we eloped—yes, I allowed myself to be convinced that was a good idea—Teddy brought along some jewels that he sold to pay for everything. It turns out that they were not his jewels to sell; they belonged to the countess. His mother and father were extremely angry."

"But why were you to blame?"

She chewed her lip.

He gave her a look of disbelief. "Tell me he did *not* say that you took them, Victoria?"

"He did."

"Good God!"

She winced at his anger and Bal bit his tongue to keep from saying more.

"It seems that Teddy took them shortly before we'd been caught together and they sent me packing. They believed I'd helped myself to the countess's jewels on my way out the door."

"The scoundrel! Did you tell them the truth?"

"No."

"*Why not*?"

"He begged me not to say anything."

Bal was speechless.

She nodded wearily. "I know, I know—I was stupid. But it was already over and his parents loathed me for being central to the scandal"—Bal made a disbelieving noise but she talked over him— "telling them that their son was a liar and thief would only sour their relationship even more. Besides, they told me they'd give me a letter of reference if I just left quietly." Her face twisted into a bitter smile. "Unfortunately, none of us knew the full extent of Teddy's thieving until after I was gone."

"Victoria, what do you mean?"

"I went to pawn the ring—my wedding ring—so that I would have enough money to go to London and look for work. The shop owner notified the authorities. It turned out the ring had been some exceedingly valuable St. John family heirloom."

"Tell me you weren't—"

"I was taken to gaol."

"*What*? I thought the earl had allowed you to go?"

"So did I. But the fact that I had that ring changed his mind."

"Good God, Victoria. How long were you—"

"A month."

"Bloody hell! *A month*?"

"He would have left me there to rot if I'd not sent him a letter threatening him that I was going to tell the truth about his son's bigamy if he did not get me out."

Balthazar just shook his head and bit his tongue, holding back the flow of crude names he had for such a cowardly, spineless ass.

"Once he managed to free me—I'm not sure what he said to get me out, I just didn't care—he helped me get a new governess position." She smiled grimly. "As far away from his family as possible. I was there for two months when I could no longer avoid the truth."

"You were pregnant."

"Yes. I should have known sooner, but I was pitifully ignorant about such matters. When my condition became evident my employers would discharge me. I knew I would not get by without help. So, once again, I sent a letter to the earl."

"Not his son?"

She made a scoffing sound. "Teddy had always outspent his allowance and I knew he would never be able to help me with money—not unless he stole more of his mother's jewels. Besides, I didn't want to see him or talk to him ever again. By that time the blinders were off and I was furious. I deeply regretted not telling his parents the truth about the theft—and I was furious at myself for being such a silly fool—but I reserved the bulk of my hatred for Teddy for being so weak and shuffling his troubles onto me."

"He should have been put in a public stockade and whipped."

Her jaw sagged. "Is that something—"

Bal laughed. "No, we didn't do that at Canoga. I'm just venting my spleen."

"It speaks well of you that you are so disgusted."

"Any decent person would find his behavior reprehensible, Victoria—anyone. But I interrupted you. Please, finish your story."

"Lord Westmoreland intimated the child probably wasn't even his grandson and I have to admit I lost my temper."

"I am delighted to hear it. Did you hit him?"

She gave a startled laughter. "No, of course not!"

"That's too bad. I think he deserved some hitting. If he wasn't already dead, I'd seek him out and do it myself."

"To give the earl credit, he did help me find the position I have now. Yet again it was the memory of my father that convinced somebody to hire me: this time the Duke of Hastings." She paused, cutting him a shy look.

"What? Why are you looking at me that way?"

"The earl decided it was better if I appeared older than I was, so…"

"Victoria?" he said when she stopped, her cheeks flaring to life in that way he adored. "How old are you really?"

"I am thirty."

Bal quickly did the math. "That scoundrel debauched you when you were only seventeen?"

"You should know that he never forced me, Balthazar. I went to him willingly—foolishly, but willingly."

"That's small consolation given the fact you went to jail for him." He reined in his anger yet again. "Go on, finish your story."

"I took the position a few months after Jamie's birth. The earl came up with the name of Dryden, somebody he knew; a man who truly had died the way I described. Westmoreland told me that if I ever told the truth to anyone, he'd lay an information against me and have me thrown in gaol for the theft of the jewels. So that is my story."

Bal could only shake his head.

"I played a role in that mess, too," she said.

"What? By marrying an ass?"

"I think you mean an arse."

He laughed. "That's right—I keep forgetting that's how you say it here. Well, I mean both. So, you've kept it quiet all these years for fear of prosecution and the loss of your son's education?"

"Don't forget all the shame associated with illegitimacy. I didn't want Jamie to have to grow up with that. I know people don't believe in marriage where you grew up, but—"

"Trust me, I'm familiar with the stigma society places on people born outside marriage. I understand why you don't want to burden your son with that." Something occurred to him. "The headmaster said the old earl had just died and the new one paid for the tuition. You said that your—er, well, *Teddy* was a younger son. Is this earl his older brother, then?"

Her eyes flickered away from his, but then came back, her expression one of resignation. "Teddy's older brother died several years ago; he is the new earl."

So, she might have been a countess rather than a housekeeper if things had been different. He wondered if that rankled.

"Is this the secret that the man who attacked you—Boyd—was talking about?" He paused. "Or are there more?"

"No," she said, her lips twisting into a wry smile. "I think this is enough for one person, don't you?"

"How did Boyd find out about your past?"

"Before you came along, he'd told me about his cousin who'd just taken a groom position with the new Earl of Westmoreland." She shrugged. "The servant network is often faster than sending a telegram." She hesitated, and then added, "I'm guessing that is how Mrs. Fowler from the King's Quarrel discovered who my father was—from Boyd."

"You never told anyone else your background?" he asked.

"No, I didn't want to give out any more information than necessary. What happened between Teddy and me was… well, the earl tried to quash the rumor, but Mr. Boyd is proof that one can never entirely hide a scandal of that magnitude."

"What did Boyd want from you? Money?"

"He never got that far, but I'm assuming that is what it was."

"If Boyd comes to you again, I want—"

"He has left. He was only here staying with his sister and her family while there was work harvesting. He does not have a good reputation in and around Symington, so temporary work is all he can find anymore. I daresay he won't return again until next year. That's providing he doesn't become worse and stop finding work altogether."

"If he or anyone else comes to threaten you, I want you to tell me. I'll make sure they never make such a mistake again."

"Thank you." She smiled. "You look quite fierce right now."

Bal growled and they both laughed.

He slid an arm around her and then pulled her closer. "This damned bustle," he muttered when he realized he couldn't get close to most of her body. He tilted her chin so that she was near enough that their noses almost touched. "I don't think any less of you because you weren't married, Victoria." He kissed her. "In fact, I think *more* of you"

"More?" she repeated, looking more than a little skeptical.

"Yes. It takes so much courage to do what you did. I hope you will introduce me to your son. I would like to meet him."

Her gorgeous blue eyes looked like a summer sky right before the rain. "Thank you, Balthazar. It means a great deal to hear you say that. And I think you would like Jamie and he would adore you. He is quite mad for inventing things."

"Malcolm Rowell told me all about him. He said Jamie is clever and already showing promise."

She gave him a watery smile. "Malcolm has been very kind to Jamie and lets him haunt the workshop he keeps at his aunt's house." A tear slid down her cheek.

"What's this?" Bal asked, kissing away the glittering drop.

"They are happy tears—*relieved* tears."

"You are glad that I know?"

"Yes. And I am relieved by your response. It is a secret that has hung over my head for almost a decade and a half. I must still keep it—for Jamie's sake—but it is a relief to share the truth with somebody."

"You've told nobody else?"

"You are the first."

***

Tori watched as a slow smile spread across Balthazar's face. "That is auspicious."

She couldn't help laughing at his adorably smug expression. "How so?"

"It speaks of trust, does it not?"

Tori nodded but felt a pang at his words.

Tell him the rest! her conscience shrieked.

But she couldn't. The fact that he accepted her status made no difference to their future together. He was still a duke's brother—and one who hadn't been raised to believe in marriage—and she was still an unwed mother who worked as a servant. He might want to take her as his mistress, but that would be worse than going to Teddy. Worse because she could see herself falling in love with this unusual, charming, and devastatingly attractive man.

"Are you hungry?" he asked, gesturing to the food.

"No. But please eat if—"

His mouth claimed hers with an urgency that shot straight to her womb and she met him kiss for kiss. When he finally pulled away, they were both breathing hard.

"I love this gown on you, Victoria, but I want it off."

Tori twisted until her back was to him.

He groaned. "Look at all these tiny buttons! There must be a thousand."

"I thought you were a mathematician; there are barely twenty."

"You've scrambled my wits so badly I doubt I could add two plus two correctly. What is it? Nine?"

"No, I think it's fourteen."

Balthazar laughed. "So, I am not the only one who has a problem thinking."

No, he most certainly wasn't. Tori's heart was beating so hard her chest hurt. Confessing the truth—at least about her past—had left her dizzy with relief.

And the thought of what they were about to do made her even dizzier.

He leaned closer, until she could feel his hot breath on her nape, which he kissed, sending shivers all though her body. She leaned back, giving herself up to the feel of his soft, warm lips, slick tongue, and the rough but stimulating graze of his teeth.

He was breathing as hard as Tori when he pulled away a moment later. "You distracted me from my herculean task," he accused, his fingers resuming their labor. "The next gown I choose will have buttons the size of chestnuts. And there will only be two of them."

For all his complaining Tori felt the bodice loosen and slide down her shoulders.

He got to his feet. "Up you get," he said, offering her a hand up and then standing behind her and sliding his arms around her waist while he lowered his mouth to the juncture of her neck and shoulder. Tori tilted her head to give him better access, sagging back against his ridiculously large chest, the rush of contentment—and the almost overwhelming feeling of security—stunning her boneless. When had she last felt so safe? Surely not since she was a little girl.

"That's better," he whispered. "You were so tense—your muscles all clenched and tight." He continued his kisses while his hands worked to loosen her skirt, petticoat, and finally the bustle beneath.

His fingers made short work of the corset laces, until all she was left wearing was her chemise and the pretty stockings and open back slippers that had been delivered with the gown.

He turned her to face him, his eyes dark when she looked up at him. "It is like opening the best present ever," he said, the earnest words surprising a laugh from her. "May I remove your chemise?"

Tori swallowed but nodded. There was no point trying to hide her body from him. She was a woman in her middle years, who'd had a baby and nursed her own child.

She was what she was.

He slid the straps off her shoulders and the plain white cotton slid to the floor without making a sound.

The noise he made in his throat—one of speechless desire—was the sort that every woman should hear from a lover at least once in her life.

He lowered slowly to his haunches and held the chemise so she could step out of it. When he stood, he took her hand and led her to the bed.

Tori hesitated, uncertain of what he wanted, and he set his hands on her waist and lifted her with no visible effort. He stepped closer, nudged her thighs apart and stood between them. "Will you undress me, Victoria?"

Tori eagerly reached for his necktie.

At the same time, Balthazar began to remove the pins that Mary had so cleverly used to style her hair not even an hour earlier.

"Your hair is even softer than it looks," he said. "Long hair is rare at Canoga. It's considered… frivolous." He met her gaze "I think there is room in life for a little frivolity; especially when it is as beautiful as this." He uncoiled the heavy rope with a gentleness that touched her; he might tower over her and be as broad-shouldered as an ox, but his hands were careful, almost… worshipful.

Tori's fingers—which were normally practical and deft—shook slightly as she unbuttoned his waistcoat, the hard, warm muscular chest beneath her hands reminding her of what they would soon be doing.

Her marriage to Teddy had lasted only three weeks and two days. When he'd taken her on their wedding night it had hurt so badly that she'd thought something had broken inside her. The subsequent nights had not been nearly as painful, but neither had they been especially enjoyable. Needless to say, her memories of intercourse—or *fucking* as Balthazar liked to call it—were less than pleasurable.

Certainly, Teddy had never made her feel the way Balthazar had that afternoon in the Queen's Suite. Even Tori, in the privacy of her own bed, had never managed to tease such a powerful climax with her furtive touches.

"Victoria?" A finger slid beneath her chin and tipped her face up. "What is it? You've gone as rigid as a post." He set his hands over hers, which had stopped on the bottom button of his waistcoat.

"It's nothing."

But when she tried to resume removing his clothing, he wouldn't let her.

"Are you anxious about what we are about to do?"

She inhaled deeply, feeling foolish for harboring such fears, but nodded. "A little."

"We don't have to do anything at all. We can just curl up together beneath the blankets, or I can tuck you in and take the other bed, or—"

"I want to lie with you, Balthazar, but it has been so many years and—well, the last time I went to bed with a man I experienced very little pleasure and came away pregnant." The words came out in a rush. Although she was mortified by making such a confession, she was relieved that she'd told him the truth.

"Did you enjoy the other day—when we were in that musty, dusty old queen's room?"

Tori pursed her lips but couldn't contain her smile. "You know I did."

"That is how I will make you feel tonight. I promise. As for the second part." He reached into the pocket of his frock coat and took out his notebook. From inside it he extracted a slim paper envelope. "Do you know what this is?" He opened the flap and pulled out a tan tube. "It's a condom—a sheath," he said, sparing her from having to answer. "I believe they are—or were—called French letters here."

"I've heard of them, of course, but I've never seen one. They truly work?"

"Nothing is entirely effective, but they are very good when used properly." He tossed the envelope and tube onto the nearby nightstand and then took her face in both his hands. "But we don't need to have intercourse, Victoria. There are other ways to pleasure each other." He leaned down and kissed her. "And there are other times than tonight. We can take all the time we need."

It was those last words that decided her.

They didn't have all the time in the world; they had only weeks. Far too soon she would be gone.

Tori slid her hands around his neck and pulled him down until she could give him a fierce kiss. When she pulled away, she held his gaze as her hands resumed their task, this time without so much as a tremor.

Once she'd unbuttoned his shirt, he shucked off all three garments with one smooth shrug and tossed them onto the bench at the foot of the bed.

Tori barely had a chance to enjoy her close-up view of his glorious chest before he bent low, unbuttoned his shoes, and toed them onto the carpeted floor with two dull *thunks*.

But when he reached for the buttons on his trousers Tori pushed his hands aside. "I'll do it," she said, her greedy gaze sliding from the heavy muscles slabbing his chest to the fascinating grooves of his abdomen all the way down to the thick ridge shoving against the black wool of his trousers. When she lightly brushed her hand against him, he hissed and jolted at the faint touch.

"Are you smiling?" he asked.

"Yes."

"You find it amusing to tease me?"

She laughed. "Yes."

"You witch," he said in a raspy voice that was punctuated by a low groan when she pushed down both his trousers and drawers and his erection sprang free.

Tori stared at him, because she couldn't help herself.

Like the rest of his body, this part of him was long and thick and beautifully masculine.

She reached for him—needing to touch him—but Balthazar closed his hand around her wrist. "Oh no you don't. I'll be embarrassing myself after all my boasting if you do that. Up on the bed—hands and knees."

She hesitated.

He cocked an eyebrow at her. "Do you trust me to make you feel good?"

She thought about that day in the queen's room. "Yes."

"Then up you go."

Feeling more self-conscious than she could remember, Tori pushed up onto her hands and knees.

"Good," he murmured, kneeling on the bed and stroking a hand down her flank. "Spread your knees. A little more," he urged. "Yes, you look lovely like this, Victoria."

Face flaming, she complied.

He chuckled when she twisted around to see what he was doing. "No peeking."

Tori felt something soft and ticklish between her thighs. She looked down and was stunned to find eyes looking back at her.

"Oh!" Her knees jerked together, smashing into his ears.

"Ow!" Balthazar slid his hands around her thighs and gently pried them apart.

"I'm sorry. You surprised me." That was putting it mildly. It was difficult to think of anything else but what his view must be.

He stroked her thighs and smiled. "No permanent damage done."

"What—er, what are—"

"Put a pillow beneath my head, love."

Tori stared.

He nodded. "Trust me."

The pillow she pushed beneath him lifted his head several inches closer to her body; closer to that private part of her—a part she'd only ever seen in passing.

"Now spread wider for me." His hands gently tugged her thighs apart.

Tori stared, her gaze riveted to his face while he spread her knees apart, until he was barely an inch from her sex.

He caressed from her knees to her bottom, his big palms settling on her buttocks and stroking and tugging and squeezing. "I'll kiss you like the other day, but this way you can control the pace and take as much as you want." His lips pulled up wickedly on one side as his finger traced down her cleft, the light yet erotic caress causing her hips to jerk, an action that pushed her against his face.

"Mmm, yes," he muttered, nuzzling the curls that covered her mound, his nose brushing against her clitoris and making her jolt again.

"Shhh, sweetheart." His hands slid around to the front of her hips and he parted her outer lips and extended his tongue, barely stroking her with the tip.

Tori bit her lip to keep from crying out. She shuddered with pleasure and the movement once again pushed the most sensitive part of her against his waiting lips and tongue.

He groaned. "Yes, sweetheart, ride my face," he urged, his soft, hot mouth closing around her bud. And then he commenced to gently suck and all thoughts of modesty or restraint fled.

***

Balthazar could come just from watching Victoria take what she wanted.

Her shyness evaporated like a drop of water on a hot stove once he put his mouth on her, her body delightfully responsive to his touch.

Her orgasm came quickly, and another, stronger climax came right on the heels of the first.

Her knees spread wider with no urging from Bal, and she grinded herself against him, humping his mouth while making the most adorable little grunts and groans.

Bal slid a finger inside her and felt the echoes of her climax squeeze him tight, his cock and balls aching to bury himself in her snug heat.

Only after her third orgasm, when she whimpered and pulled away from his questing tongue, did he give her one last gentle kiss and slide out from beneath her.

He briefly considered turning her over so he could see her face when he entered her, but he couldn't resist the elegant curve of her back and her full, heart-shaped bottom, which was canted so sweetly.

And so he knelt behind her and slid his erection between the slick petals of her sex, gently flexing his hips and stroking himself with her flesh, working himself close to the edge before he pulled away. "I want to be inside of you, Victoria."

She immediately pushed her bottom back against him.

Ba chuckled. "I'll take that as a *yes*." He leaned forward and kissed her nape and then reached for the packet on the nightstand. The condom inside was one of the newer sort that was made from vulcanized rubber. He'd heard many complaints against them—almost all from men—but believed the benefits they afforded, especially when it came to unwanted pregnancies, were well worth any diminished sensitivity.

Once he was sheathed, he teased her nipples while he slicked his cock between her thighs, thrusting until she began to rock back against him in a wordless demand for more.

Bal ached to be inside her, but she'd been so anxious earlier that he did not want to rush her.

As if she sensed the reason for his hesitation, Victoria reached beneath her body until her fingers, cool and tentative, encountered his shaft.

He smiled at her not-so-subtle hint and angled his hips so she could position his crown at her entrance.

Bal already felt ready to explode, but he *would* restrain himself. He needed to erase that shadow from her eyes, to make her forget whatever had happened during her brief faux marriage that had left her so afraid of sex.

He would make sure she had pleasure—a great deal of it—before this night was through.

***

Tori was stunned at her own audacity in reaching for him, but she knew Balthazar was thinking about her—worried about what she'd confessed earlier—and it was his very sensitivity that made her so bold and eager. She wanted him.

Badly.

His erection had looked imposing tenting his trousers. He felt even bigger in the flesh. Was she mad to want such an intimidating thing inside her? His blunt crown nudged against her entrance and Tori gritted her teeth; he felt *huge*. Fear clawed at her. *He will tear me—it will hurt like it did before. I will bleed and—*

"Shhh," he soothed, barely breaching her and then pausing. "I will go slow, darling."

Tori bit her lip and gave a jerky nod.

The feeling of being penetrated and stretched was alarming, but not uncomfortable, nothing like the searing pain that she remembered from all those years ago. Perhaps her memory had exaggerated it?

Or, more likely, Teddy had never taken his time with her.

Balthazar pulsed his hips gently, slowly inching deeper. "God, you feel so incredibly tight and hot, Victoria."

Tori was grateful he couldn't see her face. As much as his earthy language mortified her, she also loved it. Did that make her depraved?

If so, she didn't care.

"Tell me how it feels," he said, caressing up her spine with one hand and bringing goose pimples up all over her body.

"Big," she said without hesitation.

He laughed, the action causing the part of him that was inside her to flex. "Thank you, but I assure you I'm not much more than average. Are you in discomfort?"

"No. It feels… good." And it did—strange and personal and almost unbearably intimate, but good. Very good.

"Put your shoulders down lower, rest your head on your arms," he said, his hands settling on her hips while he invaded her deeper. "Yes, good girl, just like that." He groaned when her inner muscles contracted around him. "Ah, you like that, don't you? Being my good girl?"

If Tori hadn't been experiencing such incredible pleasure from his gentle thrusting, she might have protested. Was there something wrong with her? Why would being called a *girl*, good or otherwise, arouse her so?

But evidently it did. Wildly.

He gave a low chuckle. "I can almost hear your big brain working, Victoria. Relax… allow yourself to enjoy whatever you feel. It's just the two of us here—there is nobody else to please but ourselves."

Tori felt a dizzying rush of gratitude at his words. Suddenly, she *needed* him to know that she trusted him, that every part of her belonged to him—to do with as he pleased.

She could not find the words to express herself, and so she showed him how she felt with her body, canting her hips and arching her back, the submissive pose making her feel sinful and deliciously sensual.

A growl of approval rumbled in his chest. "What a good, obedient girl you are, offering yourself up to me," he praised. "Begging to be filled." He leaned low and hissed, "Needing to be *fucked.*"

They both gasped when she clenched around his shaft.

"I wish you could see what I am seeing," he said, his hips gently pumping as one of his hands moved to where their bodies were joined. He stroked her slick, sensitive flesh. "You look so beautiful taking me, Victoria." His fingers slowly slid in the other direction, moving away from her engorged clitoris.

Tori wanted to whimper and demand that he bring back his hand.

But before she could open her mouth, she felt the damp pad of his finger settle over the one part of her body she had never seen and never expected anyone else to see, either.

She gasped when he lightly stroked her there. "Wh-what are you doing?"

"Shhh, I won't do anything to hurt you, sweetheart."

His light caressing confused her. It felt so good, but it was so *wrong* to enjoy such a filthy thing.

Wasn't it?

"Such a pretty little rosette," he murmured, his voice warm and silky. "One day you will beg me to take you here."

Tori must have made some noise that expressed her disbelief because he chuckled.

"Oh, yes you will," he promised, both confident and amused as he pressed his thumb against her one last time before leaving that taboo part of her alone. Instead, he massaged her bottom in that wildly erotic way that he had—spreading her cheeks and exposing her, making her feel vulnerable yet so aroused.

"Tilt your hips up," he ordered quietly, his hands sliding beneath her, to where her thighs met her pelvis. "Yes, perfect, just like that."

He controlled her body with an ease that made her throb even harder, lifting her to meet his thrusts, filling her completely with each powerful stroke.

"Beautiful," he praised, pumping faster and harder, until the depth of penetration was almost uncomfortable. "Mmm, yes…right… *there.*" He grunted and angled his hips in such a way that his shaft rubbed against a place inside her that sent glorious bolts of lightning crackling along every nerve ending in her body.

Tori cried out when he did it again and again. The sensation was too much—the pleasure too exquisite. And yet, when he withdrew, she pushed her hips back to chase that intense bliss, shoving herself against him, needing him even deeper.

"That's right, lover, use me," he urged, his own hips immobile while she bucked against him.

Briefly, Tori imagined how she must look—needy and shameless and writhing—but decided she didn't care. Instead, she found the rhythm and angle that pleased her best and did exactly what Balthazar told her to do: she used him.

But as hard as she slammed back onto him, her climax remained just out of reach—taunting and teasing. She heard a grunt of frustration and was shocked to discover that noise had come from her.

Balthazar chuckled. "Poor baby. Here, let me help you." He slid one hand between her lower lips and pressed the ball of his thumb in exactly the right place. "Come for me, Victoria," he ordered, his firm caress catapulting her over the edge.

This time—unlike the last however many orgasms she'd had—she was filled with a hard phallus and it amplified her pleasure to almost unbearable levels, wave after wave of pleasure battering her.

Balthazar dropped onto his hands, caging her body with his far larger one, and then his powerful hips commenced to drum, his thrusts quickly becoming harder and faster, until he was slamming into her so savagely that she had to grab the bedding in her fists to hold her position, the sounds of their slapping flesh filling the room.

"Victoria," he cried out right before he buried himself deep inside her, his shaft flexing and jerking as his own climax overtook him.

***

Bal woke with a start. "Victoria?" he asked, groggy.

"I'm awake," she said, sounding alert and aware.

"Did you sleep?"

"For a little while."

He yawned and shifted, lying on his side so he could look at her, propping his head on one hand. Faint light from the street below streamed through the gap in the heavy drapes, illuminating an intriguing sliver of her neck and clavicle.

"Was I too rough with you?" he asked.

"No."

He smiled. "Do you want me to quit talking so you can go to sleep?"

"No."

"Will you tell me a little about yourself, Victoria?" he asked, fully expecting another *no*.

Instead, she said, "What would you like to know?"

"Tell me what it was like where you grew up. I want to know if your childhood was anything like mine."

She shifted until she, too, was on her side, mirroring his pose. "It sounds like you had a great many people living in close proximity?"

"Yes, that is true. All the members of the commune lived in four buildings."

"That is very different from how we lived. There was only my father and I—and a few servants. He was… distant with me and deeply disappointed that I'd not been born a boy."

Bal's heart squeezed at the pain in her voice, his anger flaring at the long dead man for disliking his daughter simply for being born a girl.

Victoria sighed. "As much as he yearned for a son, he was too ashamed of our circumstances to court a woman and bring home a wife. You see, our ancestral home was quite modest, more of an oversized cottage that could have fit into a small part of Hastings."

He chuckled. "Our entire commune could have fit into part of Hastings. Building houses that size is—well, it seems grandiose self-indulgence of the worst sort, especially when one considers all the poor and homeless there are in this country."

"Yes, it does seem indulgent," she agreed. "But Hastings Park is so very lovely, it would be a shame if such a place did not exist."

Bal didn't want to talk about architecture; he wanted to know about her—everything.

"Did you leave behind friends? Any extended family? Do you ever go home to visit? Do you miss it? Did you have a Season? Or do the daughters of baronets not get them?"

She chuckled softly. "That is a lot of questions. Let me see if I can recall them all. As poor as we were, there was still that invisible barrier between a baronet's daughter and the local gentry. Well, at least my father made sure there was a barrier. He was very concerned we keep up appearances, even though it became increasingly difficult as money became tighter. His response to our poverty was to stop entertaining entirely so that our neighbors would never see how threadbare Molton House had become. That is a long answer to your question about friends.

It was difficult to make friends when I could not have them over as guests. And we could hardly accept invitations elsewhere when we never reciprocated. So, I had no close friends."

"It sounds… lonely."

"I didn't notice how lonely until I moved away."

"When you took the governess position at the Earl of Westmoreland's?"

"Yes. As to your other questions, I have no extended family other than the cousin I mentioned. I've not gone back to visit since moving away. And no, I did not have a Season given the state of my father's finances. As to whether I miss it… Well, there wasn't anything left for me to miss after my father's death."

"Tell me about your first job."

"I'd known that I would likely need to go out and work—either as a companion or a governess—for quite some time, so when my father died, I wasn't entirely surprised. I suppose I'd hoped the Earl of Westmoreland would treat me less like a stranger given the friendship he'd once had with my father, but I hadn't considered the countess. It was immediately clear that she did not like having me in the house."

"Too young and pretty and a temptation to her sons?" Bal guessed.

"I don't know about *pretty*, but I was certainly too *convenient*."

Bal hated how cynical she sounded and almost wished he'd not brought up the subject of her faithless lover, but he wanted to know about her, so he didn't stop her when she continued.

"It was a large family. In addition to Teddy and his elder brother there were four girls—two already married and two my charges—and three younger brothers who were away at school." She gave a sigh that sounded wistful. "The house was so… alive. Even though all the siblings did not get along—I think their father played them off against each other—it was so much more interesting than my home had been."

Bal thought she sounded more infatuated with the prospect of joining her lover's family than she had with the man himself.

"I think I was interested in Teddy because of what he represented," she went on, confirming Bal's thoughts. "Deep down I hoped that if I married into that family I would finally belong somewhere." She snorted softly. "Instead, I ended up even more isolated and alone than before."

Bal reached out and laid a hand on her hip. "I'm so sorry, darling."

"It was a long time ago," she said, but he heard the sadness in her voice.

He leaned toward her and found her lips in the near darkness, pleased when her arm slid around his shoulders and she pressed her body against his.

"You're not isolated now, Victoria," Bal said.

Unlike the first time they made love, which had been hungry and demanding, the second time was slow and sensual, their bodies moving in a way that made him feel very close to her.

Afterward, it was Victoria who fell asleep.

She cozied up to him, her head resting on his chest. Although he was physically tired, his mind refused the lure of sleep. She fit so perfectly in his arms and felt so right that he couldn't be too unhappy about missing a little rest.

Bal had always enjoyed his lovers, but never before had he felt so protective about a woman. It was silly, because he'd rarely met a woman more capable than Victoria. Her story tonight had infuriated and saddened him. So much suffering and pain and rejection for one person to bear. And yet she appeared confident and fearless despite her past. Or maybe because of it. After all, it was said that adversity formed character and she'd certainly had her share of the former.

Tonight had been just as wonderful as he'd hoped their first time would be. Already his devious mind was trying to engineer another night.

At the same time, Bal sensed that he had to take care and not push. He couldn't get over the feeling that she was always poised for flight. Perhaps now that she'd confided the truth about her past, she would be more receptive to his not-so-subtle demands for more of her time.

Bal lightly kissed her head and smiled to himself, replaying the events of the evening in his mind's eye.

Things were going well between them. Bal told himself he didn't need to rush her. They had plenty of time.

All the time in the world.

Chapter 19

Bal eyed Victoria from beneath lowered lashes, trying to guess what was going through her mind. It had taken a great deal of persuasion to convince her to allow him to pay for her first-class ticket, but it was worth the argument not to be crowded in like cattle. Here there were only two others in the spacious car and one was reading while the other dozed.

He was supposed to be reading, too, but had not turned a page in fifteen minutes. Instead, he was thinking about this morning, and how Victoria had woken him after scarcely an hour of sleep.

She'd explored his body with her hands and mouth, pulling him gently from a dreamless doze. Her touch had been tentative at first but had become braver as she'd seen the power she exercised over him.

He'd made love to her in that half-awake sleep, the line between reality and dreams blurred in the crepuscular light.

Victoria had fallen asleep afterward, but Bal had reluctantly climbed from the warm bed. He'd left her to rest for a little while longer while he'd quickly washed and then dressed in the garments they'd worn the day before, which had been cleaned and pressed and laid out in the room they'd hardly touched.

He'd then rung for a servant to arrange for Victoria's new gowns and jewels to be delivered to Hastings Park, so they didn't have to take luggage back with them.

Lastly, he ordered breakfast and then went to wake his sleeping beauty.

She'd been sprawled across the bed—his Victoria was something of a bed and blanket hog he'd discovered—her hair a silky blond web across the pillows, one long, tempting, bare leg uncovered.

Bal sat on the side of the bed and laid a hand on her shoulder. "Victoria," he whispered. When she didn't so much as twitch, he gently squeezed her arm. "*Victoria...* time to wake and join the living," he teased as her sleepy eyes fluttered open and her gaze darted around, her blue eyes a little frantic until she recalled where she was. He could see immediately—by her guarded expression—that she was no longer the free spirit she'd been under cover of darkness.

"What time is it?" she asked in a sleep-roughened voice, pushing up onto one hand and rubbing her eyes.

"It is just past six. I thought we might catch the seven-fifteen."

She nodded, glanced down, and then hastily grabbed the blankets and yanked them up when she noticed that she was bare from the waist up.

Bal stood. "I'll give you privacy. I will be in the other suite, where there will be breakfast in half-an-hour."

He had adored the domestic intimacy of sharing breakfast with her and he'd enjoyed her blushes, too. Balthazar knew it might just be conceit, but he told himself that she looked relaxed, rested, and—yes—happier.

Their night together, no matter how pleasurable, hadn't just changed matters between them, it had changed him, too, and he felt the difference most acutely.

He'd never before felt such reluctance to leave a lover's side. Nor had he experienced such a strong desire to nurture and protect as he did with Victoria.

The story she'd shared about her past had been horrific. Bal saw red just thinking about her cousin and that fool of an earl—both of them, old and new—and how together the two men had terrorized and abused her. Thirteen years ago she would have only been seventeen, four years younger than Eva. Thinking about his little sister being forced to go off on her own—no family or friends—and raise a child made his blood boil.

"What is it?"

Balthazar blinked and looked up at Victoria. "Hmm?"

She glanced at their cabin mates and then leaned closer. "You're looking so... *ferocious*."

"Was I?"

"What were you thinking?"

Balthazar smiled. "You told me that was a rude question."

"See how quickly your American ways have rubbed off on me?" she retorted. And then, in a lower voice, "Tell me."

"I was thinking of you young, alone, pregnant, and afraid."

The almost playful sparkle that had glinted in her eyes faded slightly. "Ah."

"I have also been thinking I'd like to thrash that fool—Westmoreland. Has he—or his father—done anything for your son other than pay for his schooling?"

"No," she said quickly. "But that is just as well. I don't want him involved, even though I know that is not fair to Jamie. He deserves to know his father—and his family."

Bal nodded reluctantly. "You are right. He does deserve that." Jealousy gnawed at him when he considered what that opportunity would mean for Victoria. She, too, would need to see the man again. Their son was a tie between Victoria and Westmoreland that would always be there.

"What will you tell your family when they ask where you were—and if anyone notices that I was gone, as well?" she asked.

"What do you want me to say?"

"Perhaps you might just say we met on the train?"

Bal nodded. "Very well. I will tell them I stayed over in London and saw you at the train station this morning."

"Do you think they will believe us?"

"I honestly doubt anyone will even notice we were both gone." He frowned. "Well, Edith might."

She smiled.

"What?" he asked. "Why are you smirking?"

She shook her head.

"No, you don't get off that easily, Mrs. Dryden. Tell me."

"Your younger brothers and Lady Io are quite amusing when it comes to confronting Miss Barrymore. They have a way of not arguing with her and yet not complying to her wishes, either."

"I'm glad that Ares and Apollo at least get a bit of amusement from defying her draconian directives, but I fear that my twin might one day give her an unvarnished piece of her mind. And a fist to go along with it." She laughed and he smiled wryly. "That's not a joke. I'm sure you've noticed that Io can be direct even when she is not in a fury."

"She is direct, but fair," Victoria said. "Already she has helped out more than one young woman in the village." She gave Bal a significant look. "These were young girls who had nowhere else to turn, and plenty of people are aware of how much she has done to give them something to live for."

Which probably meant that Io would lock horns with Edith even more violently if his brother's fiancé discovered that his sister was championing her causes right on the duke's doorstep, so to speak.

"My twin is an impressive person," Bal said, pride for his sister mixing with worry. He thought Zeus was fair, but if Io forced him to choose between her and Edith? Well, he didn't want to think about that.

"The servants and villagers adore all your brothers and sisters," Victoria said.

"I am pleased to hear it. No doubt we provide a bit of local color."

"It is more than that; you are all kind and thoughtful."

"Thank you, I hope we are."

"And people are impressed with His Grace, as well," she added, "although most are too intimidated to say much to him."

Bal smiled at that. "For all that Zeus appears a bit stiff, he is a very good sort. He is honorable and honest, if not exactly… warm. His betrothal is"—Bal paused, considering what he was about to confide. Not that he or his siblings had hidden their feelings about Edith, as Victoria's comment had just shown.

"Yes?" Victoria prodded.

Oh, what the hell? "Zeus deserves better than Miss Barrymore for a wife. The rest of us cannot understand why they are together. If not for her presence in the house I think there would be considerably less friction."

"There does seem to be tension between the five of you and His Grace."

"I think it is getting better. Slowly. We got off on the wrong foot," he admitted, leaving the matter at that. He didn't want to delve into a subject that bothered him more than he cared to admit.

He'd come to respect Zeus and greatly appreciated the help he was giving Bal and his brothers when it came to establishing themselves. He only wished the man didn't hold the purse strings and have so much control over his future. While Bal's opposition to marriage was not as strong as it had been even two months ago it was still odious that a man who barely knew him had the final say over his choice of spouse.

Balthazar looked at the woman who was occupying not only the cozy train car but more and more of his thoughts. Would Victoria pass muster when it came to Zeus's requirements for a respectable wife?

What would Bal do if she wasn't?

***

Balthazar was eating breakfast and looking over the contract that he'd brought back from London when the storm broke.

"Leave us."

Bal's head whipped up at the sound of Zeus's sharp words. The footman who'd been lingering in the room darted out the open door and closed it behind him.

He smiled up at his brother. "I didn't even hear you enter the room I was so deep in this contract your man from the bank gave me."

"The agreement for your loan?"

"Yes. It's a bit… dense."

"Come by my study and I can explain anything you wish."

Bal was genuinely touched by the offer. "Thank you, I might just do that." He realized his brother hadn't sat down, meaning he'd not come to eat. "Did you need me for something?"

Zeus's expression tightened. "Edith brought me this." He tossed a folded newspaper onto the table.

Bal pulled it toward him. "What am I supposed to be—" His name jumped off the page at him.

What was Lord B. doing at Claridge's yesterday evening? The Wicked Spare was spotted nipping out of the deluge to procure a room. A room for one, you ask? The answer to that question is up for debate. My sources at the illustrious hotel tell me that Lord B. took two suites, one for himself and one for his mysterious guest.

But only one of those beds was slept in…

Bal filled his lungs before looking up and meeting his brother's accusatory glare.

He sat back in his chair and crossed his arms. "Well?"

Zeus's frown deepened. "Edith told me that Mrs. Dryden also stayed overnight in London. She said the two of you met by accident at the station and took the train back together."

"How observant Edith is."

"Dammit, Balthazar! This is no laughing matter."

"I agree, Zeus. Doesn't your fiancé have anything to do other than to spread malicious rumors?"

"This is in the newspaper for the entire world to see—it's hardly Edith's fault that you decided to stay overnight with my housekeeper and made no effort to be subtle about it, either."

Bal tossed his napkin onto the table, his appetite suddenly gone. "For your information, I didn't *decide* to stay overnight. The weather was bloody awful and I missed the train." That was only half a lie. "It turned out that Mrs. Dryden did, as well. Yes, I paid for her room at the hotel. Otherwise, she would have been wandering around London in the dark and rain looking for someplace she could afford. I *did* try to be discreet. These newspapermen are like rats, Zeus, they are lurking everywhere and an expensive hotel like Claridge's is probably teeming with them."

"Tell me you are not having an affair with my housekeeper."

"Quit making it sound as if you own her body and soul, for God's sake. Yes, she is your employee, but she is hardly your slave, Zeus. What she does on her free day is not your concern."

His brother's eyes narrowed and Bal knew that Zeus was perfectly aware that he'd not answered the question.

"You are right that what she does isn't my concern"—Zeus flicked an angry gesture toward the newspaper— "at least not until it brings *this* to my door, Balthazar."

He wanted to tell his brother to mind his own damned business, but he couldn't. Because he agreed with Zeus. Bal no more wanted to drag his brother's good name through the mud than he wanted to shame Victoria. Which brought up the only *good* part of this lamentable gossip.

"At least the newspaperman did not refer to the person in the other room by name."

"Yes, there is that," Zeus agreed, his voice heavy with sarcasm, pinning Bal with his uncomfortable ice blue gaze.

"What?" Bal demanded.

"How long do you think her identity will be secret? Your name has made a damned fortune for these men. They will follow the crumbs to the cheese like the rats you've so aptly called them."

Again, Bal wanted to argue but knew his brother was right.

"Is there something between the two of you that I should know about, Balthazar?"

Was there? Bal was increasingly aware that he *wanted* there to be something. But he would jeopardize Victoria's position here—one she was already concerned about—if he admitted to something and didn't even know how she felt about him.

And so, to protect her, he lied to his brother again, "I paid for her room because I wanted her to stay somewhere safe."

Zeus stared at him for a long moment—as if he could smell deception—and finally said, “She should be told there might be some trouble. Will you do it, or should I?”

“I will do it.”

“Good.” He left the newspaper and strode toward the door.

“Zeus?”

His brother stopped and turned.

“Thank you for letting me take care of this.”

Zeus nodded, hesitated, and then added, “If you have any questions about that contract you may come see me any time, Balthazar. I will always put aside my other work to speak to you.”

Such kind words coming from Zeus’s stern mouth—even after he’d come to talk to Bal about something less than pleasant—were even more meaningful.

“Thank you,” Bal said. “I will check on the Peterson farm first, and then I will come to you. That way I can bring you my assessment of their soil as well as my findings on the other two properties I’ve looked at over the past week.”

“Good. I am eager to hear your opinion.”

Once his brother left the room Bal stared at the contract without seeing it, his mind on Victoria and how she would react to the story.

He felt like a jackass ringing the bell for her—summoning her to bad news, as it were—but his memory of the last time he’d barged in on the servant area was still too fresh.

So Bal sighed, stood, and went to his study so he could summon his lover.

***

Tori knocked on the door to Balthazar’s private sitting room and entered when she heard him call out.

He stood when she entered. “Good morning, Victoria. Thank you for coming. Please, sit.”

Tori hovered by the door, uncertainty joining the worry that had propelled her up here from the kitchen where she’d been breaking up a squabble between two of the new footmen about who got to wait on Lady Evadne.

It had amused her that the Hale family were so popular that His Grace’s employees were fighting over serving them. It did not escape her notice that she, too, was fighting over one Hale albeit in her quiet, sneaky way.

Sneaky because Victoria had only scheduled the older, less attractive maids to service Balthazar's room. Not because she feared he would trifle with them—she knew him too well now to believe such a thing—but because she was a jealous old shrew who didn't want him looking at pretty women and second-guessing his seeming attraction to her.

How pathetic.

"Would you like me to call for some tea, Victoria?"

She jolted slightly at the sound of her Christian name. "Nothing to drink, thank you," she said, perching on one of the seats in front of the cold fireplace.

He glanced at the distance between them and frowned. Then he hooked a foot around the leg of one of the chairs and pulled it closer to hers. When he sat, their knees all but touched.

He reached for her hand.

Tori glanced around, as if somebody might be hiding behind the settee.

He saw the look and said, "Nobody will come in here without permission. And I may call you Victoria in my own chambers." He spoke quietly but sounded rather fierce. He lightly chafed her hand between his. "You are cold. Do you want me to light a fire?"

"No, thank you." She frowned at the empty hearth. "Did the maid forget to build your fire, my lord? They are instructed to do so at this time of year."

He smiled. "I moved here from upstate New York, this is pleasant summer weather for me, and without all the biting flies." He hesitated, his gaze moving over her face before settling on her eyes. "There was a story about me—and a mystery lady—in one of the London newspapers today."

It was the last thing she'd expected to hear. "Oh."

"They didn't know who you were."

Tori heard the unspoken word *yet.* "It won't be difficult to find out my identity if any of them come to Symington and ask around the village. My absence was noticed. And people seem to like to read about you. It will be a story worth pursuing from the newspaper's point of view." Tori gently pulled her hand away. "It is as I said. I need to find another—"

"Zeus knows, Victoria."

"*What*?"

"Edith brought him the newspaper and he did the addition easily."

"He knows that we—"

"No. Not that. I told him that we met by mistake—which is true—but I didn't mention that I purposely missed the last train to wait for you. Nor did I mention anything else."

"This is—" she broke off and shook her head. What if Teddy read about this? What if—

Balthazar leaned closer. "Victoria, if something comes out, I won't let you face this alone."

"I should leave now—"

"That's a rather extreme response."

"But I won't be able to continue working here if the truth becomes known."

"The truth that we stayed in the same hotel? So did hundreds of others that night."

"You know better than anyone that it won't matter. People will believe the worst."

"Is it your son you are worried about?"

"I'm worried about all of it." She shook her head. "I couldn't bear to be the subject of scrutiny the way you have been these past months."

"That was different; Tirzah manufactured most of those articles to titillate. This is just speculation. It is annoying and some people will assume the worst about you—"

"The way I did with you."

He smiled. "And that didn't end up so badly for us, did it?"

She gave a slightly hysterical laugh.

"Everything will be fine," he said. "I promise."

"How can you promise that?"

"I will make sure you are fine. I won't abandon you to face matters alone. But we are too hasty—as of right now nobody except a few people in this house know the truth. Let's not look for trouble where none exists."

"Yet," she said.

"Yet," he agreed.

***

Victoria had taken to avoiding him again. Short of ringing the servant bell and summoning her—or lurking around her little cottage like some sort of hole-and-corner pervert—Balthazar could not contrive a way to see her.

He tolerated her evasion until a week passed—and it was clear that the newspapermen hadn't ferreted out her identity—and then he decided enough was enough.

Unfortunately, finding a way to be alone with her was not exactly easy.

Hastings Park was a veritable hive of industry and the plans for the ball had reached a feverish level as the spectacular event was approaching with alarming rapidity.

It was Balthazar's task to see that the terrace and gardens off the ballroom were presentable and illuminated enough to prevent injuries, but not so bright as to have a deleterious effect on romantic strolling.

Or so Eva had commanded.

His younger sister was enjoying herself tremendously by *actively* observing and commanding, but holding herself removed from any actual labor.

"I would not wish to cheat you of the experience, Bal," she said when he asked if *she* might like to take over the direction of the army of gardeners hurrying to bring the rather neglected grounds up to snuff.

Io and Victoria oversaw the decoration of the ballroom and environs, an activity which seemed to involve several hundred potted plants, dozens of bolts of gauzy pink material, and more candles than Bal had seen in one place in his life.

Apollo—by virtue of the fact that he played both the violin and piano quite well while the rest of them were tone deaf—took several day trips to nearby towns to audition various orchestras, until he found one that was good enough for his sister's grand birthday.

Ares, however, contributed perhaps the most important assistance. The ballroom at Hastings Park was both enormous and spectacular. It was also terribly neglected. Cleaning the chandeliers and installing new candles alone took almost a week with two servants working full time.

The floor in the ballroom had been laid sometime in the late sixteen hundreds and there had been a leak that had gone untreated for years—decades, even. It was Ares—with the assistance of several local carpenters—who painstakingly replaced the section of floor and spent hours testing various wood stains so that the repair was undetectable.

"It is amazing," Zeus had said when he'd walked back and forth across the floor, looking for what was old and what was new. "I simply cannot tell. You are truly an artist, Ares."

Ares had preened under Zeus's praise.

His younger brother *was* an artist with wood. At Balthazar's urging Ares had approached Zeus about his idea for a furniture business.

Bal had never seen his normally lighthearted sibling get so serious about anything before. The library had been fully occupied these past weeks, with Ares busy at one table, drawing up plans for a new workshop, Apollo at another occupied by various stud journals and researching innovations in stable construction, and Bal at the big desk, engaged in correspondence directing the construction of a new prototype at Malcolm Rowell's manufactory in Birmingham.

And all of it, he had to admit, was because of their oldest brother.

He couldn't help wondering if Zeus had realized that his assistance was beginning to make Bal question whether he really needed his grandfather's money to help his siblings.

Rather than wasting their allowances on gambling or other frivolity—which is what he'd feared his rather wild twin brothers might do—they were using the money they'd been given to create something. To build a life here.

Zeus's bank—and his faith in their abilities—was extending credit that would make all their dreams possible.

His siblings seemed to be flourishing in their new environment and with every day that passed it seemed less and less likely that any of them would return to Canoga—or even America—any time soon.

Bal had believed he'd miss home, but life in England was too damned interesting to leave him enough time to miss anything.

Indeed, the only part of his life that wasn't progressing the way he'd like was the part that included Victoria. Not only was he unhappy with the snaillike pace of their relationship, but he loathed being *discreet* when that meant slinking and sneaking and fearing discovery.

It was not in his nature to dissemble—he'd hated having to lie to Zeus—and Bal doubted he could continue this way much longer.

Things needed to change. And that change needed to happen soon.

To that end, he once again summoned Victoria to his chambers eleven long days after that elysian evening in London.

"Thank you for coming," Bal said when Victoria entered his study.

She dipped a curtsey, as if he were nothing more to her than the brother of the master of the house.

Suddenly her willingness to avoid him—to do without him—irked him. No, it infuriated and insulted him! If she wanted to treat him as nothing but an employer, then perhaps Bal should bloody well accommodate her.

"Come here," he said in a cool, brisk tone that made her stiffen.

He'd risen when she entered, but he sat down again, not inviting her to do so for the first time since he'd known her.

The flush that crept up from her high-necked gown told him that his behavior was not going unnoticed. Nor did she care for it. *Good*, he thought petulantly. He didn't care for her treatment of him, either.

"You have been avoiding me, Victoria."

"Is that why you called me here… *my lord*."

He almost smiled at how grudging those last two words were, but he caught the expression in time, instead firming his jaw and lifting his chin, emulating Zeus when he became all *lord of the manor*. "Answer my question."

Her nostrils flared and she swallowed, visibly choking on her anger. "Yes, my lord, I have been avoiding you."

"Why?"

"Because—" she broke off and scowled at him in a way that no good servant would look at one of their masters. "We were fortunate to get away with what happened once. We might not be so lucky a second time."

Bal didn't answer immediately. Instead, he steepled his fingers and stared at her. Her eyes sparked with… something. Defiance? Anger? Bal couldn't read the expression. But he could see his scrutiny unnerved her, and so he remained silent. Only when she shifted and dropped her gaze did he relent and speak. "What are you saying?"

"This"—Victoria gestured between them— "it must end. I thought"—she heaved a sigh. "Oh, I don't know what I thought, but I cannot continue with this, not when there is so much to lose."

"And the potential for what we might have together is not enough for you to take a risk?"

Disbelief blazed in her eyes. "You're asking me why an affair isn't worth my reputation? My son's reputation? My *job*?"

Bal shot to his feet, no longer interested in toying with her to get answers. "When did I ever say that all I wanted was an affair, Victoria?"

Her jaw sagged. "But…"

"But?" he prodded.

"But what else would you possibly want with me?"

Bal took a step toward her. "Why do you assume the worst? Why wouldn't I look at you as something more?"

"More—what do you mean?"

"A helpmeet, a companion. A wife."

Her eyes widened. "But you don't believe in marriage."

"I didn't." The words hung in the air between them. "Not until I met you."

Her mouth opened and nothing came out.

Bal was not displeased by his declaration, even though it hadn't been his intention to blurt it out so baldly. He'd spent the better part of the last eleven damned days mulling over their possible future.

He wanted more with her.

He wanted everything.

Bal stepped toward her, slid his hands around her waist, and jerked her closer. "Have I not shown how much I like you? How much I enjoy spending time with you, and not just in a bed—although that certainly ranks up at the top of activities I love—but in all ways." He leaned down and kissed her, sighing with soul deep relief at the already familiar feel of her soft, warm lips.

She hesitated only a moment and then her arms slid around him and she returned his kiss, her mouth eager and demanding.

Thank God. The words echoed inside him like the ringing of a bell. She felt so good—so right—that he wasn't sure he could ever let her go.

But all too soon, she pulled away, her brow furrowed with confusion and her robin's egg blue eyes filled with questions, although she remained silent.

"I don't want to go to London for the Season, Victoria."

"Oh?"

He smiled at the hopeful—almost fearful—look that leapt in her eyes. "I don't want to leave you here. I don't suppose you would care to come along?"

"Oh."

He chuckled. "Is that all you have to say?"

"Are you asking me to come to London and be your mistress?"

Bal frowned. "No, of course not!"

"I—I don't understand."

"You don't understand that I want something more permanent with you?" His frown eased slightly. "Unless—is that what you want? To be lovers? Are you opposed to marriage because of your bad experience?"

"No, I am not opposed"—she stopped and shook her head, giving him an adorably dazed look. "But we hardly know each other."

"We could remedy that if you quit running away from me."

She stared at him, visibly perplexed. "I don't understand you at all. Why me? I am not a young woman—you are five, almost six, years younger than me. You are handsome and wealthy. I've seen how women throw themselves at you. Your family connections ensure you entry into any home in England. You are kind and charming and—"

He laughed. "You'd better stop or my head won't fit out the door." He became serious. "Why you? Because you are strong and clever and—yes, so beautiful you bring me to my knees."

Her jaw sagged lower.

"You are generous—I've seen you with the servants and you rule with a gentle hand, Victoria." He paused and then said, "I know that you believe in second chances. Not just pay the notion lip service, but you actually *act* on your beliefs."

"What do you mean?"

"I know it was you who hired all the servants from that workhouse outside Birmingham. I can't imagine there is another ducal housekeeper in Britain who would have given those people such a chance."

"Oh."

"There it is again—*oh*," he teased.

"Is—that is have you told His Grace that some of his employees were criminals?"

"Yes, of course I did."

She grimaced.

Bal cupped her face in his hands. "Zeus is pleased with the way you managed affairs without any other help and hardly any money, Victoria. My brother is fair and has a generous heart. He believes in rehabilitation and is proud that Hastings Park has given people a new lease on life. I daresay he will hire more employees from there as time goes on."

Her shoulders slumped with obvious relief. "I don't regret doing it—even though I know it could have gone terribly wrong. But I've never had a single problem with any of the people I hired that way. I wanted to tell His Grace the truth, but—" she gave a shuddering sigh. "I am just relieved," she said simply, staring down at the floor.

Bal tilted her face back toward his. "I was not done singing your praises, Victoria. There is more I admire and adore about you. You love your son and have sacrificed much so that he might have a better life even though maintaining a connection with the family that wronged you must be unpleasant, you put his needs first. I enjoy matching wits with you because once you forget about the *lord* in front of my name you are direct and articulate and challenging. I like you because my twin admires you and Yoyo is never wrong about people. But most importantly"—he leaned close enough that their noses were almost touching—"I believe I am falling in love with you."

Tori's eyelids fluttered closed. "You must be mad."

"Why? Because you are not worthy of love, Victoria? Did somebody tell you that—is that what your awful cousin made you believe? Or Teddy? Look at me, darling." When she did, he smiled. "You've taken up so much space in my head that I should probably be charging you rent."

She gave a choked laugh.

"It's fortunate for me that I like having you in my head. In fact, I want more of you—not just in my thoughts and dreams, but in my arms and right beside me. I want to know what your favorite books are, what music seizes your heart and squeezes it until you ache at the beauty. I want to know if you can beat me in chess or at cards. I want to know if you enjoy a hell-bent gallop or a slow meandering ride. I want to meet the son you have sacrificed so much for." He cocked his head. "Is that enough to start with?"

She blinked rapidly and laid her head against his chest and exhaled. "I think that is the nicest thing anyone has ever said to me."

"You should hear nice things every day of your life, Victoria. Because you deserve nothing less." He kissed the top of her head but only got cotton instead of her silky hair. "I hate this cap you wear." Her body shook and he realized she was laughing. "Why is that funny? You are a beautiful woman—and yes, you are still a young woman. You shouldn't cover yourself like a granny."

Her head whipped up. "Did you just say I looked like a *granny*?"

"No. I said you dressed like one." He glanced down at the snug black bodice of her gown. "Although I admit I like you in black. But I also like you in color." He cocked his head. "I picture you in a celestial blue gown—something flowing and feminine and sensual. Something with an empire waist, made of the finest silk with little puffy sleeves and darker blue velvet trim."

She gave him a sideways look. "That sounds almost suspiciously specific."

Bal laughed. "It should do. I found it in one of those trunks you located for us." He reluctantly released her and strode toward his dressing room. When he came back, the gown he'd just described was in his hands. "Napier cleaned and pressed it and even did some minor repairs. He is a most impressive man."

"It's beautiful," she murmured, stroking the soft material. "From the Prince Regent's era."

"Yes. I thought the style would suit you." He could tell by the hungry look in her eyes that Victoria thought so, too.

She wrested her gaze from the gown and looked up at him. "But—what is this for?"

"It's for the ball."

"I can't—"

"Yes, you can. And you will." He smirked. "I command it."

That made her laugh.

"I mean it, Victoria. I want you to come. I am going to tell Zeus that I am inviting you."

"Oh, Balthazar! You can't do that."

"Why not?"

"Because… Well, just because."

"Sorry, sweetheart, but *because* isn't a convincing answer."

"I am a servant, Balthazar."

He gave her a gentle shake. "And I'm a farmer, Victoria. You can protest all you want about our different social stations but the truth is that you are far more suited to the life I inherited than I am. You are a baronet's daughter. I was raised in a commune digging in the dirt and getting my hands greasy from tinkering with bits of metal. If it were my life's goal to fit into *ton* society then I would probably die a miserable man because I would be a failure. That is not the life I want." Once again, he cupped her face and held her still so that she was forced to meet his gaze. "I can, however, visualize spending my life with *you*. So, come to this party—dance with me and flirt and kiss me behind that tropical forest of potted palms you and Io have created"—she laughed at that— "and maybe it will be one more step toward deciding if you could tolerate a farmer in your life. Hmm?"

"You really are a little mad, aren't you?" she said, shaking her head.

"In America, we call it being an individual and we revere it." He grinned. "But I might be a little bit crazy, too. Will you come to the ball, Victoria?"

For a long, long moment she stared into his eyes. "If His Grace says that I might, then I will."

"Good. And will you sneak into my room tonight?"

"*What*?"

"Or shall I sneak into your cottage? Perhaps that might be better. You were a tad vocal in our room in London when you shouted out your pleasure, I wouldn't want people to come running to my chambers worried that I was being attacked."

"I cannot believe you would say such a thing!"

"My ears have finally stopped ringing. Mostly. There is no permanent damage."

Victoria laughed and shook her head, her cheeks a fiery pink.

Balthazar pulled her close and claimed her mouth, kissing her until she was pliant in his arms. "Pull up your skirts for me, Victoria," he muttered against her temple, rolling his hips so that his erect cock thrust against the hard boning of her corset.

"Here?" she demanded in a scandalized tone, but Bal heard the waver in her voice.

"Yes. Do it. I need to touch you or I truly will go mad. Go on," he urged. "Just for a minute." He leaned close to her ear and hissed, "Just until you come all over my hand."

Her body jolted at his naughty threat.

"I should not encourage you," she said, even as her hands hastened to obey his order and pulled up the front of her gown.

"That's my girl," he whispered, making a beeline for the split in her drawers, his fingers parting curls and hot, slick flesh until he found what he wanted.

He sucked in a harsh breath. "You are so wet, darling. Is that for me?" Without any preamble he pushed his middle finger deep inside her and then caressed her little nub with his thumb, the bundle of nerves swelling quickly under his ministrations. "Is it?" he demanded.

"Y-yes."

"Yes, what?"

"Yes, Balthazar."

He smirked at the frustration in her voice, her hips bucking and jerking.

"You need release, don't you?" When she merely groaned Bal paused his erotic massage and lifted one eyebrow, gorging on the taut need on her face. "Or have you been touching yourself at night—thinking of my mouth and fingers on this tight little pussy."

"Balthazar," she gasped, her cunt clenching at his vulgar words.

"Have you touched yourself, Victoria? Tell me," he ordered, carefully easing a second finger into her tight sheath.

She bit her lip.

"*Tell me.*"

"Yes… Balthazar."

It was his turn to groan. "One night I will make you touch yourself while I watch." He chuckled when she tightened around his fingers hard enough to hurt. "Did you think of me when you pleasured yourself, Victoria," he asked, stroking in and out of her snug body, the wet sound of his pumping filling the room.

"Yes, Balthazar."

"I thought of you—sometimes two or three times a night," he confessed.

She gave one of her adorable, choked laughs. "Two or three times? That's quite… virile."

"You find that amusing, do you? Thinking of me suffering with need for you?" He could see that she did, her lips curling up into a smug smile as her juices drenched his hands and her scent assaulted his nostrils.

Bal gave a frustrated growl. "I need to taste you."

Victoria shuddered when he covered her with his mouth, her tight cunt clenching around his fingers in a way that made him sorely regret he wasn't hilt-deep inside her.

She was already so close that he'd barely commenced enjoying himself when she shattered, convulsing around his fingers and flooding his mouth with her arousal.

Bal pressed his thumb against her core, easily coaxing a second, more intense, orgasm from her quivering body.

"Balthazar," she cried out, shuddering, her fingers tugging on his hair hard enough to hurt.

As he knelt before her, Bal experienced a sudden, blinding truth.

He'd told her that he was falling in love with her, but that was a mile marker he'd somehow sped past without even realizing it.

He loved this woman and he didn't want to hide his emotions from her or anyone else; he wanted to shout it from the rooftops.

Whether Victoria did or could reciprocate his affections was something he did not want to ask at this point. For the time being he would be satisfied with drowning her in erotic pleasure. But he knew himself well. Soon, he would want more from her.

He would want everything.

Chapter 20

"You look positively glowing today—years younger. Have you done something new with your hair?" Auntie Max asked.

"No, nothing new," Tori said, praying that she wasn't blushing as she thought about the true reason she was *glowing*, all six feet of whom she would see again tonight, when he came to her cottage for the fourth night in a row.

A particularly savage gust of wind rattled the shutters. "My goodness," Auntie Max murmured. "I do hope this passes over before Lady Evadne's ball tomorrow night."

Tori seized the opportunity to talk about something other than her *glow*. "I am so delighted you are coming to the ball, Auntie. Will you wear a costume?" she teased.

"Of course. What?" she demanded when Tori's jaw dropped. "You think a costume is beneath my dignity?"

"No, not at all. I'm just—er, surprised, but pleased, too. What is your costume?"

"A surprise. You are wearing one, too, are you not?"

"Yes. Many of the servants who are working during the ball will be in some form of costume," Tori hastily pointed out.

Costumes for all the servants had been Lady Evadne's idea—one which Tori had fully embraced. After all, if the other servants were dressing up then Tori would not look so conspicuous.

The youngest Hale had done a great deal of research into the sorts of traditional face coverings worn during the famous Carnival of Venice and had purchased a variety of mask styles for anyone to use. If she hadn't already been the servants' favorite, that generosity had firmly won her the role.

Maxine gave Tori a penetrating look. "There is a rumor that Lord Balthazar is especially taken with you."

Tori groaned inside, but forced herself to give the other woman what she hoped was a vague smile. "The entire family has been very kind."

Maxine paused, an uncharacteristically hesitant look on her normally forthright features. "You know I care for you a great deal—like my own daughter, Victoria."

"And you are very dear to me, too."

"Given our friendship, I hope you will forgive me for being… indelicate, but Lord Balthazar—indeed, all the younger Hale children—have a different view of the world than you or me, Victoria."

"Yes, I imagine that is true."

"I won't beat about the bush, my dear. I heard about the overnight stay in London."

"Ah, yes." Tori wasn't surprised; she knew that word of her unusual night away would pique interest. And the fact that the duke's notoriously rakish brother was gone the very same night? Well… who could resist that?

"*Have* you been foolish, my dear?"

Tori hesitated.

"You needn't say more."

"But I didn't say anything."

"Oh yes, my dear, you did." Maxine suddenly looked older.

Tori knew her face would be red with shame, a reaction that infuriated her. She was a grown woman for pity's sake! Her private business was her own. She'd sacrificed any sort of personal life over the past decade and a half, surely she deserved—

"You are angry with me."

Tori looked up from the tambor that she was clutching with white-knuckled fingers, her needle no longer moving through cloth. The frustrated fury that had seized her so suddenly ebbed when she met the other woman's worried gaze. "I appreciate your concern for me, Maxine, but there is no need for it." She set aside her needlework and took the other woman's hand. "I was going to wait and tell you this after the ball—when the time came closer—but I am leaving soon. I have found a position in London."

Maxine's eyes widened. "*Leaving*? But… *why,* my dear? Did—did something bad happen?" Her face puckered, her expression almost… guilty.

Tori stared at her friend for a long moment, confused.

No, it was not guilt she saw in Maxine's eyes—but what?

She shook herself and lied yet again, "Nothing has happened. I'm moving to be closer to Jamie. He is growing so quickly and I want to be able to see him more often." At least that was true; she would have plenty of time on her hands to visit her son. Whether he would want to see her…

Well, that was another matter.

"But—but where will you go?" Maxine asked.

"To the house of a merchant industrialist. It is not so prestigious a position as here, but the wages are very good."

As far as lies went it was simple and believable. And it was certainly better than confessing the truth: that Jamie's father was threatening Tori with gaol and pulling her son out of school if she didn't quit working as a servant—and apparently embarrassing him—and move to the house he'd chosen for her.

Maxine grasped Tori's hands, her own cold but strong, for all that the bones felt so very fragile. "Oh, my dear! *Why* won't you accept Malcolm's offer? It is my fondest hope that you two will be together. I know you enjoy his company; surely you would come to love him if you only gave him a chance? He loves you and he adores Jamie. You would make a wonderful family. It would ease my mind so much to know you would be there to take care of each other when I am gone."

Tori leaned closer to the old woman, whose eyes had become dangerously glassy. "I *do* wish you wouldn't talk about you being gone." She squeezed her hands gently. "I'm sorry, Maxine. It simply cannot be. There are reasons—"

"Your past does not matter, my dear. He would love Jamie regardless of his birth."

"My past? What do you—"

"I know the truth, Victoria."

Tori stared.

"I have known almost since the first week you moved here all those years ago. So young and pretty and brave." She gave a sudden bark of laughter. "Trying to pretend you were older than you were. As if any intelligent person couldn't see you weren't much more than a baby yourself—caring for your baby. His Grace told me the truth, my dear. He knew what sort of rumors would accompany hiring such a youthful, pretty housekeeper. He asked me to take care of you."

Tori stared. "Oh."

"You look so shocked."

"I am. Why did you never say anything to me? Tell me that you knew?"

"I didn't want to remind you of a bad time in your life."

"I cannot believe that you would still encourage me to marry Malcolm knowing the truth about me," Tori said.

Maxine made a dismissive clucking sound. "You are not to blame for what happened. Your strength and dignity these past years have been awe-inspiring, Victoria. You are exactly what Malcolm needs. He is such a dear, dear boy—the sort of son I always wished to have—and he is deeply in love with you. I want him to be happy and have what he wants," she said. "And you deserve happiness, too. I believe you would find it with Malcolm." Her lips pursed. "I think you might have accepted his offer if not for"—she broke off, her papery cheeks flushing.

"If not for what?" Tori asked, although she knew what the other woman would say.

"Lord Balthazar." Maxine snorted. "It fairly shines out of you like a lighthouse beacon, Victoria. You are in love with him, aren't you?"

Tori hesitated, but then nodded. "Yes."

Maxine heaved a sigh and shook her head. "He won't marry you, Victoria. You know his people do not believe in marriage."

"I'm not sure that is so true anymore. He—he has indicated that is what he wishes."

Maxine's eyes went wide at the news. "Indeed? But—if you return with him to America won't you have to"—she stopped, her pale, papery skin darkening. "You've read what goes on there, my dear. He would take lovers—you would be expected to, as well. Would you really wish to live there?"

Tori shook her head—as if she could shake away the thought of Balthazar with another woman. "No," she said firmly. "He does not think he will return to Canoga—or even America. I believe he is finding a place for himself here."

Maxine's eyes filled with something that looked a great deal like pity.

"What?" Tori asked.

"You must know that the secret of your past would not stay secret if you married a man like him. The newspapers *love* him, Victoria. They would dig through your past. Everything would come out. It would destroy any chances that Jamie might have for a better"—she broke off and bit her lip. "I'm sorry, I should never have said—"

"It is no less than what I've concluded," Tori said, but still felt pain at hearing her friend voice her concerns. "That is why I'm leaving to take this other position."

"And what has Lord Balthazar said about that?"

"I haven't told him. I—well, he would resist my decision." He would be furious at her and he would try to convince her and she would probably let him. And then—as Maxine said—the truth would destroy her son.

"You will leave and not tell him?" Maxine guessed.

"Yes." And it would probably break her heart.

Maxine nodded, relief in her eyes. "I think that is for the best, my dear."

Her friend's agreement caused a sharp pain in Tori's chest, as if she'd hoped the older woman would counsel otherwise.

As if there was some way that Tori might get to stay with the man she loved.

***

Balthazar pushed his damp hair off his forehead and collapsed onto his back. The rain had let up around midnight but the air was heavy with the promise of more. Not that the sweat on his body was the result of temperature. At least not entirely.

Bal turned to Victoria as she ran a firm hand over his belly, her work-roughened fingers chafing the thin skin of his abdomen as she absently stroked him.

"You seem distracted tonight, Balthazar," she said, sounding more concerned than critical.

"Did I not satisfy you, Victoria?" he teased.

Even in the firelight he saw the blush that spread from her lovely breasts up her neck. "You know you satisfied me—several times."

She rolled onto her side, so that she was facing him, seemingly unaware or unconcerned by her own nudity. It was an action which pleased him because it was so much more relaxed and confident than she'd been even a few days before. Every night that he came to her cottage Victoria became more comfortable with him. It was progress and it was occurring faster than he had hoped.

"Tell me what is bothering you," she said, her hand still caressing.

"Edith and Io had another… argument." Although that word didn't seem sufficient to describe the cold fury that had arced between the two women in the drawing room earlier that evening.

"Ahh, I'd heard that."

He smiled absently. "Of course, I should have known—they didn't wait until the family was alone. I'm sure you heard about it down in the kitchen before the fight was even over. So, you must know the subject under dispute, then?"

"Your sister is going to cut her hair shorter and dress in the clothing of your commune for the ball?" she said, her hand drifting lower.

Bal nodded and sucked in a breath, his hips lifting off the bed as Victoria absently stroked his erection, the tips of her fingers grazing all the way down to his full, aching balls.

"That is very naughty, Victoria," he said through clenched teeth.

She lowered her eyes demurely, but her lips curved into a slight but smug smile.

Tonight, as usual, Bal had brought her to climax several times while delaying his own release. There was something about making himself wait that was excruciatingly pleasurable—almost painfully so—and he knew she enjoyed teasing and tormenting him when he was in this heightened state, each night she'd become dangerously more skilled and more eager to see if she could break him.

Bal relished her efforts and suspected she would, one day soon, get her way.

"What are you going to do?" she asked.

For a moment he could not recall what they'd been talking about.

"You mean about Io and her costume?" he asked.

She nodded.

He shrugged. "Nothing. It is my sister's decision."

"And the duke?" she asked, her fingers sliding around his aching shaft.

Bal paused before he answered, thinking about his brother's reaction to the angry confrontation earlier. Zeus hadn't said a word, which was unusual as he generally tried to step in before matters could get out of hand. But his brother had looked distant and detached, almost as if some other matter was consuming his thoughts. Although how he could think of anything else when the two women—both strong-willed and neither accustomed to not having their own way—were clashing, he did not understand.

"Zeus said nothing," Bal finally answered, thrusting into her fist—which she was keeping deliberately loose to tease him. "And then Io and Edith both stormed out, with poor Miss Barclay right behind her mistress." His brother had blinked when the door slammed behind the women—almost as if he'd been in a trance—and then he'd stood and left without a word. It had been extremely odd.

Bal turned to her. "What do you think of Yoyo's costume?"

"I think it is a good idea."

Bal snorted.

"No, I really do," she insisted.

"Why?"

"Because people know about your past—it is on everyone's minds all the time. Why try and hide where you come from, as if you are ashamed? There have been dozens of descriptions of Canoga and the inhabitants. By wearing the clothing, she will rob the subject of its mystery."

He turned toward her and smiled. "That is exactly what Io said."

"Well, it is only commons sense." She tightened her grip, drawing a groan from him.

"Hell and damnation," he hissed from between clenched jaws, both of them looking down to where she pumped his cock.

Victoria shifted until she could stroke his belly with her other hand, her expression rapt as she traced the ridged muscles of his lower abdomen.

Bal preened under her admiring gaze, shamelessly flexing for her, thrilling at the way her lips parted as she stared, her blue eyes darkening with lust. He fucked her fist harder, each thrust lifting his ass and back off the mattress, wishing he were inside her body instead of—

Her hands suddenly stopped. "I want to pleasure you the way you do me, Balthazar, but it has been a long time, and I—"

"I want that," Bal said, not caring that he was rudely interrupting. He spread his thighs so she could kneel between his legs. "I've dreamed about your lips wrapped around my cock, Victoria."

***

Tori positioned herself between Balthazar's muscular thighs—which were far paler than his torso—and glanced up from his slick phallus when he dragged two cushions across the bed and tucked them beneath his head.

He smirked down the length of his body. "I want to watch."

Her already hot face became hotter and she wondered if she would ever become accustomed to his joyous, earthy approach to sex.

And then she remembered that she'd be leaving soon and would never have the chance.

"Don't you want me to?" he asked, obviously misreading her expression.

"I am not nearly so skilled as you," she temporized. "I will be a disappointment."

He laughed. "I don't think that is possible."

Tori *did* want him to watch; there was nothing more arousing than watching this strong, powerful man break beneath her touch.

She held his gaze as she leaned low enough to lick the tiny slit in his crown, taking the salty drop on her tongue.

He groaned and his hips lifted. "Fuck!"

She smirked, more accustomed to the vulgar word after spending a few nights with her verbal, enthusiastic lover.

"More," he gasped as she teased only the head. 'Take me in your mouth," he begged, his hand creeping into her hair and then withdrawing again, as if he feared what it might do there.

Tori took him by the wrist and replaced his hand on her head.

He paused his thrusting. "Are you sure? I will forget myself and become rough," he warned. "Remember that I'm not a gentleman, Victoria."

"I want you to forget yourself," she said, and then took him inside her mouth, rolling the fat crown on her tongue, flicking the underside as she'd been taught by another man so long ago.

He muttered something indecipherable and his fingers tightened in her hair, his hips lifting, filling her until she thought she'd choke.

Just as she began to panic, he eased off. His hand also loosened, fingers carding through her tangled mess of hair.

"So good," he muttered in a slurred voice, hips pulsing softly.

His fingers slid down her cheek and jaw and lightly touched her lips. his eyes slitted, his lips curved into a hungry smile as he watched her. "You look so beautiful taking me, Victoria."

She preened under his adoring gaze, lapping up his praise even as she tongued him, careful to protect him from her teeth.

"Yesss," he hissed, his hips lifting while his other hand palmed the back of her head, gently pulling her lower and filling her.

Her sex pulsed as he used her for his pleasure, taking what he wanted the way Tori did when she rode his face—which was the way they had begun every evening this past week.

She felt his knee nudge hers.

"Straddle my leg so I can feel you," he said, his lazy smile taunting as he pushed his leg against her swollen sex. "So wet and hot," he muttered when she complied, his eyelids drifting closed as his thrusting became more demanding, deeper.

Tori felt his control splinter, his thrusting becoming jerkier, the sense that he was already shattering bringing her own desire to the fore.

The sounds of their passion filled the room—rude, wet noises that should have shamed her but instead spurred her on, her hips grinding against his hard thigh even as his shaft thickened in her mouth.

"Tori," he gasped as his body arched. He tugged on her hair to lift her head—to spare her his release—but she resisted, wanting all of him, taking everything he had to give because she knew their time together was almost over.

***

Balthazar groaned and stretched, immediately aware of the small body contoured along his side.

He blinked against the candle that was still burning on the bedside table and turned his head to his lover. "I fell asleep, didn't I?"

"For a little while."

"Did you?"

"No."

He smiled. "Were you staring at me adoringly while I slept?"

She snorted. "You are vain."

"You were, weren't you?"

"How could I resist?"

He laughed and then kissed her, the light peck quickly deepening. When he reluctantly pulled away to allow her to breathe, he said, "How would you like to stare at my face every night? And every morning, too."

The laughter in her eyes drained away. "What do you mean?"

"Marry me, Victoria."

She pushed up onto her elbow. “Are you—is this a joke?”

“I have never been more serious. I know what I want, and what I want is to be with you every night. I’m sick of needing to sneak and skulk to share your bed and enjoy your body.”

She just stared at him.

“I cannot tell if you are happy or not,” he admitted when the silence stretched.

“Have you thought about this, Balthazar?”

“You mean have I thought about your past and the fact that it will likely get out if we marry?”

She nodded.

“Yes, of course I’ve thought about it. And I know it will impact your son, but I believe the home we can offer him together, and the security I can give you both, will make up for any embarrassment he might face. He cannot run and hide from who he is all his life, Victoria.”

She swallowed, but still didn’t speak.

“Why won’t you talk to me?”

“I’m just—shocked.”

“You couldn’t tell how I felt about you?”

“I didn’t know you felt so… deeply.”

He smiled. “It appears that I misspoke when I said I was falling in love with you. I have fallen, utterly and completely. I love you, Victoria.”

“Oh.”

Bal couldn’t help laughing, although there was little amusement in it. It was not the response he’d been hoping for, but there was no turning back now.

He reached up and lifted a long, curly lock of hair over her shoulder, exposing her lovely breast to his hungry gaze. “If you don’t want to marry me then I will respect your decision. You should not worry that I will make your life uncomfortable here. I’ve recently purchased a farm not very far from here. There is a nice house”—he smiled—“nothing compared to Hastings Park, of course, although it is in need of nearly as much work. But it will be a comfortable home for a gentleman farmer and there is an old barn where I can pursue my tinkering. I would like for you to share that home with me, but if you do not wish to do so you can rest in the knowledge that I will not make your life unpleasant by remaining here.”

Still, she did not speak.

Bal chuckled ruefully. "I must admit I'd hoped for a slightly different response, darling."

***

Victoria knew she was behaving like a fool, but she simply could not believe he was offering her marriage. Not only was there the matter of his past and his beliefs, but he was a duke's *brother.*

"Don't you care about what people will say?" she blurted.

"You mean about you never having been married? Or you being a housekeeper? Or Jamie?"

"Yes, all of that. You were right about the newspapers digging until they unearthed the truth. You will be in the public eye yet again."

"I weathered it once before, I can do so again—and for a much, much better reason." He slid a warm hand around her neck. "Is scandal the only objection you have to me, Victoria?"

She looked into his vibrant green eyes and saw so many emotions: love and hope were the most prominent.

But Tori saw a foreign expression, too—at least foreign to him: vulnerability. And why wouldn't he look vulnerable? He had laid his heart at her feet.

Tori suddenly imagined how it must feel to tell somebody you loved them first.

And then hear nothing in return.

She was the reason this strong, confident man was suddenly vulnerable. All he'd done since meeting her was make her feel clever, pretty, and desirable.

And how had she repaid him?

By concealing and protecting her emotions at all costs.

"I—I love you, Balthazar."

His eyes widened and his handsome face shifted into an expression of wonder.

"But I'm not sure that will be enough," Tori quickly added. "My past is so ugly. Not just the humiliation of that bigamous marriage, but there is still the issue of the theft charge and my time in gaol, which an eager journalist would be sure to unearth."

"Surely the current earl would come forward and admit his part now? Or at least insist you were innocent?"

Tori opened her mouth to confess—to say that Teddy most certainly would *not* be happy to admit that, even less so now that he was

Westmoreland—and to tell Balthazar about that awful letter and how Teddy was using the not-so-subtle threat of gaol to coerce her to quit her job.

And yet the words would not come.

"Even if he doesn't admit it," Balthazar went on when she didn't reply, "there is a time limit on such prosecutions—a statute of limitations. At least there is in America. I don't know what it is for theft, but surely it is not—"

"There is no limit here," she said quietly. "I have consulted a solicitor on the matter."

He stared, aghast. "You mean he could have you thrown in jail again?"

She nodded.

Balthazar pushed up on the bed, until he was sitting, his expression one of shock. "I cannot believe he would do that. And if he did, we would fight it. I might not be a peer like Westmoreland, but I am not without means, Victoria. And I would shamelessly exploit my connection to Zeus to fight for you. He would be on our side, too. He would not allow—"

"Think of my son having to live through such an ordeal, Balthazar. What if I were convicted?" she whispered, the possibility of such a future almost too horrible to be spoken aloud. "He already threatened to take Jamie away from me. He could do that if I were in gaol."

He stared at her, and Tori could see that he finally understood her fear. He was imagining her in some wretched cell.

And she was imagining how it would be for a young boy, away at a school where his presence was already tenuous, dealing with such scandal. Jamie would be mocked and derided. It would be miserable. Unbearable.

Balthazar heaved a sigh. "Yes, the shame and gossip would be awful for him."

"It would."

He flopped down on the bed and shoved a hand through his hair. "There has to be a way to do this that won't cause so much damage."

Victoria could have told him there wasn't.

"As for him taking your son away from you? I don't see how he could do that—unless you have acknowledged him as the father?"

"No, but his father paid for Jamie's schooling. Isn't that an admission of sorts?"

Balthazar sighed heavily. “I don’t know. I need to think about this for a while.” He turned to her, his stern expression suddenly lightening. “You love me.”

Tori smiled. “I wasn’t sure you’d heard that part,” she admitted wryly. And she probably should have kept it to herself. No, she *definitely* should have kept it to herself. Especially since she would be leaving him in barely a week.

Chapter 21

Here you are!" Bal said, and then felt more than a little guilty when Victoria yelped and spun around. "Sorry, I didn't mean to frighten you, darling." He slid an arm around her and quickly pulled her into the convenient alcove behind them.

"Balthazar, we shall be seen," she protested in between kisses.

He ignored her chiding and engaged in some of his own. "You promised not to hide from me anymore and yet you have been doing exactly that all day and all evening."

"Oh, well, there have been so many preparations and—"

"Yes, I understand you've been busy with the ball. So busy that you forgot to put on the costume I gave you."

"Oh, that."

"Yes, *that*." He pulled back and critically examined her drab gray gown and huge white apron and *enormous* white mobcap. "What *is* this outfit? Did you purposely choose this despicable head covering to torment me?"

She had the audacity to smile. "No, it is part of my costume. I'm a medieval housekeeper. This is far more appropriate to my station than the one you wanted me to wear."

"I *hate* that word."

"Housekeeper?"

"Very droll. No, I mean the word *appropriate*. I wanted to see you in that blue gown." He growled and pulled her closer. "You've disobeyed me and been very sneaky about it, Victoria."

"See what a horrid wife I would make?"

He cupped her luscious bottom—which was gloriously devoid of any bustle or cage or other nonsense—with both hands. "Actually," he said, squeezing her buttocks, "I find that I quite like this costume."

"*Balthazar*."

"Shut up and kiss me."

She did so, and several pleasurable minutes passed while they reacquainted themselves with each other after the long desert between last night—when he'd sneaked out of her cottage at three in the morning—and right now, which was the first time he'd managed to get close to her all evening.

Balthazar finally decided it was time to breathe and released her, but still held her in a loose embrace. "You promised to save me two dances," he reminded her.

"No, you *told* me to save you two and didn't wait for a response."

"You don't want to dance with me?"

She heaved an exasperated sigh. "I cannot dance, Balthazar."

His eyebrows shot up. "You don't know how?"

"Of course I know *how*. But it would be—"

"Don't say it," he said, laying a finger across her lips.

"Inappropriate," she muttered.

"You *are* disobedient. Weren't employers allowed to punish their servants during the medieval period? Yes," he said, grinning. "I believe they method of punishment was usually a good spanking."

She scoffed. "It was not."

"No, no—I'm *positive* it was. Twenty crisp swats on the offender's bottom. Their *bare* bottom," he amended, already hard just imagining the sight.

She lifted an eyebrow at him.

"What?"

"You are *not* dressed as a lord of the manor," she reminded him, plucking a piece of strategically placed straw from his messy hair. And then ruining her stern schoolmistress impression by laughing. "Wherever did you get an idea for such a silly costume?"

"Yoyo came up with it. I suppose I should be insulted that my twin thinks I make an excellent scarecrow."

"We don't call them that here."

"Ah, that's right—*hay man* is the proper term."

"We call them *murmets* where I grew up. And you are far too handsome to make a convincing one—but I think you already know that."

He grinned. "No, tell me more. How handsome am I?"

"I have to get back—"

"You are not going anywhere—not until you dance with your murmet."

"Balthazar, I can't dance out there with—"

He heaved an exasperated sigh. "Yes, yes. I anticipated your protest. Come, I know the perfect place." He took her hand and glanced around the corner of the alcove. "All is clear," he said, and then pulled her along at a trot.

"Where are we—"

"Shhhh."

Bal was no fool; he'd known that she would try and weasel out of dancing with her, so he had taken preemptive measures earlier in the day. He'd waited until the musicians had set up for practice and then found the perfect spot—somewhere he and Victoria could be private but still hear the music.

Bal stopped beside a rather magnificent, if motheaten, floor-to-ceiling tapestry.

"We can't go up there," Victoria said as Bal pushed aside the tapestry and exposed the doorway cut into the stone.

"Oh, yes we can."

"But there are all the crates and old carpets and—"

"I had them moved," he said, ushering her up the stairs and then carefully rearranging the tapestry behind them.

The staircase to the minstrel gallery was narrow and he couldn't imagine how awful it would be to tote instruments up all these steps.

Edith—whose promise to stay out of the ball planning had lasted less than a week—had wanted to put the orchestra up here, but Zeus had put his foot down after consulting Apollo, who'd assured their older brother that the orchestra he'd engaged was too large for the space.

Which had left it available for Bal's purpose.

"Oh, how pretty," Victoria said when she saw that the space was clear of everything except the candles he'd placed earlier, some in the wall sconces and some on the small round table which held a bucket of iced champagne, two glasses, and some flowers he'd pilfered from the displays in the ballroom.

"Have a seat," he said, opening the bottle.

"Did you do all this for me?" she asked, her cheeks rosy in the candlelight.

"I did it for a lady in a lovely blue gown, but she jilted me," he said, smiling to soften his words.

"I love the dress, Balthazar, but—"

"But you are more comfortable garbed as you are."

She nodded. "Yes."

"You can wear the gown when we host our first masquerade ball at Fairview," he told her, filling the glasses.

"Is that the name of your house?" she asked.

"I hope it is the name of *our* house."

She smiled and lifted her glass. "I propose a toast. To the American Hales."

"Why, thank you—I accept on all their behalf." They sipped and he set down his glass and pulled his chair closer to hers. "I know I told you that I would not pressure you to decide, but I thought I should describe how wonderful Fairview is—just in case you were swayed by spectacular views, pretty streams and a reflection pond, and an extensive rose garden that is awaiting a woman's touch."

"It sounds lovely. You will return to farming?"

"Eventually. The land has been overworked and needs healing, but in a few years I hope to be a gentleman farmer." He took her hands. "You did a lovely job with this ball, Victoria—and no, I can see you are going to try and insist you didn't do the lion's share of the work, but I *know* you did. Thank you. Eva is clearly delirious with joy.

Victoria smiled fondly. "She seems very happy—and very beautiful in that gown. The poor country lads all looked a bit dazed."

"It was a good rehearsal for London."

"Your family will leave for London soon," she said. "Are you going with them?"

"It is up to you where I go, Victoria." Before she could answer, the orchestra cued a waltz. "Ah, here is our dance," Bal said, getting to his feet and taking her hand.

She was as light and graceful in his arms as he'd known she would be, her eyes closing as he whirled her around their tiny dance floor for two.

"You are an excellent dancer," he murmured, holding her far too close to be proper on any other dance floor.

"So are you."

"You sound surprised," he teased. "I would hardly deserve my title of world-class libertine if I did not know how to dance."

She chuckled. "No, that is true. So you had dances at Canoga?"

"Oh yes, we seized any opportunity to celebrate. I also attended some grander functions when I was away at university. What about you, darling? Did you dream of a magnificent Season as a girl? Did you imagine whirling around in the arms of a handsome lord?"

"I did," she admitted, not resisting when Bal pulled her closer, holding her even more *inappropriately*.

"You never imagined you'd end up dancing with a scarecrow, did you?"

"No, I'll admit that did not enter my mind." She hesitated and then said, "But I cannot imagine anyone I'd rather dance with more, Balthazar."

Her words sent both a rush of pleasure and relief through him, all the more so because she generally was not so forthright or affectionate. True, it was not an acceptance of his offer, but neither was it an outright *no*.

It would not be easy to be patient, but Bal could wait for her.

She was worth all the time in the world.

***

Tori hurried toward the kitchen, cursing her inability to say *no* to a certain ridiculously gorgeous scarecrow. But it was almost three o'clock—the unmasking had come and gone ages ago, with Tori and Balthazar peeping from the balcony of the minstrel's gallery at midnight—and she had been missing from the ball for almost four hours now.

But whenever she mentioned returning to her duties, Balthazar would distract her with a kiss or a question or a dance or a story.

You wanted to be distracted.

That was true enough. Even though she'd been garbed in a humble gown and hidden away in the minstrel's gallery this had been the debutante ball that she'd never had.

And it had been glorious, not just up in the minstrel's gallery with Balthazar, but the ball itself had been perfect.

There was still music and dancing in the ballroom, but the older guests had left hours before. The party would go on until dawn and many revelers would stay to partake in the breakfast that would be laid out on the terrace. If it had rained last night then she would have used the dining room, but the storm had blown past, and the sky had been blue and the weather crisp yesterday.

Leaving Balthazar had been wrenching. Their evening together had been like a dream, and she hated that it had to end.

It doesn't ever have to end. You could accept his offer of marriage, brave the scandal, and live with the man you love instead of going to a man you loathe.

That argument, or some form of it, had been running through her head for days, like a catchy tune that she couldn't entirely banish.

At first, Tori had tried to resist the lure, but—increasingly—she'd come to accept that marriage to Balthazar was not quite as impossible as it seemed. After all, he was the sort of man a woman could trust. He knew about her past with Teddy and would stand by her when and if Teddy acted on his threat and prosecuted her for theft. Yes, Jamie would likely suffer shame if that happened, but he would gain Balthazar in his life.

Marry him, Victoria. You cannot seriously be contemplating moving into Teddy's house and becoming his pensioner—even if his intentions really are honorable, which you must admit is unlikely. Living such a half-life would have been miserable before. Now that you are in love with another man, it will be pure hell.

Tori stumbled as the thought slammed into her, slowing her almost headlong run to the kitchen. She stared unseeingly at the worn carpet beneath her feet, her mind reeling.

You—and Jamie—can weather any storm with a man like Balthazar Hale beside you.

Tori knew the voice was right. She'd never met anyone so fierce, confident, and steady—it wouldn't be like the last time, when she'd been alone and beholden to the old earl for whatever scraps of support he'd seen fit to give her.

This time she would have somebody to stand beside her.

She could accept Balthazar's offer and they would be happy together. They would face what came—good or bad—together.

The joy—and relief—that suffused her body at the thought was so powerful that her knees almost buckled.

She grinned like a fool. Yes, she would marry him. She would—

"Mrs. Dryden."

Tori yelped at the sound of the quiet voice and spun around to find Miss Barrymore standing behind her.

"Oh, Miss Barrymore. You gave me a start." Where in the world had she been hiding so that Tori had not even seen her?

The other woman drifted toward her, seeming to float in her severe lavender gown. The half-mourning color flattered her dark hair and eyes, making her look fragile and romantic, two things Tori did not believe she was.

Unlike the rest of the Hales Miss Barrymore had not gone to the ball, but she'd presided over the duke's dinner table, leaving no doubt in anyone's mind that she was mistress of Hastings Park in everything but name.

"You seemed quite… distracted by something, Mrs. Dryden. Happily so, judging by the smile on your face."

"I was thinking about how well the ball went," Tori lied, irked that the other woman had witnessed her brief, and private, moment of elation.

"Did you enjoy the ball, Mrs. Dryden?"

"Er, yes, thank you, Miss Barrymore."

"I saw you with His Grace's brother up in the minstrel's gallery."

Tori cursed silently; she *knew* she shouldn't have allowed Balthazar to persuade her to watch the unmasking.

"It's true that we were up there," she admitted, because what else could she say?

"Lord Balthazar is very charming." Miss Barrymore prowled around her in a circle.

The hair on the back of Tori's neck stood up when the other woman disappeared behind her, and it took all her self-control not to whip around. "Yes, all the duke's siblings are very charming, Miss Barrymore."

"But Lord Balthazar especially has an attraction for a certain kind of woman—older women, to be sure."

Tori didn't know what to say to that—at least nothing that wouldn't get her sacked. "I had not noticed that," she lied yet again.

Miss Barrymore chuckled dryly. "Oh, hadn't you? Because I couldn't help noticing that you have fallen to his not inconsiderable charms, Mrs. Dryden. As you are one of His Grace's servants, I feel that I have a duty to warn you."

"Warn me?"

Miss Barrymore came to a halt in front of her, towering over Tori by half-a-head. It irked Tori that she had to crane her neck to look up at the other woman.

"I am going to share something with you that is a very closely held secret, Mrs. Dryden. It would make my fiancé and Lord Balthazar very unhappy if it what I'm about to tell you were to be widely known."

"Then perhaps you shouldn't share it, Miss Barrymore."

The other woman's lips pursed at her tart response. "It is incumbent on me as a female to tell you. I believe all women are part of a sisterhood and owe each other certain… duties."

Tori wanted to laugh. She couldn't recall ever meeting a woman who treated other females with more suspicion than Miss Barrymore did.

"Lord Balthazar's grandfather was an extremely wealthy man—he was Horace Sinclair. Perhaps you heard of him?"

"The shipping magnate?" Tori repeated, surprised.

"Yes. He was grandfather to the five younger Hale children—no relation to His Grace, who had a different mother."

Tori was more than a little surprised that Balthazar had never mentioned his illustrious—and wealthy—grandfather. Indeed, he'd given Tori to believe that he'd been nothing but a humble farmer before the duke had brought him to England.

"Horace Sinclair made Balthazar his one and only beneficiary."

Tori waited without speaking, not sure where the other woman was headed.

"There was only one stipulation for him to inherit," she went on. "Can you guess what it was, Mrs. Dryden?"

"No."

"Horace Sinclair wanted his grandson to marry—*required* it, as a matter of fact. If you have read anything about the commune where His Grace's siblings were raised you will know that marriage is strongly discouraged." A look of distaste flickered across her cold but lovely features. "In other words, if Balthazar wants to inherit over four million dollars, he has go against his own beliefs—his religion, in effect—and marry."

Tori just stared, her mind spinning like a toothless cog as she tried to imagine four million of anything—people, stars in the sky, blades of grass in a field. No, she couldn't comprehend that number.

Four. Million. Dollars.

"Yes," Miss Barrymore said, even though Tori hadn't spoken. "It is an astronomical amount, isn't it?"

"Why are you telling me this?" she asked, a sickening sense of dread growing inside her.

"Because marriage wasn't Horace Sinclair's only stipulation. His will also requires Lord Balthazar to marry a respectable woman if he is to inherit."

Respectable.

It was like the clanking of a cell door in Tori's mind, and she was on the inside, looking out through the bars.

"Respectable?" Tori repeated, refusing to crumble in front of this woman. "Who can determine that, I wonder?"

Miss Barrymore smiled thinly. "There is a three-man group, all conservative bankers with illustrious lineages themselves, and they are the ones who will decide the matter. So, if Balthazar were to marry oh, let's say, an unwed mother or a convicted criminal—or even an *accused* criminal—the trustees would have to abide by the terms of Mr. Horace Sinclair's will and deny him the money."

Tori swallowed down the sickness that threatened to choke her. She held the other woman's gaze, looking for *something*. Spite, amusement, vindication—but she saw nothing in her opaque eyes.

"I'm not telling you this to hurt you," she said, as if she could hear Tori's thoughts. "I'm telling you because *he* won't tell you. Despite all the stories you might have read about Lord Balthazar, he truly is an honorable man, and a chivalrous one. He will rescue you—that is his nature. And later, when you find out everything that he gave up for you?" She gave an elegant shrug. "Well, I know how I would feel when I discovered that *I* was the reason my husband was a pauper. No matter how kind and good a man is, he will eventually live to regret such a decision." She smiled, the action a mere rearranging of muscles, rather than an actual expression of any emotion. "I thought you deserved to know. Good night, Mrs. Dryden."

Tori watched her leave, and slumped against the wall, not trusting her own legs to move. Her mind was a chaotic whirl where one thought gradually rose above all the rest.

Miss Barrymore had been right: Balthazar really was intent on rescuing her—regardless of the cost to him.

Nobody in their right mind would ever claim that Tori was respectable. Which meant that Balthazar had asked her to marry him even though he knew that he would lose all that money.

Tori had teased him repeatedly that he was mad.

He wasn't mad, he was a victim of his own honor.
Unless somebody saved him from himself.

Chapter 22

"I'm sorry to wake you up so early after last night," Zeus said as he and Balthazar rolled away from Hastings Park in his brother's traveling coach, the one with the escutcheon emblazoned on the sides. Beside the carriage rode four outriders in addition to the coachman and the two liveried servants perched on the back.

It was like a royal procession.

"I actually hadn't gone to sleep yet," Bal confessed, smothering a yawn.

"It was a good party," Zeus said, lazily stroking Mr. Clemens, who was sleeping up on the seat beside his brother. "You, Io, and Mrs. Dryden did an excellent job."

Bal smiled, pleased and surprised by his reserved brother's praise. "Thank you. Eva was very happy. I think she is now more comfortable about attending her first London ball."

"As am I," Zeus confessed.

"If you can go to a party dressed as the king of Olympus you should have no trouble going as a mere duke," Bal pointed out, laughing.

Zeus flashed him a rare smile. "Indeed."

Mr. Clemens looked up at the sound of Bal's laughter, yawned, and rearranged himself into a more comfortable position.

"Oh, I'm sorry?" Zeus said to the dog. "Are we disturbing you? Am I taking up too much of the seat?"

Mr. Clemens' answer was to lay his big head on Zeus's knee and go back to sleep.

Bal chuckled, amused by his brother's whimsical indulgence of the homely beast. "He seems to enjoy traveling."

"If I don't take him along with me, he makes an infernal racket—not to mention an unholy mess of whatever room he is in. So it has always been easier to bring him along." Zeus's cheeks darkened, clearly embarrassed to admit that he was at the mercy of a hound.

"I saw thousands of street curs when I was in New York City. What made you decide to rescue this one?"

Zeus stroked the dog's ears for a moment before answering. "It was a horrid afternoon—the streets jammed carriage to carriage from Wall Street all the way home. My coach paused in front of an alley, and I glanced up from whatever I was reading and saw Mr. Clemens backed into a corner by four dogs. They were taking turns attacking him, working in lethal concert—as dogs that form packs tend to do." Zeus's pale eyes looked through Bal, seeing that day. "He was so fierce. He didn't back down even though he was vastly outnumbered. And then I noticed he only had three legs." Zeus snorted. "It just seemed too… unjust to leave him there." He came back to himself and gestured to the snoozing hound. "As you can see, he has rapidly adjusted to a life of leisure."

Bal laughed. "Why did you name him after Clemens?"

"I'd met him a few times—several years before he gained national acclaim with his amusing story about the frog. He exhibited a natural tenacity that impressed me." Zeus shrugged. "Hence the name."

Bal and his siblings had read *The Celebrated Jumping Frog of Calaveras County* over and over when it came out. It was still one of his favorite stories.

"Will you tell me more about where we are going?" Bal asked. "You said there was an emergency at your estate in Wales? I must confess I didn't know you had an estate in Wales."

"It is one of three that were entailed. I already visited the one in Scotland." He frowned. "It is uninhabitable and has been for years, more of a ruin than a castle. The house in Wales, which is called—and pardon my execrable pronunciation—Golygfa Hir—has been a functioning estate with farms that have brought in just enough rents to support the property. Yesterday, however, there was a fire in the kitchen that apparently spread to other parts of the house."

"I hope nobody was hurt?"

"No, they were fortunate. But I must go and examine the extent of the damage and arrange for repairs. It is my understanding that the rains are already making things miserable. I asked you along to help not only with the damage, but I also wanted you to look at the tenant farms and give me your assessment. I suspect you will be more forthright about all the problems and money needed to fix them than tenants who've never met me."

Bal felt a jolt of pleasure that his brother had chosen to ask him along rather than his exceedingly efficient secretary.

"I felt you would be far more helpful than Masterson would be in this case." He paused, and then added, "And I also thought it might be nice to spend some time with my brother."

Based on how hot his face was, Bal suspected it was glowing, but he forced himself to meet the other man's gaze. "I would like that, too."

Zeus gave him an unprecedented second smile in one day. "Good. I probably should have confessed first that we'd be going the entire way by coach as it is not feasible by train, so the journey will be a long one."

Balthazar was glad that he'd thought of sending a brief message to Victoria letting her know that he'd left on urgent business with Zeus. Unfortunately, Bal would not be able to write to her while he was gone—at least not without embarrassing her: a letter from the duke's brother to his housekeeper would raise eyebrows.

Last night had been delightful. They had spent several hours dancing and talking in their private ballroom. While he wasn't happy to leave her today, at least things had been good between them.

Hopefully she would use the time to think about their future and conclude that marriage to him was worth weathering some scandal. Bal truly believed the storm would be a brief one and would quickly pass once they were married and settled. The newspapermen would have to find somebody else to write about once the Wicked Spare was a happily married man.

***

"Leaving? But… I don't understand, Mrs. Dryden?" Bickle's forehead was so furrowed it look like pale pink corduroy.

"I'm sorry I didn't tell you before, Mr. Bickle, but I wanted to cause as little disturbance as possible when I left."

"And His Grace knows you are leaving?"

"Yes," she said, not being entirely honest. She'd promised the duke a month before she left but given the situation with Balthazar she thought His Grace would be relieved once Miss Barrymore told him the truth about his brother's relationship with his housekeeper.

It had been a stroke of luck that Balthazar had accompanied the duke on his emergency visit to Wales. Based on what Mr. Masterson had told her, the men would be gone at least a few weeks, if not longer.

Tori would not get this chance again; she needed to leave now.

"But—all your things, Mrs. Dryden—surely you are not bringing them all on the train with you?"

She smiled at Bickle's concern. "No, I will take only some clothing. I will send somebody to collect the rest."

"Might I know where you are to settle?" he asked.

Tori opened her mouth to tell a vague lie, but then met his pale blue gaze and saw the worry that brimmed in his eyes and simply could not do it. Besides, she would not be able to keep her situation a secret once she moved into Teddy's house. "I am not taking another situation, Mr. Bickle. I'm moving to my own house."

She watched as his mind tried to work out what she meant. He would know how much money she made and wonder how she could afford a house, especially in London. Tori knew the exact moment when he moved on from that thought to the truth: that somebody else would be paying her way.

He nodded, his expression regretful, rather than accusing. "Ah," was all he said.

Conversation was stilted and awkward after that and Tori knew he was relieved when she took her leave of him.

Once she was settled in London she would write to Maxine and tell her the truth, but she didn't owe anyone else in Symington an explanation.

If Tori could have sneaked out in the middle of the night, she would have done so. As it was, she was leaving first thing and hoping not to encounter somebody she knew on the train.

Not like the last time.

Thoughts of that trip with Balthazar occupied her until she was on the platform beside her trunk and valise.

The morning was cold, but clear, and there were few people taking the early train.

Before she knew it, Tori was seated in third class, an entire bench to herself this time, no handsome, playful, adoring man beside her.

She took the most recent letter from Teddy out of her bag and studied the briefly scrawled message.

My Dear,

The house is ready and waiting for you. I've set up lines of credit for you at several modistes—your new housekeeper will give you the names and addresses—and want you to purchase clothing suitable for your new station. Unfortunately, unexpected business has taken me to

Paris. I will return to London in three weeks and expect to be received by you at that time.

Yours & etc.,

T.

No names on the letter to incriminate him. Or her, for that matter, so she supposed she should be grateful. Tori could just imagine the unexpected business that took him to Paris. Perhaps she was misjudging him, but she somehow did not think so.

Tori stared at the address of the house he had leased. It was in exactly the right neighborhood for a woman who would live her life in between worlds. Not Mayfair by any stretch, but nothing that smacked of trade. She would probably have plenty of company in the area, more *mistakes* like her who were kept neatly tucked away.

Tori replaced the letter in her bag and sighed and stared out the window. She didn't see the flickering autumn scenery. Instead, she saw Balthazar's face as he'd looked when he'd asked her to marry him, his eyes shining with love and his smile hopeful.

She knew that Miss Barrymore—for all her faults—had been correct that his smile would dim over time once he realized he'd given up millions of pounds to marry her.

Tori couldn't live with that burden. It was better to remember him as he'd been that night.

Yes, she told herself, it was better.

Chapter 23

Mrs. Dryden has gone.

Balthazar reread the line three times before it sank in. At first, he thought maybe Io was talking about Victoria's monthly trip to see her son, which would have taken place a few days ago.

But then he continued reading.

I am terribly sorry I did not notice sooner, but—well, suffice it to say I've been distracted by something. When I realized that I'd not seen her for some days I asked Masterson if she'd taken a holiday. He told me that she'd given her notice to Zeus weeks ago. Did you know about this?

No, he hadn't. Bal looked across the table at his brother. Over the past ten days he and Zeus had become closer than he'd ever expected. Behind his brother's mask of reserve was an extremely private man but also one who was warm and showed his affection, not through words, necessarily, but with deeds. Bal had known that much about him before coming on this trip. After all, it had been Zeus who provided the means for Bal and his two younger brothers to pursue their dreams.

But spending ten long, busy days together while they'd sorted out the fire damage and a hundred other small problems had made Bal see that nobody worked harder than Zeus.

His brother never complained about the long hours or the many, many people who lined up to see him day after day, every single one of them asking him for something. Almost without fail Zeus sent the petitioners away pleased and satisfied. He was generous in dozens of small, unobtrusive ways to those who worked for him, from the lowliest boot black to the ancient couple who'd taken care of his Welsh estate for decades.

Until Bal read the letter in his hands he'd been pleased to stay as long as his brother might need him. Now, knowing that Victoria had used his absence to slip away, he wanted to throttle the other man for not telling him the truth.

Zeus looked up from the copy of *The Times* he was systematically reading, one of four newspapers he read every day. "What is it, Balthazar?" he asked, his pale eyes creasing with concern. "Is something wrong at Hastings?"

"Mrs. Dryden has gone."

If he'd not been watching closely, he wouldn't have seen the shutters slam shut in his brother's eyes. "Ah."

"You knew she was leaving."

Zeus sat back in his chair, frowning at Bal's angry tone. "Yes. She gave her a month's notice. I didn't think it was over yet, but perhaps—"

"You kept that from me."

"What?"

"Why didn't you tell me she'd given her notice?"

Zeus's eyes narrowed. "First, I wasn't aware that I was supposed to report to you. Second, even if it had occurred to me that you might want such information, I would have assumed that *she* would have told you if she wanted you to know. And third—and perhaps most importantly—you told me there was nothing between you and my housekeeper, Balthazar.

Bal shoved his chair back and stood. "Quit referring to her that way. She's not just your damned housekeeper, Zeus. She's the woman I want to marry!"

His brother turned to the footman who stood beside the door—the one with his jaw hanging open and whom Bal had forgotten all about—and gestured for him to leave. Once the door closed, Zeus turned his frosty gaze on Bal.

"So, you lied to me about the two of you meeting in London."

"It was only partly a lie and I did it to protect Victoria, before you ask. We *did* meet by accident on the train down. I engineered our evening together by missing the train when I saw that she wouldn't make it."

Zeus digested that, his face once again the unreadable mask it had been before their time in Wales had brought them closer together. "Please sit down."

Bal ground his teeth for a long moment and then sat.

"How long has this been going on?"

"You mean how long have I wanted to marry her?"

"Yes."

"I asked her the day before Eva's ball, but it had been on my mind for much longer—weeks at least."

"Any time that we've discussed the subject of marriage you've indicated that doing so would be against your will," Zeus reminded him.

"Obviously I changed my mind. No"—he held up a hand—"that's not true. Victoria changed my mind for me."

"Why did you hesitate to ask her for so long?"

"Not because I worried if she'd be *respectable* enough for you, if that is what you're trying to get at," Bal snapped. "I would have said something to her before the ball, but she works all the bloody time and it's been damned difficult to get ten minutes alone with the woman." He scowled. "I despise having to hide my interest in her as if it is something to be ashamed of and I don't give a damn if she satisfies your bloody laundry list of requirements. I won't marry anyone else, no matter what you say or do. And I won't be going to London so you can parade a long line of *respectable* women before me."

"Why are you so certain that I would oppose the match—just because she is a servant?"

Bal frowned, more than a little surprised by the question. "Well… yes, that is one reason."

Zeus gave him an exasperated look. "Do you know what my Aunt Martin did before she married my uncle?"

All Bal knew about Zeus's aunt and uncle was that they'd been extremely wealthy and had raised Zeus as if he was their son.

"No," he admitted.

"My uncle met my aunt while visiting a friend from college; she was a governess to his friend's young sisters. In other words, she was a servant. And also one of the most respectable people I've ever met. So, *no*, Balthazar, I don't think being a servant precludes respectability."

Well. What could he say to that?

Zeus leaned across the table, his almost colorless eyes intense. "What I want to know is are you the reason she quit her job and left Hastings Park?"

His brother's words, although soft, cut like the lash of a whip. But it cut worse that Bal feared the accusation might be true. "I don't know."

Zeus inhaled deeply and sighed. "She rejected you?"

"She did," Bal admitted.

"Does she fear exposure of her past?"

Bal blinked. "You—er, what do you mean?"

Zeus snorted. "You needn't try to hide the truth from me, Bal. I know who she is and I also know who her son's father is."

"How in the world did you learn that?" Somehow Bal couldn't visualize his brother had been gossiping with Jo Fletcher or George Boyd.

"My predecessor left a letter for his heir. In it, he explained several matters that were too sensitive to leave for solicitors. Mrs. Dryden's situation was one of those things."

"How much do you know?"

"I know about her son being the Earl of Westmoreland's grandson. About the threat of prosecution that even now hangs over her head for stealing some of the countess's jewels. The last duke believed she was unfairly accused and—even knowing the little I do about Mrs. Dryden—I tend to agree with him."

"I can't believe the last duke knew that. Why didn't the man *do* something for her?"

"I don't know. Perhaps he felt it was not his place to act on her behalf if she'd never asked. Perhaps he felt some sense of loyalty to Westmoreland, who had once been his friend. She told you all this, or did you learn it elsewhere?"

"She told me.

"And yet you still asked her to marry you?"

Bal scowled. "Why would such a thing stop me?"

"Because you didn't know that *I* knew the truth."

It took him a second to comprehend what his brother was driving at. He snorted when he understood. "I care more about Victoria than I do about the money. Is that really so surprising to you, Zeus?" He went on before the other man could respond. "You can set the money on fire for all I care. It is no substitute for having her." Bal stood.

"Where are you going?"

"I will take a horse and ride to Hastings to see if I can discover where she went."

"If you wait until tomorrow morning, we can leave together."

Bal's entire body burned with the desire to go after her; to *do* something.

"Just give me a day, Balthazar, and then I will help you find her."

Bal exhaled noisily and stared into his brother's eyes a long moment before nodding. "Very well. One more day."

***

Tori stared at the contents of the armoire, frozen with shock. Not just at the garments hanging there, but at what an ignorant fool she had been. Not for one minute had Teddy ever intended to allow her to live a life of dignity and independence. This sordid little house told her exactly what his plan had been.

Tori turned to Mrs. Pinter, the slovenly housekeeper/cook who'd been waiting to greet her today. "Who do these clothes belong to?" she asked, even though she could guess.

"Mrs. Darling, ma'am, the, er, lady who lived here before."

"Why are they still here? Did she… die?"

Mrs. Pinter thought that was funny. When she stopped laughing, she said, "Naw. She just left. Er, sudden-like."

"Oh. And why was that?" Tori asked as she studied the brightly hued clothing.

"She 'ad a knock down row wiff 'is lordship." Mrs. Pinter chuckled again. "Them two were always goin' at it 'ammer and tongs. 'course they usually made up after—every bit as noisily"—her mouth snapped shut when she met Tori's likely furious gaze. "But you don't want to know about any of that," she said after an awkward moment of silence.

No, Tori didn't. "Why did she leave all this here?"

"She needed to find somewhere to live, first."

Tori shook her head, appalled—but not surprised—that Teddy would have thrown a woman out onto the street with nowhere to go. Isn't that what happened to her all those years ago?

"I expect she'll want everything back once she's got a new position," the housekeeper went on, eyeing the garments. "Although I s'pose you might offer her coin if you fancy any of 'em."

Tori pulled out an undressing gown in black lace and stared at it, so much anger boiling inside her that her vision darkened around the edges.

Teddy had not leased the building so that the mother of his child might live in dignity.

Teddy had kicked one mistress out—apparently onto the street, with nowhere else to go—in order to move Tori in.

Tori laughed. And kept on laughing, even though it wasn't at all funny.

"Ma'am?" Mrs. Pinter said, eyeing her as if she was not right in the head. Which Tori suddenly realized she most certainly was not. How could she have ever believed that Teddy would be anything other than Teddy? Not only had he lied about his intentions, but he couldn't even treat her decently when making her his whore.

She released the tawdry gown, spun on her heel, and marched for the door.

If you leave, what will happen to Jamie?

The question stopped her cold, her hand resting on the doorknob. If she defied Teddy and took another housekeeping position she might very well end up in gaol as he had not-so-subtly threatened.

But if she didn't, she would become a despicable creature bartering herself to a man who viewed her as no better than a prostitute. Her son might remain at Harrow, but Tori doubted that she would ever be able to look Jamie in the eyes again if she stayed in this house.

She squeezed her eyes shut for a long moment. *Think, Victoria. Think about what this will mean if you leave. You will have to take Jamie out of school. You will have to beg somebody—Auntie Max, probably—to take care of him while you go to gaol.*

Tori gritted her jaws so hard her teeth ached. *At least he won't be ashamed to claim me as his mother,* she shot back. *He is clever and hard-working. His life might not be as easy without a Harrow education, but he is intelligent enough to succeed no matter where he goes to school. And Auntie Max and Malcolm love him. Malcolm would give him a position in his business, would train him, and see that he was fed, housed, and cared for.*

But the voice wasn't satisfied. *If Teddy does what he threatened in that letter then Jamie will be branded the son of a thief.*

Far better than being branded the son of a whore.

You could always go back to Balthazar. He would forgive you for leaving. He would—

"No!" Tori shouted.

Beside her, Mrs. Pinter jumped. "I beg your pardon, ma'am?" she asked nervously.

"Nothing," Tori muttered, yanking open the door.

"Er, you want me to unpack your trunk, ma'am?" Mrs. Pinter called out behind her.

“No. Please tell Mr. Pinter to carry my trunk downstairs. I will be leaving.”

“Leaving?”

“Yes. Have your husband summon a cab for me. I will be ready in fifteen minutes.”

“But… ‘is lordship said you was going to move in. ‘ee’ll be expectin’ you when ‘ee gets back. If you’re not ‘ere… Well, ‘ee ‘as a temper, don’t ‘ee?”

Tori snorted at the thought of Teddy’s *temper.* If he were standing in front of her at that moment, he would learn that *she* had a temper, too.

She marched grimly down the stairs, heading for the small parlor the housekeeper had shown her earlier. “If you would be so kind as to fetch me paper and a pen, I will write a letter for his lordship.”

***

Thank God Tori had thought to ask the Duke of Hale for a letter of reference when she’d given her notice, not that she’d believed she would need to find another position. His Grace had instructed Masterson to prepare it and she’d been able to take it with her when she left.

With a glowing letter from the Duke of Hastings in hand it took Tori only three days to find a suitable position. Her new employers, Mr. and Mrs. Wallace Gibson, were of the merchant class and exhaustingly delighted to have a duke’s housekeeper working for them.

They were so proud of her that Tori thought they would trot her out in front of their friends and dinner guests if they could find a reason to do so.

All their enthusiasm, as draining as it was, was worth it because they had agreed to not only one free day a month, but two, so she could not complain overmuch about their rather annoying fawning and prying—especially on Mrs. Gibson’s part—or the fact that they wanted to know every last detail about Hale family and Hastings Park.

The Gibsons had been overjoyed to give her the days off to visit Jamie when they discovered that he went to Harrow. They’d even invited Tori to bring him to their home to stay over any holidays.

Their own son—a rather phlegmatic fifteen-year-old named Gerald—went to a day school. Tori knew the Gibsons were burning to know how a housekeeper had managed to enroll her son in the hallowed school of the aristocracy when even all their money had failed to buy a spot for their child.

Tori decided she would not tell her employers about Jamie's possible departure from Harrow unless it happened. After all, that matter was still undecided. In her letter to Teddy, she had strenuously and repeatedly reminded him that his father had given her his *word as a gentleman* that he would pay for his grandson's education.

She'd not been shy about pointing out how bad it would look for Teddy if word got out that he'd defaulted on that promise and was neglecting his own flesh and blood.

She had concluded her letter by telling him that it was better if they did not see one another, and that he should direct any correspondence to her solicitor.

Tori knew that Teddy wouldn't like that; he would look for her. And he would find her eventually, but she hardly wanted to help him by telling him her place of work. It was her hope that she was simply too much trouble and that he would forget about her. She knew that was probably wishful thinking, but she was done worrying about Teddy and what he would do.

Tori was done living in fear, full stop. Whatever happened, she had Jamie and the two of them would take care of each other.

It was harder than she would have believed to settle into a new job. The Wallace's house was situated in a part of town that was overflowing with the newly emerging class of bankers, investors, merchants, and industrialists. The rather ugly structure was large, brand new, and modern with conveniences like running water, gaslights, and the sort of kitchen that would have made the cook at Hastings weep with joy.

It was different from Hastings Park in every way. All those differences should have made it easier to put her old life behind her and forget about the past. Instead, the soulless new house just made her miss the creaks and groans of Hastings Park even more.

No, what you miss isn't the house; it's Balthazar.

Tori didn't bother to deny that accusation, not that it mattered.

Of all the decisions she'd made recently, leaving Balthazar before he could throw away a fortune was not one she regretted. Whatever emotions had motivated Miss Barrymore to tell her the truth, Tori had taken her warning to heart and would always be grateful to the other woman for stopping her before she'd made a catastrophic mistake.

Which didn't mean that leaving Balthazar hadn't been the most painful thing she'd ever done in her life.

Tori suspected the pain she was feeling now would be nothing compared to what she would experience when she picked up a newspaper one day and read about his betrothal to some fortunate, and infinitely more respectable, woman.

Chapter 24

Several Weeks Later

Tori popped open her umbrella before paying the hansom driver and making her way up Church Hill.

It was inevitable that the rain reminded her of another visit she'd paid to Harrow—not the last one, but the one before that: the night she'd missed the late train home.

She couldn't help smiling as she recalled Balthazar waiting for her at the station beneath his giant umbrella. Tori wished now that she had paid more attention that night—that she had known then that it would be a unique experience and the most magical night of her life. She wished that she had savored it more. Savored Balthazar more.

She still had the necklace, earrings, and gowns, even though she knew it was wrong to keep it all. One day, when the pain was less raw, she would send at least the jewelry back to him and—

"Victoria."

Tori flinched at memory of his voice, which was so sharp and clear it was almost as if—

"*Victoria.*"

She spun around so quickly her feet slipped on the wet cobbles.

Balthazar was striding toward her, carrying the same ridiculous brolly he'd had the last time. But instead of a smile, he looked every bit as thunderous as the foul weather.

"What are you doing here?" she asked stupidly.

"I want to talk to you."

"How did you know I'd be here today?" she asked, breathless from more than the walk up the hill.

"I didn't." His green eyes were far paler than usual, his pupils mere pinpricks as they flickered over her face. No sign of her gentle, tender lover remained. He was stern, cold, and implacable.

"Then how—"

"I've been here every day for weeks, waiting."

Tori stared in disbelief.

"What?" he demanded, even though she'd not spoken. "Did you think I would just forget about you? Did you think I would just forget that I loved you—and heard the same in return—and asked you to be my wife?" A jagged bolt of lightning punctuated his questions, as if even the Almighty was on his side in this discussion. He glanced irritably at the sky and gave an exasperated huff. "There is a tea shop just up ahead. Can you spare five minutes to talk to me?"

Tori hesitated.

"Surely I deserve five minutes of your time?" he demanded, his eyes so very, very cold.

She shivered beneath his chilly glare, unable to think of a reason to deny his request.

You don't want to deny it. You want more time with him—even five minutes is better than nothing. Even if what he has to say rips out what remains of your heart.

Tori desperately wanted five more minutes. She nodded.

Balthazar took her arm and led her across the street to a teashop she'd never noticed before.

The shop was humid and smelled of Earl Gray tea and sugar.

Neither of them said a word as they propped their wet umbrellas in a stand and Balthazar helped Tori off with her coat before shrugging out of his own soggy garment.

It was the wrong time of day for tea and the waitress led them through an empty seating area to a table in front of the shop's bow window.

When she would have given them menus, Balthazar shook his head and handed her a banknote that would have paid her wages for a month. "We only want to sit here out of the rain for five minutes. Undisturbed. Will this buy us that much time?"

The waitress stared at the money and nodded vigorously. "Aye, sir. Take as much time as you like."

Once she'd gone, he turned to Tori. "What in the world were you thinking? Do you have any idea how worried I've been? How could you leave without saying"—he broke off abruptly and shoved a hand through his hair. "Damn it, Victoria, you put me through hell." He shook his head, pain, anger, and disbelief in his eyes. "Why?"

"I'm sorry. I thought it was the best choice—"

"The *best choice*?" he repeated with an incredulous look. "Good Lord! What in the world were the other choices—what could possibly be *worse* by your estimation?"

"I know about your grandfather's will, Balthazar."

He sat back in his chair, his lips parting in surprise. "What? How in the world did you find that out? I never even told Io"—his eyes narrowed and an expression she'd never seen before—vicious fury—took control of his face. "That fucking *bitch*."

Tori gasped, both at his language and venom.

"It *was* her, wasn't it? *Edith*?"

She was afraid to confirm his suspicion. He looked angry enough to kill.

He snorted suddenly, as if reading her mind. "Don't worry, I won't kill her, as much as she bloody well deserves it. Let me guess—she told you that you would ruin my chance to inherit a great deal of money and you—without consulting me—took it on yourself to play the martyr?"

Tori sat up straighter in her chair, irked by his mocking tone. "I did it for *you*, Balthazar."

"Oh," he said, giving her a sarcastic smirk, "so I should thank you for running off and rejecting the offer of my heart?"

"You would grow to *hate* me if you gave up all that money. Four million dollars," she hissed. "How could I deprive you of that? And you know that if I had confronted you about it then you would have tried to talk me out of leaving—you *know* that."

"Of course I would have talked you out of leaving!"

"Can you honestly say that you would not have done the same if you were in my shoes?"

The question stopped him cold, exactly as it should have.

Tori nodded. "Yes, you see it is not so easy to dismiss when you look at it from my angle."

"I might have come to that conclusion, but I would *never* have left without saying anything to you, Victoria. I went half-mad worrying about you."

"I'm sorry about that," she said, meaning it. "I'd planned to send word to you once things had… settled."

He just snorted and turned away to stare out the window.

"Balthazar, I truly am sorry for making you worry. But I couldn't allow you to make such a sacrifice for me."

His head whipped around. "That's what you can't seem to understand, Victoria—it *wasn't* a sacrifice. I have plenty of money to live happily—I've recently bought a property that will be a wonderful home. I am not afraid of hard work; indeed, I need it to stay sane. All those millions of dollars were meaningless to me if I didn't have you."

Tori's eyes burned and she had to blink rapidly to keep from blubbering like a fool. "That's—that's the nicest—but maddest—thing anyone has ever said to me."

His lips twitched slightly. "I think that is twice you've said I told you the nicest thing you ever heard. Which means I hold both first place *and* second place on your list of *nice things*. I would say that means something; something *good*. Don't you think?"

"I just wanted to do the right thing for once in my life, Balthazar."

He took her hand and held it in both of his. "I appreciate your motivation, if not the actual outcome." He lifted her hand to his lips and kissed her gloved knuckles. "I have suffered more in these past weeks than the rest of my life combined, Victoria."

A tear slid down her cheek. "So have I."

"Then won't you put us both out of our misery, darling?" He stood, eased around the table, and lowered to one knee. "I love you so damned much. Won't you marry me?"

"Oh, Balthazar," she said, brushing away more tears. What she was about to say was wrong—and terribly selfish—but Tori couldn't stop herself. "Yes. Yes, I will marry you."

He reached up and slid a hand around the back of her head, pulling her roughly to him.

Their kiss was savage, the pent-up love and desire of weeks pouring out in a mad rush as they ravished each other.

The sound of clapping and female cheering made them both break away and turn. Their waitress, and three other ladies dressed in the garb of cooks, stood in the open doorway to the back of the shop, grinning ear-to-ear.

Balthazar chuckled. "There, you see how happy we are already making people?" He stood, bowed to the ladies, brushed off his trousers, and then took his seat.

Tori caught his hand and squeezed it until she felt his bones shift. "Are you *sure* about this, Balthazar? What will your family say? What about His Grace? Don't forget about my past and how—"

"My brothers and sisters adore you—yes, that includes Zeus." He lifted her hand to his mouth and kissed her knuckles. "It's Zeus's word that carries weight when it comes to my choice of spouse and whether she is suitable or not." He gave her a sheepish look. "I did him a grave disservice believing he would hold your position in his household against you."

"Yes, but what about—"

"He knows all of it. And no, I didn't tell him."

"Who did?"

"It seems the last duke left a letter for Zeus."

"But he didn't know the truth about the jewels—I never told him."

"I don't know how he found out, Victoria. Maybe Jamie's grandfather learned the truth about his son and told the old duke out of guilt."

Tori snorted softly at that. The last Earl of Westmoreland had despised her. He would have been more likely to send an assassin than clear her name.

"Zeus wants you to know that he will stand by us, Victoria. When this gets into the papers—and I'm sorry to say my name and reputation will almost ensure it does—he will use his not inconsiderable influence to help us. Just like he used it to ask the headmaster for your address."

"But the headmaster doesn't have my address. "

"I know that—now. But I only found that out after Zeus spoke to him, as the man refused to speak to me." Balthazar pulled a face. "He told Zeus that I had a, er, *desperate* look about me. Which I did." He cocked his head at her. "Why did you keep your address a secret, darling?"

"I made sure Jamie knew it, but I hadn't given it to the headmaster because I was going to make him promise not to release my information to"—she broke off as Balthazar's expression went from happy to stormy in the blink of an eye.

"To whom, Victoria? Is that jackass bothering you?"

She couldn't help smiling at his name for Teddy, but her smile slid away as she remembered something rather important.

Tori inhaled deeply and then let it out before saying, "I'm afraid I have a confession to make, Balthazar. It might just change your mind about me…"

Several Uncomfortable Minutes Later…

"Good Lord, Victoria! I cannot believe you would believe a word that bloody man said!" Bal's head was pulsing with jealousy and rage at the thought of anyone touching Victoria but *him.* He especially hated the thought of such a spineless weasel getting close to her.

"Balthazar. Please… won't you look at me?"

"I'm too damned angry," he confessed, his jaw clenched as he stared out the window.

"Please. I'm so terribly sorry. I know it was incredibly foolish of me to contemplate doing such a thing. I just thought—Well, I hoped he would do the decent thing. For once."

He turned to find her beautiful blue eyes imploring.

"I thought it was my only chance to keep your future safe, to keep Jamie in school, and to stop Teddy from acting on his threat."

Bal shook his head, struggling to contain his emotions. Part of him wanted to jump on the nearest horse, track Westmoreland down, and give him the beating he so sorely deserved. The other part of him wanted to grab Victoria and lock her up in his house and not take his eyes off her in case she disappeared again.

"Will you forgive me, Balthazar?" She lifted his hand to her mouth and kissed his bare knuckles.

A savage bolt of lust arrowed directly to his cock. "I should bend you over this table and take you right now to punish you, Victoria."

Her jaw dropped.

Bal smirked. "The only reason I don't do it is because nobody else is allowed to see your bare bottom. But you will have to make it up to me."

She exhaled. "Oh?"

"Yes. I will have lots of ideas about that."

"Groveling types of ideas?"

Bal barked a laugh, his rage subsiding to a low simmer. "Precisely. Naked groveling."

It would take a long, long time before he would forget, but he couldn't help forgiving her. She might have done something foolish, but her reason for doing it was sound.

"Is that all you have to tell me?" he asked. When she hesitated, Bal groaned. "Out with it. Please, Victoria. Let's clear the slate now, shall we?"

"It's… well, it's hard to describe. I've been getting letters."

"Letters?"

"Anonymous letters telling me that I'd better leave Hastings Park."

He frowned. "What?"

"Yes. I received three of them. All warning me to leave your brother's employ."

"Or what?"

"That's the odd thing; the letters never demanded money. The writer just pointed out that the duke would be shocked to find out who and what I really was."

"Do you think it was that man—Boyd?"

"I wondered about that, but to tell the truth, I'm not sure he could write even half as well, not that these letters are especially literate." She frowned. "Actually, each one seems to be written better than the last."

"Did you keep them?"

"No. I didn't want them laying around where they might be found."

"Hmm, well, there is no cause for you to worry now. Zeus already knows everything."

"Yes, I just wanted to, er, clear the slate."

"Nothing else?"

She shook her head. "Nothing else."

"Thank God." Bal took out his watch. "You'd better go. I'm sure Jamie will be waiting for you."

"I want you to come with me—to meet him."

Bal smiled, genuinely pleased. "I was hoping you'd ask me to come. Will he be disappointed that you are not with his father?"

"I told him the truth the last time I saw him," she admitted. "That I'd accepted Teddy's offer and then changed my mind. I didn't tell him why—there is no reason for him to know exactly what a—a—"

"Jackass?"

She chuckled. "There is no reason for him to know that. Although I suspect he has come to that conclusion in any case. Jamie is young, but not ignorant. He was not happy that there was no offer of marriage to go along with the house."

"Is that what you'd hoped for?"

"No. Absolutely not. I love my son dearly, but the notion of marrying Teddy—of being linked to him for life—is an appalling one. To be honest, I'd hoped that he would quickly become bored with me once he realized I would not be his lover and move on."

"How could anyone become bored with you?" Bal asked gruffly, struggling mightily with jealousy for the second time in as many minutes.

Victoria gave him a sweet smile. "I will never understand how I attracted a man like you, Balthazar. I am such an ordinary, prosaic female. While you are—"

"Yours, Victoria. I am yours utterly and completely." He once again lifted her hand to his lips and kissed her. "And you are mine. Only mine."

"Only yours," she agreed.

"Good, that is settled. Now, let us go and meet your son."

Chapter 25

Tori looked from Jamie's shyly excited expression to Balthazar's kind, interested one and said a silent, but heartfelt, prayer of thanks to be sitting with her two favorite people in the world, her heart filled almost to bursting. How had she got so lucky?

She had known Jamie would like Balthazar—how could he resist a fellow inventor? But it surprised her how much Balthazar seemed to be taken with her boy, and how easily he got along with him. Perhaps that was a result of coming from such a large family and being the eldest. Whatever the reason, he quickly charmed her normally shy, reserved son into chattering away like a magpie.

The dinner had flown past far too quickly, the two males deeply engaged in a debate about something called a *revolving hay rake*, whatever on earth *that* was.

Balthazar looked up from something Jamie had sketched on the little pad of paper he always carried in his coat pocket and caught her staring at him. He grinned. "Oh dear, we have been rude dinner guests, Jamie. Your mother does not find farm implements nearly as fascinating as we do."

Her son laughed. "She is learning more all the time. The last time she came to visit she brought me a brochure for a manure spreader."

Balthazar laughed. "I think I know the source of that document." He raised an eyebrow at her. "Mr. Rowell?"

"It is true that Malcolm gave it to me. He told me it was a sure way to Jamie's heart. And he was right, wasn't he?"

Jamie just smiled.

"I thought the sure way to a man's heart was through his stomach," Balthazar said.

She gestured to the empty dessert plates in front of the two males. "I think there has been a bit of that, too."

Balthazar turned to Jamie. "Have you had enough to eat?"

"Um." Jamie's eyes slid to the dessert tray the waiter had left not far from the table.

Tori laughed. "*Yes,* he most certainly has."

"Mrs. Dryden?"

Tori turned to find their waiter between her chair and Balthazar's. "Yes, I am Mrs. Dryden."

The man leaned closer. "There is a gentleman in one of our private rooms who wishes to speak to you, ma'am." He handed her a card, but Tori knew what name would be on it before she even looked.

She glanced up and saw Balthazar's gaze riveted to the card, his smile of only a moment earlier nowhere in sight as he lifted his eyes to hers. "Is it—"

Tori nodded. "I'd better go and see what he wants."

Balthazar's frown deepened into a glower and he began to stand. "I should go with—"

"Please, Balthazar Let me deal with this; let me finish it once and for good."

His jaw flexed and his eyes glittered with suppressed anger. "Five minutes, Victoria. If you aren't back by then, I will come in there and *finish* it."

"Five minutes." Tori agreed, standing. She smiled at Jamie, who was looking confused. "I will be right back. Everything is fine," she added when he just looked more apprehensive. "I promise."

He nodded, but she could see he wasn't entirely convinced. Fury boiled up at her son's worried expression—a frightened, uncertain look she never wanted to see on his face; this was all *Teddy's* fault.

And it ended today.

The waiter led her to a room that was on the right side of the foyer. Tori had never noticed the door before, even though she and Jamie had dined there perhaps half-a-dozen times over the last few years.

A man stood beside the door, his clothing neat and tidy, but cheap and ill-fitting. He gave Tori a bold stare that chilled her.

The waiter opened the door and Tori stepped inside.

Teddy sat on the other side of the private dining room, in front of the fireplace. "Victoria," he said, slowly getting to his feet, his eyes roaming over her body in a way that made her skin itch. "Why, you are even lovelier than you were almost fifteen years ago." He strode across the room, his hands out.

"Don't touch me," she said, stepping back, only stopping when she hit the door.

He stopped, genuinely shocked. "Why, Tori! Whatever is wrong with you? I've been searching for you for weeks and this is how you greet me?"

"Didn't you get the message I left you, Teddy?"

He laughed. "Oh, that. Yes, I received it but paid it no mind. You were just angry at the time. Your feelings were hurt that somebody else's clothing was still at the house."

"Your mistress's clothing."

"*Ex-mistress.*"

Tori snorted. "That makes no difference, Teddy. You said you bought a house in a respectable area—for the mother of your son. You did not say you were installing me in some tawdry love nest."

He shrugged, a look of annoyance flickering across his face. "I'd told her to have everything all gone by then. It is hardly my fault that she disobeyed." His blue eyes, which she had once found so romantic, drifted over her person. "That gown is rather severe. You did not take me up on my offer of a new wardrobe, I see."

Tori gave him a look of exasperation. "I didn't take your money for clothing because I never agreed to be your mistress, Teddy. Indeed, the only reason I agreed to your insulting offer was because you threatened me."

"My insulting offer?" he repeated, his sandy blond eyebrows climbing up his forehead. He was as handsome as ever, if portlier. While his well-cut coats disguised it, he had developed something of a belly and the lines around his mouth and eyes spoke of dissipation. She could only imagine how quickly his father's money was running through his fingers.

"Why is that man outside this room?" she demanded.

His smile was slow and sly. "Oh, you noticed him, did you? I thought you might prove… resistant, so I brought him along to convince you of the wisdom of obeying me."

Tori shook her head, stunned. "You really will have me dragged off to gaol for something *you* did."

Her erstwhile lover just smiled, ignoring her question. "I have looked everywhere for you. That fool of a headmaster claimed you'd left no address. I knew Jamie must have it—you would not leave him without a way to get to you—but the little bugger claimed he did not know."

Tori was always proud of her son, but never more so than at that moment. "How dare you badger my child—"

"*Our* child, and don't you forget it. I can take him from you just like that"—he snapped his fingers, the loud crack echoing in the room and making her jump.

"It's not your name on the birth record, Teddy. You have no right—"

"I have *every* right!" he roared as he strode toward her.

Tori stumbled backward, forgetting the door was behind her and there was nowhere to go.

He grabbed her chin, holding it painfully tight. "Your tongue has become waspish, Victoria. I recall even back when you were a mere girl you tended to hector." He tightened his grip, his mouth firming into a cruel slash. "If you are wise, you will temper that tendency when you are in my presence. I can be a generous lover or a severe disciplinarian. The choice is up to you."

She wrenched her head to the side to get out of his grip. "I will *never* be your lover," she hissed. "And you have no legal claim on Jamie but I will allow you to see him if you agree to comport yourself with dignity when you—"

He slammed his hands on the door on either side of her head, effectively caging her. "*You* do not tell *me* what to do." He gave her a scathing, dismissive glance. "I saw that man you were sitting with out there. Who is he? Are you already whoring yourself out?"

"What I do is no concern of—"

"The policeman I brought along is more than ready to haul you off to jail and give you your just desserts if you insist on disobeying me."

"Can you really have forgotten that it was *you* who stole your mother's jewels and—"

His fingers closed around her throat as tightly as the lash of a whip and he squeezed her hard enough to make breathing difficult. "If you repeat that to anyone, Victoria, I will see that you rot in the deepest hole—"

The door behind her shoved open *hard,* flinging Tori and Teddy—still linked by Teddy's hand—into the room.

Balthazar's green gaze went to the hand on Tori's neck and he snarled, "Let go of her, you son of a bitch!"

Teddy yanked his hand away as Balthazar all but flew across the room, landing on the other man hard enough to slam him onto the table behind him, which collapsed with a deafening *crack*.

Tori screamed just as half-a-dozen men came running into the room. They skidded to a stop near the two men fighting on the floor.

Or at least Balthazar was fighting; Teddy was just yelling *stop* and *get him off me* and *ow* while Balthazar's fists flew in a blur. He'd straddled the heavier man and pinned his biceps with his knees, his powerful arms delivering punches that should have knocked Teddy's head right off his neck.

All six men—the policeman from outside the door, the maître d, and four waiters—grabbed Balthazar's arms, struggling to lift him bodily off the prone peer.

Tori, who'd been watching slack-jawed, hastened toward them. "Balthazar," she said, setting a hand on his shoulder while he fought against the men who were trying—and failing—to hold onto him. "He did not hurt me, Balthazar. Everything is fine. *I* am fine," she added, squeezing his arm, which was like trying to squeeze stone.

His head whipped around and she flinched back from the fury in his brilliant green eyes. For a moment, he did not seem to even know her. She watched with fascination as he slowly came back to himself.

"I see red marks on your neck from his hand," he growled.

"They don't hurt. Really. I am—"

"I want you to arrest that man!"

She turned to where Teddy was being helped into a chair by the policeman, and winced at the mess that was his face. One eye was already swelling shut while blood ran from his mouth and nose.

He raised a hand to his mouth, his eyes going wide. "Goddammit! He has knocked out one of my teeth!"

And indeed, Tori saw something white fall into the palm of his hand.

Teddy's head swung up and his hate-filled eyes landed on Balthazar. "I'll show you"—he lunged for Balthazar, who was still in the grip of the four men.

"*No*!" Tori shouted, raising her heavy reticule and smacking it against his head.

Teddy roared and changed direction, lunging for her. "You *bitch*!"

Tori scrambled backward, stumbling over one of the chairs that seemed to have multiplied, and felt a slim body push past her.

"Don't you touch my mother!" Jamie shouted, wedging himself between Tori and the earl.

Teddy blinked, the sight of his son stopping him cold. "I wasn't—"

"You get away from her," Jamie snarled, sounding as fierce as he looked.

Teddy raised his hands in the universal sign of surrender and stepped back, a look of shame flickering across his face. But it fled quickly when he turned to Balthazar. "I want him arrested," he repeated. "You saw him—he was a madman."

"He was protecting me, Teddy—from you," Tori reminded him.

Teddy opened his mouth—no doubt to deny he'd had his hand on her throat—but, once again, the presence of his son stopped him. Tori was grateful for that, not just because it spared Jamie, but it also showed there was a bit of good still inside Teddy, and his son brought it out of him.

The constable or policeman or whatever he was looked from face to face, his brow furrowed in confusion. "My lord, what do you—"

"Oh, let them go," Teddy snapped. His gaze rested briefly on Tori, flickered to Jamie, and then he turned away and pushed past the waiters and stormed from the room, limping badly, and dragging one leg behind him.

Jamie twisted around and stared up at her, not needing to look up too far to meet her gaze; her little boy was now a young man. "Are you hurt, mama?"

"No." She wrapped a hand around his neck and pulled him close, kissing his forehead before saying, "Thank you for protecting me."

Whether from the kiss or her praise, his pale cheeks flared.

"You can release me now," Balthazar said to the waiters, two of whom still had their arms around him.

The men stepped back, and Balthazar straightened his clothing, his swollen, bloody knuckles the only sign that he'd just been in a fight.

"Thank you," Victoria said when he looked up.

He gave her a wry smile. "You are welcome. I heard you cry out and that is the last thing I remember clearly." He glanced at Jaime. "Are you both alright?"

Jamie nodded.

Tori met Balthazar's concerned gaze and smiled. "I am now."

Chapter 26

"That wasn't quite how I envisioned my first meeting with Jamie proceeding," Bal admitted while he walked Victoria back from the small house that her son shared with a group of other boys and a housemaster.

"It was certainly exciting," she agreed.

"I daresay we'll be reading an account of it in tomorrow's newspapers," he warned.

Victoria turned to him and smiled. "Never a dull moment with you, is it?"

"I could do with a few dull days." He stopped at the edge of the street and lifted a hand for a hansom. "I suppose you have a job that you must get back to?"

"Actually, I do have the evening free. And tomorrow, too."

"*Two* days off a month?" he asked in a mock scandalized tone. "Whatever will you do with all that time, Mrs. Dryden?"

"I am coming tomorrow to watch Jamie's rugby match. He mentioned when I said goodnight that he had wanted to invite you to come, but forgot about it in all the, er, excitement."

"I would love to go."

"Have you ever watched rugby before?"

"No, I have not had that pleasure. I'm sure you will be able to explain it to me."

"Oh, yes. I am something of an expert."

"Excellent. What are your plans for tonight?"

She smiled at him, naughty lights dancing in her blue eyes. "I have no plans."

"You do now."

A hansom stopped in front of them just as the first raindrop fell. "To Claridge's," Bal said, handing his lover into the waiting cab.

Some hours later…

Balthazar rolled onto his back and lifted a hand to shove his damp hair off his brow. "Well then, now that *that* is taken care of."

A giggle broke out of Tori before she could stop it.

He turned to her, both his eyebrows arching with surprise. "I didn't realize you could make a sound like that, Mrs. Dryden."

"Only with you, my lord." She paused and then looked down at his hips. "You've *taken care* of me—three times, I might add—but what about that?" She pointed down at the evidence of his unquenched lust, which was stiff and long and slick with desire.

He wrapped a hand around his shaft. "What? This old thing?"

Tori's sex—which had felt satiated to the point of extreme sensitivity only a moment before—tightened at the erotic sight of his big hand stroking his equally big phallus.

"You like that, don't you?" he asked in a taunting voice, the tendons in his arms taut beneath the tanned skin as he thrust into his fist.

Tori nodded dumbly, too entranced to speak.

He continued to pump himself, the tiny slit in the crown beading with clear liquid. She reached out and dipped one finger in the glittering jewel and then lifted it to her tongue, savoring the salty musk of him.

"Good Lord, Victoria!"

She couldn't hold back her smile.

Balthazar laughed. "You like to tease me."

"I do," she admitted without shame.

He growled and released himself. "I like it too. Too much. But I don't want to come on my belly or in my fist. I want to spend inside you."

Tori swallowed convulsively, both at his words and his hot, black stare.

"We've not talked about children, Victoria. You already have one. Do you want more?"

"Do you?" she countered.

"I would love children. I greatly enjoyed my position as the older brother to my younger siblings"—he laughed—"well, except for Yoyo, of course."

"Why do you call her that?"

"Eva couldn't say her name when she was a baby, so she called her Yoyo and the name stuck." He grinned. "She used to hate it so of course the twins called her that all the time. Now I don't think she minds so much. But you didn't answer my question."

"I would love more children," she said. "I hated growing up an only child."

"Do you want to wait?" he asked, stroking her belly lightly, his eyes drifting over her body in a way that made it hard to concentrate.

"I will be one-and-thirty on my next birthday, so I think I do not have much time."

"Tirzah—the woman who wrote those articles—is pregnant even now. And she is forty-two."

Tori's heart thudded to a screeching halt, as if somebody had pulled a handbrake. "Is it—"

He frowned. "Is it what?"

"Is it yours?"

"Is her baby *mine*?" he repeated, looking so shocked it would have been comical if not for her fear. "Of course not! I told you, Victoria: I've never had intercourse without a condom. I am serious about children being a woman's choice."

"I'm sorry, I just—I was worried." Not to mention she'd been seared by a bolt of jealousy so fierce her skin should be smoking.

"You have nothing to be worried about, darling. We can enjoy a wonderful and varied sex life without me ever ejaculating inside you," he said, oblivious to the torment she was experiencing imagining him with his lovers.

"Why are you blushing so hard?" he asked, leaning close to scrutinize her.

"You are so… direct when it comes to speaking about such matters." That was the truth, if only part of it.

"Don't you like it?" he asked, amused rather than offended, his sneaky hand sliding down her belly toward her mound. "Am I too vulgar for you? Your wet pussy says otherwise."

A wave of heat swamped her.

He chuckled. "You *do* like it, you dirty thing. I felt you tighten."

"You know I do," she shot back, wishing she did not color up like a schoolgirl. "But that doesn't mean it doesn't embarrass me."

His eyelids lowered and his eyes smoldered. "I love making you blush."

"I *know*."

He stroked a finger between her lower lips, rubbing her lightly and avoiding the source of her pleasure. "I have all sorts of filthy words to share with you," he said in a voice that was half purr.

Tori spread her thighs like the *dirty thing* she was, her eyelids fluttering and hips jerking when he flicked a light touch over her engorged bud, shivering at his teasing caress.

"You've made a study of filthy words, have you?" she said in a voice that was ragged and breathless with want. "It is good to know you've used your time responsibly, Balthazar."

He laughed. "I haven't had to study it. Eva shares most of her best research with the rest of us."

Tori's eyes popped open. "*That* is the sort of dictionary she is compiling?"

"Mm-hmm," he hummed, his finger swirling with intent now. "What did you think *street cant* meant?"

"I don't know—I guess—*urgh*," she groaned when he rubbed her in *exactly* the right spot.

"Hmm, what was that? A word Eva needs to add to her lexicon? *Urgh*. I don't think I've ever heard that before." He chuckled as his wicked finger destroyed her.

When he moved to withdraw his hand, she grabbed his wrist with both hands and held him where he was.

"You're so greedy, Victoria… I love it. I also love this tight, wet cunt," he hissed, leaning closer and sliding a finger inside her while his thumb assumed a position that gave her exquisite pleasure when she rolled her hips.

It didn't take long for her to shatter yet again, the orgasm sending her into a dreamlike state.

When she came back to herself it was to find him between her spread thighs, his hot soft tongue gently licking her—cleaning her, and moving lower and lower, until the wet tip prodded at the taboo part of her.

He laughed when Tori jolted. "Ah, you are back, are you?" he asked in a slightly breathless voice, and then licked her again, harder this time, his prodding more insistent.

"Balthazar," she gasped, horrified by what he was doing—and yet… *terribly* aroused by the feel of his mouth on that filthy part of her.

"Does it feel good?" he asked.

"I—I don't—this is so *wrong*!" The last word tore out of her like a groan as he probed her again.

Balthazar chuckled and Tori didn't know whether to sigh in relief or beg him to continue when he finally moved away from that part of her.

"Was that wicked of me?" he asked.

"Yes," she answered without hesitation.

He grinned. "But you liked it, didn't you?"

Tori could not help herself; she nodded.

"I have so much more planned for you, darling—so much pleasure to give you. But that is for another time—not tonight. I've been dreaming about filling you up—claiming you—for weeks now. Coitus is such a primitive act, is it not?"

Tori knew exactly what he meant. When he was on top of her, and inside her, she was reminded of just how much bigger and stronger he was. And yet he gentled that strength and never hurt her.

"I want you inside me, Balthazar. I want you to fill me and claim me as yours."

He smiled. "As excited as I am I fear I might pop off like an adolescent."

"So?" she murmured, stroking her fingers over the chiseled grooves of his abdomen. He was her own work of art, a perfect body inhabited by a generous, loving heart. "We can always do it again, can't we?"

A low laugh rumbled through him and he positioned himself at her entrance. "Indeed we can, my love. We can do it as often as we like."

And then he filled her to the hilt with one powerful thrust.

***

Bal had to pause after he entered her, waiting a moment while he struggled to regain control of his body.

Her hands, firm and confident, slid down his lower back and landed on his buttocks.

"Mm, that feels good," he said when she squeezed him. He chuckled when she tugged his cheeks apart—the way he enjoyed doing to her when he imagined her tight pucker exposed and full of his cock.

Bal withdrew slowly, astonished by the intense sensation. He shivered when one of her slender fingers grazed the entrance to his body.

She jerked her hand away. "I'm sorry."

Bal just smiled. One night soon he would have to teach her about the pleasure a man could experience when a lover penetrated him just so.

"Does it feel different for you—without a barrier?" she asked, caressing his back.

"Oh, yes."

"Better?"

He just laughed.

"Is it really that much different?"

"It is quite remarkable," he said through gritted teeth, his hips speeding, his thrusts harder, deeper. "I won't last," he warned her.

"You don't need to. Take your pleasure, Balthazar." Her hands moved again to his buttocks and she slid a hand between his thighs, her fingers lightly caressing his sac.

And that was all it took for his control to snap. Bal stroked into her hard thrice more and then buried himself deep and emptied inside her body.

***

Balthazar had fallen asleep, still inside her, his shaft half hard. He was heavy, but Tori loved being crushed by him.

If she had ever felt more contented in her life, she could not recall when. She watched him doze, his beautiful face younger in sleep, more boyish and less mischievous.

She still couldn't quite believe this was real—that she could have her son *and* the love of her life. Teddy might cause more trouble before everything was over and done, but she wouldn't face him alone.

Balthazar shifted and then opened his eyes. "I'm amazed you can breathe," he said, rolling them—their bodies still joined—onto their sides before she could protest that she *loved* the weight of him.

"There, that's better," he said, his lips curved in that lazy smile that she adored. "So, do you get to be Lady Victoria once we are married?"

Tori laughed. "No, I'm afraid not."

He made a face of shocked amazement. "What? You mean nothing magical happens to your name?"

"I get to be Lady Balthazar Hale—Lady Bal to my intimates," she said, employing the clipped, haughty accent of a royal duke.

He laughed at her imitation, carding his fingers through her messy hair and carefully teasing out some knots. "It hardly seems fair that you don't get a title all your own," he insisted.

Tori gave a dramatic sigh. "Such is a woman's lot in life, my lord."

Rather than laugh, his expression turned serious. "I have been so busy trying to convince you to marry me that I haven't really thought about you, have I?"

Tori frowned. "What do you mean?"

"I mean marriage will take away a good many of your rights. As your husband I may beat you, lock you up and feed you bread and water, or even put you away in a lunatic asylum, and nobody will stop me."

Tori gave him a sidelong look. "Er, are those things you're planning to do, Balthazar?"

"No, of course not. But the institution of marriage can be a barbaric one for women. That is one of the main reasons it is frowned upon at Canoga. It is fine for men, but it can be hell for their wives. I have always supported my sisters' decisions."

"Do neither of them wish to marry?"

"I doubt Yoyo will ever marry, but I believe Eva wouldn't mind. She is mad for babies. That was her job at Canoga, working in the nursery and taking care of the infants and toddlers. She often became… attached. I don't think she considered having children at Canoga because she wouldn't have wanted to give up her child to be raised by another."

"Neither would I," Tori admitted.

His vague gaze sharpened and he smiled, pulling her hips closer and gently thrusting his rapidly hardening erection. "Before I met you the prospect of allowing a child of mine to be raised by my community was not an unappealing one. Now… well, I want us to have that pleasure—to share that intimacy. And then there is the child's future, which if we do not marry"—he broke off and grimaced. "I'm sorry. That was insensitive." His arms tightened around her. "I hope you know I will treat Jamie as if he were my own. He will never want for love or support."

"Thank you, Balthazar—that is a burden I am grateful to share. But even though his future will be secure, I can't help being concerned about the stigma he will face if his illegitimacy becomes known."

"Things are changing faster than ever. The world is growing and the modern way is more… pragmatic. A man is important for what he does, not the legalities of his birth."

Tori hoped that was true but wasn't so optimistic. "I worry he will one day hate me for his lack of status."

"I have only met Jamie once, but he seems too kindhearted and intelligent to harbor such resentment." He smiled. "He is a scientist and he is intelligent; he will view the matter sensibly."

Tori chuckled. "One of your people, in other words."

"Just so."

"As I am going to be a part of your family, will you tell me about meeting your brother for the first time? I read about it in the newspaper, but—"

"But they probably exaggerated matters," he finished for her, a wry smile on his lips. "It was an enormous shock to the five of us—our father had never even hinted that he'd been married before. Evidently, Zeus's mother had died shortly after he was born and her sister and brother-in-law took charge of him while my father"—he broke off and frowned. "I don't know how my father justified abandoning his child."

Tori heard real pain in his admission. "Perhaps he knew he couldn't give him the care and love he needed. Were His Grace's aunt and uncle kind to him?"

"Zeus has only ever mentioned them with fondness." He gave her a wry look. "But he couldn't have been reared more differently than we were. A stern, protestant upbringing compared to the five of us, who might have been raised by wolves as far as my upright brother is concerned."

"Surely he never said that?"

Balthazar chuckled. "I'm sure he's thought it more than a few times. Things were… rough between the six of us at first." He suddenly scowled. "And made worse by Edith." His entire body stiffened, not just his delightful erection. "Just wait until I tell Zeus that the shrew knew why you had left Hastings all along. She sat there while we discussed it and looked as if butter wouldn't melt in her mouth."

"You think it wise to tell him?"

"Of course I do! What?" he said when she gave him a doubtful look. "You don't think I should?"

"She will be our sister-in-law, Balthazar."

"Not if I tell my brother what a vindictive bitch she is—it might just be the straw that breaks that camel's back. Those weeks Zeus and I spent together in Wales were very enlightening as far as he is concerned. Not only is he remarkably kind, but the man *oozes* honor. I tell you, Victoria, I am positive he does not love her—he is betrothed to her because of some warped notion of honor. Her brother was his closest friend. The two of them even went to war together and Edith's brother died of his war wounds. I suspect—although I have no proof—that Zeus promised the man on his deathbed that he would take care of his unpleasant sister."

"If his betrothal is born of honor that makes it even less likely that he will end things between them—no matter what you tell him."

Balthazar inhaled deeply, his powerful chest pressing against her breasts, the wiry dark hairs tickling her nipples. "I suppose you are correct."

"That sometimes happens."

He gave a bark of laughter. "I daresay it happens a great deal."

Tori just smiled and curved her palm around his left pectoral muscle and gently squeezed the hard, satin flesh. It was the most perfect example of that muscle that she'd ever seen—and she had done her share of gawking at farm workers over the years. She stared at his tiny brown nipple; would he think her odd if she just… licked it a bit?

"Mmm, your hand feels good," he murmured, shifting slightly, so that his tempting nipple was even more accessible. "Suck me, Victoria—the way I lick and tease your breasts."

Tori swallowed the moisture that flooded her mouth at his graphic command, leaning closer and lightly brushing the little disk of flesh with her lips.

"Yessss," he hissed, his hips rolling lazily, his hard phallus thrusting in and out of her at an exquisite angle.

Tori closed her lips around him and sucked, beyond aroused when he moaned and jerked beneath her ministrations, every muscle in his big body tensing.

"Are you trying to make me come again?" he whispered, his hips pumping harder now.

She smiled against the thin, sensitive skin.

He chuckled. "You *are*. Mmm, that won't be difficult." He pulled her closer, his thrusts sharper and less controlled as his hand slid between them, his skilled touch pushing Tori over the edge she'd been teetering on.

"I love you so much, Victoria," he said as his big body stiffened, his shaft swelling and spasming inside her, jetting heat and—yes, possibly even new life—deep inside her.

Tori was so happy she wasn't sure her body could hold all her joy.

Suddenly she thought back to the day she'd first met him—the Wicked Spare—the man the newspapers had warned would be the scourge of English maidens everywhere.

"Are you laughing?" he muttered into the top of her head, his sleepy voice thick with disbelief.

"It is happy laughter," she assured him, her heart so full it hurt. "I love you Balthazar Hale." She felt his lips curve against her scalp.

And then the only sound was his gentle snore.

Epilogue

Balthazar watched his wife of less than one hour smile and converse with his older brother.

Victoria had surprised him—in the best of all ways—by wearing the celestial blue gown he'd wanted her to wear to Eva's costume ball. If anyone thought it odd that she was garbed in a style from sixty years before, nobody was foolish enough to mention it. Not even Edith, who'd worn a sour expression from the moment Bal had returned to Hastings Park and announced the news of his impending nuptials.

Bal had considered getting his brother's fiancé alone for a few minutes and sharing a piece of his mind with her, but he'd ultimately decided that Victoria was right: Zeus would probably marry Edith and Bal had better think about his brother rather than exacting revenge.

Victoria looked every bit as delicious in the empire waist gown as he'd known she would, the elegant style perfect for her hourglass figure.

And there would be no pesky bustle for Bal to wrestle with later.

Even though Zeus and his younger siblings were going to London tomorrow—their departure to London having been much delayed for one reason and another—his brother had insisted on hosting their wedding breakfast today, regardless that the whole house was at sixes and sevens as servants scurried to pack.

Bal and Victoria had been married in the tiny chapel attached to Hastings Park, a church that nobody had used in at least two decades.

He and his two younger brothers had spent the days before the wedding working with a carpenter, roofer, and a half-dozen laborers whom Zeus had brought in specially to prepare the chapel for the ceremony.

Bal had spent almost every day in the tiny old church following Ares's directions, just like the other laborers. His younger brother was a brutal task master, but Bal had been grateful for the distraction.

Because Victoria was ethical, she had given her employers two weeks' notice, which meant that Bal hadn't seen her since the night they'd spent together in London.

He'd wanted Victoria to come back from London immediately and stay at Hastings before the ceremony, but she had rejected the idea.

"I can't do that, Balthazar, it wouldn't be proper! Besides, I owe the Gibsons notice. They helped me when I needed it."

"They got plenty out of having you in their home," he'd groused.

But she had stood firm so he'd not seen her for weeks.

Even though she'd come to the village four days ago, she'd chosen to stay with Maxine Rowell before the wedding—so they'd *still* not seen each other.

When Bal had complained to Io about it, his traitorous twin had agreed with Victoria. "It's bad luck to stay under the same roof before you are married."

Bal had spluttered at her pronouncement. "Says who?"

She had shrugged. "Everyone knows that."

"You don't know the first thing about weddings! This is the only one you've ever been invited to."

"So? Just because *I* haven't experienced it doesn't mean it isn't true. After all, I can't see gravity but I know it exists."

Her unexpectedly scientific retort had momentarily surprised and impressed him.

But then the truth had struck him. "Ha! You're just hoping it's bad luck because Edith is living under Zeus's roof."

His exceedingly practical, unsuperstitious sister had grinned. "One can always hope."

In any event, Io and Eva had spent a night at Mrs. Rowel's the night before the wedding while Bal, Ares, Apollo, and yes, even Zeus, had retired to the King's Quarrel where they'd stayed too long, drank too much ale, and had an all-around marvelous time.

As for all their worrying about the Earl of Westmoreland and what sort of revenge he would exact?

What actually happened had been blessedly anti-climactic.

While there had indeed been stories about their scrap at the restaurant, the earl had obviously exerted his influence—not to mention paid a great many bribes to waiters—and the newspaper coverage of the ugly affair had been brief, merely stating that Lord Balthazar Hale and the

Earl of Westmoreland had exchanged heated words in a restaurant not far from Harrow School.

Word of Bal's marriage to his brother's housekeeper had been a seven-day wonder. Evidently it wasn't nearly as lucrative to write about a reformed rake, even if he married a servant.

Thankfully most of Victoria's fears about her past coming to light never materialized. The story Jamie's grandfather had put in place all those years ago—about Victoria's marriage to Mr. Dryden—had held water and there had been nothing in any of the newspapers about Jamie's real father or her time in jail.

The rare sound of Zeus's laughter broke into Bal's thoughts, and he smiled when he realized that Victoria had said something that made his stern brother laugh.

Bal was amused at how the conversation around the rest of the table stuttered at the unusual sound, more than one person gaping in wonder.

"Well, would you look at that?" Io murmured. "Your new wife can even make a stone statue laugh."

"He might look like a statue, but he bleeds like a man, Yoyo. You might consider giving him a chance."

She cut him a dry look. "Oh, Bal; always the peacemaker." Her eyes narrowed. "So, tell me, what does it feel like to be a millionaire, brother?"

Bal heaved an exasperated sigh. "I wish you would take your share and—"

"Oh, hush. I'm teasing, Bal."

"You say that, but you are hurt by our grandfather's actions, I know it."

She patted Bal's hand with her far smaller one. "His actions scarcely matter as you are so determined to share the wealth with us."

He glowered at her. "Not that any of you will take it."

Indeed, all four of his younger siblings had rejected—with varying degrees of politeness—his offer to share the money. Bal didn't care; he'd had Zeus's bank set up four accounts in their names. Whether they ever touched the money was up to them. He'd experienced an almost dizzying sense of relief after splitting the monstrous sum five ways; nobody should have that much money.

Bal followed his twin's gaze and wasn't surprised to see it settled on Masterson, who was seated beside Edith, who wasn't just talking to the secretary, but—shockingly—smiling at him.

"What in the world do you think he is saying to make the gorgon look almost pleasant?" Io asked in a tone of disbelief, her face tight with poorly suppressed hostility as she stared at the duo.

Bal ignored his sister's invitation to sharpen his claws on Zeus's betrothed. Instead, he glanced around the table, his gaze lingering on Edith's cousin.

For once, Miss Barclay was seated too far away from her employer to be summoned quickly. She was between Ares and Apollo, both of whom must have been teasing her about something because she was smiling, her normally pale cheeks flushed with happiness.

"She's quite pretty," Bal murmured, surprised.

Io knew who he was talking about. "She's also clever—a woman of hidden depths."

"Are you hoping that Ares or Pol will rescue her from her life of drudgery?" Bal teased.

"It wouldn't be the worst thing to happen."

Bal tried to imagine either gregarious Ares or saturnine Apollo with the timid Miss Barclay and could not visualize it.

Io turned to him. "Are you *sure* you don't want to come to London with us? Just for a few weeks?" she wheedled.

"I'm sure. I want to settle into Fairview before the first snows come."

"It's not like home, you know. There won't be fifteen feet of it here."

"I know that. I'm just eager to get started." Bal bumped his twin's shoulder. "You won't need me with you, Yoyo. You will have a wonderful time in London."

She clucked her tongue. "Sometimes I think you don't know me at all, Bal."

"What? You don't think there will be talks and museums and more history than you can shake a stick at?"

"You can't really believe that we will get any time away from balls, routs, breakfasts, et cetera, et cetera, to do any of that, do you?" she retorted, scowling down the table at Edith. "She has already informed me and Eva how things will be for the next four months."

"Look on the bright side, Yoyo. She's still in mourning, so she won't be able to go to many of those functions you just mentioned."

"Somehow I think Edith will twist the rules of mourning to suit her needs."

Bal suspected she was right.

"I will miss you, Bal."

"And I will miss you, too."

She snorted. "Liar. You're so in love you hardly notice anyone else exists."

Yet again his face heated.

"Don't be embarrassed," she said, patting his hand. "I'm delighted for you. You deserve happiness and she is lovely."

He smiled as he stared down the table at the woman in question. "She is, isn't she?"

"Yes. And not just on the outside," Io said. "Her son is also delightful."

They both turned to where Eva and Jamie were seated, the two laughing hard at something and then smirking like a pair of conspirators.

"Why do I think that Eva is going to make sure Jamie returns to school with an entirely new vocabulary?" he asked.

Io laughed. "She has always wanted a younger sibling. I suspect she will spoil him horribly."

"He's a good lad. I doubt he can be spoiled." Bal meant that. He'd spent the last few days with his stepson as their wedding coincided with the boy's winter break. Jamie would be joining them at Fairview for a few weeks before returning to school. Bal knew that Victoria had been concerned about having her son stay with them immediately after their wedding, but he thought having Jamie around right from the beginning was the perfect way to start their lives together.

Besides, Fairview was a large house. They would spend their days with Jamie, but their nights would be for the two of them alone.

"You have that fatuous smile on your face. Again," Io said.

He laughed. "I won't apologize for it."

"You don't have to. Be happy, twin."

Bal smiled at her and squeezed her hand. "You, too, twin. Give our brother—and London—a chance."

"I'll try," she said, glancing toward the other end of the table, her mouth and eyes narrowing at whatever she saw.

He couldn't help noticing that his sister wasn't staring at Zeus, but his secretary.

Bal grinned. He somehow suspected that Mr. Masterson had some very trying times ahead of him.

***

"It was kind of your brothers to take Jamie with them to the King's Quarrel for a game of darts," Tori said as they both mounted the stairs to the family wing of the house. For the first time ever, she wasn't intent on an errand, or service, but headed to her husband's room, which they would share for one night before they left for their own home tomorrow.

"Don't worry," Balthazar said, setting a light hand on her lower back as they reached the landing. "They won't teach him bad habits." He chuckled. "At least not too many."

Tori was still a bit in awe of Balthazar's almost too-perfect looking brothers. Although Ares and Apollo had never been anything but courteous and polite to her, she'd already heard tales of how they were both working their way through the female population of Symington. Not that the female population were reluctant in the matter. Tori didn't consider herself a prudish woman, but the way so many women chased after the brothers was rather shocking.

Balthazar opened the door to his chambers and Tori caught her breath. "Oh, Balthazar! It is lovely."

"Thank you."

She turned to him. "*You* did all this?" she asked, gesturing to the vases of roses on every flat surface and the trail of rose petals that led to his bed chamber.

"You sound so surprised. Do you think I lack the ability for romance, Victoria?"

"No, it's just—"

"It was Eva's idea."

She laughed. "You rat. For a moment, I believed you." Tori lowered her nose to sniff the roses. "Where did you get these at this time of year?"

"I have my ways, darling. And I *was* the one to get the roses. Eva just took charge of the decorative strewing of them because I wasn't doing it correctly." He picked up a bottle that had been chilling in a wine bucket. "Champagne?"

"I shouldn't—I've already had two glasses."

"We only have one wedding day."

"You just want to get me flawd and take advantage of me."

He paused in his pouring. "*Flawd*? No wait, let me guess: Eva."

She laughed. "Yes, she taught us a great many useful words last night at Auntie Max's."

"I'll just bet she did." He handed her a glass and raised his. "To us."

"To us."

Once they'd taken a sip, Tori set down the glass and Balthazar sat beside her on the narrow settee, their bodies touching from thigh to shoulder.

"This reminds me of that first ride we took together—when you brought me back to Hastings in that gig." He bumped her shoulder. "After you'd been caught ogling my wares."

Tori choked on a laugh. "Your *wares*?"

"Don't deny it."

"It was difficult not to look at your *wares* as you were strutting about like a peacock."

Balthazar gave her a lofty, affronted look. "Strutting? I was working hard, breaking a sweat."

"You were *strutting* because you knew the shrubbery was loaded with gawking women."

He laughed. "To be honest, I only knew about Miss Brower. She almost fell out of the second-floor window the first day." He shifted her around until she was facing him and then lifted her legs up and draped them over his thighs. "Better."

"I have something to tell you, Balthazar. But I don't want you to be angry."

He narrowed his eyes. "My God. If you tell me that *arse* Westmoreland has contacted you after—"

"No, no. It has nothing to do with Teddy. It's about those letters I received—the anonymous ones."

"Did you get another?" he asked, instantly concerned.

"No. But I discovered who sent them."

"Who."

"It was Maxine Rowel."

"*What*?"

"I know, I was shocked, too."

"But why?"

"You won't believe this." Even though Tori's dear friend had confessed the truth three days ago, *she* still could not believe it. "She hoped that if she drove me from my job at Hastings that I would relent and accept Malcolm's offer of marriage."

Balthazar stared at her for a long moment and then said, "Huh."

She laughed. "*Huh*? Is that all you have to say?"

"It rather defies common sense or criminal sense or any kind of sense I can think of, Victoria. Didn't she consider the possibility that such letters might drive you away from the area entirely?"

"No, I don't think she did. I don't think she was thinking straight, at all. She is not well, Balthazar." Tori chewed her lower lip, not wanting to voice her worries aloud, which would somehow make them more real. Although Maxine hadn't said so, Tori thought the older woman was very ill, perhaps even dying.

She should have known that Balthazar would see how she felt without her even saying the words.

"Oh, darling," he murmured, gently squeezing her hand. "I'm so sorry."

"So am I, Balthazar." She sighed. "I feel terrible that I couldn't give her what she wanted. Maxine is an old lady who loves her nephew madly and just wants to see him happy. People do odd things for the ones they love the most."

"Like running away from them?" he taunted, pulling her closer and kissing her savagely to dull any sting from the accusatory words.

"Yes, just like that," Tori said when he released her.

"You were not tempted to marry Rowel?" Balthazar asked, carefully plucking the pins from her hair.

"No. He is my friend, but I don't love him. Malcolm knows how I feel and never asked me to marry him again after the one time. I believe he has moved on in his heart. At least I hope he has."

"Wouldn't it have been better marrying him than going to Westmoreland and trusting to his kindness and honor?"

Tori knew this was dangerous ground—that the wounds on Balthazar's heart were still raw—but she wanted him to understand just how little Teddy meant to her. "Teddy was a means to an end, Balthazar. I didn't care for him, nor did I feel guilty for agreeing to take what he essentially forced on me. With Malcolm I always would have felt guilty that I didn't love him. He is a wonderful man and deserves a wife who loves him, not one who merely needed him."

He tossed the last pin onto the end table and unraveled the thick plait that she'd worn in a simple crown today—regardless of how much Maxine had begged her to add a few ringlets.

"This is so gloriously heavy," he murmured, combing out the thick hank of hair with his fingers. "This dress looks beautiful on you. I like you in colors. But I think right now I'd like to see you in nothing." He turned her so he could access the tiny ivory buttons that ran the length of the bodice. He sighed. "Buttons."

Tori laughed.

For all his complaining, he had her down to her chemise and hose quickly.

"Up," he murmured, pulling her to her feet, and then pushing down her chemise.

She stood before him naked but for her stockings and garters.

"We will leave those on," he said, his eyes so hot she swore she could feel them burning her skin. "You are so lovely, Victoria." He slid his hands from her waist to her breasts.

She arched her back and closed her eyes, offering herself to him. Wet heat lowered over a nipple and she moaned as he caressed and kissed the sensitive flesh until the tips were pebbled.

"I want to feel all of you—skin against skin," he murmured.

Tori nodded dazedly. "Yes."

"Go lay on the bed."

Tori was intensely conscious of his gaze on her naked back and bottom as she scrambled up onto the high mattress and then propped herself on her side so that she could watch him disrobe.

"Very pretty," he said, his lips pulled into that lazy smile, his eyelids heavy as he stripped for her, his movements deliberate rather than hurried. He sat briefly to remove his shoes and pull off his stockings. His coat, waistcoat, shirt, and tie he tossed over the back of a nearby chair.

And then he came closer to her—close enough that she could reach out and touch him.

He gave an appreciative growl when she traced his erection, long, thick, and thrusting against the fine wool of his wedding trousers.

"I've missed you," he said, pushing down both his trousers and drawers with one smooth motion.

Tori's breathing quickened at the sight of his arousal. She had seen him fully naked and erect before—more than a few times—but she still could not believe that this beautiful, sensual, generous man was hers. All hers.

"Stroke me," he murmured, pushing his hips toward her. He hissed when she curled her fingers around his hot, hard length.

Tori worked him from root to tip, her fist tight. She was fascinated by the moisture he produced and entranced by the way the muscles in his belly and chest rippled and flexed beneath her hand. As big and powerful as Balthazar was, *she* was the one who felt strong and fearless with all his masculine beauty at her command.

His fingers closed around hers and halted her caresses and he climbed up on the bed, pushing her thighs wide and lowering himself between them.

He kissed the spot where silk met flesh, tracing a finger over her garters, a smile curving her lips. "These are pretty."

They were embroidered with roses, the stockings the finest she'd ever owned. Although she was well past the age of such flights of fancy—or at least she should be—she'd felt like a princess when she'd looked at her reflection in the mirror today.

And now, the way her husband was gazing at her body—consuming her—made her feel like a queen.

Tori gave herself up to pure sensation, responding to him without any fear of judgement or shame, opening herself and taking everything he had to give.

Only when he'd brought her to climax twice did Balthazar kneel between her spread thighs and plunge deep inside her, the echoes of her orgasm all the more powerful for being joined with him.

Balthazar paused, his heavy body holding her pinned. "I love you so much, Victoria. Thank you for marrying me and making me happiest man in Britain."

Tori cupped his face as tears of joy welled in her eyes. "Thank you for being my knight, Balthazar; you rescued me when I'd given up on girlish dreams of love. I'm so happy it almost frightens me."

"We rescued each other, sweetheart," he murmured, his hips beginning to move. "You don't need to be scared, Victoria, I'm here for you, darling. Always," he said, taking both her hands in one of his and holding them above her head. “Tonight is the first night of the rest our lives, and it will be glorious.”

And then Balthazar once again showed Victoria just how glorious…

The End

Dearest Reader:

Well, that was an odyssey! Starting a new series is always nerve-wracking. In this case I didn't just start a new series, I picked a new era and began the story on a different continent!

This was a challenging book in a different way from any book I've written before. I've mentioned before that I'm a savage cutter of words—often hacking out hundreds of pages at a time. BALTHAZAR was no exception. The weird part this time was where I cut the words: right from the beginning, something I've never done before. I usually start my books exactly where I want them to be (I've been lucky!) But my luck ran out this time and I ended up cutting the first 86 pages!

And it just about killed me.

The book originally began in the Canoga colony right before Balthazar and his siblings meet Zeus for the first time.

There were oodles of details of life at the commune, information about Charles Hale—the father of all the Hale kids—tons of early clashes between the various Hale sibs and Zeus.

And yes, lots of arguments with Edith that I instead distilled into a few flashbacks when I ended up changing the beginning.

Unfortunately, in that iteration of the book Victoria and Balthazar didn't even meet until page 91, LOL. That sort of story structure used to work in the olden days—Victoria Holt had the hero and heroine meeting at the halfway point in several books—but modern readers like to get the H/h together on the page ASAP, so I knew something (a lot of somethings) had to go.

And so I killed my darlings, as we say in the writing world. I was, in fact, a serial killer of darlings.

In any case, I was guided in my decision by my writer guru and pal, Jeffe Kennedy.

Jeffe is that friend who steps into an overwhelming situation, rolls up her sleeves, and gets down to business without making a fuss.

THANK YOU, JEFFE!

This is a family saga, so the first book is, by necessity, full of details. I wanted to flesh out the Hale siblings' world without writing myself into a corner, later. To that end, I left some questions unanswered—like how Zeus and Edith met—and offered only minimal background information about the Hale siblings or the book would have been too long. Never fear, there are five more books to learn every single detail about all the Hales.

Back when I taught American history one of my favorite periods was the mid-nineteenth century. The religious history of the United States is especially rich and interesting and I've always been intrigued by the utopian societies that sprang up during that time. At first, I was tempted to use an actual community, but after reading Ellen Wayland-Smith's fabulous book, ***Oneida: From Free Love Utopia to the Well-Set Table***, I decided it was wiser—and more respectful—to create a fictional community for the book.

Ms. Wayland-Smith is a decedent of the family that founded the Oneida community and I realized it would be all too easy to step on toes if I used an actual religious commune and meddled with the structure at all.

In any event, I drew heavily on the liberal ideology of many of these communities—especially their position on gender equality and their suspicion of the institution of marriage.

Yeah, I also had fun with all that free love, complex marriage, and coitus reservatus stuff, too, LOL.

I'm sure most of you reading this book already know this, but I'll say it just in case: THIS IS NOT A HISTORY BOOK! So, if you are interested in any of the subjects mentioned herein, I strongly suggest you get your hands on an academic work.

I love writing alpha heroes and I kept trying to make Balthazar an asshole, but he stood up to me and refused to do it. That happens sometimes—a character seizes the reins and shows me who is the boss.

Bal ended up being the sort of guy who'd lived his whole life loved and secure, so he was the perfect foil for poor Victoria who had a horrible father figure—because she was female—and then was used, cast aside, and betrayed by her reckless first lover. I think she wouldn't have liked Bal very much if he'd been all alpha and not a sweetheart who was unafraid to lay his love on the line for her.

I consoled myself by thinking about the next book, IO: THE SHREW, which features Corbin Masterson as the hero. Yeah, you KNOW Corbin's an alphahole. Luckily Io can handle that sort of man with one hand tied behind her back.

Or so she thinks.

I'm already getting excited about writing that story.

The next book of mine to launch is THE DUELING DUCHESS, book 2 in THE WILD WOMEN OF WHITECHAPEL, which is out only a few days after BALTHAZAR! Yes, you can grab a copy of that on May 23, 2023.

After that is SELINA, book 3 in THE BELLAMY SISTERS, which will be out August 18, 2023.

In September and October, I will launch the first two books in my science fiction/fantasy series THE TIME CONTROL trilogy. This is a Regency Era meets post-apocalyptic space opera. There is action and a lot of romance and it's STEAMY. Not only that, but the Duke of Wellington is one of the main characters. Yes, for real! I put him through the wringer and drag him from the battlefields of Europe to 24th century Britain.

This book won 1st place at the Rocky Mountain Gold Contest for best speculative fiction, which was a pretty fabulous honor for my first science fiction.

Anyhow, if that is your jam please check it out. I've got links to all the books I just mentioned listed below.

I'd like to give a shout out to those lovely, lovely readers who sent me emails that kept me scribbling away over here. Yeah, YOU know who you are! Thank you so, so, so much for taking the time to send me some positive vibes.

Thanks to all you fabulous readers who keep me so busy writing new books. I've got a busy year ahead, so I should have something to keep everyone satisfied.

I know every author begs and nags for reviews, but they really do matter, even if a book already seems to have hundreds. The 'Zon cares about "freshness" so if you've read and enjoyed one of my books and haven't dropped a review, please consider jotting down a few words.

I'm including an excerpt from a book that somehow gets buried beneath all the dukes and billionaires, but the hero is truly one of my favorites, Hugo Buckingham from ***HUGO AND THE MAIDEN.*** Yeah, Hugo is quite a trip, but he is hilarious and watching him fall in love is a treat.

So enjoy the first four chapters on me…

Until next time, take care and have a fantastic summer!

Xo

S.M.

Who are Minerva Spencer & S.M. LaViolette?

Minerva is S.M.'s pen name (that's short for Shantal Marie) S.M. has been a criminal prosecutor, college history teacher, B&B operator, dock worker, ice cream manufacturer, reader for the blind, motel maid, and bounty hunter. Okay, so the part about being a bounty hunter is a lie. S.M. does, however, know how to hypnotize a Dungeness crab, sew her own Regency Era clothing, knit a frog hat, juggle, rebuild a 1959 American Rambler, and gain control of Asia (and hold on to it) in the game of RISK.

Read more about S.M. at: www.MinervaSpencer.com

Minerva's OUTCASTS SERIES
DANGEROUS
BARBAROUS
SCANDALOUS

THE REBELS OF THE *TON:*
NOTORIOUS
OUTRAGEOUS

INFAMOUS
AUDACIOUS (NOVELLA)

THE SEDUCERS:
MELISSA AND THE VICAR
JOSS AND THE COUNTESS
HUGO AND THE MAIDEN

VICTORIAN DECADENCE:
(HISTORICAL EROTIC ROMANCE—SUPER STEAMY!)
HIS HARLOT
HIS VALET
HIS COUNTESS
HER BEAST
THEIR MASTER

THE ACADEMY OF LOVE:
THE MUSIC OF LOVE
A FIGURE OF LOVE
A PORTRAIT OF LOVE
THE LANGUAGE OF LOVE
DANCING WITH LOVE’
THE STORY OF LOVE*
THE ETIQUETTE OF LOVE*

THE MASQUERADERS:
THE FOOTMAN
THE POSTILION
THE BASTARD

THE BELLAMY SISTERS
PHOEBE
HYACINTH
SELINA*
AURELIA*

THE HALE SAGA SERIES: AMERICANS IN LONDON
BALTHAZAR: THE SPARE
IO: THE SHREW*

THE WICKED WOMEN OF WHITECHAPEL:
THE BOXING BARONESS
THE DUELING DUCHESS*
THE CUTTHROAT COUNTESS*

THE BACHELORS OF BOND STREET:
A SECOND CHANCE FOR LOVE (A NOVELLA)

ANTHOLOGIES:
THE ARRANGEMENT

Made in the USA
Las Vegas, NV
25 June 2023